KILL OR BE KILLED

Cobb licked his lips. Why had Wolf given back his gun?

"You told me you'd do whatever I said if I let you live," Wolf said. "Do you remember?"

"I remember," Cobb said as he buckled on his gunbelt, the Colt still in place in the drop holster.

"Then you decide whether to keep that promise or not."

"If I decide not to?" Cobb asked.

"Then I'll kill you," Wolf said. "That's *my* promise."

Slowly Cobb moved his hand toward the holstered Colt. "How do you know I won't kill you first?"

Wolf didn't move, just watched, his dark eyes narrowing. Then he said, "You might try, Cobb, but you can take my word for it—that would be your last mistake."

DAN PARKINSON
A MAN CALLED WOLF

ZEBRA BOOKS
KENSINGTON PUBLISHING CORP.

To the class of '53

ZEBRA BOOKS

are published by

Kensington Publishing Corp.
475 Park Avenue South
New York, NY 10016

First printing: October, 1989

Printed in the United States of America

I

December's dusk lay bleak upon the land, chill wind-fingers groping southward beneath a leaden sky, across sandhills where tendrils of gray dust swirled knee-high among lonely spines of brush. Random snowflakes drifted by, caught up and lost in the whispering, shifting sand.

Beneath the bank of a dry wash, Wolf pulled his blanket tighter around his shoulders and peered at the lowering sky. North and west the gray deepened toward a black horizon. Everywhere the light was fading. He stood, feeling the bite of chill winds. He stamped his feet to relieve the set-in cold, rubbed raw hands and pulled his hat down low over his eyes. Long raven hair blew free beneath it.

"It's time to move," he told the others. "It isn't far now."

Reluctantly they stood, holding their blankets about them as shields. "Could have used a fire," Trooper growled. "My toes are about to break off. Maybe they already have."

Shanty huffed and blew into his cupped hands, then clambered to the top of the bank. Cold wind ruffled his red whiskers. "What I could use is a drink. How far back do you think they are?"

5

Wolf came up beside him. "An hour, no more. With horses, they'll close fast." He turned his face to the cold wind and the dark horizon, and set off, long legs straining against the hard gusts, soft boots silent and sure on the shifting sands. Dark eyes on the move, missing nothing, he led, and the others followed close behind him. Trooper peered ahead into the darkness. "I don't see anything. If we're that close I should see something by now."

"We're close," Wolf said. "Look." In the lee of a low dune there was a mark on the sand, an undulating thin line as though someone had dragged a reata.

"Snake track," Trooper said.

"And there." Wolf pointed. A few feet off was another mark, this one deeper, better defined. "Big one there. Diamondback."

Interested, Shanty studied the dim ground around them. "Hey, there's a lot of 'em."

"That's right," Wolf said. "And all going our way. Come on."

"Ain't it somebody else's turn to carry this sack?" Trooper paused to shift his load. "Damn thing's heavy."

Shanty shrugged, then stepped closer to him and took the leather pouch. He slung its strap across a thick shoulder. "Gold usually is," he said.

The dark, shrouded sky seemed closer now, and more snow was falling, sand-dry flakes like birdshot hurled on the gusting wind. Wolf held his pace. Trooper turned to glance back and veered aside a few steps. He turned back, yelped and sidestepped, nearly falling. He raised his carbine, and Wolf snapped, "Don't shoot. Just watch where you're going." A yard from Trooper's boot a huge rattler slithered away, sluggish with cold but moving determinedly. It was nearly six feet long, its diamond-covered girth the size of a man's forearm.

"Old man of the breaks," Wolf said. "Let him alone. He knows where he's going."

"Well I sure as hell don't want to go where he's

6

going," Trooper rumbled.

Wolf glanced back at him, dark eyes searching. "That's where we *are* going, Trooper. We're going with him."

Trooper shook his head. "Will you just once talk straight out and say where in hell we're goin'? This whole thing is the craziest mess I ever heard of."

"Never heard a grown man complain so much," Shanty muttered.

"Well, it *is* crazy. Hell, we knew how many of them there was back there. Twenty. *Twenty men!* So what does this'n here do? Why, he just walks right in like he outnumbers 'em an' walks out with a forty-pound sack of gold coin. Crazy! An' us freezin' our butts out in a damn gully while he does it."

"We know all that, Trooper."

"Yeah, but how can you not think about it?" Trooper shook his head. "Jesus! So then what does he do, after he gets in an' out an' nobody's gunned him yet? Sets fire to th' damn house! I still can't believe it. We could have just got on our horses an' been gone, but he has to set fire to the house! So now our horses are still back yonder someplace, and there's eighteen armed men that *do* have horses comin' after us. And now he tells us we're followin' a damn rattlesnake."

Wolf glanced around. Shanty thought there was a touch of amusement on his dark features, but he couldn't be sure. The light was fading. Winter night came on suddenly when the dark clouds settled in.

"I just don't understand it," Trooper pressed on. "We could have been long gone with all this gold, and good horses under us. So why in hell aren't we?"

"That isn't what we came for," Wolf said softly, letting the wind carry his voice back. "We came to stop Purdue."

"Well, it's a fine job we're doin' of that. In just about half an hour Purdue is goin' to be on top of us with

7

seventeen men at his back—"

"Eighteen," Wolf said.

"Seventeen. Shanty and me killed one apiece when they came boilin' out of that house."

"Shanty killed one. You only creased yours."

"I saw him fall!"

"I saw him get up again." In the gloom they passed another big rattler going the same direction. "See you there, Old Man," Wolf said.

"He's crazy," Trooper told Shanty. "That Injun is crazy as a loon."

"Crazy like a wolf," Shanty said.

They topped a rise in the prairie, and ahead of them was a hump. Too low to be a hill, it was just a big, flat-topped rock, a shadow in the gathering darkness. "That's where we're going," Wolf said. "Better step it up now."

Winds whipped at them as they hurried on, directly into the teeth of a rising storm. "Norther," Shanty said. "Might be a bad one."

As they closed on the bulking hump of rock, Wolf raised a hand. "Can you smell that?"

Shanty and Trooper lifted their heads, sniffing the wind with frozen noses. "Yeah," Trooper said. "Somethin'. Kind of a sweet smell, but like putrid and sweet both. What is it?"

Wolf pointed to one side. Three more rattlers were there, scurrying toward the rock. "Them."

"Jesus," Trooper whispered.

"Rock's full of them by now. It's where they winter. Come on, we'll circle around. Watch where you step."

Eyes scanning the snow- and sand-misted ground, Wolf made a wide circle around the rock to approach it from the north. Up close, it looked in the dusk like a huge buffalo chip, maybe seventy feet across and ten at its highest point. Dark porous stone left by some upheaval in a long-gone time, it was a beehive of holes, cracks, tunnels and declivities. Its north face was nearly hidden

8

by piled tumbleweeds, stacked and held there by the wind.

"This will do," Wolf said. "Shanty, give me the sack. You two clear a space right up against the rock. Pull the brush away. I want a dozen feet of clear ground."

Two more rattlers passed them, coming from the north. One had to swerve to go around Trooper's boot. They disappeared under the piled weeds. Trooper shuddered. "I ain't puttin' my hands in there. Clear it yourself."

"Use your rifle barrels," Wolf said, his tone icy now. "Get it done." He turned away, disappearing into the gloom.

Carefully, Shanty and Trooper approached the tumbleweeds and began clearing them aside, working with extended gunbarrels. There was a buzz, and something hit Trooper's gun. He jumped back. "Jesus!"

"Careful," Shanty warned. He pulled away a matted cluster of thistles, and several snakes slithered for the rock, their rattles whirring. One coiled, reared and buzzed, then looped around and disappeared into a hole in the rock.

Trooper discovered that he was sweating. Despite the biting cold, his hands were clammy, and moisture dripped down his face. Carefully and steadily they worked, and with each move of brush there were dark shapes whirring and wriggling away. In minutes they had a wide opening through the brush, right up to the face of the rock. Wind whined and sang in the porous surface in front of them.

Wolf came back with an armload of dry buffalo chips. He looked at what they had done and nodded. "Shanty, get off around there and watch for Purdue's bunch. They should be coming over that rise in a few minutes."

Shanty hurried away. There was yet a little light in the sky to the east and south. He would be able to see them when they came.

"They're gonna ride right in here and gun us down."

9

Trooper glowered.

Wolf ignored him. He crouched on the cleared sand a few feet from the rock. With a handful of pale, dry grass he started a little fire, shielding it with his hat. When it was going he crumbled a buffalo chip and fed it, coaxing the dim, blue blaze until it was a small fire. Its light in the storm-dark gloom threw his shadow hugely onto the face of the snake-infested rock behind him. Again he fed the fire, then he stood, removed the heavy leather sack from his shoulder and opened it. Slowly, stooping, he poured gold coins onto the ground behind the fire, spreading them wide across the cleared area. In the dancing firelight they shone like little yellow mirrors in the sand. Trooper watched in amazement.

Shanty hurried around the rock. "They're comin'! The whole blasted lot of 'em, just like you said."

Wolf's eyes glinted in the firelight. He emptied the rest of the gold from the sack in a spreading sweep and tossed the sack aside. "Come on," he said. At a run he led them away from the rock, out to where an abrupt gully cut the prairie, fifty yards away. They slid to the bottom and crawled back up to peer over its rim, the wind at their backs now and snow sticking to their hats and blankets. Beyond them the snow was a whirling thin mist, scudding over the sand, driven by the wind. It was nearly full dark.

The big flat rock stood dim against the sky, the little fire winking at its base, dwarfed by the great piles of tumbleweeds on each side. To the left, beyond, shapes moved against the dim low horizon. One, then another, then more—riders coming around the rock.

Winking firelight gave a slight glow to the swirling snow, and they slowed, moving cautiously. When they were even with the north face and could see the fire, they stopped, bunching there. Two of them broke off and came forward hesitantly, leaning in their saddles, straining to see beyond the spark of firelight. Others followed, one or two still holding back. Slowly they closed toward the little fire, peering around in the blowing gloom. One man dismounted then and went forward on foot, crouching, gun in hand, ready for trouble.

"They think it's a trap," Wolf said softly. "But they can't figure it out."

The man on foot reached the fire, looked all around and glanced down. Stooping, he picked up a gold coin. It glittered in his fingers. He raised it for the others to see, and in an ebb of the wind his voice came to the gully. ". . . gold. Scattered all over . . ."

Most of them moved in then, eagerly. Two still held back. Wolf sucked breath through his teeth. "That's Purdue. And Cal Salem. Go on, *chitos*. Go and get your gold." Trooper and Shanty glanced at him, noticing the sleek revolver in his hand. Neither of them had noticed him drawing it.

Again the wind ebbed, and they heard bits of voices. ". . . it's all over here . . ." ". . . tossed around . . ." ". . . too dark. Can't see . . ."

"Use the weeds," Wolf murmured. "Make some light."

The hard voice of Jack Purdue rode across the wind. "Pull some of them weeds onto the fire! Get some light there! Gather all that up! Don't miss any!"

Men hurried to pull loose armloads of the spiny thistles, fighting them as they tried to sail in the wind, forcing them down onto the little fire. They smoldered for a moment, then blazed, tendrils of bright flame racing upward through them, exploding into a fierce blaze. Suddenly the scene was as bright as a sunny day, and men scampered and crawled around the base of the rock, picking up coins as the wind took the flame and smoke from the pyre and rolled it back upon itself, to billow around the face of the honeycombed rock . . . blinding the men there with smoke. They bumbled around, arms over their eyes. Purdue swung down from his horse,

11

exasperated. "Oh, for God's sake!"

A scream lanced through his words as a man near the fire straightened suddenly, thrashing his arms. From his face hung a writhing, coiling snake. Next to him another cursed and doubled over, reaching for his ankle, then straightened and ran screaming into the darkness. Suddenly the whole face of the rock was a coiling, dripping, chirring mass of angry snakes. The ground all around the men was alive with them. Hundreds upon hundreds of them, coiling and striking, serpentine arcs hitting legs, arms, backs, their hum was a buzzing of bees on the wind. Some of the men fell where they were, awash in serpents. Some tried to run, rattlers clinging to them like writhing whips. Their screams drowned the howl of the gusting wind.

At the gully's edge Shanty stared, color draining from his big face. "Jesus," he whispered. "Jesus." Trooper, for once, was speechless. Mouth hanging open, he simply stared. Yet with the interested detachment of a craftsman testing a new device, Wolf watched the spectacle and kept count. He counted them as they screamed, counted them as they ran, counted them as they fell.

Ten yards from the fire, Jack Purdue stood frozen for a moment, then turned and ran for his horse. The man still mounted held its reins, but he had his hands full. There were snakes everywhere now, and the horses had gone mad.

Stumbling and cursing, Purdue managed to catch his reins and swing aboard. The horse pitched, swapped ends and pitched again, but Purdue stayed on, hard-reining for control in a spinning dance that brought him closer and closer to the dark gully.

Finally he had the animal under a semblance of control. He started to turn toward the fire and heard a voice close at hand—slow, precise and colder than the wind. "Jack Purdue," it said. He whipped around in his saddle, clawing at his gun. But Wolf's gun was already up, pointing at him. "Good-bye, *chito*," the cold voice said. Flame blossomed from Wolf's hand, and Purdue pitched backward over the quivering rump of his horse.

Someone else fired then, and Wolf heard a slug clip air alongside his face. Then Trooper's carbine roared, and a mounted man just at the edge of the firelight was slapped from his saddle.

"I didn't miss that one," Trooper yelled.

Running hoofbeats sounded in the darkness, and Shanty's rifle spoke from beside him. There was a thump, and the horse veered away, riderless.

"Seventeen," Wolf said.

For a moment the firelight dimmed, quick-flaming tumbleweeds dissolving into showers of ruby sparks on the wind. Then another mass of brush blazed up against the face of the rock. In the brightness more angry snakes poured out from the clefts. Dark, writhing heaps here and there showed where men had fallen. From the darkness beyond the rock, dim in the wind, hoofbeats sounded, and the three men caught a glimpse of two riders going away. Only a glimpse, then they were gone, and a thin voice drifted back against the wind. ". . . remember! I'll see you dead for this. . . . !"

Shanty came up beside Wolf. "Could you tell who that was?"

"Jack's brother. Evan Purdue. Maybe Salem with him."

Trooper came over to them, his craggy face gaunt in the dancing, dying firelight. "Jesus," he said, gazing at the scene there by the rock.

With cold fingers Wolf reloaded his spent chamber and put his gun away. "Let's catch up some horses," he said.

Shanty glanced at him. "Where we goin'?"

"Back to Purdue's. There's a wagon in that barn. We'll come back in the morning and pick up what's left."

Trooper scowled. "You're goin' to leave all that gold

13

just layin' out here?''

"Do you want to go over there and pick it up?"

There was no answer. Dim light from thistle coals and showering, swirling sparks illuminated the slithering, coiling dark mass beneath the rock.

II

"Methods of locating vary with the occasion," the speaker said. "But the truth of it is that no person has ever been so lost that he can't be found. Every human presence leaves traces. No one is invisible. As with any animal, a man impresses himself upon his surroundings, and each impress is unique. Each man has patterns, habits, reactions not quite like anyone else. Know the person you seek, and you will find him. Of course, if he does not want to be found, then you will have that to deal with when you find him. Or if someone else doesn't want you to find your man—or wants to find him first—that also is part of the situation and must be considered."

He paused, giving them time to weigh what he had said, to match it to what had gone before. And as they studied him, he studied them. A mixed group, most would never become adept tracers. Six policemen, a pair of army scouts, three detectives employed by a private agency, two sheriffs from nearby counties, a federal marshal, a prison guard seeking promotion in rank and pay, and three who had paid for the course without stating the reasons for their interest. Two of these he identified as would-be bounty hunters dreaming of large sums to be collected through the recovery of fugitives. A mixed bag. For most, the best he could wish for them was to never have the opportunity to pursue a real-life trace. A few, though, showed promise. Eighteen people, gathered in an out-of-use courtroom—sixteen men and two women— each was present now to gain the arts of tracing, to become adept at finding people who did not want to be found. Two or three might learn the rudiments here. Their real education, of course, would come out there— by doing.

Most of them disliked him. It was plain in their eyes and in their attitudes. They disliked what he was, and they resented his being better at what they wanted to learn than they were. Yet each of them had paid to be here, and he would make sure they got their money's worth.

A hand went up . . . one of the sheriffs. "You say people leave impressions of themselves wherever they are, like that's more than footprints or spoor. Well, I've sat here for an hour today, listenin' to you. Are you sayin' that when I'm gone you could tell that I'd been here?"

He had anticipated the question. Someone always asked it. "Very easily. You came in with dust on your trousers. A little of it has fallen to the floor. There is a heel mark in it, right there by your foot. You see?"

"I see a heel mark."

"You also see that the mark was made by a man of about six feet in height, who sits quietly and tends to cross his left leg over his right. You see that he has recently walked past a lumber shed or a sawmill. You see that he smokes panatelas and uses a penknife to trim the ends—"

"Where do I see that?"

"You dropped an end under your chair. You also see that the man is younger than middle age, that he arrived here last night by coach from the northwest—the dust tells you that—and that the cobbler who put new heels on his boots recently was left-handed. That's a beginning. There may be more there if one takes the time to

15

study it."

The reactions were varied. Some—a few—saw what he saw when he pointed it out. The younger of the two women studied the heel mark and telltale dust for a moment, then glanced toward the rack where the men had hung their hats. Then she looked at him, raising a brow.

"Yes," he told her. "That is how I know that he came here by coach. There is a bit of the same dust under the hat rack."

"So he traveled by dusty conveyance, Mr. . . . ah . . ."

"Call me John Thomas if you like, Miss Larkin."

"John Thomas, then. Still, how do you know the conveyance was a coach?"

"There is no rail northwest from here. So he traveled by coach or carriage. Carriage seems unlikely for this distance, this time of year."

A clever one, he thought. She learns to make the connections, to see how one thing fits with another. But why was she studying the arts of trace? A pretty young woman, unmarried . . . never married, subtle things about her told him. Urban-bred, educated, perhaps of a good family—yet here she was, using a week of her time to learn what she could of the ways of hunting for people. She was one of the unidentified in the group, and the only one who posed a puzzle to him. All the rest, in one way or another, he understood.

"Well, you've buffaloed me, John Thomas," the sheriff admitted. "Everything you say is right; and how you come to it makes sense. But I still don't see how you do it."

"The same way you can. You have eyes. Use them."

"Comes natural to his kind," one of the policemen muttered to another.

John Thomas looked at the man, dark eyes narrowed. "That's a myth you'd better get rid of," he said. "Some people have more talent for the hunt than others, but the skills have to be learned. Nobody is born with them." A

16

slight smile touched his cheeks. "Not even *my kind.*"

"And you intend to teach us those skills in a week," one of the detectives said, frowning.

"Of course not. Just some basics. The rest you learn by doing."

The man stared at him, not trying to disguise the contempt in his eyes. "We'll see. But I ain't sure I'd be here if I'd known about you."

"That is your problem," John Thomas told him. "Not mine. I know what I am, and I know what I can teach. Whether you learn is up to you."

"Well, how much do you think I'm goin' to learn?"

"Not very much." John Thomas shrugged. "You aren't well equipped for learning."

"Now hold on!" The man came upright in his chair, burly shoulders pulling his coat tight. "I won't—"

"You paid money for a training course without investigating who would teach it. Then when you came in here you made up your mind about me without knowing anything about me. Then to top it off, you've waited nearly an hour to make your protest. Face it, Mr. Sloan, you aren't very bright."

There was usually one. In John Thomas's opinion it was best to weed that one out immediately. The man would either leave now, angry and fuming, or—as sometimes happened—become enraged and attack him physically. Either way, it would clear the air, the troublemaker would make no more trouble and the rest would be more attentive for the remainder of the week.

But the second woman in the group, an older, studious-looking lady from the same detective agency, turned to the man and said sharply, "Sloan, shut up. The man is right. You aren't very bright." Abruptly, almost miraculously, Sloan subsided, and John Thomas added some notes to his mental inventory of Catherine Grimes. That one would stand watching.

17

The army scouts grinned at each other, and one of them shrugged. They knew about John Thomas. They had heard the stories. They had been hoping to see him at work.

"If there are no more questions, then we can proceed," John Thomas said. "Generally speaking, persons who disappear come in two categories: those who choose to, and those who do not choose to. For the time being, we will concentrate on the first category. In most respects, from a tracer's point of view, they are far more interesting."

These preliminary portions of the course, though critical, were elementary, and John Thomas could deal with them in his sleep. Still talking, he strode to the courtroom's big double-hung window and gazed out. The streets of Leavenworth lay bleak beneath January clouds, and those who were out pulled their coats tightly about them. Why were they out there, on a day like this? Were they paying off debts? An interesting notion—a thing that would motivate people, would put them in places where they did not choose to be, doing things they did not choose to do. The paying off of debts. He could not discount it as a significant motivation. Of all people, *he* could not discount it.

He turned back to the group. Some were making notes, some not. Some were looking at him, some not. Why had the brute—Sloan—not released his anger in the usual ways? Was Sloan paying a debt? Did he owe something to Catherine Grimes?

More often than not, John Thomas knew, people were exactly what they seemed, provided one's judgment of what they seemed was sound. Sometimes, though, there was more to them, and that made things interesting. Supposing Sloan were to disappear and a tracer be set to find him . . . the thought brought a private smile. Ten minutes' effort. Background, past and present associations, natural habitats, probable reason for disappearance

18

and a knowledge of the man's pattern of needs—for one who knew these things, it would take ten minutes to list the places where Sloan might hide, and Sloan would be found in one of those places. But only if Sloan were acting on his own initiative. If someone else were involved, it might be an entirely different matter. And if a person owed a debt, the creditor was always involved.

"Habitats are essential," he was telling them. "Without restraining circumstance, a fugitive tends to seek the habitat most familiar to him. A person of the streets will hide in cities; a person of the frontier will seek frontiers; a person of any strictured culture will try to hide within that culture. By the fact of being a fugitive, a person who hides is seeking solitude. He will look for it wherever he has found it before. To know a fugitive's own definition of solitude is to know where he will hide. Know that, and then you can go and find him."

Know who he owes his greatest debt to, he thought, and that person probably can tell you exactly where he is. He glanced out at the cold, blustery streets again. Colonel Britten knows exactly where I am. In winter storage. Imparting arcane wisdoms to paying customers to pay for my own storage until he needs me to solve a problem for him.

"About six times out of ten," he told the group, "a person in hiding or on the run is where he is because he has stolen something . . . or at least he believes that he has. And in about half of those situations, he will have with him the thing he has stolen. Upon occasion one can trace the person through the thing. A fairly recent example was the tracing of the Purdue gang after their raid on Three Bridges."

"Heard about that," a sheriff said. "How was that done?"

"One of the items they took was a large sum in gold coin, freshly minted in Philadelphia. One of those coins turned up at Dodge City. From there it was only a matter

19

of knowing the sort of habitat Purdue might select and where such a place might be found, within a two or three days' ride of Dodge City."

"Heard how they was brought in, too." The sheriff's eyes glittered. "Most of 'em died of snakebite . . . in December."

"Even the most experienced fugitive can be careless sometimes," John Thomas said.

"Makes it easy on the courts," the sheriff allowed. "Fourteen cases of snakebite and four of lead poisoning . . . sure doesn't leave much work for the hangman when things work out like that. You have any notion how such a thing might have happened?"

John Thomas shrugged, dark eyes hard and as cold as the winds beyond the window. "I imagine a person would have to have been there to know that."

The pendulum clock above the bailiff's bench toned. Another hour had passed. Beyond the gilded glass of the courtroom door a shadow moved restlessly. John Thomas glanced at it curiously. The person waiting out there had been there for nearly ten minutes. A tall man, the shadow told him. Long coat, hat not on the head but in the hand, and held casually as one long acquainted with the civilities. Soft boots or shoes that did not scuff the dusty floor or echo from its surface. Two other things the shadow told him: The person there knew that whoever he was waiting for was in the courtroom, and he knew that John Thomas was aware of him. He did not turn his profile to his revealing shadow even when his stance would have done so naturally. A very, very careful person.

Footsteps passing in the hall outside he recognized. A records clerk from the tax assessor's office. The footsteps did not hesitate or change their tempo. Therefore, the person waiting beyond the door did not seem out of place there, nor was he a person the clerk would recognize.

"A bit later we will discuss how things a fugitive does

not have with him can lead to his whereabouts," John Thomas said. "But it is now eleven o'clock, and the eating places nearby tend to fill early. We will break for midday and resume at two."

They gathered up their things and filed out, several of them eyeing him as they passed, sizing him up. Sloan's glare was dark and hostile, but Catherine Grimes shepherded the burly man out adroitly. Gail Larkin hung back for a moment, until the others had passed. "You goaded that man," she said quietly. "Will you tell me why?"

"Curiosity, as much as anything." He shrugged. "And a preference for solving problems as they arise rather than leaving them until later."

"Will he be a problem for you?"

"Probably." He turned away, gazing out the window. He heard the hesitance in her steps, the realization of dismissal, the firm tapping of her heels on the way out. When she had gone he said, not loudly, "You may come in now, Mr. Joy. We are alone."

The softest of footsteps sounded behind him, then the door closed. "You knew it was me, then."

"You knew I would. What are you doing here, Mr. Joy? Leavenworth is a long way from Georgetown." He turned and noted the fatigue on the tall man's features.

Joy looked around at the empty courtroom, tired eyes searching for any open doors, cracks in the walnut paneling, any place where someone might listen.

"We are secure here," John Thomas said. "I've tested it."

"Very well," Joy said. "You are needed, John Thomas."

"And *you* came? Colonel Britten could have—"

"We don't know where Colonel Britten is. We tried, but he has disappeared. The Director asked me to come personally."

"My only arrangement is with Colonel Britten," John

21

Thomas reminded him. "I am not involved in anything else."

"No. Of course you aren't. But I want you to talk with the Director, John Thomas. I persuaded him to agree, and that under the circumstances, we might contact you directly. As I said, John Thomas, you are needed."

"Under the circumstances? What are the circumstances, Mr. Joy?"

In a face that had trained itself for a lifetime to reveal nothing, suddenly there was expression—a sadness too deep to contain. "I came because there was nothing that could be trusted to the wire or to a messenger, John Thomas. We have information—reliable information, I'm afraid—that Ernest Kichener is dead."

For long moments, John Thomas stared at the older man, dark eyes seeking a confirmation or a doubt. Then he turned away, to look out on the gusty grayness of Leavenworth January. The question was needless, but he asked it anyway. "Are you sure?"

"As sure as we can be, John Thomas. He was . . . on a mission."

"And did not complete it. That's why I'm needed. Is that right?"

"Precisely," Joy said.

"My commitment here—"

"Will be upheld," Joy said. "I have already contacted Jay Merrill. He will be here in time to step in for you this afternoon. Also, while I was waiting, I sent word to your Irishman to prepare for your departure. There is an eastbound train leaving at two forty-five. I can't force you to be on it, of course, but under the circumstances. . . ."

Under the circumstances. Ernest Kichener . . . dead. "I am not Ernest Kichener," he said.

"No, you aren't," Joy agreed. "But you *are* John Thomas Wolf."

III

"So you are John Thomas Wolf," the Director said. He had not bothered to stand when the two entered the inner office in the secluded house at Springfield. He had simply listened to Joy's introduction while he stared in distaste at the newcomer. He noted the long, raven-black hair, the ruddy chiseled features, the placid dark eyes and coil-spring vitality of the man before him, and chose to disapprove. "The late Mr. Kichener's protégé," he added, seeking response. The dark eyes simply regarded him, unwavering. "Expert tracer, they tell me. A problem solver, they say." Still John Thomas said nothing. The Director glared at him. "Well?"

John Thomas turned to the tall, dour man beside him. "How long has this man been in charge here, Mr. Joy?"

"The Director was appointed in June, John Thomas. Personally appointed by the President, of course."

"Six months," John Thomas said. "One of the Civil Service Reform appointees, then. I'd heard that the results of that act had been disastrous. Does he know anything about his organization?"

The man at the desk stared at him, his eyes turning hard. "Now see here. . . ."

"The Director has all of the records and reports at his disposal, John Thomas," Joy said.

John Thomas turned his gaze on the Director again. "You sent for me. Why?"

"Now see here, I am not accustomed to being addressed in such manner. Especially not by an—"

"An Indian, Mr. Director?"

"—an amateur, Mr. Wolf. Yes, I have read the reports—what there is to read—on both yourself and your Mr. Kichener. Frankly, I do not approve. Not in the slightest."

"Why did you send for me?"

23

"Under certain conditions, and with certain understandings, I am prevailed upon to give you an assignment. There is a task that—"

"No."

"What?"

"I said no. I accept no assignments, Mr. Director. I do not work for you. For that matter, neither did Ernest Kichener. Your reports should tell you that."

"My reports tell me only that my predecessors have, upon occasion, had the bad judgment to entrust matters of great urgency to outside amateurs."

Joy raised a hand. "Mr. Director, Ernest Kichener was no amateur. Neither is Mr. Wolf. Free lance . . . but hardly amateur."

"Nonetheless, I certainly do not choose to operate in that fashion, sir. This organization is—"

John Thomas leaned hard knuckles on the desk, and suddenly the dark eyes that had seemed so placid were no longer placid. They burned with a cold fire that was like a physical force boring into the other man's soul. *"This organization* is eighty-six years old," he said. "You have been its director for six months. If you have something for me to do, I will consider it. But only on my own terms. If that doesn't suit you, then you have wasted my time and your money."

The Director tried to speak, swallowed and started again. Never in his life had he felt such force of presence . . . as though something dark and violent had been released, just for an instant, and he had felt its hot breath upon him. It left him shaken. "My orders from President Cleveland are very clear," he said, faltering. "The method of directing this organization is—"

"Cleveland," the dark man chopped the name off short. "The President. Commander in Chief of the armed forces. Do you know where the combat strength of the United States Army spent the past summer, Mr. Director? Five thousand of our best troops coordinating

24

their efforts with nearly twelve thousand soldiers of the Mexican Army? In the southwest deserts, Mr. Director, helping General Nelson Miles track down a man named Goyathlay."

"Who?"

"Geronimo, Mr. Director. His real name is Goyathlay, and his 'bloody army'—which nearly a third of the United States Army spent the summer running to ground—consisted of twenty-four warriors. George Crook could have brought him in within a month, with no more than a company of cavalry. But Crook isn't a Cleveland man. Miles is."

"Those numbers are classified information," the Director snapped. "How do you know them?"

"Professional secrets are secrets kept from professionals. As you said, Mr. Director . . . I am an amateur."

Joy turned away, stifling a smile. He had done all he could, persuading the Director to at least interview John Thomas. The rest was up to them.

For a long minute there was silence. Then the Director sighed and pointed to a chair. "Please sit down, ah . . . Mr. Wolf. Possibly we can begin again, with a slightly better understanding of each other. The thing I want you to understand is that I can't do things in the way my predecessors may have done. Even if I were so inclined, it would not be allowed. There have been changes in the rules of government in this country. Persons in public service no longer have the discretions that they once had. The new Civil Service System carries with it levels of responsibility and answerability that apply to everyone now. The days of the private adventurer sanctioned by a public trust are gone. I am sorry to hear of the death of your Mr. Kichener, but surely you can see that the man was an anachronism. There were never any real controls upon his methods, or even upon what he chose to do. Every . . . ah . . . task he ever performed for this organization, he did for reasons of his own."

25

"And did he ever fail?" Indian eyes regarded the man closely, testing him.

"Apparently not . . . until now, that is. However—"

"The thing *you* need to understand, Mr. Director, is the nature of the mechanism you direct. This was never intended to be a military unit, or a judicial arm or a legislative or even executive function. You speak of new systems, but the very reason for this organization's existence is that no system is perfect or complete. President Jefferson knew that when he created it. Ernest Kichener was fond of likening our society to a fabric. A tapestry, he called it—threads woven this way and that, each becoming a part of the overall weave, each working with and drawn against all the others to make a vital whole. But a tapestry is complete in itself, Mr. Director. It has no control of elements beyond its plane . . . not even its own loose threads. That is why this organization exists—so that there will be someone in position to operate outside the fabric and trim off those loose threads."

"But we can't have free agents running loose, doing whatever they please with our sanction. It just won't do."

"It won't work any other way." John Thomas shrugged. "Now are you ready to tell me why you are playing this game?"

"Game?"

"If you didn't know the unique nature of this organization, you wouldn't be in charge of it, Cleveland or no Cleveland."

The Director turned away, a quizzical expression on his face as he looked toward Joy.

"I told you," Joy said.

The Director sighed again. "God help this country if we must solve our problems in such manner."

"God help us if we ever forget how."

The Director thumbed open a file, glancing at it. John

26

Thomas Wolf, protégé to the half-legendary Ernest Kichener. John Thomas Wolf, age thirty-six, educated at Sheffield and Fairmont with additional degrees from St. Ives and three other universities. Professor emeritus and expert on field maneuvers for three military academies— including West Point, an institution he did not even qualify to attend because of his race. John Thomas Wolf, manhunter, tracer and academician. John Thomas Wolf . . . Indian. He did not read the words in the file. He knew them by heart, and more besides.

There were some, they said, who had known Ernest Kichener as Nemesis. Those who knew of John Thomas Wolf had another name for him. They called him, simply, Wolf.

It had been his fervent hope never to meet either of them—never to have occasion to need those skills they could uniquely offer. But now he did. Nemesis was gone. That left only . . . Wolf.

He looked up. The Indian was watching him, patiently now, letting him make up his mind.

"If you'd had any other choice, you wouldn't have sent for me," John Thomas said. "So you might as well tell me about it."

The Director closed the file and squared his shoulders, wondering if his career would survive what he was about to do. "Very well," he said. "Have you ever heard of the Mask of Montezuma?"

There was a knock at the office door, and Joy went to open it. Voices, then he closed it again. "Message from the gate, sir. The house is under surveillance."

"Description, Mr. Joy?"

"Yes, sir. Gate says it's a young woman in a carriage. Shall we have a look?"

"By all means," the Director said, standing for the first time since they had entered. He glanced at his guest. "Come along if you like. Since you know so much about us here, I'm sure you know about our observatory."

From within an ornate tower atop the house, they scanned the public road with fine telescopes, and John Thomas's jaw tightened as he studied the fur-muffled face in the shadows of a closed carriage, a face whose eyes were intent upon the house.

"I've seen her," Joy said. "Somewhere recently."

"At Leavenworth." John Thomas nodded. "She was in that group I was teaching when you arrived. Her name is Gail Larkin."

The Director and Joy exchanged a glance. "Larkin's daughter," Joy said. "So that's where she went."

"Apparently. Then followed you and, ah . . . Mr. Wolf all the way here."

John Thomas was still studying the face in the carriage. Not once on the trip eastward from Leavenworth had he suspected they were being followed. Whoever Gail Larkin was, she was good. "Who is Larkin?" he asked.

Joy frowned. "A missing person. One of several, lately."

"The group you were teaching?" the Director asked. "Which sort of group?"

"A mixture. It's a thing I do sometimes, when I'm not doing something else. I teach people the craft of hide-and-seek."

"Should we bring the young lady in, sir?" Wide-lens nautical glasses scanned the public road beyond the gate: tracks in the snow from the day's traffic, lone carriage standing beyond the gate, its dray horse stamping idly while the single passenger sat motionless in the hooded shadows . . . beyond only an undisturbed field of twilit snow with the gray mist of winter trees in the background.

"How could she have followed you?" the Director asked. "Was she on the same train?"

"No," John Thomas said. "She wasn't."

"Then, how could she find her way here?"

28

"I can think of a dozen ways. I think you should bring her in. It's cold out there."

"Have her brought in, Mr. Joy," the Director said. "Ask Maude to serve tea in the parlor, where Mr. Wolf's . . . ah . . . man is waiting."

"This Larkin," John Thomas asked, "is he in any way connected with the business you need me for?"

"I'm afraid he is, yes. That's what worries me."

"And with Ernest Kichener?"

"Most likely. We think he was one of the people Mr. Kichener had gone to find. Frederick Larkin—*Doctor* Frederick Larkin—is the man who first told us about the Mask of Montezuma."

"We don't know exactly what the mask looked like," Joy said, leafing through stacks of careful notes, "except that it was made of gold, with embellishments of red and green stone, and it was thought that wearing it—under certain conditions—made its wearer the embodiment of the god Huitzilopochtli, the primary deity of the Aztec pantheon. Hernan Cortes actually saw the mask. It is described in his letters to the Holy Roman Emperor Charles V. But it disappeared during the siege of Tenochtitlan. It was never in the inventory of prizes returned by Cortes."

"Three hundred and sixty-seven years ago," the Director added. "But legends have persisted all that time, in Mexico, that one day Huitzilopochtli will return to bathe in *chalchinatl* and give domination of the world to his faithful subjects."

"*Chalchinatl?*"

"Huitzilopochtli's favorite nourishment. It means 'precious liquid.' The Aztec word for human blood."

"Most of this we have from Frederick Larkin," Joy explained, "although we have added extensive details from our research. It seems that Moctezuma Xocoyotzin, the second King Montezuma of the Aztecs and the one Cortes defeated, was quite a despot among his neighbors and a real zealot for keeping the sun god well nourished. Dr. Larkin estimates that at one point, human sacrifices at Tenochtitlan reached more than a thousand a day. The victims all died the same way. Their hearts were torn out."

"To please a god."

"Well, partly," Joy said. "As a matter of fact the ceremonies were an excellent way to keep the populace in line. Montezuma II wasn't the first Aztec king to rule by terror, but he probably perfected the system. He was killed by his own people, you know."

"Not by the Spanish?"

"No. Cortes was a wise conquistador. While he was demolishing Tenochtitlan and starting to build Mexico City on the ruins, he sent Montezuma out to face his people. They met him with stones and arrows."

"Come to the point, Mr. Joy," the Director said.

"Very well. The point is, John Thomas, the cult of Huitzilopochtli—the sun god—never died out in Mexico. It simply went underground. But nearly a million people in Mexico still speak Nahuatl—the Aztec language—and our scholars believe that generations of people have simply waited for the coming of an old prophecy their priests foretold after the Spanish defeated them: the coming of the double god, they say, when the archenemies Huitzilopochtli and Quetzalcoatl—the sun god and the plumed serpent, the gods of day and night— join forces to bring back the glory of the Tenochca—it means 'chosen people' or some such. The Aztecs often called themselves that.

"The sign they wait for is the coming of Quetzalcoatl in the guise of Huitzilopochtli. The symbolism is that Quetzalcoatl will sustain his old enemy long enough for the people to arise again and furnish the sun god with the nourishment he needs."

30

"Human blood."

"Exactly. The blood of enemies, and a lot of it."

"Go on."

"The plumed serpent is only one of Quetzalcoatl's incarnations, John Thomas. In another, he is seen as a white man with a red beard."

John Thomas gazed around at the lantern-lit study, a sanctuary deep within the house, its walls lined with cabinets and bookshelves. A dozen times in forty years, he knew, Ernest Kichener had been in this room . . . and had gone from here to find answers to problems that had no answers, to create solutions to situations beyond solving through any normal recourse. Now they said that Ernest Kichener was gone. And now John Thomas Wolf sat here, putting together the pieces of a situation that had no proper answer. And as the pieces came together he felt a coldness in his belly.

"Quetzalcoatl in the guise of Huitzilopochtli," he murmured. "A white man in the sun god's mask."

"Exactly," Joy said.

"Where is Montezuma's mask?"

"We don't know, John Thomas. But we know that there is someone searching for it. Some of the Apaches brought back from Mexico have spoken of it. A young chief named Emilio, for one. He says the Indians in Mexico told him of a man in Mexico, a leader, who claims to be Quetzalcoatl—a powerful man, they say, with influence and much wealth. He has promised to appear as Huitzilopochtli and lead the Nahuatl speakers to a new Tenochtitlan from which they can conquer the earth, as their sun god promised them."

"A lunatic?"

"We don't know. Ernest Kichener didn't think so. He felt it more likely a gambit by some individual or group to gain a base of power. This all surfaced nearly a year ago. Eight months ago Ernest left here, for the southwest. That . . . that was the last time I saw him." Joy took a

31

deep breath, his chin on his chest. "Ernest was sixty-five years old, John Thomas. He should never have gone."

"What evidence do you have that he is dead?"

The Director pushed back his chair and stood. "This," he said. He strode to a wall where a small, ornate tapestry hung between laden cases, and raised the fabric. Behind it on the wall were characters, ranked like squared glyphs, drawn on the plaster surface with something dark that might have been dried blood. "Yes, it is blood. We confirmed that. No one has access to this room, John Thomas. No one except those who belong in this house. And yet here it is. The tapestry had been thrown aside and these symbols painted here. I found it myself, one morning about ten days ago."

"The symbols are *Nahua* glyphs," Joy said. "We brought in a translator. A scholar. He thinks it says, 'The hawk has fallen. This is his blood. Send no more hawks, or everyone will die.' The symbol there beside the characters is the symbol of the god Quetzalcoatl, the plumed serpent."

The hawk. Ernest Kichener. Nemesis. John Thomas nodded. "Where does Frederick Larkin come in?" he asked.

"Larkin is a scholar of history and archaeology. He learned—quite by accident—that evidence had been uncovered in Mexico that might lead to the wherabouts of the Mask of Montezuma. Some of Montezuma's followers, it seems, may have spirited the thing away and gone north with it, then sent back word that it had arrived safely in Aztlan . . . according to Aztec legend, the land where they originated."

"And where is Aztlan?"

"Larkin felt—*feels*, if he is still alive—that Aztlan may have been somewhere in the Arizona Territory. He went to search for it, and we think Ernest Kichener went to find him."

For a long time then, they sat in silence, while John

32

Thomas sorted through the pieces he had been given, letting them fall into an order in his mind. It was a hunter's trick—a tracer's trick—test the terrain, the situation, then just let it fall into place before reviewing detail. Sometimes patterns emerged that the detail mind might never see for being too close.

"What would you like to see happen?" His question was aimed at the Director.

"We would like . . . for nothing to happen, Mr. Wolf. We would like for this entire business to vanish as a nightmare vanishes. The Mask of Montezuma is lost. All things considered, we feel it best for all concerned if it remains lost forever."

"I agree, John Thomas," Joy said. "Our country—all of our countries—has all the trouble it can handle without some devil, be he lunatic or prophet or simply a power-mad schemer, bringing back the days of a sun god nourished by human blood."

"I might go and have a look around," John Thomas said. "But I want it understood, *if* I do, that anything I might do will be done my way."

The Director sighed. "Understood," he said.

"Is your housekeeper still entertaining the young lady in the parlor?"

"Maude is something more than a housekeeper," the Director said with a trace of smugness. He pulled a sheet of paper from his lapel, unfolded it and glanced at the writing on it. "Gail Larkin is twenty-six years of age, unmarried, resides with her father in a house in Emporia, often accompanies him on his travels and acts as his secretary. She took the train that left Leavenworth three hours after your train, and traced you to this house through two inquiries—one of a station attendant and one of a carriage handler who recalled hearing your destination when you boarded your hackney. She knows you are here and desires to speak with you." His eyes gleamed with triumph. "We are very good at gathering information here, Mr. Wolf."

"Not bad," John Thomas agreed. "Does that tell you why she followed me here?"

"No. She didn't say."

"Didn't say? Then how about where her father is, or where Ernest Kichener went?"

"Ah . . . no, Maude didn't want to seem to be inquiring."

"I see. Well, do we know whether she knows where her father is?"

"No, we don't know that."

"I see. Is my man still in there with them?"

"He was. He had tea, then he went to the gallery to play with the stereopticon. He was evidently bored with the women chattering."

John Thomas turned away, and Joy thought a trace of smile had tugged at his wide Indian mouth. "Can you call him in here, please?"

The Director shrugged, and Joy left the room. He returned, followed by the hulking Irishman.

John Thomas glanced at Joy, then asked his attendant, "Shanty, did you listen to the conversation in the parlor? The two women?"

"Sure I did, Wolf. I was there."

"Why is Miss Larkin here, Shanty?"

"She followed us. Took a separate train, but she read our sign pretty good."

"Do you know why she followed us?"

"Same reason she went to Leavenworth. She wanted to size you up, then maybe get you to find her daddy for her. He's missin'."

"Then she doesn't know where he is?"

"She only knows where he was goin', is all, but she figures you could find him if you took a notion to. She's heard about you. Little scrap of paper in her handbag says, 'G . . . no wire beyond here . . . K told you of Wolf . . . find him Leavenworth . . . I fear for K. . . .' That's

34

all it says, Wolf. She don't know I read it."

"Anything else?"

"Bits an' pieces. I don't know."

"Thank you, Shanty." He turned to the Director. "Kichener talked with Miss Larkin before going in search of her father. He mentioned me to her. Her father sent her a message, but it was incomplete. All it tells us is that Kichener did find Larkin, then separated from him, and now Larkin has gone where there is no telegraph and is afraid something has happened to Kichener."

The Director was staring at the burly, shaggy Shanty.

"My sources of information also are very capable," Mr. Director," John Thomas added.

"Well, shall we go talk to Miss Larkin, then?"

"You talk to her," John Thomas said. "Then send her home. See that she gets aboard the next train bound toward Westport Crossing. See that she is on it."

"You aren't going to talk with her?" The Director seemed stunned. "After all this, you don't even want to interview her?"

"Just do what I asked," John Thomas said. "I've been here long enough. I need to be on my way. Mr. Joy, show us out a back way, please. We'll use the carriage we came in. Mr. Director, this has been . . . interesting. Good-bye."

"What do you mean? You can't just walk away now! Don't you understand; this is a crisis! You have to accept this assignment!"

"I don't accept assignments, Mr. Director. I told you that. And I don't *have* to do anything." Without further words, he strode from the room, Shanty following after him.

The Director stared at the closing door, his mouth still open. "Well of all. . . ."

"I told you about him, sir," Joy said.

"Does that mean he won't. . . ?"

"It doesn't mean anything, sir, except that he is

35

leaving. If John Thomas wants to tell you something, he says it. If he doesn't say it, then it isn't implied, either way. I'd better hurry, sir. If I don't show him the back entrance, he'll find it for himself."

"But there were files I wanted to show him . . . other things to discuss . . . he doesn't have any of the intelligence documents . . . he didn't take anything!"

"No, sir, he didn't. I shall be back shortly, sir." Joy hurried out to catch the guests, not looking back. No, John Thomas Wolf had taken nothing, but the Director would notice soon enough that all the documents he had collected so carefully were gone. Joy had seen—barely seen—Shanty gathering them up while the Director's attention was on John Thomas.

Six months was a very short time to learn a great many things about an organization, and a totally inadequate time to learn about the people the organization relied upon. Still, John Thomas had said it as clearly as anything. Whatever he might decide to do, he would do it his own way.

IV

Iron wheels on iron rails clattered mournfully as the train crossed the iron trestle into Missouri. There the bleak rails would climb onto new roadbed for the two-day run westward to Kansas, where portions would be shunted off and recoupled for the journey to Leavenworth. In the rearmost passenger coach John Thomas gazed out at the winter land, high bluffs ahead crowned by snowy flats and the mist-gray of winter forest, rising from the frozen banks of the big river. Rail travel had become a wonder in the past three years. The wonder was what could be bought with the capital generated by a hundred and fifty million acres of public lands granted to the railroad companies.

What was it Emerson had said about railroads? He tried to remember the words . . . Emerson's essays had fascinated him during his years at academy and university, giving him his first clear concept of how the minds of "white men" worked. As Emerson had studied Coleridge, seeking avenues of understanding, so John Thomas Wolf had studied Emerson. As Emerson sought evidence of a spiritual relationship between man and nature, so John Thomas Wolf sought evidence of a spiritual path that might lead a red man into the patterns of the whites. And in Emerson's essays he discovered a profound irony. The further Emerson pursued his notions of individualism and self-reliance, the more Emerson—to John Thomas—approached the Indian ways of thinking. One more Emerson, he had decided, and the white people would all be trying as hard to be Indians as the Indians—a few at least—were trying to be white. For years the idea had amused him.

Americans take to railroads, Emerson had written, as though this little invention were the cradle to which they were born.

The "little invention" had come of age in recent years. Rails went almost everywhere. Yet *almost* was not everywhere. For a tracer, more often than not, the end of rail was the beginning of the trail.

Cold air eddied through the swaying coach, and Shanty entered from ahead, ducking to pass from the frigid bellows-way, seeming to fill the narrow aisle with his bulk as he headed back to where John Thomas waited. He dropped into the aisle seat and rubbed his eyes with big knuckles. "She's still there, Wolf."

"She didn't see you, did she?"

"Aw, Wolf." The big man frowned. "You know me better'n that."

"I don't suppose it would matter now, anyway. There's nobody else on this train to worry about. It is just as well, though, if you stay out of sight for a time. Our next stop is at Haven. You'll get off there. You know what to do?"

"Sure, Wolf. Like you told me."

"Those telegraph messages . . . don't send them from Haven. Wait until you get to Harpersville. There's a wire there."

"You think somebody's got eyes on us, Wolf?"

"It's just a feeling. But somebody obviously knew all about the house at Springfield, and how to get inside. Whoever it is, I don't want to underestimate him."

"Do you think Kichener is dead, Wolf?"

"They think he is. Joy knew him better than anybody else who's left from the old days. If Joy thinks he's dead, then maybe he is."

"But *you* don't think so, do you?" Shanty raised a heavy eyebrow.

"I don't know. Kichener has been dead before. Several times. But maybe his luck ran out." He folded the sheaf of papers he had been reading, replaced them in their leather wallet and handed them to Shanty. "I've learned all I can from this. When you get to Harpersville, mail it back to Mr. Joy. I don't imagine it's good for the Director's nerves to have such things out running around. It isn't tidy." He stood and edged into the aisle, past the massive legs of the Irishman. "Will you have any problem with Trooper?"

"No more than usual. He'll whine and grumble, but I guess he'll be glad to see me." A cruel grin split his fiery whiskers. "Near a month in an eight-by-ten cell, I 'spect he's ready to be glad to see most anybody."

Taking his hat and valise, John Thomas went forward to the front passenger coach. Ignoring the disapproving stares of several passengers in rear-facing seats who saw him enter, he went forward to where the girl was seated, tossed his valise on the opposite bench and sat down,

38

facing her. "Where was the message from your father sent from, Miss Larkin?"

For a moment she only stared at him, then her hand went to the handbag at her side.

"I know what it says," he told her. "But I don't know where he was when he sent it. Where did it come from?"

"Why didn't you see me in Springfield? That house . . . I know you were there and I waited. . . ."

"Too many eyes," he said. "It's better to talk here." He saw her furtive glance at the various passengers around them in the coach and added, "Only two of these people boarded after you, and they are in another car. It's fairly safe."

"Then, you know I was followed."

"Yes, of course. But the man who followed you isn't aboard. He is probably still in Springfield, recovering from a severe headache."

"And you know why I followed you there, don't you?"

"Yes. Where was the wire sent from, Miss Larkin?"

"Tucson. It's a town out in the—"

"I know where Tucson is. I also know there is wire west of there, so I gather your father was going either north or south. Which was it?"

"Are you going to help me?"

"I don't know. Why should I?"

"Because that man who came looking for my father—"

"Kichener?"

"Yes. He told me about you. He made a point of telling me. He said if he couldn't find my father, then you could. Then when the message came, my father's message, he said to find you. At Leavenworth. How do you know about the message? It hasn't been out of my bag since I received it."

"Yes, it has. Do you know what your father was looking for out there?"

"Yes. A mask. An old Aztec artifact. He felt he knew

39

where it was, at least the general area."

"Where?"

"Out there. North of there. He was going north . . . if he could. I don't know what happened, John Thomas. The message wasn't completed."

"Why didn't you come directly to me at Leavenworth, Miss Larkin? Why the game of enrolling for my course?"

"When Mr. Kichener told me about you, he didn't mention that you are . . . ah . . ."

"An Indian?"

"Yes. And I was being cautious. I wasn't sure what to do. I thought if I could just watch you for a bit. . . ."

"It wouldn't have mattered. I was not intending to take on any odd jobs. I just finished one a month ago that wasn't very pleasant."

"Those Purdue people, the gang that was broken up. Was that you? Sheriff Decker told Catherine Grimes that he thought you were the one who . . . did that." She shuddered as though chilled.

He glanced out the window at the frigid landscape beyond. The rails had entered hills, and the train was straining upgrade. As it slowed at a bend, he saw movement behind—a quick glimpse of a man rolling in the crusted snow. He leaned closer to the window, peering back. A burly, coated figure appeared at the corner of a rolling coach, leaning outward to look back. Shanty.

Farther back, the rolling man was on his feet and running, away from the rails. In woodland beyond, John Thomas saw movement that gave the impression of men with horses. The train was still pulling upgrade, aiming at a cleft between ridges just ahead. John Thomas squinted in thought, then glanced at the overhead rack. "Is that your luggage? Do you have any more?"

"No, just the one bag. I left in rather a hurry when I learned you had gone."

"Do you know how to open the diaphragm between

40

cars? The bellows cover?"

"I've seen it done. There is a lever that looses a section of it."

"Right. Now listen carefully. In a moment I am going to steal your bag off that rack. I am going to stand, then grab it and run, back through this car to the one behind. When I do, I want you to scream and point at me."

"Point at you?"

"Shout and point. Say 'that Indian stole my luggage,' or something. Some of these men will chase me. When they do, you follow behind them, into the connecting corridor. Then you open the hatch and jump . . . not on this side of the train. On the other side. Jump out, get down and hide."

She was staring at him. "Just do it," he said. "It is important." Without hesitation, then, he stood, grabbed her satchel from the rack and ran. He heard her scream behind him and saw men coming out of their seats as he passed. At the connecting door, he pushed through, crossed the rocking corridor in a stride, and slammed through the door beyond to spring the length of the middle coach. He heard men entering the car behind him, shouting and cursing. At the end of the car he pushed through the door, closed it behind him and flipped the side railing around to block it. A tug at the diaphragm lever and he was through, clinging to the outside of the shifting, tarred canvas bellows as he pulled the hatch closed behind him. A car length ahead he saw Gail Larkin leap from the train and roll into snow-brushed growth beside the roadbed. Holding her bag and his valise, his hat firmly on his head, he jumped. He lit running, and a moment later he dived into brush cover beside the girl. The train streamed by, clattering on frozen roadbed, its engine already topping the grade, starting down the other slope. As the caboose cleared past them he saw horsemen at a distance, up on the far ridge, riding hard, paralleling the direction of the train. The caboose topped the rise

41

and disappeared beyond it. For a moment there was only the receding song of the rolling stock, the whine of cold winds through denuded hills, and silence. Then the hard ground beneath them flinched at a shock wave, and the blast of an explosion carried back on the wind. Lazily, somewhere beyond the tracked rise, smoke rose in the sky to feather and flare on the morose wind. Distant keening of steel wheels braking on iron track drifted back from beyond, then silence.

Gail Larkin's eyes were huge in a face as pale as sundown drifts. "What happened?"

"They've blown the track ahead, to stop the train. Come on, we have to move. They'll be back this way when they don't find us."

"Who?"

"Whoever those men are. We're the ones they're after." He stood, gathered up belongings and helped her to her feet.

She gazed around. Everywhere was winter-locked wilderness and silence. "Where can we go? How?"

"Just follow me." Climbing to the heaped roadbed he started uphill, alongside the tracks, walking fast. She hurried to keep up. Just ahead, before the crest of the rise, a little trestle crossed a runoff gully. He angled downward toward it.

She glanced back. "You aren't going to fool anybody this way," she said. "We're leaving tracks that a blind person could follow."

He ignored her, went on down the side of the gully and stopped at its bottom. Hard, clear ice lined the rocks there where snows had thawed, run and refrozen. When she reached him he pointed to the right, toward the trestle. "We won't make tracks now. Stay on the clear ice. Come on, hurry."

Almost running, they reached the trestle and passed under it. He set down his burdens and began sweeping crusted snow off the timber risers at its north shoulder.

"Climb here," he told her. "Go right to the top and step over onto the ties between rails. Don't leave prints if you can help it."

She climbed, and he came up behind her, dusting snow back over the timbers as he passed. "Now this way," he said.

"This is the way we came. Why are we going back?"

"Just keep up with me if you can. These ties are clear, step on them, not the ground between." He ran silently, downgrade, nimble as a dancer on the rail ties, with the girl running like an antelope behind him, squinting with concentration to step where his feet had been. They passed the brush where they had hidden, the telltale scuffs of snow where they had left the train, and went on . . . two hundred yards, then three hundred. He stopped, and she almost piled into him.

On the north shoulder, snow was scuffed and tumbled, and tracks of a running man led off toward the forest fifty yards away. "Here," he said. "Be careful. Step in the man's tracks." Again he led and she followed, slowly now, stretching and balancing, matching the single trail that was there. It seemed to take a long time to reach the shelter of the woods.

Just beyond, the ground was disturbed where horses had milled, and they noticed the bootprints of several men. From screening brush John Thomas eased out to peer back up the grade. Five riders were at the crest, coming down along the embankments, leaning to look at the snowy ground. "Get low," he told the girl. "Stay out of sight and wait."

He saw them find the walking prints, then saw them gather on the grade to look toward the gully. Four of them dismounted then, guns in hands, while the fifth held their reins. The men on foot started away, toward the iced bottom. One of them turned to wave a hand at the mounted man, then went on. When they were out of sight the rider swung his mount and, leading the other

43

horses, crossed the tracks and came downslope to a point opposite where John Thomas crouched. There he turned, following the set of prints in the snow, and headed for the brush. He entered the bare forest, leaning low in his saddle, and straightened as a sound touched his ears. He started to turn when a lithe figure burst from the underbrush at his side, coming upward at him. A hard hand closed on his throat, pulling him downward, and something hard exploded behind his ear.

John Thomas calmed the five horses, gathered in their reins and said, "Come on. We don't have all day."

While the girl mounted one of the horses, he strapped their belongings onto another one, then paused to roll the man on the ground into the cover of a snow-topped thicket.

"Is he dead?" she asked.

"Not quite. He was lucky this time." He swung into the saddle of a tall bay, gathered the reins of all the others and led the way back into the forest, climbing northward toward the distant ridge. She followed, and where the forest cleared in a crusted meadow she rode alongside him.

"I never saw anything like that. You came out of that cover like a—"

"Like an Indian?"

"—like a wolf bringing down an elk. It was so fast. I don't think he even saw you."

At the ridgetop he crossed over, and an hour later, with the winter sun low and smudgy in a frozen sky, they came to a road that wound westward through a valley. A mile along it was a fork where a second road curved away toward a shelf. Smoke from a farmhouse curled above the bare trees there. John Thomas reined in, handed his reins to Gail Larkin and shucked the saddles and gear off two of the horses. He slapped their rumps and set them off toward the farm. Then he remounted and regained the single lead horse with their gear and the few extra things he had selected from the others. At the next rise he pointed ahead and to the left. "Town off there. That's Haven."

"Good! I'm so cold and sore I might not move for a week."

"Oh, we're not going there," he assured her. "That's where they'll expect us to be. We're going cross-country, right up through those hills. Cold and sore is one thing, dead is another. We're taking no chances."

"Who were those men back there? Why are they after us?"

"When we learn that, we'll know a lot more than we know now, won't we?"

When the mounted men had gone, after searching the train, Shanty walked through the passenger cars, shouldering aside shaken, jabbering passengers and a busy train crew. At the front car he stepped out and walked ahead, past mail coach, tenders and steaming engine, to look at the hole in the ground ten yards away, twisted rails and thrown ties littering it. "Dynamite," he muttered. It would be a while before this train moved again.

Back on the train he retrieved his pack, slung it on his shoulder and picked up his repeating rifle. Without looking back he went out again and set out, past train and steaming locomotive, past the blasted track, his face westward.

"You!" someone shouted.

He turned. A trainman had come to the pit and was gazing across at him. "Where are you going?" the man asked.

"I don't have time to wait," Shanty said. "I guess I'll walk."

V

"Three People and the Dutchman told my father about the mask," Gail explained, a bit amazed at how comfortable a few blankets and a little fire could make a shallow limestone cave on a cold winter night. "The Dutchman—I've never heard why he calls himself that; I understand his father was a White Mountain Apache and his mother was a gypsy from Jalisco—he worked as a guide for my father in the first expedition with the army surveyors into the Tonto Valley. Father considers him reliable when he's sober. Three People was an Englishman at first—Oxford and all that—but he is fond of Zunis and decided to be one. Father says it's the climate. What kind of Indian are you, John Thomas?"

"American. Did they tell him where it is?"

"What?"

"The mask."

"Oh. No, I don't think they know. If they did, they would have gotten it long ago. It would be worth a lot of money, you know, a thing like that. They just got to talking about it. The Dutchman had heard of the old ones from his mother . . . she learned *Nahua* in Jalisco and gathered the Aztec legends. She was a healer of some kind. And Three People knew about it from studying the old Spanish letters while he was in Europe. The story is that after Montezuma was killed, some of his priests took the mask away and carried it home. They decided that "home" must mean Aztlan, where the Aztecs believed they came from. It was my father who developed the theory that Aztlan was in what we now call the southwest deserts."

"How did he come up with that?"

"He has studied the Toltecs. They were the ones who brought the Aztecs into Mexíca—Mexico now. They hired them as warriors and guards for their empire. He

46

patterned the empire and decided that the Aztecs had to have come from the north, beyond its borders. There are some linguistic connections between *Nahua*—the Aztec language—and some of the tribal tongues there as well. Ute, for example. There are similarities. So, he feels that Aztlan may be some part of western New Mexico or Arizona. And the Dutchman says there are stories among the Apaches about others who were there a long time ago . . . great warriors who sacrificed to the sun."

"That covers a lot of territory."

"Yes. Well, Father has worked a long time to narrow it down. He has a fairly good idea now where it might be hidden . . . if there is such a thing at all."

"You doubt it?"

"Everybody doubts it . . . well, everybody except maybe Hall Kileen. He swears the mask exists. But he's a lunatic. Father was associated with him in one venture, in Mexico. He won't have anything to do with him again. Kileen—" she shook her head—"lunatic? The man's a maniac. They were digging in the Yucatan, had found some good Mayan pieces. Then Kileen ruined it all. He started a peasants' revolt, and it took the Mexican troops to put it down. It's a wonder we weren't all shot or thrown into a prison. We haven't been back to Mexico since then."

"Where is Kileen?"

"I don't know. Probably still down there someplace. He's a Mexican national."

John Thomas turned cuts of meat on a willow spit over the little fire. "If your father knew where to look for the sun god mask, why did he wait to go after it?"

"With the Chiricahuas running loose? Nobody has gone into that country lately, John Thomas. Not until a few months ago. As soon as he felt it was safe, he went."

"And didn't take you."

"My father is a stubborn man, John Thomas. What's safe enough for him isn't necessarily safe enough for me,

47

in his opinion."

"Did Kichener tell you why he was looking for your father?"

"Not exactly, but it has something to do with that mask. I gather my father isn't the only one looking for it." She watched as he mixed flour with salt, saleratas and a bit of water, rolling it up into a ball on a slab of sycamore bark. The meat, high over the little flame, was beginning to glisten in the light. It had been a fat rabbit, and she had no idea where or when he had gotten it. They had ridden steadily through the daylight hours, winding westward among the winter-bleak hills, stopping only twice to rest their horses and themselves. Yet when he had chosen this secret place to stop at nightfall, he'd had the rabbit on his saddle, already skinned and gutted. Now he was mixing biscuit to go with it, and herb tea simmered in an open canteen. "Those men back there, who stopped the train . . . they have something to do with all this, don't they? With the mask and all?"

"For the moment it's a safe assumption." He drew the dough into strips and wrapped them on the ends of willow sticks, which he handed to her. "Keep these over the fire, and keep turning them until they crust. It's called bannock. Tell me about Hall Kileen. Describe him to me."

"Well, he's a tall man, taller than most. He'd be about fifty now, I suppose. Thin hair, kind of long and wispy, so blond that it almost looks white. Blue eyes, pale and always watery, though his eyesight is excellent. He doesn't look at all like a fierce man, or a cruel one, though I've seen him be both . . . not cruel for the pleasure of it, perhaps, but terribly cruel. Indifferent to others. It's as though he is the only one in his world who matters, and everybody and everything else is just there for his convenience."

Shadowed agate eyes in a dark, firelit face shifted to study her, eyes that seemed to see deep inside her. She felt herself blushing and shrugged. "No, there was nothing like that. No personal insult or, ah . . . offense. It's just that at one time I thought Hall Kileen was the greatest historian of his time. I mistook his . . . single-mindedness for dedication, I suppose. Then I learned what it really was. He is power-crazy, wealth-crazy, influence-crazy. Very simply, the man is crazy."

The bannock had turned gold on the willow sticks, and it steamed as he pulled it free, two puffy gold biscuits the size of his fists, each with a hole through the middle. He split them, loaded strips of broiled rabbit between the halves and handed her one of the sandwiches. It was hot and delicious, and she realized she was ravenous. For a time they ate in silence, listening to the lonely wind in the barren winter wilderness just beyond the stretched blanket.

"John Thomas," she asked finally, "do you want to help me find my father?"

"Not especially."

"But—" she sputtered and started again. "You mean after all this . . . and after those men at the train and . . . and everything . . . you don't intend to help?"

"I didn't say I don't intend to. I said I don't especially want to."

"Well, will you or won't you?"

"I don't know. I might see if I can find out what happened to Ernest Kichener. I guess I owe him that. I don't owe you or your father anything. If it takes finding your father to find out about Kichener, then maybe I'll do that."

"Good," she spat. "Because I can't think of any other way for you to proceed."

"I can think of several." He shrugged. "But tracing through Frederick Larkin is probably the best, at least to begin. I'll get you back to Leavenworth, then I'll see what happens from there."

"I know what will happen from there."

49

"Oh?"

"Yes, you and I will head for the southwest territories by the most expeditious transportation and—"

"No."

"No what?"

"No, *you and I* will not. I choose my associates, Miss Larkin. I do not choose you."

"Is that so?"

"That is indeed so."

"In that case, neither of us is going to accomplish much, *Mister* Wolf. Because I know where to look for my father, and you don't."

"Easily remedied. You tell me and—"

"No."

"No?"

"Absolutely not. I came to you as a tracer because of my father's message about you. But if you refuse to take me along, I shall just have to find someone else. Suit yourself."

"Unreasonable, Miss Larkin."

"But final, Mr. Wolf."

But he wasn't listening. Abruptly he had turned, his eyes narrowing, a hand up. For a moment there was silence, then he said, "Stay here. Be quiet and don't move." Fireglow glistened on a gun in his hand. She hadn't seen him draw it, but it was there. Then he pulled aside a corner of the shielding blanket and was gone. It was as though he had never been there at all, and Gail pulled her wrap more tightly about her, wondering what sort of person could move so quickly and make no sound at all.

The lowering clouds that had been a gray shroud over the land all day were breaking up now, and frosty stars glinted here and there. Wolf squatted on a knob watching other lights, little bobbing glows below and to the east, and the coldness he felt came not from the chill winter wind but from within. The ones who sought them were more than he had suspected. Audacious enough to blow out a track and stop a train in broad daylight, cunning enough—or well-connected enough—to penetrate a secret room in a secret house and leave threats written in blood, they were also tenacious enough to have not stopped their search with the end of daylight. They were out there now, with lanterns, reading the sign of his passage. How many were there? He had seen five—had taken their horses. But there were more than five now. A lot more. And they were on his trail. He had believed they were safe until morning. Now he knew they weren't. Following a cold trail at night . . . the men down there had trackers with them and good ones. Within the hour, they would be on the trace directly below. They would find the horses, then they would find the little cave.

Kichener, he asked silently, what kind of ant's nest have you stirred up this time? Maybe your last one . . . maybe not. But it is a big one to reach so far with such force.

He had no doubt that those below knew him, knew who he was, probably knew the girl as well, and were after both of them. They had closed his only option then—to turn his back and ignore the whole thing. He would not be allowed to stay out of it. Having been contacted, he was in, and to those down there that meant he must be eliminated.

And the same, obviously, applied to Gail Larkin. An intuition he had long ago learned to trust told him they had been marked even before leaving Leavenworth.

With one more glance at the bobbing distant lights he stood and returned to the little cave. The girl's startled eyes said she had not heard him coming.

He gathered up the things they had there, doused the tiny fire and took down the stretched blanket. "We're leaving," he said. "Follow close behind me and try not to make any noise."

51

In the sheltered cleft where he had left the horses to crop winter graze he saddled two of them, leaving the third. As he was tying gear onto the saddles the girl saw the lights moving in the distance, and her indrawn breath was a sharp hiss. "Are those the same men?"

"Among others. We seem to have become quite popular, Miss Larkin. Which resolves one item in your favor. Unless I can find a safe place to put you—or *until*—then I suppose I'm stuck with you."

"Well, you needn't be so overjoyed about it."

"You shouldn't either, Miss Larkin. I have a hunch this is not going to be a church social."

There was no point in circling back or confusing the trail now. The thing they needed, John Thomas knew, was distance . . . all the distance they could get. On horses that had had an hour's cold rest they headed westward, following the contours of the wild land, and the pace he set would spend their mounts by morning. For a time Gail rode essentially blind, wondering how the Indian could see where they were going. Then there was moonlight, pale on a ghostly cold land of hills and ridges, forests and breaks where the steam of the horses' breathing hung like misty tendrils behind them.

He glanced back, upward at the unwelcome moon, and she saw a fierceness in his eyes and knew what it meant. Darkness had given them an advantage. With moonlight the advantage was gone. If those following had fresh mounts, they would close in soon.

The trail they followed entered a road, and for a time they followed it; then from the crest of a rise appeared lantern glows ahead, and he swung to the right, across a field of stubble and into wooded lands beyond.

"Was that more of them?" she wondered.

"They're scouting the road. The others must have wired ahead."

"Who are those people? How can there be so many of them?"

"I don't know," he said. "That's something we need to find out."

"We can't go much farther this way, John Thomas. These horses are nearly exhausted."

Another mile and they were in hills again, rising, wooded crests between moonlit white valleys. From a high place they looked back and saw a dark mass of riders coming toward them. Wolf muttered something under his breath—something distinctly not in English—and they pushed on. From another rise they saw, ahead and to the left, maybe a mile away, the dark buildings of a sleeping little town—no more than a hill village—where no lights shone and the only sign of life was tendrils of smoke from a few chimneys. John Thomas studied the place carefully, then turned them toward it. As they neared, a dog began to bark, then another. He reined in at a shadowed cut where a road ran below them. "I'll need a few minutes without interruption," he said. "You hold those dogs' attention."

"How?"

"Ride through town. Just take the main road and go right on through at a walk. No faster unless you have to. Don't stop, and if anyone hails you, don't respond. Just go on through, out the other side. Get out of sight and wait for me. I won't be long."

"What are you going to do?"

"What Indians do." He shrugged. "Steal things. Now move."

Moonlight bathed the frozen mud street of the little town as she rode along it, holding her mount to a steady walk. A pair of dogs had come out to meet her, and now they paced and pranced alongside, barking to tell the people in the dark buildings that a stranger was here. A shuttered window grew little yellow streaks as a lantern flared behind it; then the shutters opened, and lantern light fell rosy upon the street. Ahead and on the opposite side she heard a door open in shadows. "Dogs!" someone

53

shouted. "Quiet!" Then, "Who's that? Who's out there?"

She kept her face straight ahead, a blanket pulled over her traveling hat, and kept going. Another voice, somewhere, called sleepily, "What's it, Jud? Who's out at this hour?"

"Hey!" the first one shouted. "Say who you are!"

She kept going, the horse at a steady walk, and felt their eyes following her. Well, at least when they looked at her, they weren't looking at John Thomas . . . wherever he was.

"Hell with 'im," the first voice grated. "Cold out here."

She heard a door slam, then silence behind her. The dogs had wandered off, going toward the buildings where people were. A hundred yards more, and the town was behind, the last pole barn receding behind her in moonlight. Where the road curved she looked back, then guided the horse off the road into a stand of winter-bare elms. If she had expected a long wait, she had underestimated John Thomas. Only minutes passed; then she saw movement in the shadows across the road, and he emerged from a thicket there, looking bundled and laden.

"Come on," he said. "We can make it to the river."

First pale dawn was in the sky behind them as they came down from the hills and saw a river in the flats below, a pale curving surface bordered by skeletal brush, with cultivated fields on either side. There was enough light now for her to see the things he carried: a small wooden crate on one side, behind his saddle, a dark, boxy-looking smaller thing on the other side, a pair of tow sacks hanging from his saddle horn, and a large roll of bright wire carried over his shoulder. The crate had lettering on it, but she couldn't make it out.

"It's called straight dynamite," he said. "Or sometimes forty percent dynamite. There are lead mines up in those hills. I assumed that where there were mines there would be mining equipment. Sure enough, there was."

She waited for him to continue, but he said no more, just concentrated on guiding them toward the frozen river ahead. Cold, tired and irritated, she kept her peace.

Their tracks across the cleared fields were a trail a blind person could have seen, but he did nothing to hide it, seemed indifferent to it. It occurred to her that he was not trying to lose their followers now, at all. It was almost as though he was inviting them on . . . leading them.

At the river's edge the horses scrabbled down hard banks, and their hooves crunched in crusty ice at the water's edge. Horses less tired might have balked there, or bolted, but John Thomas pushed his mount forward with hard heels, and Gail's followed. Past the thin edge crust, the ice thickened, a flat, snow-blown sheet from edge to edge of the watercourse. He led out onto it, and it supported their weight—although every few steps the ice seemed to sing, high little crackling trills that raced off into the distance. In midstream he dismounted and handed his reins to Gail, then opened the crate and displayed dozens of brown, waxy cylinders packed in wood shavings. From one of the totes he took a hand drill and a mallet, and stopped to drive a hole into the ice. Capping a stick of explosive, he attached wire to the cap and thrust the stick into the hole, scuffing snow over the top of it. With Gail leading his horse they proceeded across the ice, the Indian stopping every dozen paces to plant another wired cylinder. At the far bank he climbed into the brush, unrolling wire behind him, then unstrapped the small box opposite the dynamite crate. "Take the horses downstream a little way." He pointed. "Stay out of sight and wait for me."

"That isn't going to do any good, you know," she said. "You might break up the ice here, but all they'll have to do is just go and cross somewhere else."

He glanced around at her, dark eyes smoldering like

coals in a firebox. "Just do what I told you. Now go."

When she looked back he was kneeling in the frozen brush, attaching wires to the little dark box with the crank lever on its side. And beyond the river, coming across open fields, were mounted men, a dozen or more that she could see.

In good cover she dismounted and tied the reins of both horses securely. She put her hands over her ears and waited. Moments passed and nothing happened. She wondered if he were having trouble with the detonation device . . . or if maybe the dynamite had become wet and unusable. Something was wrong. It should have blown by now. Across the river, the mounted men were out of sight, though she could see their tracks down through the open field. Then she saw them, one and then another and then several more, coming through the brush at the riverbank. They paused there, looking across, then one in the lead rode out onto the ice, circled his mount and waved an arm. In a ragged, close column, two and three abreast, they began crossing, and Gail's eyes widened in horrified understanding. She knew why John Thomas had not yet blown the ice. He was waiting for them. As one in shock, she watched them cross, watched the lead riders reach midstream, then those behind them, nearer and nearer to where the Indian lay hidden in the brush.

With a muffled roar that echoed back and back across the valley, the ice beneath their hooves reared slowly upward, splintered into fragments and fell back to immerse a screaming tangle of horses and men in frigid undercurrents. Their cries rode the echoes of the explosion, highlighted by a shrill, rending ring of sound that danced and raced upstream and downstream—the keening of splintered ice on pounding water.

Ice fell like winter storm upon the thrashing, screaming chaos in the river, screening details from view. Here she saw a horse plunging madly upward, pawing at broken ice . . . there a man clinging to a bucking fragment which reared and capsized atop him. The quiet that followed was unearthly: receding echoes, lapping water, small grindings of ice against ice in the current, here and there a splashing as man or beast still fought the deadly cold of the water. Near the bank a man came upright from the water, head and shoulders rising above it as he fought his way toward the bank . . . then stopped and fell backward as a gunshot ripped the chill air, followed by John Thomas Wolf's voice, a deep murmur which yet carried in the bright silence. "Too late, *chito*. Sorry."

Gail Larkin was still staring at the peaceful, lapping, ice-strewn water when brush rustled and John Thomas stepped out to untie the horses' reins. He handed one set to her. "Let's move along now," he said. "We have a long way to go."

VI

"I just can't for the life of me see how a person could do something like that."

Until she spoke, he was not aware that she was awake. She had slept for two or three hours in the stable loft outside Colville Station, then had gone back to sleep almost as soon as they had boarded the single coach on the milk-and-mail Westport Limited. From Wolf's standpoint it was just as well. He had things to think about and had not needed conversation. But now, obviously, she was awake. He turned from his scrutiny of the night-dark countryside flowing by outside. "Like what?"

"Like what you did back there . . . I mean, all those men and horses, just . . . just bang. Bang, splash, gone.

How could a person do that?"

"It seems to me that was the sort of thing they had in mind for us, Miss Larkin."

"Well, that may be. But . . . well, *all* of them?"

"Should I have let one or two of them go, then? To carry the news to others, so they could take up the pursuit where the first group left off? Things like that can get to be a real nuisance."

"It was cold-blooded murder. I guess you know that."

"Absolutely. Miss Larkin, those people who signed in for hide-and-seek—"

"For what?"

"My course of instruction, The Tracing Arts. At Leavenworth. Did you know any of them before?"

She thought about it for a moment, then shook her head. "No, not really. I had met Mrs. Grimes—the lady from the detective agency in Kansas City. But none of the rest, that I remember."

Thoughts aligned themselves in Wolf's mind . . . bits of a puzzle shifting for review. "Tell me about Mrs. Grimes."

"Oh, I don't exactly know her," she said. "I only met her briefly. It was in Emporia, right after my father's message came . . . about finding you, I mean. She was at the depot when I made my travel arrangements. I . . . well, I was upset and I turned around and bumped into her. Then of course I helped her pick up her packages, and we introduced ourselves. I was surprised to see her again at Leavenworth; but of course I hadn't known that she was a detective, and detectives would be interested in your course of instruction, I'm sure."

"What exactly were you doing when you turned and bumped into her?"

"What was I doing . . . oh. I had just sent my wire to enroll in your course. I was at the telegraph window and she was behind me."

"I see."

"You see what?"

He gazed around him at the empty carriage, letting pieces fall into place. They were the only coach passengers. The little Limited carried few people in the winter. "I see how we were tagged," he said. "Whoever is out there looking for us, your friend Mrs. Grimes set them onto us. Maybe just to find out what they could, at first, but when we went to Springfield, somebody decided the safest thing to do would be to eliminate us."

She paled. "Mrs. Grimes?"

"Distinct possibility. I'm wondering right now if there is a connection between Mrs. Grimes and Hall Kileen."

"Hall . . . now whatever would make you think that, John Thomas?"

"Curiosity. Since you paid for a few lessons in tracing, Miss Larkin, here's one. When you're on a trail you don't look just where the trail is. You look at all the country around, everything you can see as you go. Landmarks often do more than just outline a path. Sometimes they direct it."

She had no idea what he was talking about, but before she could ask, the door at the front end of the car opened and a man wearing a badged cap came in. "We're comin' up on Holcomb in a few minutes, Mr. Wolf. You want me to stow that parcel for you now?"

Wolf stood and took down Gail's luggage. "Go with him," he told her. "From here on, you are property of the United States Postal Department. You'll be riding in the mail coach."

"She's the parcel?" The man took off his cap and grinned at her. To Wolf he said, "I thought I'd be totin' U.S. Mail. You didn't say it was U.S. Female."

She stared from one to the other of them. "I don't understand. What are you doing?"

"Keeping you safe and out of sight for a time, Miss Larkin. Just go with the man and do as he says. I have other things to do, and you are an impediment."

59

"How long must I ride there?"

"Until I come to collect you. I'm mailing you to myself."

"*Collect* me? Where?"

"General delivery." He shrugged. "Come along now. Time's short."

As the postal guard hustled her out of the coach, toward the secured mail coach ahead, she glanced back. John Thomas was moving along the passenger coach aisle, systematically extinguishing each of the little lamps that lit the inside of it. By the time the guard pulled the door closed behind them, the car was dark.

The Limited carried no passengers when it made the first of several scheduled stops in western Missouri. Its single passenger coach was empty and dark, its only attendants its crew and the postal guards in the mail car. Were anyone watching the train for passengers, they saw none, for there were none to see. Two flatcars carrying farm equipment were coupled in at Halsey, and the train crossed a trestle bridge in midmorning and entered Kansas, bound for the yards at Osawatomie.

At about the same time, many miles away, a hooded surrey rolled into the dooryard drive of a large stone house in the hills near Columbia. The man who stepped down from it wore a long coat with a high-turned collar, a muffler covering his lower face and a wide hat shadowing his eyes. He looped the reins to the ring of an ornamented hitch-post and strode to the house to rap at the wide front door. To the old black man who responded, he nodded and said, "Good morning, Covey. Is Dr. Gleason at home?"

The Negro squinted up at him, then his face broke into a wide grin. "Why, my land, suh! It's you! He sho' is here, suh. You come right on in."

Inside, he took the visitor's hat and wraps, then went to a door standing partly open to the entry hall. "Mistuh Gleason, suh, you have a visitor. Mistuh John

Thomas Wolf."

While Covey went for tea, they sat before the fire in Professor Gleason's big study, saying little, each noticing how little the other had changed in the years since they had last met.

The wispy halo of hair outlining the old man's bald head was perhaps even thinner now than before, but his round cheeks were as ruddy as ever, his eyes as bright and curious, his smile as quick and ironic. How could so many years wash across a man, John Thomas wondered, and leave so little trace of their passing? Except for the scarcity of his hair and the wisdom in his eyes, this could be the face of a child . . . a child ravenous for answers to all questions in a world full of questions.

"It has been a time, John Thomas," Gleason noted. "But you aren't much changed, at least on the surface. A bit more craggy, perhaps, another scar here and there, I suppose? Yes, and maybe a few more inside, where they don't show. What service can an old scholar provide for you, to bring you here today?"

John Thomas smiled slightly. No, Gleason had not changed. Ever direct and to the point. A writing tablet lay on the table beside his chair, and he took it up and began drawing on it, using a steel pen. Covey came with tea and biscuits, served them and withdrew, grinning at John Thomas, and still the pen traced symbols on the paper, symbols in a line that became two lines, then three, then four. Finally he blew on the pad to dry the last of the ink and handed it across. "This," he said. "Can you decipher it?"

For a time the old eyes studied it, moving from one symbol to the next, then Gleason glanced up. "Was it written in more than one color?"

"It was written in blood, on a plaster wall. Possibly done with a painter's brush."

"Two colors." Gleason nodded. "The blood and the plaster. That has to do with the translation, you know.

61

They used color to make meanings."

"Who?"

"Those who communicated in this manner, the speakers of Nahuatl. The people of the Triple Alliance, John Thomas. The Aztecs."

"You can read it, then?"

The old man studied it at length, tracing here and there with a finger, nodding at some symbols, puzzling over others. "It isn't really writing, you know," he said. "Not writing as we know it. It is rather like word pictures, instead. Pictures of meanings that may vary according to what is around them and how they are placed . . . even to what colors they contain, as I said. This symbol here, for instance, you can see that it is a bird, but done in this manner it doesn't represent a bird so much as a person whom both the writer and reader will recognize as being associated by them with a bird. And yet it isn't a name. More a . . . an aspect of the person it represents. The bird is a hawk, by the way. You see? It is shown in stoop. Still, what follows does not indicate stooping—a plummet from the sky to strike at prey—but rather that it is falling. Has fallen. Is dead. Then this next part, this string here, is an imperative. It makes a command and theatens punishment, that what has happened before will happen again. Now, this symbol here is the word *chalchinatl*. It can have three or four meanings, but generally it means human blood. You said this was written in blood, John Thomas?"

"Yes. That was verified."

"Well, this says—indicates—that the blood of its *tlaxtl*—its substance, what the writing was done with—is the blood of the person who is symbolized by the fallen hawk."

"And the command? The imperative?"

"It warns that no more hawks must . . . come, but it does not say where. It indicates that all who come will fall." The old man looked up. "Are you sure you did this

62

correctly, John Thomas? Exactly as it was?"

"I think so. Why?"

"This part here, where the glyph's perimeter is open and seems to flow into a separate pattern below, so that the next is not so much a separate glyph as it is an extension of the first. Could you have been mistaken about this?"

John Thomas studied it, then shook his head. "I remember it. This is how it was."

"Well, then, this is a very odd message. I have the feeling that two people are speaking here, somehow. The message of all the rest is very clear, the warning and all, and no indications of exception are given. Yet this last part adds to what went before and changes the sense of it. The message, to here, says to send no more hawks. Yet this last small thing—the little circle with cones above it—it was a sign meaning coyote or dog in the *Nahua* picture writing. The three lines radiating say it is larger than what is indicated. . . ." He looked up, bright eyes inquisitive on the Indian's face. "It says send no hawks. Then it is appended to suggest a wolf."

The old man wanted him to stay for a time, to speak of the old times when Wolf was a student at St. Ives and Gleason was a teacher there—times that had been different from the times now. But John Thomas had little time, so their conversation was brief. Still, as they finished their tea, Gleason asked, "Tell me this, John Thomas, have you lived up to the potential you once showed me?"

"I've never been sure what that potential was," he said with a shrug. "Some said I should be a soldier . . . and of course they laughed when they said it, at what a joke they had made. Others, well, they suggested all sorts of things. And the man who should have had the choice—"

"Ernest Kichener," the professor breathed, raising a brow.

"Yes. Kichener. But he never guided at all. He just said

I'd know it when I found it. I don't know if I ever have."

"How about the potential I once suggested to you, John Thomas? That you study the dimensions of things that others might miss, for lack of a second viewpoint?"

"If I ever completely understand what you were talking about"—he grinned—"then I'll let you know whether I have achieved it or not."

Before returning John Thomas's sketch to him, Gleason glanced at it again. "You haven't said why you came here, John Thomas. Or what this might be about."

"No."

"Ah. But still, the inquisitive mind knows no civilities. How many times—when I've heard him mentioned at all—have I heard people describe Ernest Kichener as a hawk in stoop? Slight acquaintance of the man seems to have left a similar analogy in the minds of a remarkable variety of people . . . very much the way I have known people to know you by name before they ever knew your name. Wolf is more than a name, of course. It is an appellation. But I can't help but wonder, seeing this. . . ."

John Thomas said nothing, only listened, and Gleason's eyes sparkled. "You haven't changed very much with the years, young man. You say nothing more or less than you choose, do you? Very well, I'll let it be an old man's fiction that the stooping hawk here might relate somehow to Ernest Kichener . . . and the wolf suggested here might be you. But it does raise an interesting question, doesn't it?"

"Yes."

"If Ernest Kichener is dead, as this might suggest, then how can Ernest Kichener use his murderer's announcement of that fact—which this message could be construed to be—to send for his own replacement?"

"I don't know." John Thomas shrugged.

"But you intend to find out."

"Possibly."

Gleason chuckled. "Of course." Pushing up from his chair, he crossed to the wall opposite the hearth—a wall that was shelves from floor to ceiling, shelves for books, notes, artifacts, shelves for all the things left from all the years of life of an avid collector. John Thomas followed him there, waiting while the old man scanned books on a shelf and selected one. "Since you don't tell me, John Thomas," he said, "then I shall not assume that this has to do with the sun god legend or the lost mask of Motec'zoma—Montezuma the Younger—any more than I would have assumed that Ernest might be looking for the same thing—" he thumbed pages—"but I have heard some things these recent times. Disturbing things. Ah, here it is." He spread the book open on a reading table. "One thing that can be said for the friar-scribes who accompanied the conquistadors, John Thomas. They were exceedingly thorough. Just on the off chance that your inquiries might pertain to Montezuma's mask, here is a drawing of it."

The illustration was a carefully rendered drawing of an elaborate mask, its center a shaped eagle's head, upper beak outthrust, its radian a wide, circular shield covered by rings of elaborate designs, those in turn surrounded by a fringe of flame shapes, a representation of the sun. It was nearly circular, open only at the bottom, from the eagle's beak downward, a flaring cleft between sculpted plumage.

Beneath the drawing and on the following page were flowing lines of elaborate, careful Spanish script.

"It was made of beaten gold," Gleason said. "Brightly polished and emblazoned with red and green gems. The later Aztec emperors, especially the two Motec'zomas and a particularly bloody old tyrant named Ahuitzotl, who ruled between their times, venerated the god Huitzilopochtli above other gods. He was the sun god, of course, though the Aztecs didn't consider him the sun— Tonaiu—but rather the god whose duty it was to keep the sun nourished and healthy and reliable. The Aztecs—or Mexíca as they more often called themselves—had quite a penchant for the ceremonial and practical spilling of blood. Most of their ceremonies involved sacrificial death, and most of their gods, at one season or another, were given substantial feasts of blood. But this one, Huitzilopochtli, was particularly ravenous. The Aztecs conducted regular wars against their neighbors for no other purpose than to collect human beings for sacrifice to him."

"And the mask was lost."

"Quite a lot of the booty that Cortes saw and recorded never actually made it back to Spain. Much of it wound up in the mud beneath a lake one day—his own soldiers dumped it there, inadvertently—but this piece was not part of that shipment. A lot of people have tried to figure out where that mask went. It has significance far beyond its value. Religious significance, of course. . . ."

"The Aztecs are still there, waiting?"

"Yes. They are. Probably millions of them. And having religious significance, it has political significance."

"You, said you have heard disturbing things."

"Yes. The legends were that some of the Aztecs spirited this mask away, for safekeeping . . . back to Aztlan, where they supposedly came from originally. Now it seems that there are people seriously searching for it, and possibly with some idea where to find it."

"Who?"

"Well, for one, an archaeologist named Larkin. Good man. I've met him on a few occasions. Possibly a bit radical in his theories, but—"

"Who else?"

"Someone else, I'm not really sure; but he seems to have a base in Mexico, and the word is that he has very big powers behind him. I've never heard his name, but I understand some of the Mexicans refer to him as

Kukulki." He closed the book, glanced up at Wolf and scowled. "The distressing thing is, he's no treasure hunter. I hear he intends to start an uprising of some sort."

"Revolution is no stranger to Mexico."

"I didn't say revolution, John Thomas. And I didn't say Mexico."

As the miles clicked by beneath iron wheels, Gail sat huddled among rocking mail sacks under the admiring gaze of a strapping young postal clerk named Cyril and under the glowering protection of the distribution agent, Booker Sims. Her first tirade of questions had been largely ignored as the two wrestled hook sacks into place for the dozens of drops at small stations bordering Westport. So, as mile succeeded mile, measured in the enclosed car only by the clacking of rail and the signals of the engine's whistle, she subsided into a confusion that resolved itself into intense irritation, and kept an eye on a bulky sack labeled for Emporia. At least, the sack told her, the train was going in an appropriate direction.

She had resigned herself to being in fact a prisoner of the United States Mail Service at least until she could escape, but questions swarmed through her mind for which there were no helpful answers. How could a person be "mailed" to anyone?

"Discretionary delivery," Booker Sims had grunted to that. "It's in the postal regulations."

"But not for *people!*"

"Doesn't say not." The man shrugged. "Was you livestock, say, or high explosives or corrosive liquids, then we couldn't accept you for delivery. You're not any of them, though, so we can on discretion."

"Whose discretion?"

"Postmaster General, Secret Service, Federal Revenue

agents or anybody that carries a seven-A-one clearance code."

"What's seven-A-one?"

"I don't know, miss. All I know is, if you have one, you can declare discretionary mail . . . long as it isn't livestock or high—"

"I know. High explosives or corrosive liquids. Which of those is John Thomas Wolf?"

Cyril chuckled. "Seems to me he'd be a toss-up between high explosive and corrosive liquid."

"Cyril, be quiet," Booker said. "Don't confuse the mail." To Gail he added, "All I know is, he carries a seven-A-one and uses it now and again."

"Then, he's done this sort of thing before? Mailed people?"

"Usually just himself. Says it simplifies gettin' around sometimes. Turkey?"

"What?"

"We got some cold turkey whenever you get the need to eat a bite. And that bunk yonder, you can rest there if you want to. No sense bein' uncomfortable. The Postal Service takes care of its mail."

She had the freedom of the car as long as she stayed out of the way, and as long as she kept out of sight of the door when it was open. Twice the train stopped, once for shunting to another line, and she could hear the car being uncoupled and recoupled to another train. Each time, for at least a minute or two, the door was open and she thought about jumping and running. But each time either Cyril or Booker was there, keeping an eye on her. They didn't mistreat their mail, she decided, but neither did they take chances on any of it walking away.

The bit of sky visible through the high windows turned from gray to dark gray to dark as the car clicked on, and finally she slept. When she awoke the Emporia sack was gone, and sky patterns said the train was still going west.

"Where are you taking me?" she demanded.

"You're General Delivery, miss," Booker explained. "So unless the party you're addressed to shows up before we get there, I expect we'll haul you all the way to Arkalon."

"Where is that?"

"End of track. At least, this month it is."

Having no choice in the matter, Gail decided to be philosophical about it. It was just as well that she hadn't managed to get off at Emporia, she supposed. If there really were massed villains out there looking for her—and that did seem to be the case—then they certainly would have been lurking at the town where she lived.

VII

They were waiting in Leavenworth, as he had known they would be. At the depot a train arrived and departed, and by watching the people watching the train, he identified three men who probably were looking for him and the girl. There would not be another train for several hours, so he left them there to watch for nothing. Two others were outside the courthouse, and he knew there would be at least two inside. At the boardinghouse where he had a rented room he walked openly to the side door, stepped inside and waited in shadows beside the door. Moments passed, then the door opened slowly and a man leaned inward to peer at the stairs. Wolf's knuckles took him in the temple, just above the cheekbone, and his other hand caught him before he could fall. To anyone outside, it would have appeared that the man simply stepped inside and closed the door behind him.

He left the man doubled over in a tiny broom closet and went up the stairs on silent feet. In the narrow hall above he stopped just short of his own room and waited, listening. How many would there be waiting inside? Probably only one, yet the adversary seemed to have plenty of manpower, so he couldn't be sure. Being careful not to shadow the crack below the door, he knelt and peered at the little length of twine barely visible from the doorframe to the bottom of the door, on the hinge side . . . just a half-inch of string, which no one would notice unless one knew it was there. The string that was visible was dark green. It had been red when he last left the room. The twine rolled from a little spring-fed spindle inside the frame. It was dyed in six colors at one-inch intervals. He pulled it out an inch to see the next section. Yellow.

The door had been opened eight times in his absence. Four of those times would have been the woman who came to clean. The remaining four would be since her last visit, two days ago. Instinct and educated guess said there was one man inside now, and he had been there since morning. He started to rise and heard a muted sound. Someone had snored.

A slight, cruel grin pulled at his cheeks. He stood, stepped past the door, hit it once—a hard, echoing blow—then flattened himself against the wall. Beyond the door there was a snort, then the creaking of bedsprings and shuffling footsteps. As the door opened inward he whirled around the frame, hitting it with his shoulder, continuing inward in one sweeping motion that focused its force on the fist that came up from his knee and collided with a heavy jaw. The man toppled, sprawling in the middle of the room, never having seen what hit him. Wolf closed the door quietly and looked down at him, grinning. "I told you before," he said. "You just aren't very bright, Mr. Sloan."

Relieving the unconscious bruiser of two guns and knife, Wolf collected his few belongings from the room, packed them in a leather shoulder pack and went back

70

downstairs. Mrs. Wallace stood at her open door, scowling at him. "I heard noises upstairs, Mr. Wolf. Did you drop something?"

"Nothing important," he assured her. He handed her a few bills. "I'm checking out, ma'am. This should cover everything."

She looked at the money, then up at him. "I expect it will. Why are you leaving? Is there something wrong with the room?"

"You might want to check it for vermin" was all he said.

Leaving the house by the side door, he crossed quickly to the little house across the way, where tracks said the first man had come from. The door was unlocked, and he stepped inside, looked around, then waited by the door, listening. It was only a few minutes until he heard the boardinghouse door slammed open and Mrs. Wallace's shouting voice. He closed the door and went out the back, smiling coldly.

From the shadows of a cold portico, he watched the two men who had been outside the courthouse hurry past, and a bit later those he had seen at the depot. Two others joined them on the street, coming from a hotel across the square. When they had passed he headed for that hotel, staying to shadows, slipping like a ghost from cover to cover. When one of the spotters from the courthouse hurried across the square and into the hotel, Wolf was already inside, waiting.

Cold dark eyes watched as the man took the lobby stairs two at a time, watched as the clerk at the desk turned to see what was happening, then strode to the frosty front window to look out at the street. As soon as the man had turned away, Wolf went up the stairs, silent as a forest hunter.

The man went along the hall, glanced around nervously, then rapped at a door. When it opened he removed his hat and spoke quietly with someone inside.

71

A moment later the door closed, the man turned, put on his hat, hurried to the stairway and went down almost at a run, oblivious to what was happening behind him.

Catherine Grimes had barely closed her door and turned away when it opened again. No sound told her that, only the shift of air currents in the room, the flutter of the blaze in the little fireplace hearth. She spun around and gasped. John Thomas Wolf stood inside her closed door, smiling gently at her. He walked past her, glancing around the room, and turned away. . . .

For just an instant, the Indian turned his back, an instant in which his ears heard the flutter of the woman's hand at the fold of the heavy robe she wore. An instant, then he spun abruptly. A hand like cold steel clutched hers, immobile, and with his other hand he removed the little revolver she had drawn.

"Just one final test, Mrs. Grimes," he said softly. "I wanted to be sure."

"I don't know what you're talking about. Turn me loose."

"Yes, ma'am." He released her hand, again looking around the room: fireplace, nightstand, thick braid rug on the wood floor, drawn blinds at the double windows, a high bed with a tall oaken headboard and footboard, each ornately carved with floral designs spreading from an oval center cutout. "Comfortable," he said. "Expensive and comfortable."

She backed away from him, rubbing her hand. "What are you doing in my room? I demand that you—"

With a stride he caught her shoulders, turned and lifted her and threw her onto the bed. She hit rolling, almost escaping him as he pinned her there . . . a strong woman, surprisingly strong, quick and agile. Not at all what she appeared, but then he had suspected that before. By main force he rolled her over, turned her and thrust her head through an oval cutout in the footboard, then dropped to a crouch on the floor beyond it, his fingers wrapped in her hair, his other hand covering her mouth.

"If you scream or struggle," he said softly, "I will break your neck." He looked into her eyes for a moment, then added, "No, that won't do, Mrs. Grimes. You know I will do exactly what I say. You didn't come here without knowing that."

Her eyes told him clearly that she knew. He removed his hand from her face. "I don't intend to waste time here, Mrs. Grimes. So you will answer my questions promptly."

"I don't know what you want," she hissed.

From his coat he drew a small knife, razor sharp. "Yes, you do. First, where is Hall Kileen?"

His face was close to hers, his eyes studying her eyes. He saw the refusal there, a stubborn shutting down within her eyes, and he touched the point of the knife to her lower lip—only a touch—just to raise a single welling drop of red blood, just to let her taste it on her tongue. The refusal in her eyes became panic. "You understand me, don't you," he said.

Where her hair was clutched in his hand, its strands were tight, seeming to lift the scalp beneath where a little line of flesh showed between separated roots. Shifting the knife, he touched it there. "Have you ever seen a scalped person, Mrs. Grimes? People have been scalped and lived. It doesn't even do serious damage to their health necessarily. But it changes their appearance for the rest of their lives. Without the top scalp, all the skin falls. The features sag; the forehead rests on the nose and almost covers the eyes; the cheeks hang below the chin. . . . Where is Hall Kileen, Mrs. Grimes? Tell me now."

"I don't know," she gasped. "West somewhere. They didn't tell me."

"What *did* they tell you, Mrs. Grimes?"

"Only . . . only that I was to find you . . . verify who

73

you are . . . keep you under surveillance . . . until—"

"Until what?"

"—until they could come and deal with you! That's what they said . . . deal with you. I didn't know—"

"Yes, you did." Again the knife touched the taut skin of her head, and now there was blood among the hair.

"All right . . . please! Please don't! Yes, I knew. They didn't want to take a chance on your getting a message. Then when you disappeared, and we learned you had gone to . . . please! Oh, God, please don't. . . ."

"Was it just me, Mrs. Grimes?"

"You . . . and the girl. They said both."

Again the knife touched scalp, its razor edge breaking the skin delicately. "Do you know where Aztlan is?"

"No . . . please, no . . . I don't know about any of that . . . I don't want to know. Oh, God, please!"

Her eyes said she was telling the truth, and he believed her eyes. "Just one more question, then, Mrs. Grimes. Is Hall Kileen Kukulki?"

The panic in her eyes became a dazed disbelief. "No," she stammered. "Oh, no. He's just . . . Kulkulki is Kukulki. He is—" Abruptly her mouth snapped shut, so hard he could hear her teeth grinding together, and the fear and shock in her eyes reflected a cold resignation. She had already said too much, and a specter lurked there that she feared even more than she feared him and his knife. Far more.

But his cold smile told her that he knew, and there was no drawing back.

"Yes," he finished for her. "Kukulki is Quetzalcoatl."

He released her and stood, putting away his knife. With a sob that was half-muted scream she pulled her head from the footboard cutout and drew herself across the bed to huddle at its headboard, her hands in her fallen hair. Then she sat pale and dazed, as one in shock, staring at the blood on her fingers. "You're an Indian," she whispered. "You're a damned heathen savage Indian."

"Yes, ma'am." He nodded. "I am."

She barely saw him when he strode to the windows, pulled back one of the blinds, lifted a sash and was gone. Chill winter winds billowed the blinds that closed behind him, but for a time she simply sat, her hands clutched on her head, rocking and stifling sobs of awful dread. The blood on her fingers—blood from what was really only a pair of tiny, shallow cuts that would heal in days—was so like the blood they had shown her in that closed foundry in Kansas City, when they had come to hire her. They had taken her there to show her what happened to those who worked for them and failed.

The man she had seen there . . . he had still been alive when they opened his chest and tore out his heart. She knew he was alive. She had seen his eyes when they showed his heart to him.

In a hidden place in the cold dusk of evening John Thomas Wolf watched them gather at the depot, those who would be the messengers. He watched until he knew what train they would take, then he turned away. It was as much as he needed to learn just now.

Catherine Grimes had surprised him. Just his words and his manner should have set her to singing like a bird, but even when he drew blood she had told him little . . . or thought she had. The woman was obviously terrified of someone or something, and he was beginning to guess at that something's magnitude at least, if not its very nature. Far more than lawbreaking was involved here . . . but then he had already known that. If Kichener had been on it, it was more than could be dealt with by the law. The answers lay far to the west somewhere, probably in Arizona Territory. And a key to it was a man named Kukulki. As he saddled a horse in the shadows of a private stable at the edge of town—one of the stalkers had led him to the horses, and the man lay still now in the loft while Wolf took possession of the best of the mounts—he turned over in his mind the woman's odd reaction to his simple statement about Kukulki's name: Kukulki is Quetzalcoatl. The words had evoked a blind terror in her eyes. She had heard far more than he had said, and he pondered it. Kukulki is Quetzalcoatl. Kulkulki was the Mayan word for the old Toltec god-chief, just as Quetzalcoatl was his Aztec name. Yet it meant far more than that.

The Mask of Montezuma. The Aztec sun god mask. Huitzilopochtli's mask. And the legend of Quetzalcoatl returning as Huitzilopochtli—to bathe the earth in blood. What, among such dusty old legends, would have sent Ernest Kichener off on a quest at his age? One thing would, he told himself. If the legends and the evil occurring around them were not analogies at all, but boded a literal reality.

Nature, Emerson had said, is not separate and remote from the doings of man. Nature is, each day, the result of what has occurred the day before, and if that occurrence is by the arts of man, then nature is man's creation to that extent.

In ancient times men invoked their gods to intercede on their behalf, and the memories lingered. Could someone now invoke those memories?

Again there was moonlight, and the mount he had taken was a good night-horse. By a little after midnight he was at the town of Oscaloosa. A half-mile westward an old barn stood at the back of an overgrown field. Beyond its little passway door, its interior was dark and silent. For a moment. Then, distinctly, there was the sound of a hammer being drawn to full cock, and he raised his hands, still standing in the passway, silhouetted against the moonlit icy ground outside.

"It's me, Shanty," he said. He stepped through, closed the passway behind him and waited while a match flared and was set to the wick of a lamp.

76

The Irishman raised the lamp and hung it on a pole hook. Its light blazed on his fierce whiskers. "I knew it was you, Wolf. Just bein' cautious."

On a cot beyond him a second large figure sat up, blinking at the light, rubbing his eyes. "I ought to skin you alive, Wolf," Trooper said. "Leavin' me in that stinkin' jail all that time. Why didn't you come get me?"

"Safest place for you," Wolf said. "When you're in jail it keeps you out of trouble."

"I didn't get in trouble!" Trooper growled. "Sumbitch tried to cheat me, was all. Quoted me a price on supplies, then tried to charge me more."

"Matter of judgment, Trooper. A two-dollar over-charge isn't reason enough to tear down a general store. Anyway, we have things to do now."

"Like what?"

"Old gold, old gods and bad people." He turned to Shanty. "Did you get everything we need?"

"All yonder." The Irishman pointed. "Horses out back. Judge Halsey racin' stock. Best there is."

Wolf inspected Shanty's acquisitions carefully, then nodded. "Everything bought legally?"

"Near enough." Shanty shrugged. "When do we leave?"

"You leave now," Wolf told him. "Take the horse I rode in on. You'll be in Burlingame by morning. Leave the horse there. Take the first westbound train and pick up our mail. She'll be waiting at Arkalon."

"She?"

"Gail Larkin. I mailed her. You accept delivery for me and get her on out to Black Mesa. You know where that is?"

"Sure I know. Highest point in the pit of perdition. What do I do there?"

"You wait. We'll be along directly. We're going to stop off to see Windwagon Willie."

Trooper curled his lip in disgust. "What do you want

77

with that old loon, Wolf? He's crazy as a coyote . . . not to mention bein' older'n dirt."

"He knows the territories. Get up from there, Trooper. I want to sleep for an hour. You can get us packed and loaded."

Obediently, though with a running rumble of curses, Trooper deserted the bunk. Wolf sat on the edge of it, pulled off his boots and lay down, pulling a blanket over him. Trooper shook his head in wonder. "Would you look at that? Flat out sound asleep, just like that. Like we didn't have a worry in the world. An hour, he said. An' sure enough, in an hour he'll be wide awake an' ready to go. Just like a damned Injun. Not a worry in the . . ." Behind him the passway door opened and closed. Shanty was on his way to Burlingame to catch a train.

VIII

His name was Willie Shay, though few called him that. Few, in fact, called him anything anymore, because it was common knowledge in various places that Windwagon Willie had been dead for years.

Old-timers around Concordance and Medicine Bend had the clear of it, honed and reclarified through many tellings in the afternoon shade in front of general stores and post offices. "Seen it all myself," they'd say. "Back about fifty-seven or -eight it was, this bowlegged feller turned up at Cross Point (or, some would say, Helmsley or maybe Baker's Store) with a busted up old wagon and a load of drag poles and canvas. Moved into the old smithy yonder (or old man Cole's abandoned barn, or maybe the shed across from Loomis's house) and went to work on that wagon, an' it were a sight to behold, yessir.

"What? Why, he'd taken out the axles and put in new 'uns better'n twelve feet long (or fourteen, or maybe eight). Then he hauled her out an' mounted masts on her. Yessir, that's right. Masts, just like on a sailin' ship. Two of 'em, they was (though some would say one and others three), an' a big ol' juttin' jib out front. 'Member that in particular 'cause th' first time he run a sail up from that jib th' wind caught it an' that wagon, why, it tipped right up on its nose an' sat there with its back wheels just a-spinnin' in the wind. So after that he run a pole out from th' tailgate an' hung a counterweight on it. 'Bout eight hundred pounds of rock in a double tote sack (or, some said, a pair of plows, or maybe a brace of anvils). Hell's fire, it don't matter what it was, it kept that contraption from standin' on its nose, didn't it? Had him an anchor, too, with a rope tied to it.

"Anyways, come a day that we had a right good breeze out of the northeast (or maybe the southeast), that feller hauled that thing out, right yonder in that very street (or, some would say, in the pasture past Preacher Parsely's place, or maybe the flats past Goat Creek). Then he kissed as many of th' ladies as he could catch, tipped his hat to th' gentlemen, said they was a fair tide a-runnin', and climbed aboard. An' land but when he run up his sails that thing began to movin'. An' th' farther it went th' faster it went, an' I guess th' last any of us seen of him he was just a-sailin' out across the prairie yonder, headin' west."

There were those who swore that they had later seen his scalp hanging from a Comanche lance (or Cheyenne, or maybe Kiowa) and others who would testify that the windwagon had run off into the Arkansas River (or maybe the Cimarron) and Willie had drowned, though it was reported that he and his contraption had been seen as far west as the foothills of the Rockies, and one or two were sure he had made it to California.

Windwagon Willie, they named him. May God have

mercy on his soul.

On a bright, chill morning Willie Shay sat in his rocking chair, on his roof, a buffalo robe wrapped around him to ward off the high prairie cold. Rheumy eyes that sometimes saw farther than other people's eyes peered eastward across the desolate miles. "Company comin', Dog," he said.

Dog's ears twitched and his tail switched from side to side, but he had no other reaction. If the old man said company was coming, then company was coming. But not necessarily today.

"Recollect another time we had company," Willie went on. "Fifth day of July it was, eighteen and eighty-two . . . or -three. Waste of time. Been a day earlier we could have got drunk an' celebrated, but I don't hold with celebratin' the fifth. Nothin' ever happened on the fifth of July." He pulled his buffalo robe more tightly about him and nodded emphatically. "Nor ever likely to, either."

Fifty feet away, Willie's windmill squealed as a fresh gust caught its tarred canvas fans on their wooden poles and propelled them into unlikely motion, driving the wooden rod to send gouts of dark water into the ice-filled tank. It was a stubby windmill, built of lashed poles that had once served as sail masts, and its fan brace and armature were wagon wheels. On a clear day a body could see nearly twenty miles from Willie's roof, and that was what there was to see—twenty miles in any direction, except south where there were hills and breaks. All the miles a man could want to see and think about. And the only permanent man-made features in those miles were Willie's soddy, shed and windmill. If there was any other scenery it was ephemeral: a few buffalo straggling past now and then, or Indians dropping by to gawk at the windmill and at Willie, or sometimes a feather of dust on the far horizon westward where the Indians told him white men passed sometimes driving *wo-haws* northerly

80

. . . and just now and then a trace of smoke to the south where the railroad now had track. Generally, though, there was nothing about but miles, and Willie was content with that.

"Reckon what they want?" he grumbled. When Dog's ears twitched he added, "The company that's comin'. Reckon what they want here? Not Injuns. It's company. Folks."

He shook his head moodily. "Well, I won't celebrate with 'em. Nothin' to celebrate. They've missed Christmas by six weeks, an' I don't know anybody that's real sure when Easter is."

In mid-afternoon Willie climbed to his roof again, Dog following at his heels. Together they peered eastward across a blown and frozen land where listless winds gathered among the ivory grasses, gaining strength to tickle Willie's windmill. "Ain't company atall," Willie decided after a time. "It's that Injun an' his varmint. What you reckon they want way out here?"

Dog sat expectantly, his ears up, gazing off where Willie looked. He, for one, didn't see anything at all out there, but if Willie said someone was coming, then Dog knew somebody was coming. His large, sensitive nose tested the wind, but it came from the northwest and told him only that somewhere behind them, a long way off, buffalo were drifting southward.

"If that big varmint gets to whinin' like he done last time," Willie decided, "you can chew on him a little bit. But don't go tryin' to chew on that Injun. He's mean."

Dog wagged happily and licked his lips with a wide red tongue.

"Salt pork and onions," Willie muttered. "Why would a man complain about salt pork and onions? Been all right had he stuck to complainin' about how hot it was an' all. That was all right. It *was* hot. August the twenty-seventh as I recollect, eighteen and eighty-three . . . or four, maybe. An' I didn't mind him bitchin' about the

81

flies none, either, or gaggin' on the well water. But who ever heard of anybody that would raise a ruckus about salt pork and onions?" He spat, then muttered, "Varmint."

By last light of day Willie took his rocking chair down from the roof and tied it to the doorpost so it wouldn't blow away in the night. He broke ice on the tank for a bucket of water for the house, hauled a blanketful of chips in for the evening fire, then went out and stood on the roof again, pointing. This time even Dog's near-sighted eyes could see tiny movement in the ruddy gray distance.

"Be here 'long about breakfast time," Willie decided. "Reckon what they're doin' way off out here this time of year? Last time John Thomas Wolf showed up he was wantin' me to show him where all them old Spaniards had buried theirselves. You recollect, Dog? Land, but didn't we show them some sights! Best I recollect, we was gone nigh four months. Barely got back here in time for Christmas. December the nineteenth it was, eighteen and eighty whatever that year was. Reckon what he wants me to show him this time?"

As they entered the house Willie added, "I want you to behave yourself this time, too, Dog. Diggin' up buried Spaniards is one thing . . . chewin' on them is another. You could'a broke half th' teeth in your head." As was his custom, he left a lantern burning atop his flagpole.

As dusk faded to darkness Wolf reined in and pointed. "Willie's light," he said.

Trooper squinted, trying to see it—a tiny, dim spark still miles away.

"He knows we're coming," Wolf said. "We'll camp here, give the horses a rest. There's a gully just over there, and water—or ice at least."

"How could he know we're comin', Wolf? Nobody can

82

see that far."

"Willie can, sometimes. I don't know how. He probably doesn't, either. But he can."

"That old coot is crazy as a loon," Trooper growled. He stepped down, gathered reins and led the tired horses off where Wolf had pointed. For a moment longer Wolf stood gazing at the distant light, his lips pursed. With darkness the prairie wind was rising, its chill becoming a hard cold. Not a night when anyone would likely be out and around, and certainly not out here—this far north of the rail and the little string of settlements that followed it, far north even of the few newly organized counties. Nobody lived out here—nobody but the scattered, migratory tribes and, of course, Windwagon Willie. Yet now there was not only one light out there, but two—the second one several miles from the first, off to his left, just the faintest glow of firelight. The angle and the apparent distance would put the fire about at Willie's Digs.

It had been several years before, when Wolf first came across the old man. Some wandering Kiowa had told him about the "crazy-wagon" man, and Wolf had gone to see for himself. The Digs were where he had found him—the place where his old wagon had finally destroyed itself a long time before, and where the old man had literally buried the contraption by dismantling it and caving in a gully wall to hide it. Fifteen years earlier.

In those years Willie had wandered on westward, as far as the Painted Desert, then southward into the mountain lands below the Mogollon. Better than anyone else he knew, Willie had learned the desert lands. Nobody had bothered him out there, and he had wandered at will, doing a bit of prospecting sometimes, now and then hide-hunting to pay for his few provisions, trading occasionally with various Indian tribes. The Apache, it seemed, had just accepted Willie as they would accept a falling star or an eclipse or a camel—as something harmless but wholly unaccountable and therefore not to be harmed.

To the Navajo he was a source of good stories to be told on dark nights, to the Zuni he was a mystical being to be portrayed in picture writing, and to the Yaqui he was one touched by the finger of a dark god.

How many years had Willie spent roaming the remote lands? He didn't know. Willie never forgot a date, but he could never remember years.

Eventually, though, he had given in to some strange urge to settle down and have a home of his own. So he had wandered eastward, across the mountains to the high plains, and returned to where he had buried his wagon. Willie's Digs. He had spent a year or two there—had even dug a deep well—before deciding he didn't care for the scenery and moving a few miles northward, to build his soddy.

Not many people knew about Willie. To most of those who did, he was an oddity—a mystery. Yet the old man was no mystery to Wolf. The old man was like the land. He had his seasons and he had his reasons, and that was enough.

But now he wondered, who *did* know about Wind-wagon Willie? A few Indians, but it was not Indians who made that distant speck of light. Maybe a few buffalo hunters who traded hides down where the iron rails ran. But those were not buffalo hunters over there.

Instinct as keen as the cutting edge of the night wind told Wolf the answer. Those out there, warming their hands over a secretive fire at Willie's Digs, were some of *them*—the ones with whom he was playing hide and seek.

He had broken the trail at that river in Missouri, then given them a new trail to puzzle over at Leavenworth. He had broken that trail, he thought, at Oscaloosa—but they knew his direction, and there seemed no quick limits to the manpower they could expend in their search.

Who would know about Willie? Who would have known about the secure house at Springfield? Who would have known about the organization, whose only credential was an apparently meaningless code in the huge bureaucracy of a nation—the seven-A-one discretion?

They knew. And they surmised that he might go after Willie because maybe they knew that Willie knew the territories. Had he been them, he realized, he would have surmised the same.

In the frozen gully Trooper had broken ice away for the horses to drink from the turgid water beneath. Wolf walked among them in the darkness, his fingers and ears determining which two were fittest. "This one and that one," he told Trooper. "Get saddles on them. We're going to pay a call. Leave the rest here, with the packs. We'll come back for them."

"Be easy as anything just to go around those jaspers and get on where we're goin'," Trooper groused as they rode across the sighing, crackling prairie with only starlight to guide them.

"They'd just follow us," Wolf said. "And get word to others about where we are."

"Not if they didn't know we was here. You said yourself they'd be lookin' for Willie."

"And if they find him they'll find us. I need Willie, and I don't need them. Hush, now. We're close." The errant wind brought a scent of smoke. Another half-mile passed and Wolf reined in. "The Digs are right over there." He pointed. "That's where they are, probably down in the old pit, staying warm." He dismounted and handed his reins to Trooper. "Circle around. Get north of them, this far away. You'll know if I need you."

"It's cold out here, Wolf. You sure that old coot is worth the trouble?"

There was no answer. Wolf was already gone, ghosting away into the flitting shadows of night prairie. Trooper swore under his breath, then turned his horse, heading north.

Wolf circled the Digs, close in, searching. He found

85

five horses close-herded in a gully, held there by a corral made of rope. For a moment he crouched there, letting his senses tell him the position of men and equipment, a shadow among shadows. Faint fireglow flickered on the gully's wall at a sharp bend fifty feet away. He climbed the flat prairie above and crept toward it until he could look over the rim. Four men huddled there in silence, either asleep or nearly so, resting on their saddles, blankets pulled around them against the cold. A packframe lay nearby. The depression where they lay around their little fire was the hole where Willie's remarkable wagon had lain buried for all those years.

Beyond, the only visible feature against the dark horizon was the four-foot-high ring of stones that was the top of Willie's old hand-dug well. He had gone twenty feet down, he said, before deciding that an auger-bored well with a windmill was what he wanted, instead.

For a time Wolf crouched above the men at the fire, studying them, wanting to hear them talk. Three were of a type, frontier toughs, the class of man Ernest Kichener had referred to as ten-or-nothing men—a charitable man might pay ten dollars to have them buried. Most would leave them where they fell and pay nothing. But it was the fourth one who held Wolf's attention. A small, blocky man, he sat apart from the other three, ebon eyes in a ruddy face staring into the fire. No hair showed beneath the dark hat pulled low around his ears—no sideburns, no scruff, not even brows over the eyes. But it was the face itself that held Wolf's attention. The man could have been sixteen or sixty; his face showed no indication of age except a slight gauntness of the cheeks. Yet his eyes seemed to smolder in the dull firelight, almost to have a light of their own. And the wind carried an odd, rancid stench. . . .

Wolf made up his mind. Edging away, he circled back to the men's horses, placed himself upwind of the animals and emitted a low growl, the sound of a hunting

86

wolf. The horses responded, pawing and peering, first one and then another speaking its concern in a loud whinny. Wolf crouched and waited. Beyond the bend shadows moved, faint voices carrying on the wind. A moment later a man stepped around the bend, his gun in his hand, peering with fire-dimmed eyes into the darkness. He came toward the horses, investigating, and Wolf let him pass, then stepped up behind him and snapped a blow into the back of his neck, speared knuckles striking upward to the base of his skull. As the man started to topple, Wolf stopped and caught him, hoisted the limp body to his shoulder, then headed back the way he had come.

At the lip of the wagon dig he put the man down silently and crept forward for another look at the rest. But only two remained now, crouching by the fire, glancing worriedly off toward the horses. The small ruddy man was gone. Cold premonition crept up Wolf's spine. Even from beyond the bend he should have known if one of them had moved away. Keen-honed senses—senses upon which his life so often depended—should have told him. Yet the man was gone, and nothing had told him so. He backed away and stood, turning slowly, searching in the night. Nothing.

With a shrug of irritation he raised his head and barked a coyote call, a thin, keening sound that seemed to come from a distance but carried in the wind. He called again, a slightly different call, a coyote somewhere else responding. Then he strode to the brink of the wagon cut, pushed the unconscious man over the edge and drew his gun. The two below gawked as the body rolled and jostled into them, then jumped to their feet, eyes searching, hands on their guns.

"Freeze, *chitos*," the cold voice above them commanded. "That's right. Pull those guns out nice and slow. Now toss them aside. Trooper?"

"Right here, Wolf." The voice came from the other

bank. "I heard you callin'."

"There's another one someplace, Trooper. Circle for him."

Hooves scuffed in the darkness as Trooper vaulted to his saddle, then drummed a quick tattoo on the hard ground. "You two stand very still," Wolf told the two below. "You're not going anyplace." He studied them, puzzled, seeing their faces for the first time, then he squatted on his heels at the edge of the dig, a cold smile playing on his dark face. "Well, look who we have here. Hello, Evan. Had any snakebites lately?" To the second one he said, "Hello, Cal Salem. You don't know me, but I know you. My name is Wolf."

Quiet hoofbeats sounded behind him, and Trooper said, "Not a sign, Wolf. Nothin' that I could see, anyhow. He musta' got away."

"There are five horses just past that bend, Trooper. Bring them up here."

"Yeah, I saw 'em. But there aren't five, Wolf. Only four."

So the strange little man had gotten away. A touch of admiration tinged his annoyance. "Then bring what's there." He let himself down the cut bank, revolver holding steady on the men by the little fire. "You boys are keeping strange company nowadays," he said. "Tell me about it."

Evan Purdue's hard eyes glittered with hatred. "They told us who they was after, Wolf. Mainly you. So we decided to buy in."

"What did you buy into, Evan?"

"That's all I intend to say. They're gonna kill you, Wolf. They're gonna bend you over backward and cut out your heart and the last thing you're ever gonna see is your own heart, still beatin', right in front of your eyes."

Wolf's grin was cruel and cold. "You've developed a vivid imagination, Evan. Just like your brother Jack used to have. You've become a nuisance, too." The revolver tilted toward him, glinting in the firelight. "I said tell me about it."

Hard eyes and silence. Wolf shrugged and rolled the unconscious man over with his toe. "Who is he?"

Purdue glared at him, tight-lipped, but Cal Salem said, "Nobody much. Name of Fletcher. Considers himself a hard man."

"Thank you. And the other one? The one that slipped out and left you here?"

"He's the one who'll kill you, Wolf. Him or another one just like him. You don't know what you're into this time, Injun."

"I asked for his name."

Again Purdue went silent, but Salem the gunfighter shrugged. He was staring death in the face, and with the resignation of his craft, he knew it. "His name's Tactli . . . something. I don't know the rest of it. He's an Indian. But not any kind of Indian I've seen before . . . except there are a lot of them now, and Evan's right. They're going to kill you, mister. They surely will."

"Who hired you on? Him?"

"Another one like him. I told you, there are a lot of them now. They come in from the south."

Purdue hissed. "Shut up, Salem. We don't have to tell this stinkin' Injun trash anything."

Salem glanced aside. "What difference does it make, Evan? We're dead, either way. You remember." He looked again at Wolf, but his words were words to himself. "Better his way than theirs, I guess." Abruptly he dropped to the ground, rolling, reaching for a discarded gun. Wolf's bullet took him through the ear, and he twitched once and lay still.

Purdue's face had gone very pale, and his knees were trembling. Wolf gazed at him. "Why did he do that, Evan?"

The man's hard eyes were wide now—the same insane

89

fear Wolf had seen in a woman's eyes in Leavenworth. "He . . . God, he was right!" With a lurch like a man drunken he flung himself at Wolf, across the fire. The Indian dodged aside and clubbed him with his gunbarrel. Purdue toppled, sprawling across the unconscious Fletcher.

On the lip above, Trooper said, "I believe that's about the dumbest stunt I ever saw two men pull. Want me to finish 'em, Wolf?"

He shook his head and put away his gun. "Salem's as dead as he'll ever be." He began collecting dropped guns. "We'll just leave these others. Maybe they'll wake up eventually. It was the other one I wanted."

"Well, he's gone. What do you want me to do with all these horses?"

"Pick up whatever's useful here and pack it on them, then you might as well take them on up to Willie's house."

"I'm not goin' up to that house at night," Trooper spat. "I know better than that. That damn dog the old coot has—I never saw any son of a bitch that big."

"Then take them back where we left our others." With a wave of dismissal Wolf crossed the dig and climbed its other bank to gaze off into the midnight darkness to the west, thinking.

Tactli, Salem had said. The little dark man's name was Tactli something . . . or something Tactli. The name rolled around in his mind, the taste of it on his tongue. It didn't have the sound of any plains tribe, or of any desert tribe that he knew. Possibly a Ute name, but the man had not looked like any Ute he had ever seen.

Possibly Ute, though . . . or more possibly it was a Nahuatl name—the language of the Aztecs.

IX

They came to Willie's house at first dawn, two riders leading seven spare horses, and the old man was waiting for them with a breakfast of salt pork and onions. It was not a happy meal for Trooper. When he sat down and Dog sat up, they were practically eye to eye. Dog's tongue lolled from his wide mouth as he exposed great fangs in a happy dog-grin. Trooper shuddered and tried to concentrate on his salt pork and onions.

"I ain't set foot in Arizona in years," Willie told Wolf. "Nice enough country, but it gets tiresome after a bit. Only places in the whole territory that a man can see some real scenery without mountains and piney woods gettin' in the way is down along the Gila or up on the Mogollon. Gila country's all red an' gray. Everywhere you look, red an' gray . . . 'cept if it rains; then the cactuses bust loose, an' the whole shebang looks like a French whorehouse.

"Up on the Mogollon, that's all right, 'cept it looks a good bit like western New Mexico, an' I'd already saw that. What are you lookin' for out there, anyway?"

"Aztlan."

"What?"

"The place the Aztecs came from, before they went to Mexico."

"Musta been before my time," Willie decided. "What do you want it for?"

"I want to find out if Ernest Kichener is dead . . . and maybe stop a revolution or something. I'm not real sure. First step is to get out there."

"Aztlan," Willie muttered. "I don't know, John Thomas. I was out there quite a while, back then. Shoot, I didn't leave 'til September the twelfth, eighteen an' . . . ah . . . some time. Maybe eighteen-twenty year ago. If Aztlan is out there, then I reckon I seen it one time or another, but if I did I didn't know what I was lookin' at."

"We'll track for it. There's been others looking too. I want you because you know the terrain."

"Fine with me. When do we start?"

"Now. Soon as you're ready."

"Nothin' to bein' ready. Just bring in my rockin' chair an' lash up my windmill, is all. You got your Irishman around someplace, or is it just th' four of us?"

"Four?"

"You, me, Dog an' whatsisname there. Less you still got your Irishman."

"We'll swing down to Black Mesa. He's waiting there, with a woman."

Willie's ancient eyes widened. "A woman? Land, I ain't had me a woman since the second day of February, eighteen hundred and fifty-one . . . or maybe fifty-two. An' that one was a Paiute squaw with a notched nose. Fine woman, though. Been thinkin' maybe I'll get me another one some day." He cocked an eyebrow at Trooper. "You ain't said a word about what fine salt pork an' onions this is."

Trooper growled. Dog came to his feet and bristled happily. "It's fine," Trooper said.

From Willie's they rode west across trackless, climbing plains that seemed wider and emptier by the day . . . well clear of the settled lands of the organized counties. On a brilliant morning when the cold wind hung suspended and the silence was as vast as the land itself, Willie rode out ahead with Dog trotting along beside. A few miles on they came up with the old man, standing beside his horse, looking westward. "This is the seventh day of February," he announced.

"Happy tidings," Trooper snorted.

Willie looked up at him crossly. "Trouble with you is you don't keep track. That's why you ain't any better than you are." He pointed at the ground at his feet. "You know what this is, don't you?"

92

"Dirt." Trooper shrugged.

"Varmint. This here is the Colorado line. One more step and I won't be in Kansas anymore, 'til I come back. So I hereby cross this here line on the seventh day of February, eighteen hundred an' . . . what year is this?"

"Eighteen eighty-six," Trooper said.

"Eighty-seven," Wolf corrected. "It changed while you were in jail, Trooper."

The big man shrugged again. "Eighty-seven, then. What difference does it make? What makes this old coot so sure this is the Colorado line, anyway? Nothin' here to see."

Willie looked up at him again, exasperated. He turned to point south. "Line comes from straight yonder"—he swiveled to point north—"and goes straight on yonder. Straight as a string, an' I'm standing here square on betwixt them two directions. So this is the Colorado line. No sense fussin' about it; it just is."

Trooper gazed around at the endless, featureless rising plain. "So what difference does it make?"

Willie shook his head. "There's those as knows where they are, and there's those as don't. If you'll hush an' listen, I'll tell you right where you're at on the seventh day of February, eighteen hundred an' eighty-seven. One day you might want to look back an' recollect that once in your life you knew exactly where you was." He pointed. "Yonder 'bout sixty miles, south an' a little west, that's the bad end of No Man's Land. Right at th' end of it is Black Mesa." He turned to point west. "An' yonder 'bout th' same far is Twin Buttes. Big cattle trail runs north between here an' there, but there's nobody on it this time of year. Nobody around here at all to amount to anything. Now, if Wolf here hadn't left his Irishman to wait for us at Black Mesa, we could cut out past Twin Butte and be at Trinidad in time to get drunk an' celebrate George Washington's birthday. But since we have to go down to Black Mesa first, then we'll head over

93

an' go west by way of Raton Pass an' Glorieta Pass."

"No good," Wolf said. "Glorieta's a perfect place for a trap. They may not know where we are right now, but they know where we're going."

"Well, that's the scenic route." Willie shrugged. "You want to go on down an' cross this side of the Gallinas?"

"Better."

"Wild country."

"Good."

"Fine." Willie nodded. "This bein' the seventh day of February, eighteen hundred an' eighty-seven, I hereby cross this line." With a flourish, Willie stepped from Kansas to Colorado. The ceremony ended, he swung into his saddle—a wizened, white-bearded monkey of a man still lithe as a Comanche buck. "What are we dilly-dallyin' here for? Let's get to Black Mesa so's we can go to Arizona."

On the vast plains, riding good stock and switching off at each rest, throwing their saddles on fresh mounts each time and spreading the pack load lightly, they had made a hundred and twenty miles in two days. But now as they headed southwest, the plains became more broken, more rolling and cut here and there by canyons leading down toward the breaks of the Cimarron. "Badlands," Willie explained contentedly. "Nothin' like the badlands we'll see later, but these are for practice. That's why God put 'em here, so's folks can get the hang of badlands before they get to the real thing."

"Thoughtful of him," Trooper grumped.

"Anyways, yonder is Black Mesa."

"Where?"

"Right yonder. Too far for you to see it yet, but there it is, right yonder."

They were busy then for a time, pulling their mounts and lead stock down the steep sandstone steps of a winding canyon, making their way along the bottom until they found water, then stripping them down to rest and graze for an hour. Wolf scouted impatiently, on foot, a mile up and down the canyon, then returned to the little rest camp. Hunch and premonition told him that they were not as alone as they seemed, that the enemy was close at hand here, but he found no trace of anyone.

"Wolf, I'm gettin' awful tired of that coot," Trooper told him. "I wish he'd just shut up."

"About what?"

"Everything. Like a while ago, sayin' yonder is Black Mesa, like there it was, right there in plain sight, when we can't see it yet."

"You can't see it yet," Wolf said. "Maybe he can." He walked over to where Willie was sitting under a bare-branched cottonwood, with Dog's head on his lap. He sat beside him. "There are people nearby, Willie."

"Could be." The old man shrugged. "Road just ahead, forks off toward the settlements yonder and down into No Man's Land. Hay road for some, hidin' road for others. Folks come by now and again."

"Where does it go?"

"Trinidad."

"Somebody moving west from End of Tracks, is that the road they'd use?"

"If they wanted to use a road, they would. It's the only one around."

Wolf checked the loads in his gun, then dropped a second gun into his coat pocket. Striding past Trooper, he said, "Stay down here. You'll know if I need you."

"Aw, Wolf, I'm gettin' awful tired of that crazy coot and his animal. Why don't I—" He turned, raising a hand, then stopped. Wolf was gone. Not even a rustle of brush betrayed his passage.

Up on the flats again Wolf crouched in brush, dark eyes searching. Ahead was a rise and, beyond it, a steep bluff rising toward cedar-strewn slopes beneath a flat-top limestone cap. He looked away from it, scanning distances, then shifted his sight abruptly back to the rise and up to where cedars hid a sway in the bluff's eroded slope. He felt it there, the little tingle inside the scalp that said there were eyes there, looking back.

Flattening behind the brush he paused a moment, then eased to the side . . . once, then again, and again . . . quick, sure movements from cover to cover with pauses between. Angling forward, yet not directly toward the cedar cover, he moved seventy yards and then did the scan and quick-sight thing again. Yes, there was someone there. But now the eyes were not on him. Whoever was up there wasn't quite sure where he was.

A few more darting moves and he was hidden by the rise. Carefully, crouching, he ran. Minutes later he crawled to the edge of the limestone cap and looked down. Directly below him a man in overalls and wool coat crouched behind the screen of cedars, bobbing this way and that as he tried to see all of the open areas below and beyond. Beyond a hard curve in the bluff's face was a screened cove where a hay wagon sat, wheels braced against the grade. A boy of ten or twelve stood by the draft horse's head, holding its bit, his free hand stroking its muzzle. At the foot of the slope were waves and swathes where they had been cutting winter-dry hay. And just beyond, a few hundred yards out, was a wagon road. Where it forked there was a little mound of fresh-dug earth.

Only one weapon was in sight—an old rifle lying on the ground beside the hidden man.

Silently, Wolf eased himself over the edge of the caprock and lowered himself to the slope below. Silent footing on the steep grade, littered with shards of broken stone and scattered brush, was tricky. But it was a thing he did well. Out of sight of the boy with the wagon, he eased down behind the man crouched and took away his rifle. The man spun around, almost losing his footing. His eyes were round, and the blood drained from sun-weathered cheeks.

Wolf regarded him coldly. "Why were you watching me?"

For a moment the man just stared, then he raised a hand defensively. "Please, mister. I was just tryin' to keep out of the way. I didn't see nothin'. Really."

"Who are you?"

"Curt . . . Curt Olmstead. I just come out for a load of hay. Listen, I swear to you, I don't know nothin' about it. I didn't do it and I didn't see who did and I won't talk to nobody about nothin'. I promise."

Wolf set the man's gun aside, out of his reach, and squatted on his heels, eye to eye with him. "Tell me what it is you don't know anything about, then."

"That feller down yonder. We just found him there, and I buried him because I didn't like seein' him lay out there that way. But he was dead when we found him, an' I didn't see nothin' else."

The man was faltering and trembling, his face pallid.

"Well, whoever you buried, Mr. Olmstead, I didn't kill him either if that's what you're thinking. I just got here. You know that. You were watching us before we ever came to that canyon over there."

Olmstead gazed at him, trying to read his eyes, then seemed to relax just a bit. "Yeah, I did. I . . . I was afraid you might have been them, comin' back."

"Who?"

"Whoever . . . done that."

"Somebody killed a man down there, and you found him and buried him."

"That's right. Look, that's all I know about it, honest. Not the first man I've found dead out here, either. This ain't that far from No Man's Land. But I never . . . well, I never seen nothin' like this before."

Wolf held his eyes, saying nothing.

"I mean . . ." Olmstead stuttered. "Well, I mean what they done to him. Like . . . well, I could see that you was

97

a Injun—no offense, but you look like one—and, well, I never heard of a white man doin' nothin' like that. I tried to keep the boy from even seein' it."

"No, I didn't do it, and I don't intend to harm you, Mr. Olmstead. But what did they do?"

The man gulped, licked his lips and shook his head. "He was layin' out there half-naked and pinned to the ground. And his whole chest was open, and his . . . his heart had been just sort of tore out of him. It was layin' on his stomach."

"Huitzilopochtli," Wolf breathed. "Mr. Olmstead, have you seen any strange people around here lately?"

"Strangers pass through here all the time. That road down there—"

"No, I mean *strange* people. Strange looking."

Olmstead blinked. "Well, there was those Mescans a couple days ago."

"Mexicans?"

"I guess. I didn't see 'em close. There was a big bunch of riders come by our place, goin' west. Twelve or fourteen maybe. But I noticed four of 'em because they was little, funny-lookin' men, all dressed alike. All wearin' black hats an' long black coats. Thought for a minute they might be preachers, but they all looked Injun or Mescan or something. Short little fellers. Looked like maybe they didn't have any hair under their hats."

Wolf watched while Olmstead and the boy got their rig down from the cove, and watched them head off eastward. When they were gone he raised his head and sang the coyote bark, hearing its distant echoes. A few minutes later Trooper rode up from the canyon, followed by Willie and Dog and the spare horses. When they were at the foot of the bluff Wolf joined them and swung into his saddle. He rode ahead, down to the road where the little hump of fresh earth marked a grave. He knelt beside it, letting his eyes rove the nearby ground. Olmstead had spaded dirt over the large, dark stain where a lot of blood had pooled and seeped into the cold ground, but he could still see its pattern. Slowly he worked out the scattering of prints: Olmstead's fresh prints, the wagon's some distance away, and the older confusion of tracks of many hooves and many feet. Among them, dim from the passage of a day, were smaller prints, almost like a child's feet, yet deep and solid in the earth. He thought of the strange little man by the fire, the man who first was there and then was not. Four of them, Olmstead said he had seen.

By the time the others came up to him, he had worked out a pattern. Fifteen riders in all, four of them the little men with little feet. They had paused here to commit murder. Then they had split up. Most had gone on west, toward Trinidad. But five—one of the little men and four others—had headed south, away from the road. They had gone toward Black Mesa.

X

When Shanty arrived at the little town of Arkalon he nosed around for a while, quietly, then rented a buckboard and team from a sodbuster, loaded it with sacks of grain and other supplies, tied a pair of good horses on behind and drove two miles out to the dugout and sod shed where Morton Bean was breaking out a quarter-section to farm. At the dooryard he hollered until Bean came out of his hole, gun in hand, then he stepped down.

"My name is Shanty," he said. "Man in town said you have a grown boy who'll hire out."

Bean squinted at the big man with the wild red

whiskers. "That'd be Buck. What you want with him? He's a hellion."

"Man in town said he can take care of himself. Where is he?"

"In the shed yonder, with a rifle pointed at you." Bean grinned. "You sure he's who you want?"

"Seems like it to me," Shanty assured him.

Bean hawked and spat, then turned. "Come out here, Buck!" When the son appeared—a big, strapping youth with quick eyes—Shanty sized him up. Bean said, "Son, this here feller says he'll pay wages. You want to work for him?"

"Doin' what?"

"Driving that wagon there," Shanty said. "Can you drive a wagon?"

"I can do any damn thing I set me—"

"Shut your damn mouth, Buck!" Bean roared. "What'd I tell you about that kind of language? Shit."

"Man in town said you're a hand," Shanty told the youth. "Said you can take care of yourself, too. Can you?"

"I sure as hell can." Buck grinned.

"Show me," the big man said.

Buck's grin widened. He glanced at his father, then set down his rifle. "Sure will," he said. With a single long stride and a leap, he launched himself at Shanty, big fists swinging. A second later he was flat on his back on the cold ground.

"Not too bad for a young fellow," Shanty admitted. "I guess you'll do. Can you leave now?"

"He can leave whenever you say . . . sir," the father said, trying to understand what he had just seen.

"Good." Shanty helped Buck to his feet, brushed him off and handed him his rifle. "Climb up there. I'll pay a dollar a day . . . two if you have to get shot at."

Buck gave him a dazed look. "Yes, sir. Uh, where we going?"

"West a ways," Shanty said. "You'll be back in a few days."

With a nod at Morton Bean, Shanty climbed into the buckboard beside Buck, turned the team and headed back into town to pick up Wolf's mail.

Wolf's mail on that day was in her second week of protective custody, in the solicitous but unwavering care of Section Clerk Booker Sims, and she was in a snit. First there had been that long, tedious journey by closed mail car whose only windows were high, narrow glassed slits through which one could see nothing but the sky. Then there had been the arrival at End of Track, the waiting while the car had been shunted onto a side track, the hours while the section clerk's assistant hauled a wagon load of bagged postage into town to trade with the local postmaster for an update of all the current goings-on in the area, the worried glances of the two men as the assistant reported back to Sims in a monotone not intended for her ears, and then the announcement by Sims, "Been strange folks snoopin' around here lately. Postmaster recommends Rule 41."

"And what is Rule 41, Mr. Sims?"

"Rule 41 says that if a general delivery parcel's not readily deliverable to its addressee and is of such nature that regular processing through the local post office—involving public view and temptation—might endanger delivery, then the responsible official is bound to make such arrangements as will keep the parcel out of public view and temptation until such time as delivery can be made."

She sighed. "What does that mean, Mr. Sims?"

"It means I got to keep you in the holding barn until your addressee shows up."

The holding barn—a nondescript, fortresslike little building a mile from town—proved to be comfortable enough for temporary residence, though she seethed at the manner of getting there—in a mail sack in the back of

101

a wagon, stacked among other mail sacks, some of which contained her luggage. But then there had been more tedious days of waiting, enclosed in a building as confining as the rail car had been. Any container designed to keep people from seeing what was inside, she decided, also kept anyone inside from looking out. Gail had developed an advanced case of cabin fever.

Thus when a large and grinning young man showed up at the holding barn with a loaded buckboard and a pickup order from the Arkalon postmaster, she responded with mixed emotions.

"I shall be delighted to get out of here," she assured Booker Sims. "But I'll be damned before I'll get into that box."

"It's a ventilated box, miss," he said, indicating the large crate he had brought in from the fenced yard. "See, there's plenty of room inside for you, and we'll put down some excelsior for you, and parcel pads. You'll be fine. Land, I've shipped as many as four pigs in a crate like this, and they came out just fine."

"I will not be hauled in a pig crate!"

"It ain't a pig crate, miss." He looked pained. "This here is a Live Consignment Container, Model 38-B. The very best the department provides."

"A pig crate! No, Mr. Sims, this is going too far. I absolutely refuse."

Sims shook his head sadly and turned to the large, grinning young man. "I guess you'd better give me a hand here, Buck."

It took both of them more than three minutes to get her sealed into the M38-B LCC, and they were panting as Booker Sims buckled the straps around it while Buck sat on its lid.

"I never knew women used that kind of language," Buck admitted. "I guess I got a lot to learn yet."

"Won't hurt to try." Sims shrugged. "But most folks never do manage to learn about women. Not a whole

102

lot, anyway."

"I mean about language," Buck said. "Land, I've done heard some words I never even knew there was."

"Well, don't use 'em. It ain't gentlemanly to swear. She sure enough got cantankerous, didn't she?"

"Yes, sir." Buck's grin returned. "How does a fellow get into the post office business, Mr. Sims? I believe I'd like to try my hand at it."

"Used to be easy. All you had to do was know how to read an' get on the good side of the right politician. Nowadays they got something new. It's called Civil Service. You have to take an examination or something."

It was a noisy and bumptious crate they loaded onto the buckboard; but there was no one within earshot to hear the commotion, and if anyone was watching from a distance, they saw only a pig crate being loaded onto a farm wagon.

As Buck climbed up and took the reins, he mused, "Here I thought all mailmen ever handled were letters and hatchery chicks. Never figured on anything like this."

"That's the Postal Service," Sims admitted. "Adventures in mailing. How's come John Thomas got you to pick up his parcel, Buck?"

"Who?"

"John Thomas Wolf. The fella that crate is for."

"That his name? I don't know. I'm just hired on to drive."

He headed west, skirting the town, attracting no attention. At the railhead he took the left fork to head southwest and had to haul rein abruptly when a large band of riders crossed in front of him at a lope, heading westward on County Line Road. Beer City toughs, most of them looked like, from down in No Man's Land—hard men for hire to any bidder. Yet among them were others—one or two a cut above the rest, and four who appeared distinctly different. Small men . . . little dark-

103

faced men like broomcorn Indians, but all dressed in flat black hats and long black coats, and all with oddly childlike features and no hair to be seen.

Buck had seen one of those before, a strange little not-quite-Indian man standing on a short boardwalk in town, watching people go by. He hadn't realized there might be more than one.

The riders passed him with no more than a glance, their mounts kicking up dirt on the hard-frozen road. He watched them for a moment as they streamed westward, and shook his head. "Wish Pa'd been here to see that," he told himself. "He wouldn't believe there was Mescan snake-doctors up here."

The harsh, muffled response from behind him startled him—he had almost forgotten about the mail in the crate—and he swiveled around. "You just keep yourself quiet, ma'am. I got my orders from John Thomas Wolf to keep you out of sight until he says."

Again the crate spoke, and he repeated, "John Thomas Wolf . . . big bear of a man with a red beard. He hired me on."

He listened to the muffled string that followed, then shrugged. "No, ma'am, he didn't tell me that's who he was. But that's th' name Booker Sims said, an' Booker Sims ain't often wrong about who somebody is."

He switched up the team and drove on, southwest toward the territory line. In an hour he came in sight of the new town being staked out just north of No Man's Land, and swung wide around it to cross the Cimarron North road and head once again southwest, now following no more than an old buffalo trail. Miles away to his left was the tiny cluster of shacks and tents that was called Beer City, the gateway to No Man's Land, the neutral strip between Kansas and Texas . . . the zone where there was no law of any kind except what each man enforced for himself.

In another hour the wagon rattled across a shallow

gully, and he turned to get his bearings on the other side. Beer City was due east now, barely visible in the distance. He was leaving Kansas, crossing into No Man's Land. He checked the loads in his rifle, then shagged up the team and turned due west. Periodically the crate behind him in the wagonbed complained audibly, but he did no more than reach back to give its lid a reassuring pat, then travel on.

Afternoon was waning into overcast evening when he drove along the upper steps of the Wolf Creek watershed and angled upward over the mile or so of high flats which shouldered the maze of cuts and shallow canyons called Plum Breaks—a barely passable area of maybe two hundred square miles extending northward. Somewhere near now, out across there, was the boundary between Kansas and Colorado, but he wasn't sure exactly where it was. Out here boundaries hardly mattered, because there was no one around to care where they were. Since mid-afternoon, Buck had not seen another person or even evidence of any; and he was beginning to wonder about people who mailed women to the wilderness and didn't show up to take delivery.

But as he drove along the shoulder of a rough wash, brush parted and the big man rode up to flank him, leading a second saddle mount.

Shanty glanced at the young man and frowned. "Where's the girl?"

Buck shrugged, starting to tip a thumb toward the crate behind him, but the crate spoke for itself. The diatribe that erupted from it made up in volume what it lacked in discernible words.

"How come she's still in that box?" Shanty demanded. "That's no way to treat a lady."

The crate agreed with him volubly.

Buck shook his head. "Mr. Sims got me to help put her in there, and I come on out the way you told me to; but didn't anybody say I was supposed to let her out."

Shanty sighed and stepped down, tying his reins. "Well, what's done is done. Let's get her out of there. Hasn't been anybody around to hide her from for forty miles."

It was a stiff, rumpled and thoroughly angered Gail Larkin who emerged from the confines of the Model 38-B LCC, and both males backed off several steps for the time it took her to elaborate her attitudes regarding each of them, the U.S. Postal Service, John Thomas Wolf, Model 38-B Live Consignment Containers and the institutions of slavery and capital punishment. Shanty hung his head, and Buck stared at her in wonder while he added new words to his vocabulary. She completed her dissertation by planting a resounding kick on the side of the crate, then toppling into it when the buckboard team shied at the noise. As they lifted her out a second time she glared at Shanty. "Just who the hell are you, anyway?"

"I'm Shanty, ma'am. I look after Wolf and do errands for him now and again."

"Wolf!" she fumed. "This is all his fault. Where is he?"

"Oh, he'll be along directly. But don't you worry, miss. I'll see to you until he catches up."

"Me, too," Buck breathed.

Shanty had found a sheltered campsite in a deep canyon, and they followed on foot, leading the saddle mounts, while Buck eased the wagon down a series of slopes.

"We'll be comfortable here 'til morning," Shanty said. "Then tomorrow we ought to get to Black Mesa in time to fort up and wait for Wolf."

"I think you're all crazy," Gail fumed. "And Wolf is the craziest of the lot. I've never in my life—"

"Yes, ma'am," Shanty agreed. "There's no disputin' that we might be crazy. Plenty have said so. Trooper swears Wolf is, says so all the time. But we're still around . . . and there's some others that aren't. Wolf's only got one way of doin' things, and that's Wolf's way."

"Crazy," she repeated.

"Yes'm. But Wolf thinks there's some others out there that just might be a lot crazier than us."

Forty miles north, across the breaks and the hills that rimmed them there, other travelers made camp in the lee of a bluff overlooking the fork where trails led west to Trinidad and Placo, east toward the Kansas settlements —the way they had come—and southeast into No Man's Land. Just before sundown the trailing cloud cover broke to the west, and cold, bright sunlight slanted across the winter land. One of the small, dark-clad men in the party stared for a moment into the sun, then raised a hand to halt them. In a singsong voice he chanted, *"Ayyo, Tonaiu . . . ayyo, Tonaiu . . . aya ya nexcha Huitzilopochtli . . . nocipa Huitzilopochtli . . . ayya, chalchinatl."* Then he pointed a small finger at the red sun and said, *"Tonaiu."*

The others dismounted, the little almost-Indians silently, the rest with the usual grunting, cursing and clamor of men preparing to camp after a long day in the saddle. One stood apart from the rest—a tall, ascetic-faced man with long blond hair and a drooping mustache. He seemed disinterested in the rest, almost unaware, as one in a trance. One of the little dark men came to him and pointed at the sun. *"Tonaiu,"* he said. *"Krell pictlin, Tonaiu."*

As though obeying an order the tall man knelt, his eyes still on the lowering sun, their pupils tiny in gray irises. The little dark men gathered around him, and one produced a small hide pouch from which he drew a thing no larger than the end of a finger—a dull gray button. The kneeling man opened his mouth, and the little man fed the button to him. He chewed and swallowed, then knelt for a long moment rocking back and forth. Finally

107

he stood, turned and beckoned, and a pair of burly men came to him. He spoke to them quietly, and they walked to where others were preparing a camp, paused, then sprang upon a man just laying down a saddle. They pinned his arms, relieved him of gun and knife, and dragged him back to where the tall man stood. For a moment the captive had sagged between them, stunned, but now his eyes widened in terror as he saw the tall man waiting for him, flanked by the four little men in black. "Krell," he gulped. "Wait, you don't understand. I—"

The tall man pointed an accusing finger. "Evan Purdue, the chance was yours. You came back alive, and our enemy still lives."

Purdue gasped in panic. "We can still get him, Krell. I told you, I just need another chance."

"You failed," Krell said in a dead voice, his eyes seeming not to see Purdue at all. "I told you, just as the Taltzin told me . . . the double failure. You did not kill your enemy, nor did you force him to kill you."

"But that's crazy," Purdue interrupted, struggling. "You can't mean that stuff. Nobody thinks like that!"

As though he had never spoken, Krell continued, "The sun is Tonaiu, and now Tonaiu speaks to me. His master Huitzilopochtli awaited his feast, and you failed to serve him. Now Huitzilopochtli hungers and Tonaiu is red, like *chalchinatl* . . . like human blood. Prepare yourself, Purdue. You will be honored—" he turned and pointed at the red-washed cold prairie where the trails forked— "there."

Purdue screamed and pleaded, but they did not hear him. He was carried down to the forking of trails, and his shirt was ripped from him, baring his chest. He was pinned on his back on the hard ground, and sharp pegs were driven through his hands and the backs of his ankles, holding him there. While the others stood back, wide-eyed, the four little men gathered around him, one at each point of the compass, and said in unison, "*Ayyo,*

Huitzilopochtli . . . chalchinatl." Abruptly then, they knelt, and one drew a wide-bladed black knife and thrust it into the man's chest just left of the breast bone. With a heave he forced the blade downward and turned it, opening a huge, bleeding hole. Another reached his hand inside, twisted, and pulled forth an object the size of a fist . . . an object that jumped and pulsed in his hand, spraying livid blood. He raised it high. *"Ayyo, Huitzilopochtli,"* he said. *"Ayya, Tonaiu."*

Around them several of the rough men staggered back, their faces going pale. One turned away, hurried off a few steps and was sick in the brush.

Krell turned full circle, staring at them with unnatural eyes—eyes that seemed to have no pupil at all, only disks of black agate where once had been gray iris. "He was told," he said in his dead voice. "You all were told. There can be no failure in the service of the sun god. Either way, he will be served."

They left Purdue there and broke camp before daylight. Most of them continued west. Five, though—the priest Ixtituatl Mictoc Malinali and four of the hired toughs—turned south, toward Black Mesa.

XI

During the night the wind shifted southwest, and with dawn came warm breezes to soften the chill of the air. Spring was still a month away in the central plains, and winter would strike again—as winter usually did after the first false warming—but now for the first time since December the weather was bright and balmy, and the only traces of lingering snow were little crusts dripping quietly away under rims where the winter sun did not reach.

Shanty brought his charges up from the breaks at first dawn and headed west again, guiding by the sun over his left shoulder. Out here, climbing gradually toward the high end of No Man's Land, trails were rare and roads were none. On the horizon now, huge and squat though still miles away, stood the final landmark of the neutral strip, Black Mesa. Beyond was New Mexico and that land of breaks that some honest Frenchman long ago had named Purgatoire—the region called Purgatory.

When they stopped for their noon rest Gail demanded of Shanty, "Why would John Thomas have sent us to Black Mesa? It seems to me if I were those . . . those people . . . and were looking for us, I certainly would scout out Black Mesa. It is so obvious."

"He didn't say." Shanty shrugged. "Though I expect he'd hope they were smart enough to do that, because once we're past there they haven't got a chance of heading us off 'til we get to where we're goin'."

The answer puzzled her. Worse, it worried her. But the big man didn't have anything more to say on the subject. He didn't choose to share his conjectures, and as far as what Wolf might intend next, his only comment was "I don't know, miss. Generally he doesn't say much about what he's got in mind."

Late sunlight was in their eyes when they rimmed the Cimarron Valley and looked across at the big, flat rise a mile away, its western face glowing softly in the warm sunlight. "Black Mesa," Shanty said. "We'll hold up here for a bit."

Then he began doing things with the contents of the wagon. From a burlap sack he took items of clothing, men's and women's, various lengths of wood lathe and a ball of twine. With his knife he cut the ties on one of the bales of straw. While Gail and Buck watched, fascinated, he packed straw into the clothing, inserted lathe to stiffen portions of them, and tied it off with twine to

110

create two surprisingly realistic dummies, which he bound into place on the wagon seat. When that was done he circled the wagon, studying the effect, then nodded his satisfaction. To Buck he said, "I told you I'd pay double if you get shot at, but no sense takin' too much chance of gettin' you hit, right?"

With strong twine he spliced onto the team's reins just behind the harness rings, and ran the twine across the wagon seat between the dummies. "This may smart your fingers a bit, son, but a mile or two won't do you serious damage. What I want you to do now is get up here in the wagonbed, flat-out on your belly, and drive with these strings. Oh, don't worry, it'll look just like this fella here—" he indicated the male dummy—"is drivin' the team. You just keep your head down. You can see enough to drive, just lookin' between the bench and the footboard. It's an easy crossing."

"What do you think is going to happen?" Buck wondered.

"Well, one of two things. Either you'll drive down across that river and up the other side, to where the trail veers off—it bends right, by the way, just past the far crest—or, maybe, someplace between here and there, somebody will ambush you and probably just kill the hell out of these innocent folk up here on this bench. In which case, you just stay down until they finish shootin', then you do whatever seems right."

Buck shrugged. "Generally if folks shoot my direction, I'd think the thing to do is to shoot back."

"Fine with me." Shanty nodded. "How many loads in that rifle?"

"Fourteen."

"That'll do for starters." The big man opened one of his saddlebags, rummaged inside and came out with a large revolver. "Keep this with you. It doesn't have the range of that rifle, but it's fit for social work."

"Where will you be?"

111

"Close by. Don't worry. Chances are there's nobody yonder at all. But if there is, I might try to keep one or two, in case Wolf wants to talk to them."

When the wagon rolled over the crest and headed down the slope toward the distant river bottom, it looked for all the world as though there were two people aboard—a man at the reins and a woman sitting beside him.

"Wolf said you ride just fine, miss," Shanty told the girl. "So climb up on that horse and let's get to moving. We'll cross a little farther up, then circle back. No sense anybody knowin' that we're around. It would just confuse folks."

"You really are crazy," she allowed. "Every one of you."

"Yes, ma'am."

At a place where cedars screened the view, beyond a shoulder of the wide valley, they crested and dropped down toward the distant river—just a ribbon of water winding across hard sand at the bottom of the wide valley. Shanty set a mile-eating pace, and Gail had her hands full staying on the horse and trying to keep up with him. Not until they came out on the level floor of the valley, with the river hidden ahead by groves of trees, did she have a chance to look downstream. But even then she couldn't see Buck's wagon. Shanty's chosen route was out of sight both of the trail crossing and of the mesa itself.

Nearly an hour had passed when they topped out again on the north ridge, and Shanty led into a cross canyon that wound eastward. "Keep moving," he urged her. "That wagon's across the stream by now, and I'd like to see th' rise before he gets there. Do you know how to shoot a pistol?"

"Of course I do."

He hauled up for a moment and found another revolver—smaller than the one he had given Buck, but

112

still a lethal-looking implement. He handed it to her. "Thirty-two-twenty," he said. "Use it if you need to." Then he was off again, and she drummed heels to keep up.

They came up onto the foot of the mesa between the shoulders of a cut, with the low sun directly behind them, and Shanty slowed to listen and look, getting his bearings. Satisfied, he put his mount into a high lope and headed upward toward a jumbled rise where the towering bulk of Black Mesa began. Following him as best she could, Gail squinted upward at the climbing steep grade ahead and to her left. From here the top of the great mesa looked unattainable—sheer canting walls of cedar-strewn climb that looked as though it had been devastated by some ancient catastrophe. Rugged, broken terrain that stood on end and seemed to defy the world to assail it. From miles away it had been obvious that it was a mesa—a massive highland with its top flat as the top of a table. But here, at the foot of its soaring broken face, the top was not evident. That insane clutter of standing land seemed to go on up, right to the sky. A person on foot might climb that face—might walk or crawl or scrabble to the top of it—but no wagon would go there, not even a horse.

Forty-five miles long, her father had said of Black Mesa—forty-five miles east to west, with its ramparts in No Man's Land and its bulk extending over into Colorado and New Mexico. A mile wide at its narrowest, seven or eight miles some places. And on top—grass. Just grass, blowing in the wind on a surface as regular as a dooryard lawn.

The path Shanty followed was no path at all now, just a twisting, turning course among broken slabs and rises, but always upward, aslant, higher and higher toward the steeps that loomed above.

The immediate surroundings changed wildly with each turn—now a crack between cleft stones, with footing

113

barely wide enough for their mounts to high-step past their own feet, then a thread of trail clinging to a rutted cliff where masses of tumbled stone poised above and jagged chaos waited below . . . then, briefly, a wide, easy slope slewing out from the mesa's face, then a vertiginous dip where the horses scrambled to keep their footing and the trail curved away around a shoulder with nothing but air beyond.

Still the big man barely slowed his pace, even when it seemed impossible to go on, and at each turn and wind there was a new obstacle.

"Crazy," Gail muttered to herself over and over. "They're just plain crazy."

Twin pillars of eroded stone, like squat mushrooms thirty feet tall, stood like archposts at a place where the path rose and then dipped out of sight, and here Shanty slowed and raised a cautioning hand. Gail waited while he walked his mount forward to the crest between monuments, then eased up beside him. The buckboard wagon was only a few hundred yards away, coming up a gentle rise where a vague trail climbed toward a shelf—the same shelf they were on—and turned east, away from them. The straw and rod "passengers" startled her for a moment. In the horizontal light of last sunshine they were as real to the eye as real people would have been.

"Well," she said, "so far so—"

The crash of a gunshot, echoing instantly among the rocks, cut her off. The straw driver shuddered, and a second shot followed, then another and another, their echoes a rolling thunder. The male-dressed dummy seemed to explode and toppled backward into the wagonbed. The other—the woman—turned half around, its arms swinging outward. Then its head burst into a cloud of straw and dust, and it pitched over the far side of the wagon.

The shots seemed to have come from above and ahead, but Gail couldn't be sure. The echoes were stunning and

114

confusing. She was still staring around when Shanty jumped from his horse, handed the reins to her, said, "Stay here," and sprinted around the left monument to disappear into tumbled rocks above. Ahead, the buckboard's team had just reached the shelf, both horses dancing and shying in their traces, and veered toward the right, following the dim trail there. But instead of bolting, they stopped, held in check by invisible twine reins from the wagonbed. For a moment there was silence, except for the shifting of evening breezes upon the face of the mesa—breezes that brought a startling and puzzling scent, an under-odor pervading the tendril whiffs of gunsmoke. Gail swung down from her saddle, holding two sets of reins, and edged forward, trying to see what was above. Rock shards erupted beside her, and a bullet whined away across the valley beyond. The reins she held almost jerked her from her feet as both horses shied back and away. Then there was a rolling tattoo of hard cracks that went on and on, and she glimpsed Buck in the wagonbed, firing upward with his rifle, spent cases glinting like golden spray as he levered and fired. Almost drowned in the thunder was a high, drawn-out cry and a rattle of rock. A man plunged into view, somersaulting from above, thudded onto the path and lay still, a broken heap.

Farther out, on a broken shelf of rock above the turning trail, she saw a man's head and shoulders rise into view, saw the glint of a gun as he leveled it downward toward the young man in the wagon. Somehow, there was a gun in her hand—the thirty-two-twenty Shanty had handed her. Without thinking she raised it, sighted and fired. Ten yards below the gunman, flint outcrop erupted in a burst of shards, and the man's shot went wild as he ducked back. Only for an instant, then he pointed again . . . and doubled over to sprawl across a slanted stone as Buck's shot found him. Even at that distance, Gail saw the young man grin as he tipped a salute

115

toward her.

Two dead men lay in plain view from the shelter of the twin spires, and quiet breezes played around the twisted rise of Black Mesa. And again, as the acrid hints of gunpowder drifted away, there was another odor on the wind, and she toyed with it, not really thinking about it. There might be a dead animal nearby, decomposing, but it was not that exactly. A carrion odor, but not the fetid sweet-sour of decaying flesh . . . not exactly.

Where had Shanty gone? Were there others around? She listened, noticing Buck still in his wagon, turning carefully this way and that to scan the rocky slopes. Silence and the evening winds. Abruptly there was sound, then, a piercing scream, a man's voice high with terror. The scream seemed to float, to fly, then suddenly rushed nearer as a cartwheeling form plummeted from above somewhere to thud and splatter among the cold rocks to the right of the trail. For a moment a hand reached above the rocks, fingers outstretched and quivering, then it relaxed and collapsed, seeming to sink into sleep, the fingers curling against the rock. Thin and far away, Buck's voice drifted back on the shifting breeze, "Good Gawd a'mighty!"

Then the last of the sunlight was gone, rose-gold colors climbing away up the face of Black Mesa. Appalled at the death before her on the trail, Gail backed away, through the monument gate and down the rising path, a step at a time, edging between the two horses, turning them and leading them back. Distant, faint scrabbling sounds came down the steep face of the mesa, and she glanced up. High above, silhouetted against the slivers of evening sunlight haloing the crest of the malpais pass, she saw movement. After a moment she could make it out—a man, far above, climbing. Far below him she saw the massive figure of Shanty going after him. Sprinting and clambering, the big man angled up the sloping shoulders, heading for the sheer cliffs above. But the fugitive was too far away, and as she realized that, she saw him realize it too. Even at that distance, his massive shrug was visible as he stopped, turned and started back down.

The errant breeze shifted again, and suddenly that odd, tenuous odor in the air was a hot, reeking presence near at hand. She raised her head, wrinkling her nose. Where had she smelled that before? Images fell into place and she knew. It was the smell of a slaughterhouse—the smell of blood, fresh blood flowing across cold, coagulating blood slippery on the black residues of older, dried blood beneath. She couldn't hear Shanty's voice, but she knew he was shouting . . . and pointing. She turned.

Twenty feet away, a small black-clad figure was coming at her, running at a half-crouch, bobbing, scuttling like a crab up the path, one hand high and waving a shining black thing. The breeze at his back carried to her the heavy reek of thick, drying blood. He came upright as she turned, and charged, his reedy voice chanting words in a strange, clicking, singsong tongue.

She wasn't even aware of the pistol bucking in her hand, only that bright spray erupted from him . . . from a shoulder, from the side of his head—his flat black hat spun away, revealing a head as bald as an onion—and from behind him as a high-speed bullet mushroomed in his chest. Behind her the led horses reared and backed, jerking her backward as part of the man's face disappeared in a welter of spray. A shot whined away across the face of the mesa, and she sat down abruptly, one arm stretched back, reins whipped from her fingers, and the gun clicked on a spent chamber. For an instant he was over her, almost on her; then he crumpled and sprawled, and the thing in his hand slid across gravel to come to rest against her thigh—a wide, black obsidian blade with a stubby handle wrapped in rawhide.

The sprawled, gurgling body twitched, seemed to shrivel, then lay still, and the odor of bloody carrion was a heavy evil in the still air. Vaguely aware of Buck

117

scampering up the far rise, heading off panicked horses—
of Shanty half-running, half-sliding down the broken
face of Black Mesa—Gail turned away, got to her knees
and crawled, not looking back, until the odor of death was
dispersed by a vagrant breeze. Then on hands and knees
she simply waited, head down, rocking slowly, trying not
to be sick. As though in the throes of a nightmare, she
heard again the strange, high, clicking chant of the little
madman, and syllables rang familiar in her shocked
mind. The language was Nahuatl—ancient and still-
living tongue of the Mexíca, the people called Aztec.

Beneath the high halo of the last red rays of Tonaiu,
the setting sun, the creature had come with an obsidian
knife and a chant of worship to the sun god, the drinker
of blood, Huitzilopochtli.

Big hands raised her gently and guided her away to a
place upwind where tumbled rock shielded the view of
the death-littered trail. Strong, gentle fingers pried loose
the empty revolver from her hand, and Shanty eased her
down to sit with her back against a rock, sheltered from
the evening breeze. "You did right well there, miss," he
said. "Devil took a lot of killin', but you brought him
down. I'll put some fresh loads in this, and you can hang
on to it; but I don't reckon you'll need it again right away.
There was five of 'em and we got four. Th' other one went
over the top. I couldn't catch him."

"That little . . . man. . . ." she whispered, then cleared
her throat and took a deep breath, trying to still the
shakes.

"Yes'm. I've seen a few of them around. Don't know
exactly what he was, but—"

"Quatemál."

"Ma'am?"

"Quatemál. A kind of Indian. They come into Mexico
sometimes, from the south. But . . . not like that! I don't
know . . . I don't know what he was."

Shanty shrugged. "I guess Wolf can figure it out. But

118

whatever that was, that's what we're up against."

Buck came then, from somewhere, his eyes wide with wonder in the fading light. "I'll take that double pay, mister. Damn, what a set-to. You both all right?"

"We're fine. Did you catch those horses?"

"Yours and hers. I left them yonder with the wagon. If those jaspers had horses, I couldn't find them."

"Probably up on top. From the north, a horse can get up there."

"Well, there's four dead people on that trail. Or else three dead people and a dead . . . somethin'. What kind of critter is that back there? He's shot all to—pardon, ma'am—and he stinks to high heaven. What is he, anyway?"

"Miss Larkin says he's a . . . Kwatamaul?"

"Quatemál," she said, standing and brushing dust from her coat.

"Quatemál. That's some kind of Indian, from way off. I don't know what else he is. Wish I could have caught that other man. Maybe he could've told us something."

"I know what he was," Gail said. "At least, I think I know. He was a priest. An Aztec priest."

"Aztec?" Shanty frowned.

"Not Aztec race. Aztec religion. That knife he had—"

"Yeah, I picked it up. It's made out of black flint or something." Buck handed the object to Shanty.

"Obsidian," Gail said. "That's a sacrificial knife. A *cholotl*. I'm afraid my father was right. Someone is trying to bring back the sun god."

Shanty squinted at her, then raised his head and turned, listening. "Did you hear that?"

"Coyote," Buck said.

"No, that wasn't a coyote, and maybe that last one didn't get away after all. That was Wolf. He's up there." He pointed at the mesa top, distant and dark against a deepening sky.

XII

The man's name was Cecil Cobb. He was a drifter, a brawler and sometimes a thief. He had hired out as muscle and now and then had hired out for his gun. But now, as he dangled head-down from a rock outcrop, trussed like a slaughter-hog, while Wolf built a small fire a foot below his twisted face, Cobb was full of repentance and panic. Tears streamed down his forehead, and the realization that there were worse ways to die than what the little Indians had done to Evan Purdue was a knot in his throat. He wasn't even sure that those little black-clad, stinking maniacs were Indians. But the one kneeling beside him now, preparing to roast his head, was. Cecil Cobb's entire miserable life paraded before him, and he regretted.

And nobody was going to help him. The crazy old man with the wild white hair stood a few steps away, watching with clinical interest while the monstrous beast he called Dog sat by his side, waiting happily for table scraps. Beyond, in the distance, the big, sulking man with the lever carbine had joined an even bigger man with red whiskers at a campsite where there was a wagon and a lot of horses. There were others there, too—a young man and a young woman—but they were all ignoring what was going on here.

Cobb had told the Indian called Wolf everything he knew. He had pled for mercy, had sworn and blustered and wept, had promised to change his ways . . . promised to do anything he was told to do. But Wolf wasn't satisfied. All he had said was, "Maybe you know a little more. Now we'll find out."

"I seen Yaquis do that to a man one time, Wolf," the old man said. "Trouble was, after a while his head blew up. Made a gawdawful mess. You sure you wouldn't rather just let Dog chew on this jaybird for a while?"

"Dog isn't precise," the Indian said. "He might kill him too soon. I want to hear the rest of what he knows." With sticks and tinder he assembled a little teepee just below the crown of Cobb's trembling head, then built a neat pile of additional fuel to one side.

"I don't know *anything* else," Cobb wailed. "There ain't any rest of it. I told it all. I told you 'bout Krell an' the little buzzards that feed him cactus buttons, an' what they done to that Purdue back yonder, an' how Krell paid us to ride with him to track down a Injun an' a woman . . . oh, my God. Was that you all?"

"Who is Krell working for?" Wolf asked, unwrapping a packet of matches.

"I already told you I ain't got the slightest idea," Cobb blithered. "Wait, don't do that! If I knew I'd tell you. Hell, I'll tell you anything you . . . oh, God! Don't! . . . anything you want to hear."

Wolf struck a match, let its flame grow on its wooden stick, then held it to the tinder. Wisps of smoke stung Cobb's eyes, and he struggled, lurching, swinging this way and that on the rope holding his ankles. When his wild struggling subsided, Wolf steadied him, stopping the swinging, and now Cobb felt the heat of first embers against his scalp.

"Pretty quick his hair'll catch on," the wild old man said. "That'll singe him pretty good. May take an inch or two off his ears, too, if it burns good enough. Way them Yaquis done it was, they—"

"Please!" Cobb sobbed. "Tell me what to say. I'll say it. Anything!"

"How much did Krell pay you?" Wolf asked quietly.

"A hundred dollars! I told you. A hundred for each of us, an' five hundred when we got to Aztlan, plus a thousand bonus for the man that brought you down an' a thousand on that woman."

"Where is Aztlan?"

"Dammit, I don't know. Ow! Jeez, that's hot! Nobody

121

ever told us, except it's west someplace . . . an' Krell said be glad it's winter because it's hell out there in th' summer. God, mister, don't do this to me! Please!''

"Yaquis kept that feller turnin'," the old man said. "That way he didn't cook just on one side. Sort of roasted nice an' even, right down to his nose an' his earlobes. Only got messy when his brain boiled an' blew up his skull. You want some more firewood, Wolf?"

"What would you have done if I hadn't caught you?" Wolf asked casually.

Cobb was rolling his head this way and that, trying to find clean air to breathe. His hanging hair had begun to smolder. "I don't know," he coughed. "Hid out, maybe . . . tried to get east someplace . . . get away . . . maybe stole some money to get out of th' country. I seen what they do to people who fail."

"Like Evan Purdue."

"Yeah. Jeez, put that fire out. I'm roastin'!"

"Krell and the rest, where did they go?"

"West. I don't know. We was supposed to look around here, then meet them someplace called Rock Point. Past Trinidad, down toward Santa Fe."

"You haven't told me anything new yet," Wolf said. He added a stick to the fire.

"I don't *know* anything new!"

"That feller the Yaquis had," the old man said, "he kept shuttin' his eyes that way, too. So they propped 'em open with cactus spines. There's some prickly pear right yonder. . . ."

A tendril of matted hair caught and blazed smokily, the flame climbing toward Cobb's skull. He screamed at the intensified heat, and in the wagon camp in the distance, faces turned toward them. The young woman stood and started up the rise, but the big red-beard caught her arm and led her back. They wouldn't interfere.

Casually, Wolf reached out and snuffed the blazing hair strand with calloused fingers. "What would you do

122

for me if I let you go?"

"Oh, Jeez! Anything! You name it! Anything!"

"Spoke like a true hothead," the old man chuckled. "That feller th' Yaquis had, he even promised to teach 'em all how to fly. Then he said he'd kill President Grant for 'em. I believe it was Grant then. What year was that? I recollect it was the ninth of May . . ."

Wolf nudged Cobb's shoulder with a stick, setting him to spinning slowly. "Would you help me find Krell?"

"God, mister, didn't I tell you? Those people are crazy. They'd cut my heart out, just like they did to—"

"Hard choice to make, isn't it?"

Fresh wood caught and sputtered, and again there were smolders in Cobb's hair. "Oh, God! Please!" he sobbed. "Yes, I'll help you. Yes! Whatever you want!"

Wolf shrugged, stood and scattered the little fire with a boot toe. "You've made a deal," he said. "The worst mistake you could ever make would be to go back on it." He drew a knife and sliced the rope at Cobb's heels. The bound man thudded onto hard ground, rolled over and moaned. Wolf tossed the knife to the old man. "Cut him loose, Willie. Then clean him up a little and bring him down to the camp."

"I could let Dog teach him a few manners. . . ."

"Dog may have his chance later. Right now, just cut him loose."

Without a backward glance Wolf strode off up the slope, making for the turn-trail Shanty had showed him, where the assassins had jumped the wagon. He wanted another look at the bodies up there—one of them in particular.

They had come around the east promontory of Black Mesa at dawn, Wolf in the lead, the trussed captive riding behind him on a led mount, then Willie Shay clinging monkeylike to his saddle, and Trooper bringing up the rear and pushing all the extra animals—the ones they had brought from eastern Kansas and those they had

123

collected along the way. It was becoming a sizeable herd. They had already collected the five atop Black Mesa by the time Cecil Cobb, panting and wheezing, had clawed his way up the southeast steep and into Trooper's waiting hands. The only way to bring horses down, though, was the north slope, not quite as steep and rugged as the south and east prominences. So it had taken several hours—in the dusk of evening and the dusk before dawn—to come around to where Shanty waited with his charges.

Now in good light Wolf walked the turn-trail, studying the bodies there one by one. Shanty had already collected their various hardware, but left the bodies where they fell. The first three, two of them shot by Buck's trusty rifle, the third thrown off a cliff by Shanty, were men of the general cut of Cecil Cobb—prairie drifters, bush-whackers gravitated to No Man's Land or the Kansas frontier or Colorado's badlands, just some more of what Kichener called ten-or-nothing men. Men who would hire out to most anybody to do most anything if the price was right. Only this time, somebody had hired a lot of them. Maybe hundreds.

The fourth dead man was different—maybe the same little black-clad man he had seen and lost at Willie's Digs, or maybe another like him. It was hard to tell. But now with the sun on him and the air turning warm, the miasma of blood and old death hung over him like a stinking fog. A smell to turn the hardest stomach. Wolf's nostrils twitched and he frowned, steeling himself as he approached. He turned the body over and knelt beside it. Gail Larkin had shot away large pieces of the man before he fell. Wolf smiled grimly, wondering what condition she had been in thereafter. Shanty hadn't said much, only that she "wasn't in very good shape for a while." And Wolf hadn't talked with her yet. He and Willie had stopped upslope from the wagon camp to deal with his prisoner. He would as soon have done that alone, but

124

when Willie Shay took a notion to watch something, it was no use arguing with the old man.

The little man had the features of Indian ancestry, but not the craggy, stolid lines of the plains tribes or yet the chiseled features of a Cherokee or Cheyenne, or any of the Iroquoians. His features were neither the wide, sturdy planes of an Algonquian or Ute face, nor the hawkish lines of the Apache, Creek or Comanche. He had the face of a child, as though age and experience had left no imprint, though Wolf judged him to be in his thirties or older. Nowhere on his body was there visible hair except for a faint, dark fuzz above his eyes, and the lashes on his eyelids.

The coat he wore was filthy, stiff and reeking with matted dark stains on the black fabric. Beneath it he wore a pullover garment so soiled that its original color was lost, and under that, fouled leggings of wool or loose felt and a loincloth of soft tanned hide. The shoes on his feet were plaited sandals with rope soles.

He was scarcely more than five feet tall, and could not have weighed more than a hundred and twenty pounds. and his skin color, flushed now with the relaxing of rigor mortis, was a light rose-gold where his clothing had blocked the rays of the sun.

Wolf thought of the jungle tribes—little bands of primitives hidden away in the rain forests of Central America. The man was not—at least racially—a descendant of Aztecs. The Aztecs, though of no unusual stature, had been rugged, sturdy people, fierce warriors who had conquered a land in their time. In this man, Wolf saw the results of centuries of semi-starvation—and, his hunch told him, a keening fanaticism that, itself, had become part of the breed.

What have you gone after this time, Kichener, he asked in his mind. What monstrous thing have you found? Are you still alive somewhere, or have you finally encountered the evil that could overcome you?

125

Maybe it was only a matter of time.

Repulsed and revolted by the thing at his feet, he stood and backed away, drawing from his pocket the stone knife that Shanty had handed him. It seemed to be the only implement the creature had carried—a wide, razor-edged blade of black obsidian with a stubby handle. A thing designed for the butchering of living people. The man might not have been Aztec, but the weapon he carried was. Whatever his ancestry, and however unlikely after three centuries of oblivion, the rites of Huitzilopochtli were alive, and he was one of those who worshipped the old god. An Aztec priest.

Feeling cold inside he gazed toward the west, beyond the looming mass of Black Mesa. Out there somewhere, past the first ranges of mountains, secret armies were being amassed. He had the feeling he had seen only glimpses of the total: armed toughs and hoodlums, ten-or-nothing men in large numbers and well organized, penetrating into even the sedate and civilized lands of the east under the leadership of others more devious—men like Krell—and these others somehow controlled by still others, with somewhere at the center of the growing web a person who named himself Kukulki—Quetzalcoatl. A person who intended to raise the blood-drinker from the past and use him—and all who would follow him—to gain whatever ends he had in mind.

And through it all—throughout the web—creatures like this one existed . . . intense, bloodthirsty little fanatics in stinking black coats, seeking fresh blood to nourish the god of the ancient sun.

He shook his head, gazing at the dead creature a few feet away. Not Aztec—but more than Aztec. No, he thought, your ancestors did not escape the fury of Cortes and Alvarado to hide in the jungles to the south. Your ancestors were already there when those refugees came, and they learned from them. They learned all of the evil that was the old Triple Alliance, with none of the

126

experience of civilization that had been part of it—nothing to soften it, nothing to balance it. How many generations did it take to produce you? Fifteen? Twenty? Generations isolated and hidden in the killing jungles, devoted to the worship of a god whose only hunger is for human blood . . . insanity as a way of life.

And what kind of man would have found you and organized you and set you loose?

Who is Kukulki?

Resolve that had already been there now firmed itself in his mind. Somewhere west—looking for him and the girl—was the man called Krell. And Krell could lead him to Hall Kileen, and Hall Kileen could lead him to Kukulki. What had been hunch had grown to a certainty, and he had no need to add up the clues to it. It was a white man's tendency, the analytical amassing of evidences before admitting to a fact. Wolf knew. He had been fascinated by Ralph Waldo Emerson's need to explain the obvious. Emerson had been right . . . but too white to ever be sure of it.

Krell to Kileen to Kukulki. And Kukulki to the mask of the sun god, and thus the answers about Ernest Kichener.

Wolf knew.

Morning sun was full on the east face of Black Mesa now, and with balmy winds still coming from the southwest the air was losing its winter chill. Already, a pair of buzzards had begun to circle, high up near the rim, drawn by the death on the slope below. Three ten-or-nothing men and a bizarre little creature from another time. The killing was ended for here and now, and it was time for scavengers to clean the field. Wolf pocketed the obsidian blade and walked away, downslope. Willie Shay and Dog were just herding a shaky Cecil Cobb into the camp, and Wolf could see Trooper fingering his carbine, glaring at the three of them equally.

When he came down to where they waited, Trooper

confronted him. "What do you want with that damned outlaw, Wolf? Soon's we turn our backs, he'll either try to shoot us or else just hightail it."

"If he does," Wolf said, "kill him." He turned to Shanty. "Has your driver earned his keep?"

"He sure has, Wolf. Kid's good. And he's a hotshot with that rifle. Two of those up yonder are his."

"Then pay him what you agreed. Hold out the best dozen of those horses and get packs on five of them. Then make out a holder's deed on the rest and give it to Buck. They're his if he can get them home. In return I want him to take a message to the telegraph operator at Arkalon and get it off for me. Do you think he can do that?"

"He can."

"Good. I'll work out the message before he leaves. But I want him gone before we start out. We've broken all the trails now. Let's keep it that way."

"Sure, Wolf."

Gail Larkin was waiting for him by the buckboard, pale and fuming. "It's about time you showed up," she snapped. "Do you have any idea what all I've been through since you turned me over to those . . . those postmen?"

"Chalk it up to your continuing education," he said. "Some time back, you told me about a man named Hall Kileen. You said he was a lunatic . . . or a maniac . . . and that he tried to start a revolution when you and your father were in Mexico with him."

"We weren't *with* him; we were just looking for the same things."

"But you got caught up in it."

"When Hall Kileen decides to make trouble, everybody gets caught up in it. It's how he is."

"Did you ever hear of a man named Krell?"

"No." She shook her head. "No, I don't think so."

"How about Kukulki?"

"Kukulki? That's a Mayan word or something. It

128

means the same as the Nahuatl word Quetzalcoatl."

"I know that. Do you know of anyone who calls himself that?"

"Well, yes, but it's sort of a joke. There was a Mexican general down there then—Don Juan Ascencion Acuna— a petty little tyrant who used to strut around the villages in Zacatecas and San Luis Potosi, bullying the people there. He liked for people to call him Kukulki. It was a nickname, I guess."

"Was there a connection between him and Kileen?"

"Well, yes. Acuna was the one Hall tried to get to revolt."

When Buck was gone, with the buckboard, an assortment of second-hand horses and a coded message that he swore would be sent as Wolf directed, they saddled and headed west, skirting the sweeping foot of Black Mesa. Nearby were the decades-old ruts of the Cimarron Cutoff, one of the routes of the old Santa Fe Trail.

They had gone four miles when Windwagon Willie held up his hand and reined to a halt. He walked his horse to the head of the file, looked around, went a few steps more and proclaimed, "This here bein' the twelfth day of February, eighteen hundred an' whatever, I hereby cross this line."

Trooper scowled, staring at the featureless land beneath the old man's horse. "What line is that old coot talkin' about now?"

Willie glanced around. "Varmint," he muttered. Then with a flourish he added, "At this hour of this here day I hereby cross from No Man's Land, which ain't fit to be in anyways, into th' territory of New Mexico, which is a sight worse some ways." The ceremony attended to, he glanced back at the rest of them. "Well, come on. We ain't got all day."

XIII

"Nice country out here," Willie Shay chatted as they crested a rolling ridge with the white-topped blue swell of the Sangre de Cristos to their right. "Not too many folks, an' a man can be sociable or not, as he pleases. Follow th' trails an' sure enough you'll get th' chance to howdy just about ever'body there is, 'cause that's where they'll all be, one time or another. But stay off th' trails an' it's downright peaceable . . . barrin' Injuns or hardcases or drunk miners or such." He pointed off to the left. "That jumbley-lookin' stretch yonder, that's where th' Pecos River heads up. Don' amount to anything as rivers goes; but it meanders all the way down through Texas, an' there's folks down yonder that say it's th' beatin'est river they ever waded acrost. Now, over yonder, them is the Sangre de Cristos. I've heard folks say those are the purtiest mountains God ever put on earth . . . 'course, some folks will say anything when th' spirit is on 'em . . ."

A short way back Trooper sighed and shook his head, like a buffalo troubled by flies. "Doesn't that crazy old coot ever shut up? He's been talkin' non-stop for nine days that I know of. I don't know why Wolf doesn't shoot him, just for some peace and quiet."

"He's been isolated." Shanty shrugged massive shoulders. "Got a lot of talk built up that he needs to get rid of. Just ignore it if you don't like it."

"How can I ignore it? He never stops. And most times he doesn't make any sense anyway. I swear he talks in his sleep—"

"I don't know if he sleeps."

"Well, if he does he talks in his sleep."

"Maybe you ought to pay attention to him," Shanty suggested. "Wolf does."

"Hell, I think half the time Wolf's crazy, too."

His voice had risen in exasperation, and Willie glanced back, scowling. "Varmint," he declared. "Yonder's Glorieta Pass," he told Wolf. "Maybe you can't see it yet, but yonder it is. You still want to go around?"

Wolf nodded. "We'll make for the Gallinas, Willie. How long to Arizona?"

Willie gazed into the distance and shrugged. "Maybe ten days, maybe a month. That North Plains country is funny this time of year. If it's dry we'll move fast. If not, we'll hole up someplace an' wait 'til it is. I'd say it's dry right now . . . we'll see."

For five days the weather had remained clear, a steady southwest wind bringing warm temperatures each day, although the nights were still chilly. Two days out from Black Mesa they had angled south, staying off the Cimarron Cutoff Trail to skirt Rabbit Ear Mountain, then made due west to the Canadian Crossing.

High, blue mountains had grown ahead and to the south as they circled wide around the village of La Junta to rim the Pecos Valley at its upper limit, rough country where a man could see what wasn't hidden but could hide from being seen. Twice they had eased into cover to avoid being seen by riders in the distance, relying on Willie to tell them when someone was out there. Not even John Thomas Wolf could spot movement at the distances Willie was accustomed to.

And each time, when it was clear, they had gone on—a string of people and animals tiny in the wide, creased lands—with Wolf setting a steady pace that put the miles behind them but preserved the strength of their mounts. Usually Willie led, sometimes with Wolf beside him, at other times with Shanty there. Dog scouted constantly, trotting off in great, looping circles ahead, always to home again on Willie before starting over. Gail Larkin held a little back from the leaders, at Wolf's orders. And behind her came Cecil Cobb, nervous and pale, and Trooper alternately bringing along the pack animals and

131

keeping an eye on Cobb. Six people in all, plus twelve horses and Dog. Shanty had noticed as the days and evenings passed that Wolf rarely glanced at the hardcase Cobb, hardly seemed to notice him at all. Shanty took his signal from this and passed it along to Trooper. Give the owlhoot all the rope he wants. Wolf wants to see what he'll do.

A dozen times in those few days Cobb was all alone, separated by terrain and space from the rest, and could have gotten away . . . or at least would have thought he could. And as many times, in evening camp, there was nothing to keep him from picking up a weapon and using it . . . or he at least thought so. Yet the hardcase clung to them as a drowning man clings to a raft, and his gaze when he looked at the distances was not the yearning of a man thinking to get away. It was the worried gaze of a man expecting enemies from out there and ready to pull in close to the group for safety. For a time he could not bear to wear a hat, and there were blisters on his scalp where some of his hair fell away. But whatever he had found among these people, there was worse waiting out there somewhere.

Noons and evenings, and when they paused for water or good graze, Wolf often was distant from the rest, withdrawn, roving the area afoot, head high like a scenting predator or bowed in thought. At other times he fired questions at Gail Larkin: Why was she sure the little priest had been Quatemál? What were the distinguishing characteristics? What further details did she know— from Frederick Larkin or from accompanying him—of the rites and rituals of the Aztecs? Had they ever been underground people? Were any signs of them ever found in caves? Were their structures of original design, or copied from the earlier Toltecs and Mayas? What colors predominated in their designs? When they prayed, or worshipped, what was their preferred direction to face? The Nahuatl language was still spoken in Mexico in various forms, but how varied were they? Was there evidence that the language was still a consolidated tongue? What was the evidence? Why did Frederick Larkin believe the mask of the sun god could be found? What had he said about Aztlan? What clues had he given her?

She had few answers, but he returned again and again to the questions, to the point—she felt—of inquisition. Yet when her annoyance boiled over he simply gazed at her, stonily, until she ran down . . . and then started again. When her father first started thinking about Aztlan, what artifacts was he studying? When he left that last time, what artifacts did he take with him?

Only one, she said, so far as she knew. A little medallion of carved jadestone—the snake medallion, she had called it, because of its odd design. It was oval in shape, with a natural pattern in the stone that had been honed or cut through, so that an undulating opening wandered from one end to the other of the stone—a slit maybe a sixteenth of an inch across, from about a quarter-inch inside one short end of the oval to about the same distance from the other. The cut had made the stone very fragile, and it was in two pieces when Frederick Larkin found it among shards at a dig south of Lake Texcoco. He had repaired it for study. The undulating slit across its face was like the track of a drunken snake, wavy and irregular.

He had her draw him a picture of it, from memory, then when she was done, he put it away and had her draw it again . . . and again and again.

"The mind has more memory than it knows," he said. "Among these is a match for the original stone."

Then at other times he would be huddled with Willie Shay, talking about Arizona as the old man remembered it. Had Willie ever gone directly north from Tucson? What had he seen there? What had he seen the first day out? And the second . . . and the third? Where were the

133

watercourses? Where was grass? Where there was volcanic stone, in what direction had it flowed? Where did it look newest? Describe the horizons . . . there, and there, and there. Did he remember seeing two peaks that looked like twins in the distance? Where? And where did he see them from?

Even Willie had become irritated once or twice at the Indian's painstaking inquisitions. "By damn, Wolf," he complained, "you're worse'n sand fleas when you get aholt of somethin'. If you know what we're lookin' for, just come out an' tell me; then I'll tell you if I saw it or not an' where it is! Land, it taken me years to see Arizony. If I could tell you ever' step of it in a hour, then it wouldn't have took me that long, would it?"

But Wolf had wandered away, and Willie found himself complaining only to Dog, who had no response except a tongue-lolling grin.

At one nooning Windwagon Willie sat on a rock eating salt pork and onions and leering at Gail Larkin, when suddenly his eyes widened. He finished his meal and beckoned to Wolf.

"You see that there woman?" He pointed.

"I see her," Wolf said.

"Well, sir, lookin' at her got me to thinkin' 'bout them twin peaks you been onto me about. You recollect talkin' about twin peaks, don't you?"

"Yes."

"Well, I don't know when I seen a nicer set, though what with all th' clothes white women wears, it's hard for a body to tell for sure. What do you reckon she's got on that makes 'em poke out like—"

"Willie?"

"Huh?"

"What about twin peaks?"

"You mean hers?"

"No. What about what you were thinking about?"

"Oh. That. Well, I just plain don't recollect ever seein'

a pair of twin peaks out in th' territory, not like you asked about. But how 'bout valleys?"

"Twin valleys?"

"Yeah. It's all in how you look at it, don't you see? Now that woman there . . . well, think about her a'layin' on her back an' th' sky above her. . . . Land, just think about that. . . ."

"Willie!"

"Huh? Oh, yeah. Well, then sort of turn her over like, an' think about when she bends down sort of, an' think how it would be if *she* was th' sky. I mean, what you might expect to see of her was she to do that, imagine that's the sky an' what's around it is horizon. . . ."

"You hear that?" Trooper whispered to Shanty nearby. "Didn't I tell you the old coot's crazy as a loon? I never heard such a notion in my life."

"Shut up," Shanty suggested.

"Twin valleys," Willie said. "That's what you'd be seein' then, was you to look at it thataway."

"Have you seen them?"

"Naw, I keep lookin', but she never takes off any of them clothes when I'm around."

"I mean the valleys, Willie." Wolf's voice was strained. "Twin valleys."

"Oh, sure. Out in Arizony. Sixteenth day of August it was, eighteen hundred an' . . . I forget. . . . Anyhow I come up on this little squatty peak and out there ahead was th' purtiest set of twin valleys you ever did see. Old volcano sittin' right between 'em, an' the peak I was on wasn't any peak at all. It was more like a ridge runnin' right on up to that cone, except I'd come on it from th' end and didn't see it that way right off. Anyways, it seemed like the good Lord had decided to take a right smart valley an' make two valleys out of it, an' come out with twins. That's just how it looked to me."

"Where was that place, Willie?"

"Oh, yonder. We can go there if you want to see it. I

135

reckon I can find it again, all right."

"Which way were you going when you found that place?"

"Mostly north. I'd been down in the Sierritas, gettin' along all right 'til the Pimas started gettin' wooly, so I hauled out an' went to see what the Mescals looked like. It was on up that way that I found that place."

"In the Mescals?"

"Shoot, I don't know. Maybe, or on past maybe. You know they don't put names on those mountains out yonder." He paused, then grinned crookedly. "'Cept one that I know about. I come across some pilgrims out there, and they said, 'What mountain is that yonder?' and I said, 'Why, that there is Jerusalem Mountain.' An' I heard later on that they'd lit there an' spent near a year spellin' out *Jerusalem* in rocks afore the Apache run 'em out. Religious folks, they was."

When they were moving again, Wolf rode alongside Gail Larkin. "How did you know which side of the stone was the top?" he asked.

She stared at him. "What?"

"Each time you drew that stone for me, you drew it the same way. I watched. You drew it with the two major arcs bending upward, with the smaller, irregular waves leading downward on the left and upward on the right. How do you know which was the 'up' side?"

She shook her head. "I don't know. I guess that was the first way I saw it. Does it matter?"

"It might."

"Do you think that stone is some kind of a map? How could it be? There's nothing on it to indicate any point of reference. If the opening is a line, then it could be anywhere."

"Maybe not a map." He shrugged. "Maybe a template, recording landmarks."

"Template? How . . . oh. Oh, yes. A horizon. Like two peaks against a horizon that rises from left to right. Yes."

"Or turn it over and it's two valleys with a peak—or a crest or cone—between. And if you are looking toward the north, the elevation would rise from west to east."

"There's nothing on it to indicate direction, though."

"No, but if you are going south and want to remember where you have been, then when you look back to see the landmarks there, they are north of you."

"And you assume the stone is a landmark record for Aztlan?"

"Your father assumed that, I think."

"It's a pretty theory, John Thomas," she sighed. "But the Tenochca are thought to have traveled for decades—maybe for generations—before they reached Mexico's central valley and became the Aztecs. That stone might be just one of hundreds, recording their travels."

"No."

"Why 'no'?"

"The Aztecs were a very methodical people, Gail. They counted everything, recorded everything. They were obsessed with numbers. If that were one record of many, it would be numbered. But you say there was no mark on it."

"There was one, but it was only a sun-sign." She looked at him archly. "You asked which was the top, but you didn't ask how I knew which was the front and which was the back. Furthermore, now that I think of it, I'm sure that was how we—or how I—decided which way was up. They would have shown the sun in the sky, wouldn't they?"

"Not necessarily. If it were a place they had left—a place they consigned to their past—they might have shown the sun as set."

She thought about it, then turned again to stare at him, defiant and accusing. "Is that how you do it, John Thomas? Is that how you—as you say—play hide-and-seek? Guesses and intuition? Word games?"

"That's some of it," he admitted. "Hunches are the

137

difference between a clever amateur and a professional when it comes to tracing people. Not word games, though. Mind games. Think as they thought, if you can."

"But it's only *guessing*, John Thomas. There isn't enough real evidence to even—"

"Evidence is for white people," he said. "It's for courtrooms and bank transactions. If you can't know a thing without being able to prove it, you don't belong in the world I know."

"That is pure arrogance, John Thomas. Tell me this . . . if the Indian ways of thinking are so superior to the white ways, then why is it the Indians are being forced onto reservations and not the white men? Why is it that you have taught yourself to be white, instead of me teaching myself to be Indian?"

He shook his head, and a twitch that might have been an instant's smile touched his cheeks. "That's simple. There are a lot more of you than there are of us."

She sneered. "Sophistry. Pure sophistry. John Thomas, are we looking for my father or not? Exactly what are we doing out here?"

"We may find your father, if it comes to that. But we won't track him or anyone else unless we can first backtrack the trail of a people who migrated southward at least five hundred years ago. Maybe your father knew how to find Aztlan. If so, then that's where we will look. But first we have to know where to look for Aztlan."

They made camp that evening in a hidden canyon east and a bit south of Glorieta Pass, only a few miles from the old trail where it swung northwest toward Santa Fe. John Thomas gave them all time to eat and rest, then when a bright moon hung over the east rim of the canyon he roused Shanty. "Put saddles on the two best night horses," he told him. "I'll be taking Cecil Cobb with me."

Shanty didn't ask questions, but a grim smile lifted his whiskers as he walked toward the rope corral. Wolf had let Cobb live, had given back his life instead of taking it.

138

Now it was time for Cobb to earn the favor.

While he waited, Wolf went to Trooper's bedding and shook the big man awake. He had instructions for him.

XIV

Ten riders had gone to Trinidad—four of the black-cloaked Quatemál-Aztecs and six others, led by the man called Krell. They had gone there searching, but from there they would have turned south. Their last, best chance of ambushing Wolf's party now, they would reason, would be at Glorieta Pass.

Wolf counted on their reasoning it so. Since Black Mesa he had estimated the miles and the days, trying to know at each turning where the searchers would be, what they might do next. Trinidad to Raton Pass, from the pass to Wagon Mound, then up through the Cornudo Hills to Las Vegas. Would they have split their forces there? Wolf thought so. He would, had he been them. But Krell was the leader. He would have gone on. And now, somewhere in the funnel that was Glorieta Pass, he would be waiting—gambling that his prey would come to him. And probably the little priests were giving him the cactus buttons, the gray bits of desert magic that some believed could make a man wiser than any man could be. Wolf hoped they were. If Krell was hallucinating, he would be easier to take. A man collapsing the thoughts of a day into what seemed to him an hour might feel very wise indeed, but in fact he was very slow.

The peaks ahead were looming, bright patchworks—moonlight on snow and deep shadow—as they came up out of the gully lands aiming for the rising ridge that was the south shoulder of Glorieta. Shanty had chosen their

139

mounts well, big, powerful horses surefooted in the silver light and not inclined to shy at shadows. Wolf set a pushing pace and Cecil Cobb followed, wide-eyed and frightened but thoroughly cowed by the Indian who set his path for him. Near midnight they hit the first slopes, beyond which rose the climbing Sangre de Cristos, and Wolf reined to a halt for the first time. As Cobb came up to him he turned, agate eyes shadowed beneath his hat brim but seeming to burn with reflected cold light. "Do you know where we're going, Cecil?"

"No. You didn't say."

Wolf turned to release the buckle on a saddlebag, reached into it and drew out a handful of leather and metal—Cobb's own gun rig, oiled shell belt and drop holster, the Colt still in place. Cobb licked his lips.

"You told me you'd do whatever I said if I let you live," Wolf reminded him. "Do you remember?"

"I remember."

Wolf held out the gun rig, offering it. "I'm taking you at your promise. If you put this on, you're mine."

Cobb hesitated. Why was the Indian giving back his gun?

"Take it," Wolf said.

"Then what?"

"Then you decide whether to keep your promise or not."

"What if I decide not to?"

"Then I'll kill you. And that is *my* promise."

Cobb took a deep breath, then accepted the belted gun. But still he hesitated, afraid to put it on. "How do you know I won't kill you first?"

"You might try, but it would be your last mistake. You can take my word for that or not, just as you choose."

"What do you want me to do?"

"I think Krell is up there, ahead of us. I want him. I want you to help me bring him out."

"You're crazy!" Cobb's eyes were saucer-wide in the

moonlight. His hand twitched, and he almost dropped the belted gun.

"I'm giving you a chance to stay alive," Wolf said. "Without me, you have no chance. Even if I didn't kill you, you *know* they would."

"But there's ten of them! And there's those . . . those little ones. . . ."

"I don't think so. I think Krell is up there with two hired guns and two of the Aztecas—"

"The what?"

"The little men. Aztecas. They think they're Aztecs. They're priests, not fighters."

"I saw what they did to Purdue. God! Mister, I can't—"

"You have a gun there in your hand. Drop it, use it or put it on and follow me." The agate eyes were beads of cold fire in moonshadow. The voice was a deep purr. Cobb's hands shook as he buckled on his gunbelt. He wanted—more than anything he wanted—to draw and fire, to see Wolf fall before him . . . then to ride away. But he wouldn't. Somehow he knew, Wolf's promise was just that. It was truth. Slowly he drew the revolver, noticing that Wolf didn't move, just watched. And that, just that, said he would never get it done. He checked the loads in the gun and put it away.

For a moment longer Wolf regarded him, then he reined around and headed upslope, turning his back on Cobb. Cobb gritted his teeth . . . and followed.

Whatever fear those others had planted in him, it was nothing compared to the awe he felt for Wolf. Indian, white or whatever, he had never met a man who could seem so deadly.

Through an hour or more of frosty silence they climbed, up and up, first along the sweeping slope of Serafina Ridge, then following a moondust path of switchbacks and humps where refrozen snow crunched beneath the shod hooves of their mounts, finally emerging atop a breakaway where a mile of the old trade trail lay small below them.

Cobb looked along the trail, one way and then the other, and at the precipice before them. "How are you gonna find anybody up here? They could be anyplace."

"Not just anyplace. There are only two spots where an ambush from cover would have a chance. They'll be camped between those spots. Come on."

Again they climbed, but now at a gentler rate, angling up forested mountainside away from the breakaway. Ahead and below, walls of sheer stone bulged inward on both sides, funneling the trail. The south wall was fifty or sixty feet high, capped off by sparse stands of dark cedar and tumbled rock from the higher slopes behind it. If he set out to bushwhack someone coming up that trail, Cobb decided, it would be hard to find a better place. But Wolf barely paused, looking down at the jumbled cap, then moved on, staying to the forested slope. The moonglow seemed to brighten, taking on a hint of color, and Cobb glanced back, eastward. First dawn was in the clear sky there. Another quarter-mile of steady, zigzag travel, following the slope's contours, and Wolf stopped. He raised his head, his nostrils twitching. Cobb sniffed the air but found nothing.

"There they are," Wolf said. He pointed and Cobb followed the point. He saw nothing there, just a shadowed cleft between outthrust slopes, a deeper slope that fell away to a brushy darkness above the barely visible trail.

"What do we do now?" Cobb twisted in his saddle nervously.

"We wait. It won't be long."

They stepped down and squatted on their heels, watching the sky take on the colors of dawn. They held the reins of their horses. Vagrant breeze drifted up the face of the slope, and Wolf raised his head again, testing the air. "Do you smell that?"

Now Cobb caught the scent—just a suggestion of smoke, as from a dying campfire. That and something more—a sweet, sickly odor that seemed to override the smoke, a cloying, rancid taste to the air that he recognized.

"Jesus," he whispered.

"The Aztecas." Wolf nodded. "You've smelled that before."

Cobb shivered. He had smelled it before, all right. He had the feeling he might smell that odor all the rest of his life.

"The other likely ambush is just up the trail," Wolf said. "Maybe three hundred yards, just past that bend up there. It's a ledge with good cover and an easy slope behind it."

Cobb said nothing, but his fingers caressed the butt of the Colt at his belt. It should be so easy, he thought. Just slip the gun out, cock and fire. Point blank range—

"Don't even think about it," Wolf said, not looking around. "I told you before, I'll kill you if you try."

"I wasn't—"

"Yes, you were. But you won't. You had your best chance at me when I first gave back your gun. You didn't have much of a chance, but it was the best one you got. You didn't take it. If you had, you'd be dead now."

Again, somehow, Cobb knew that the words were literal truth.

There was movement in the shadowed cove below, and a man stepped out from the cover of cedars. Cobb realized that he could see the camp now, with the improving light. Back among the trees, in a little pocket on the mountainside—horses just beyond in a sheltered clearing. He knew the man who had stepped out into the open.

"That's Benning," he whispered. "One of Krell's gunnys. He used to run with Charlie Coe over in No Man's Land."

The sky had brightened further, and dawn was sliding

143

down the slopes to the west. Abruptly Benning paced off toward the out-facing ridge, looking back, and a pair of small, dark figures scurried from the cedars to climb the shoulder of the cove. At its top they stood on a bare rock and faced eastward.

"They're waiting for the sun," Cobb hissed. "They always do that."

The man called Benning had turned away from the bizarre pair and was studying the trail below. Two other men were visible now in the cove.

"Which one is Krell?" Wolf asked quietly.

"Tall one there with the gray coat. The other one—I don't know his whole name, just Pete is all. I think he's a wanted man. He doesn't say much."

"Aren't you wanted?" Wolf's glance at him was almost a sneer.

"Not like he prob'ly is. Sheriff or two might want to talk to me, but I never done anything real bad that I know of."

"Not until you got mixed up with this bunch, Cecil."

"Yeah. Maybe so."

"Who's the most dangerous? Benning or Pete?"

"Hell, I don't know. They both are. Maybe Pete's the worst, but Benning's a slick hand with a gun. What do you think you're going to do?"

"I'm going to take Krell out of here alive. But he's the only one I need. You can have the rest."

"*Me?*" Cobb's face paled in the dawn light. "What do you expect me to do?"

"Kill Pete . . . or Benning, whichever one is handiest. And any of the others you have a chance at. That's all."

"*Me?* Hell, mister, given half a chance either one of them can—"

"Then don't give them half a chance. I wouldn't."

"Yeah, but how—?"

"Shut up. Listen."

On the rim above the trail, below them, Benning had

144

turned abruptly, looking off to the east. Slightly above him and off to one side, the black-coated Azteca pair stood like statues, seeing nothing but the brightness on the far horizon where the sun was heralding its appearance with shafts of golden light. Then, far down the trail, nearly a mile away, there was movement, and a rider came into view, coming uptrail.

Wolf watched those below intently. He saw their movements, heard their voices, thin in the distance, as Benning called to those in the cove and they hurried out to join him. Would they take ambush position, either left or right? No, they wouldn't. They weren't looking for a single rider. But they would want to watch him pass.

The sliver edge of a new day's sun topped the hills to the east, and the black-coats on the rock raised their arms in unison and began a singsong chant. Krell and the gunmen glanced around at them, then concentrated on watching the tiny figure coming up the trail. He came on, making good time, and Wolf clenched his teeth. Not so fast, he thought. A traveler on a tired horse doesn't set a pace like that. Still, it was dawn. And it was time.

From a pocket Wolf withdrew a small, silvered mirror and held it to his eye, sighting through a small hole on its back cover. Three times he veered it toward the rising sun, then back to the approaching rider, then he put it away. "Come on," he told Cobb. "We'll leave the horses here."

Keeping to cover, they worked westward along the slope until they were above the uptrail shoulder of it, then Wolf pointed at the shoulder. "Get down there, Cecil. You'll be behind them there. They're all looking east."

Cobb's face was pale, and despite the chill air he was sweating. "What do I do?"

"Do as much damage as you can to those two gunhands. Leave Krell to me."

"You sayin' I shoot those men in the back?"

145

"That's up to you. Face them if you want to, but if they kill you it's your own fault. The party starts in about three minutes. Get going."

Cobb eased down the slope a few steps, screened from below by out-hanging brush, then turned . . . but he was alone. There was no sign of Wolf. He could turn and run now, he knew. He was alone. Wolf was gone and those below didn't know he was here. He could just slip away . . . or could he? Could he really get away from Wolf? Could he hide so the Indian couldn't ever find him? He knew the answer to that. No. He couldn't. With a sigh of resignation he eased down the slope toward the bulging shoulder of the hidden cove.

On the trail below, Trooper had seen the flashes of Wolf's mirror, and he fixed the place in his mind. He rode steadily forward, his carbine resting across his saddle, and kept his gaze ahead, not seeming to look at the ledge above where men now stood: three men, two with the look of hardcase about them, the third with the bearing of gentry . . . and some distance away, back from them and above, a pair of small, dark figures standing side by side on a rock outcrop. He shuddered. Damn it, Wolf, he thought, are you trying to get me killed? The three on the ledge were watching him curiously, trying to decide if he was of interest to them.

He held his pace, pretending he didn't see them. He closed to a hundred yards, then seventy, then fifty. On the ledge he saw the gentry type turn his head, saw him saying something to the others, saw their hands go to their guns.

"Wolf," he muttered, "damn you, you're crazy." With a single fluid motion he raised the carbine and fired, at the same time kneeing his horse to the right, bolting toward a little brushed gully across from the ledge and almost directly below it. The carbine's bark echoed back and back between slopes, and he saw the nearest gunny pitch backward as though a large hand had slapped him off his feet. The second had his gun out and was raising it as other gunfire rang amid the echoes—two fast shots, or three, he couldn't tell. But the second gunman jerked abruptly upright, staggered forward a step and fell, bouncing and rolling on the slope below the ledge. Trooper's horse took the gully at a bound, down and twisting right, seeking the cover its rider's knees demanded. Even as it turned he hauled rein, skidded the animal around and swung to the ground, carbine at his shoulder.

The gentry type was just drawing a gun from beneath his coat, slowly it seemed, his movements strangely sluggish. For an instant he stood there alone, bringing up his gun. Then like a dark shadow, silently and efficiently, Wolf was on him. Trooper couldn't see what Wolf did, but the gentry type simply crumpled and fell. Now his gun was in Wolf's hand, and Wolf was turning toward the two black-coats above, silhouetted against the red sky of dawn. They had spun around at the gunfire, turning as one, still side by side, like Siamese twins. Their hands dipped to their coats and came out with objects that glittered in the sunlight. Wolf's shot and Trooper's were simultaneous, a double roar that racketed and rang between the crowding slopes. One of the little men was lifted from the rock and flung backward, and a second later Trooper saw his body rolling in brush beyond, to thud against a standing stone. The second—Trooper blinked. It was as though there had only been one of them. The second had disappeared.

Leaving his horse, Trooper sprinted across the trail and began to climb. Above he heard Wolf's voice, cold and chiding, "You missed your timing, Trooper. You were moving too fast. They didn't believe you."

Clambering from stump to rock, cursing under his breath, Trooper struggled upward. "Give me a little credit, Wolf, damn it. I stopped to watch another bunch like this, off yonder past the trail. I think they spotted

Shanty and them. I had to hurry."

Wolf knelt to drag the big man up the final few feet to the ledge. Beside him, the gentry type lay unconscious, curled like a child in sleep.

"How many?" Wolf asked.

"Five, I think. They was a long way off, comin' along the trace, but then they veered off. I think they saw our bunch."

"The rest of the party, then. The ones they left at Las Vegas—"

A gunshot blasted, close at hand. They spun around, raising their guns. Up on the shoulder of the cove, Cecil Cobb screamed and fired again, and something bulky and black sailed from cover to lock itself upon him, a big, busy black spider clinging to his chest and . . . doing something. Another gunshot sounded, muffled as though silenced by pillows, and the figure on the shoulder staggered and fell, the black thing on his chest falling with him. Trooper didn't see Wolf go up the slope, but when he got there, the Indian was there ahead of him, looking down at what lay at his feet.

Cecil Cobb's eyes were wide open, staring blindly at the sky. The little man sprawled atop him had fist-sized red holes in him, two in his back, one in the back of his neck below his stiff black hat. His right hand was flung out, and the fingers of it clenched an obsidian blade drenched in blood.

All about them hung a stench like rotting blood.

Wolf knelt and rolled the little man off Cobb's body, and Trooper felt sick. There was Cobb's gun, between them where it had fired its last muffled shot. And just under it, Cobb's chest had been laid open from breastbone to backstrap, ribs pushed apart, and the little man's left hand was thrust through, out of sight, deep in the drifter's chest.

"He always was more afraid of these than he was of the gunslingers," Wolf said, as though to himself.

148

XV

Shanty was unhappy. As they skirted the final slopes of the Sangres and angled southwestward, aiming at the saddlelands between the Manzanos and Los Pinos ranges, they rode hard and made good time. But still Shanty looked back over his shoulder, and his scalp itched each time they skylined on a ridge or mesa. It was more than instinct. It was something Willie Shay had said.

"Mighty lot of traffic yonder," the old man had allowed casually, looking back a half-day out of the camp where Wolf and Trooper had left them. When Shanty asked him about the comment, though, he just shrugged and said, "Just had me a notion there was folks way off yonder an' they was lookin' at us, that's all."

Two days had passed since then, though—two days and a hundred or more miles. Yet each time they skylined and each time they rested, Shanty had the sensation of being followed. Followed or pursued. And Willie was no help now. Though Shanty had insisted a dozen times that the old man find a high place and read their backtrail, it came to nothing. "This ain't far-sight land," he said. "Back yonder in Kansas, now, I could see a far piece now and again. Don't work like that out here, though. Things way too humped up out here. All th' scenery gets swallowed up in itself."

"You think somebody's following us, don't you?" Gail Larkin asked him finally. It was the first halfway civil sentence she had spoken since the morning she woke up and found Wolf gone again and herself back under the guardianship of Shanty—this time with the dubious additions of Windwagon Willie Shay and Dog. It hadn't helped any that Shanty had assigned her to lead the packstring, but her real snit was, Shanty decided, because Wolf routinely neglected to tell her what he was doing or planned to do next on what she considered *her* expedition.

Now, though, she had sensed his concern and was willing to share it.

"Yes, ma'am," he said. "I don't know for sure that somebody's after us, but I feel like there is. Willie thinks so, too, but his eyesight doesn't work right where there's mountains."

"Well, what are we going to do about it?"

"Wolf said for us to aim for Arizona and keep going, so I guess that's what we'll do. We're well mounted and making good time, so if there's somebody back there, it will take a while for them to catch up. Wolf will be along eventually. He'll know what to do about it."

"Oh, I know what John Thomas would do," she said flatly.

"You do? What?"

"He'd dynamite a river under them—"

"We're a little short on rivers out here, miss."

"—or something equally violent. He isn't really civilized, you know."

"He isn't?"

"Not in my opinion."

That was her final word on that subject, at least for the moment, but it did set Shanty to thinking. If they were being pursued, then obviously something had gone amiss. Wolf's orders hadn't included anything about how to deal with pursuers. Wolf was not a man to leave out instructions that might prove vital. Therefore, Wolf hadn't expected anyone to follow them after he left for Glorieta with Trooper and the hardcase Cobb. So what, then, *would* Wolf do if he were here now?

For more than five years, Shanty had worked for the Indian—since the day Wolf had shown him the error of his ways. Shanty had been riding with Zeb Copeland then, and Zeb Copeland had made a deal with Silas Hartnett to wreck a train. Shanty recalled having some misgivings about that, but the way Copeland explained it,

150

everything had sounded all right, at least at the beginning. The train belonged to Silas Hartnett, as did the rails it ran on and the two bridges the rails crossed. And Hartnett was losing money on his investment. But he had a mail contract from the government, and on the basis of that contract he had been able to acquire a lot of insurance on his little railroad enterprise. If a mail train were destroyed he could collect enough to turn a handsome profit.

They were already into the operation before Shanty learned that part of the deal was that the train crew would go out with the train, and that bothered him. Shanty always wondered if it was he himself who had let it slip about what the Copeland gang was up to. He'd never been sure.

The arrangement was that the train would leave New Burdick station on schedule, en route to Peoria, and the Copeland bunch would board it when it stopped for water at Hartnett's private tank just east of the Sand Gully Bridge. Once across Sand Gully, with Hartnett's highly insured Walnut Creek trestle three miles ahead, the gang would show themselves, take over the train, knock all the crew members in the head and drive the train on to Walnut Creek, where they would stop it atop the trestle, get off and blow up the bridge, train and all. It was nice and neat. A robbery and wreck by parties unknown, with no witnesses. Hartnett would collect a fortune in insurance, and the Copeland bunch would share in it.

Nice and neat—except that there was an Indian aboard the train, an Indian who wore a tailored suit and talked like a college professor and caught Shanty alone at the water tank and bounced the big man around the way a cat might bounce a mouse, then stuck a pistol barrel into his mouth and explained to him that the time had come for him to change sides.

Shanty had changed sides. With his help, the Indian had spirited all the crew members off the train, then watched as the rest of the Copeland gang crept aboard. With Shanty at the throttle, the train had pulled out just as though nothing had happened. But it hadn't gone very far. The Indian had made a believer of Shanty. The Indian had said to jump off the train and hide before it reached the Sand Gully Bridge. Shanty had jumped. It wasn't the Walnut Creek Bridge that blew up that night. It was the Sand Gully Bridge. The outlaws hadn't been aboard more than three minutes when the train rolled out onto that structure, the structure went up in smoke and the train fell a hundred and twenty feet into the gully, taking the entire Copeland gang with it.

Silas Hartnett had been convicted of so many things that he probably would never see the outside world again. And Shanty had decided that the only sure way to avoid ever running afoul of John Thomas Wolf again was to work for him.

The Larkin girl was right about one thing. Wolf had his own ways of doing things. What would Wolf do about the people following them, if Wolf were here now? Shanty puzzled over it. The facing of a situation without Wolf's planning made him distinctly unhappy.

Another day put another fifty miles behind them, a long arc of space that Willie chose because it was a route he had traveled before. They made camp for the night in a little cove on the south face of a brushy ridge where there was good graze for the stock, and Shanty slept fitfully, awakening often to scent the breeze and look out across the silvered, rolling lands. His restlessness had infected the others, as well. Gail slept off and on for a few hours, then wrapped herself in her blankets and went to sit on a rock, her pistol in her lap. Willie dozed, slept a bit, awoke with a snort and tossed around, trying to go back to sleep. Finally he sat up. "Ought to be able to see them folks," he muttered. "I swear they ain't that far away."

And through the night Dog came and went, prowling the cove and the ridge, raising his head often to sniff the air, a growl rumbling in his throat.

Dog came in at dawn and nuzzled Willie, tugging at his boot heel with large, gentle teeth. Willie sat up, stretched, and stood. "All right," he grumbled. "Give me a minute, will you?" He waved at Shanty. "Dog wants to show me somethin'. Be back directly."

Gail had a little fire going and coffee on to boil when the old man returned, running down the slope faster than she would have believed he could. He hauled up by the fire, his eyes bright. Shanty had been out in the brush, but he was headed in to see what the trouble was.

"Them people you wanted me to try to see," Willie told him. "Well, I can see 'em now all right. They ain't but maybe five miles back, an' comin' on. Five of 'em, I make it, an' a pair of 'em is them little jaspers like that one th' lady here shot hell out of that time."

Shanty stared at him. "Five miles? How did they make up that much distance?"

"I don't know. Killin' their horses, maybe. Then again, maybe they figgered out where we was aimin' and rode straight through. Might be a trail they knowed about that I didn't."

"I thought you knew all this country out here!"

"That's a fool notion. All I ever done with New Mexico Territory was just to cross it a few times, like we're doin' now."

Gail stood hugging her pistol, staring out at the distances beyond the cove. "What are we going to do?"

"I don't know, miss." Shanty shook his head. "I sure wish Wolf was here right now."

But Wolf was nowhere near. It had taken a surprisingly long time to get all the information from Krell that Krell had to give him. The man rambled, hallucinated, was lucid one moment and off in lunatic regions the next, and had seemed for the most part impervious

153

either to fear or minor pain. Wolf was certain the cactus buttons weren't the only thing his Quatemáls had been feeding him.

Finally, though, he had put it all together. He had been right in his assumptions. Krell belonged to Hall Kileen, and Kileen was no longer in Mexico. He was in Arizona. Krell had been a recruiter for him, gathering a small army of gunslicks and frontier toughs, organizing others in various places, making contacts by mail and telegraph, and orchestrating various interesting things in various places.

Krell hadn't been east of Kansas. That had been others, working out of Kansas City; but they were Hall Kileen's people, and Krell had directed them. Great amounts of money had been spent to buy that much firepower, but Krell felt it was a drop in the bucket. There was much more where that came from.

Wolf was satisfied that Krell knew little about the source of the funding, except that it was from Mexico, and that a man called Kukulki was behind it. And the more he learned from Krell, the more Wolf marveled at the scope of this thing . . . this plot that centered around the legends of the vanished Aztecs. No wonder Ernest Kichener had gone after them. The scheme was enormous. And not the least of what Wolf had now was a list of names—a long, frightening list of people in high places both in Mexico and in the United States—a list of people who, in one way or another, were connected with the man called Kukulki. As far as Wolf could tell, Krell did not know the man's real name. But that didn't matter. Wolf knew it. Don Juan Ascencion Acuna. Kukulki. The man who would be Quetzalcoatl.

The sun was barely above Cibola Crest, and the sleepy Western Union telegrapher had just opened his office in the village of Albuquerque when an Indian strode through his door and locked the door behind him.

The clerk frowned at him, wondering if he was drunk,

154

yet noting that his buckskin shirt and leggings seemed clean and new. Even the beaded band around his head seemed to have been just finished, bright and unstained. The Indian stepped to the desk and slapped down a sheaf of papers. "Send this now," he said in perfect English.

The clerk glanced at the papers, then looked again. They were handwritten in the flowing script of a person of education. He started counting words.

"Send it," the Indian said again. "Count the words later." He placed a stack of bills on the counter. "This will cover it."

"Yes, sir," the clerk said. "I'll get it out as soon as the night traffic has been sent."

"Send it now," the Indian said, agate eyes becoming hard and piercing. "Or stand aside and I'll send it myself."

"Send it . . . yourself?" The clerk goggled at him. "But you . . . well, I mean, you wouldn't know how. . . ."

"Send it or get out of the way," the Indian said, starting around the counter.

"I'll send it now," the clerk said.

It was a long message, direct wire to someone named Joy in Illinois, with transmittal to a separate address in Maryland. The telegrapher understood very little of it and paid no attention to any of it. His eyes read the letters of the words, and his fingers tapped them out on his key, while his mind occupied itself with rethinking everything he had thought he knew about Indians. It was the first time he had ever had a customer listen to his code . . . and understand it. Not until he had completed the message and the bug had clicked acknowledgement of receipt at Springfield did the Indian move, and then it was to come around the counter, retrieve his papers and put them away in his clothing.

"You aren't supposed to take those," the telegrapher said. "I'm supposed to keep—"

The Indian reached past him to activate the telegraph

155

key. With sure touch he tapped out, "Previous message clearance seven-A-one. Acknowledge."

Minutes passed and the clicker was silent. Then it came to life. One word only, "Acknowledged."

"Thank you," the Indian said, heading for the door. Then he paused and turned back. "A word of advice. Don't tell anyone about this. Not a single soul. The very least that would happen if you did, would be you'd lose your job."

Trooper was waiting at an old barn beyond the edge of town, with their horses. "You took long enough," he grumbled. "I was beginning to think somebody had recognized you."

"I expect everybody who saw me recognized me," Wolf said, stripping off his buckskins while Trooper dug out his travel clothes. "They recognized me for an Indian. You know how it is, Trooper. When you've seen one Indian you've seen them all."

They rode away from Albuquerque going west, but once beyond sight of the town they turned south with Manzano Peak as a landmark. Somewhere past there, probably less than two days' ride, they would find Shanty and his charges.

"Still think you should have let me shoot that fellow Krell," Trooper said after a while. "Lord, he's got th' stink of those little jaspers on him so bad it'll never wash off."

"No need to shoot him now, Trooper. He's no threat to anybody, anymore."

"Well, I'd have enjoyed it."

Among the rugged slopes and canyons above Glorieta Pass, the man who had been Krell wandered aimlessly, unfocused eyes dull from chill and exposure, sometimes falling, sometimes stopping to sit and stare at the sky. What reason the drugs of the Aztec-Quatemál priests had

156

left him, the interrogation of John Thomas Wolf had taken away. Yet when he turned and saw the sun, he let it burn into his eyes while his hoarse voice whispered words that had no meaning . . . that had never had meaning but seemed now as though they should.

"*Tonaiu,*" he rasped, not particularly aware that he was speaking. "*Ayyo, Tonaiu . . . ayyo, Tonaiu . . . aya na nexcha . . . Huitzilopochtli . . . nocipa Huitzilopochtli . . . ayya . . .*"

XVI

From the rim of Cuero Bluff, Bull Mason watched the fleeing riders, and a grin spread across his whiskered face. For a month now, ever since Krell had hired him on, Bull had felt like he was living in a nightmare. But now it was about over, and he could almost taste the money that would come his way. He had made up his mind weeks ago that as soon as this chase was ended—whether or not he shared in the pay—he was going to get himself so far away from Krell and his weird playmates that no one would ever find him. He had even been thinking about just riding away from the whole mess—the babbling, stinking little Indians with their glittering eyes, their chants, and the things they did to those who got afoul of them, the endless chasing around, from telegraph to railhead to high country trail . . . and from Krell himself. Bull had thought at first, when Krell hired him on, that Krell was drunk. But Krell wasn't drunk. He was addled. The little black-coats fed him things to keep him that way, and Bull had decided that the whole mess of them were crazy.

All this chasing around—Bull had worn out five

horses in the past month. Somebody was paying out a lot of money for bounty on two people, and Bull didn't know who it was or why. He had about decided to light a shuck on the whole mess. But now . . . now there was bounty to be had, and it was within reach. Those people out there, a big Irisher, an old man and woman, they wouldn't get away now. He had them. And he knew beyond a doubt that the woman was the one there was bounty on. The Indian wasn't with them—maybe Krell had bagged that one—but the bounty just on the Larkin girl would set Bull up to live in style for years . . . far away from Krell and his gunsels and his stinking little crazy Indians.

It had been just luck that he had seen this bunch at all. Luck that he had decided to pull out of Las Vegas and head for Glorieta. Luck that he still carried the telescope he had taken off that drummer in Trinidad. Luck that he had happened to pull off the trade route back there east of Santa Fe to have a look around. And luck that the bunch out there hadn't taken a straight path but had circled around instead, giving him and the four with him a chance to ride straight through the Manzanos and overtake them. Probably they didn't know about the trail through the mountains, but he did. A man who made his living on the other side of the law in country that was starting to settle in—that man had to know the terrain.

So Bull had led off on the mountain trail, and they had come out almost on top of the quarry, covering in sixty miles or so the same distance that had taken those people out there more than a hundred. And to top it off, he and his men now had fresh horses, thanks to that Spaniard they had found in the Manzanos. The Spaniard would never object, either. The little Aztecas had seen to that . . . in that special way they had.

Those out there, they knew now that they were being pursued, but it wouldn't matter. Bull's group would overtake them by noon, probably. Kill the Irisher and the old man, give the girl to the Aztecas—he wondered what special ways they might have of dealing with women—then all he had to do was find Krell and collect his money. *His* money. Not his and Jake's and Henry's. He had already decided that Jake and Henry wouldn't be around when he collected. And the stinking Aztecas wouldn't mind. They seemed oblivious to what white people did to each other, as long as they could have their sun-chants and a regular supply of people to kill with those black knives of theirs.

Bull put away his telescope and turned. "It's them," he said. "They're leading extra horses, but there's only three of them out there. A big redbeard, an old man and a woman. Watch out for the redbeard, he has a rifle."

Jake and Henry glanced at each other and grinned. So the man had a rifle. So did they. Off to one side—downwind where Bull tried to keep them—the two little bald Indians sat their saddles as they always did, not seeming to care anything about anything, not even seeing what was around them, for all Bull could tell. Bull had tried once, early on, to communicate with them, but it was useless. They didn't speak English—hell, as far as he could tell they didn't even speak Spanish. Their language, what he had heard of it, sounded like gibberish with clicks and gargles thrown in.

Bull had tried once—when Krell seemed relatively sober one morning—to get the man to tell him something about the little black-coated demons . . . who they were, where they were from, what a white man was doing mixed up with the likes of them, anything. Krell had just stared off into the distance, shaking his head. Finally he had said, "Get used to them, Bull. They're going to run the show before too long."

"What show?" Bull had asked.

"Why, maybe the whole show, Bull. Won't that be something?"

Something. Yeah.

"Come on, then!" Bull told Jake and Henry. "Let's get

159

this over with."

Out on the rolling plains they were strung out for a quarter-mile—Windwagon Willie out front, with all the extra horses on leads, Dog loping alongside, and some distance back Gail and Shanty, trying to catch up. Willie hadn't waited around for them, just shouted, pointed toward a pair of peaks a couple of miles away, said, "There used to be a ranch yonder," and was gone. All they could do was follow.

Bent low over her saddle on the big bay Shanty had chosen for her, Gail rode as though the devil were on her tail. Once she glanced around and could see them, far back but coming on, a tight-packed group of riders coming down from the slopes beyond the cove where they had camped.

Shanty saw them, too, and spurred the powerful black which thundered beneath his weight. Drawing even with Gail he gestured back, the wind whipping his whiskers. "Fresh horses! They have fresh horses!"

"So what do we do now?" she shouted back.

"I don't know," he rumbled, and she could barely hear him.

What would John Thomas Wolf do if he were here?

The gap Willie aimed for was a narrow, high-walled cleft between capped peaks, with sky beyond it. Lower lands on the other side, she thought. Grasslands and open spaces. No place to hide. A ranch, Willie had said. Maybe a house? A place to fortify? But how far? What about the peaks themselves? But they seemed to offer no cover, no defensible place, only a trap should they try to hide there. What would John Thomas do? Wildly she searched the approaching peaks, imagining that the Indian might somehow contrive to lead the pursuers in there, into that gap, then bring a mountain down on them or something. She could see no such possibilities. There were a few

160

boulders on the slopes above, but not many, and none of them looked ready to fall. Possibly a man as big as Shanty might loosen one of them . . . but what would that do? Those were not avalanche slopes. He might drop a rock, yes. But that would be about all of it. One rock, maybe some debris with it . . . she tried to find other avenues of thought and gave up.

"Shanty!" she yelled.

He eased over toward her, still watching the path ahead.

"Do you see those boulders up there? Above the cut?"

"Yeah."

"When we go through there, could you circle back, up to where they are?"

"I don't know. I might. Why?"

"I was just wondering if you might roll a rock down on top of those people."

He squinted ahead, at the slopes above the cut, then squinted at her. "I don't know if I could. Even if I did, what's the chance of me hitting any of them?"

"I don't know. I was just wondering."

But it gave Shanty something to think about. It was just silly enough, to his view, to resemble something that Wolf might ask him to do. Maybe . . . his eyes brightened . . . maybe he couldn't actually drop a rock on those owlhoots back there, but maybe he could block their path, give the girl and Willie some time—and maybe get off a shot or two in the confusion.

"Forget it," Gail said.

"What?"

"I said, forget it. It won't work."

But the wind was in his ears, and he couldn't hear what she said. Ahead of them Willie was approaching the cut, not running the horses now but still moving smartly, making time. The land on both sides was rising now, and the two peaks no longer seemed separate. This close, they appeared to be a single crest that in some ancient time

161

had split apart, the tops of the break shearing away to make high slopes above nearly vertical walls that pinched together as they led away, climbing for a quarter-mile, then dropping off beyond. Gail followed Shanty into the opening, noting how the cut narrowed ahead, how a wall of stone rose into view as they climbed, seeming to block the end of the path. But ahead, Willie and the spare horses were still going, and as Gail reached the crest of the walled trail, they vanished around a turn. Whatever was ahead, Willie seemed to know the way.

The air was colder in the pass, and crusted snow lay in drifts where the sun had not reached it. Minutes passed, and tens of minutes; then the pass widened and turned again, and the walls of it stepped down to head-high banks with strewn slopes above. Shanty slowed and waved her past. "Go on," he said. "Willie knows the way. Stay with him."

"Where are you going?"

"Don't wait for me," he urged. "I'll catch up." He leaned to swat the rump of her horse, and she clung as it bolted ahead. Another turn, and the walls were only a few feet high, the trail widening and descending, its far opening in sight, a wide shelf sweeping away toward a valley beyond.

Willie was just ahead now, and she came up to him where the trail widened. Dog had gone on ahead somewhere.

Willie glanced back as Gail came up to him. "Where's that Irishman?"

"He's right—" she looked around. Shanty was no longer behind her.

"Oh, I see him," Willie said, looking upward. She followed his glance. Shanty had left the trail, jumping his mount to the low top on the left, and was working back and up, on foot now, his horse waiting between rocks at a fold of the slope.

"What does he think he's doing?" she demanded.

162

Willie shook his head, not slowing down. "Beats me. Buyin' us some time, maybe."

"But they'll trap him up there!"

"Mebbe so." He peered ahead. "Seems to me there used to be a ranch yonder in that valley. Slap-up little place on a rise. Do you see anything?"

The trail had widened more now, coming out of its cut in the split peak, sloping gently downward into a wide valley—a slope where cattle grazed on grass newly uncovered by recent warm sunshine. Dog was out there on the slope. He had found the cattle and circled them, then had decided to harass them, working them as his distant and smaller ancestors might have worked sheep.

"Let 'em be, Dog!" Willie shouted as the big creature romped and circled around a bunched group of a hundred or more rangy cattle, daring their horns. "Damnation, you'd think you never saw cows afore!" He glanced around at Gail apologetically. "He's prob'ly hungry. Ain't had time to find hisself a meal yet today. Son of a bitch gonna get himself hooked if he's not careful. Dog!" he shouted again. "Go find yourself a deer or somethin'! You can't eat folks' cows!"

Beyond the grazing slope, nearly a mile away, blackened stubs stood above a rock foundation. "There's the ranch you were looking for." Gail pointed.

"Well, hell's afire," Willie sneered. "That ain't gonna do us any good. 'Paches prob'ly got 'em."

"Then what are we going to do?"

"I don't guess I rightly know, miss." He slowed his wheezing mount, then stopped. "Only place I know about between here and the Gallinas where there might have been folks. I thought maybe we could sort of fort up 'til Wolf finds us. Now I'm fresh out of notions."

Up on the slope above the cut, Shanty was still visible, working his way along, sometimes sliding and scrambling, then climbing again. Back there, Gail thought, if he slides

163

over that edge he'll be killed. Those walls are high.

Beside a large, tumbled boulder he stopped, looking eastward, then turned and waved his hat over his head three times.

"He's seen 'em," Willie said. "Says they're about three miles back. They'll be startin' through in a little bit." He lifted his old rifle free of its saddle thongs. "I don't see how we're gonna get out of this, missy. We got no place to go nor any place to hide. And th' only way Shanty's gonna get a shot at them is to get right down to th' top of that cut, an' if he does that they'll have a better shot at him than he'll ever have at them. Damn fool'd be better off down here with us."

"Look what he's doing." Gail pointed. Her eyes widened. Shanty was working at the base of the boulder, digging and scooping. "He can't move that rock . . . can he?"

They watched, fascinated. For minutes the big man dug around the toe of the rock, dirt and gravel flying. Then he climbed behind and above it and braced his shoulder against it, and even at that distance they could see his feet dig into the slope as he pushed. The rock held firm; but bits of shard erupted from its top, and seconds later they heard the distant whine of a ricocheting bullet.

"They see him up there," Willie said.

Again Shanty braced and pushed, then he scurried around to the downslope face again and resumed his digging. Dust flew from the slope just below him, as a bullet struck there. Another minute passed, and two more shots. Then Shanty climbed again to the upslope side, braced himself and pushed again.

"I be danged," Willie said. "I believe he moved it a little bit."

Another bullet whined overhead, spent with distance. "They're waitin' to see if he can roll that thing," Willie said. "Out of range yonder, where they are, but they're just shootin' for the fun of it."

164

Shanty strained at the huge rock, and slowly at first, it moved, teetered and began to tip. Gail held her breath, biting her lip. The rock seemed to hang, off balance, then it leaned outward and rolled . . . one turn, then skidded to a halt, wide-side down.

"So much for that notion," Willie sighed. On the distant slope Shanty stood and picked up his rifle, and they could see the defeat in his sagging shoulders. He turned toward them, raised his hat once more in salute, then started edging down the slope toward the top of the cut.

"They'll kill him," Gail said. "They'll come through and . . . and just kill him when he shows up. They know where he is."

"I reckon," Willie said. "Not much we can do, neither."

"Well, I'm not going to just sit here and wait," she snapped. "Come on. Let's see if we can chase some of those cows."

"You want to chase cows?"

"Into the cut. Up the trail. Maybe they'll give Shanty a diversion up there."

She sprinted her horse around the clustered cattle that Dog was circling happily, and Willie followed. "How many do you want to chase in there, miss?"

"All of them! How do we make them start?"

"Oh, that's easy enough," Willie drawled. "You ease on around that side and I'll hold this side, then we'll let Dog do it."

When they were in position, one on each side of the mass of cattle, Willie whistled. Dog started toward him and Willie pointed. "Set yonder, Dog!"

Obediently, Dog moved to a point downslope from the bunched cattle and sat down, watching Willie.

"You ready?" Willie called.

"I'm ready!"

"Then watch this here!" Willie raised his arm and

165

lowered it, to point to the cattle. "Dog!" he shouted. "Varmints! Git 'em!"

Dog came unwound. The happy, sitting canine disappeared, and in its place was a raging, ravening monster twice the size of any wolf the cattle had ever encountered. As one they bolted, bellowing in fear, a running, thundering mass of beef and horns aimed the only direction open to them—directly into the mouth of the cut.

The five had paused on the slope, the three gunmen scanning the terrain while the two Aztecas sat their mounts to one side, expressionless and patient, simply waiting.

Crazy little bastards, Bull Mason thought, glancing sourly at them. It was like having a pair of vultures following along, just waiting for him to kill something for them. Sometimes they gave him the shudders.

"Anyplace in there they could lay for us, Bull?" Jake asked.

"No place we wouldn't see them first. It's just a gap, sheer walls on both sides with slopes above. I've been through it before."

"What's on the other side?"

"Nothin'. Used to be a little cow ranch over there, couple of idiot brothers from back east someplace. But Injuns burned the place to the ground, with them inside."

"We goin' on through, then?" Henry fidgeted, his eyes flicking toward the little black-coated men a few yards away. "I'd as soon get this done and get rid of present company. They make me sick, just smellin' 'em."

"Yeah, we're going through," Bull said, lifting his reins. Then he hesitated, squinting. A long way off, on the slope above the cut, he saw movement. "Hold on," he said. He got out his telescope, extended it and peered.

"Well, I'll be damned. It's that Irishman. What does he think he's gonna do up there?"

They rode on up the slope, the Aztecas following along placidly behind them. Where the cut's walls began to rise Bull reined in. The Irishman was closer now, less than a thousand yards away, kneeling at the base of a boulder, doing something . . . digging.

"What's he doin'?" Jake squinted at the distant figure.

"I'll be damned," Bull snorted. "That . . . boys, I believe that man is going to try to block the cut and make us go around the long way."

"Well, maybe I'll change his ways for him," Jake said. He hauled out his rifle and adjusted its peep sight.

"You can't hit anything from here," Henry said. "You'll just waste bullets."

"I got plenty," Jake said, leveling the gun. He took a breath, held it and squeezed the trigger. The rifle bucked against his shoulder. An instant later rock shards sparkled in the sunlight above the man upslope.

"Close," Henry said. "Try again."

"He's behind the rock," Jake said. "Wait . . . oh, there he is. He's pushing on that thing. Can you believe that?"

He sighted and fired again. A little cloud of dust blossomed near the distant man. Jake levered the rifle and fired again. The man up on the slope continued his efforts, ignoring them. Jake fired twice more.

"Henry's right," Bull said. "You're wastin' powder, Jake."

Then they watched, wide-eyed, as the great rock teetered and began to topple. "My God," Jake breathed.

It fell, skidded and stopped. Bull grinned. So much for that foolishness. "Let's get on with it," he said.

"What's to keep him from snipin' at us from up there, Bull?"

"Because he can't see the trail from up there. I told you, I know this route. Just keep your eyes open. If he

167

comes down to where the wall starts, kill him."

Without further words he led out, between the rising slopes of the split peak and into the cut.

They had gone about a thousand yards when a large silhouette appeared at the top of the left sheer and a shot crashed and echoed in the cut. Jake's rifle was up and coming level, but he was an instant late. The bullet that hit him slapped him from his saddle. But it had given Bull time enough to react. Lightning reflexes raised and aligned his handgun, and triggered two shots that multiplied the echoes. He saw his second shot hit the man above, saw him flop back from the ledge, out of sight. Gravel chittered down the wall, and a large arm came into view, dangling limply over the edge above.

Bull holstered his revolver and turned to gaze at what was left of Jake. The Irisher's bullet had taken him at the base of the neck and come out the far side of the hip. Jake had never known what hit him.

Fair trade, Bull decided. The Irishman had been the main problem with overtaking the people ahead. And Jake had been his main problem in planning how to rid himself of partners to share the money. Henry would be easier.

Henry had Jake's horse in tow, and the two little Aztecas had stopped directly above Jake, looking down at him, their agate eyes glinting at sight of the blood there. In unison then they turned and looked up. A large drop of blood formed on the dangling fingers above and fell off, and they watched it all the way to the floor of the cut.

Christ! Bull turned away. Henry was right. Those two could make anybody sick. "Let's go," he told Henry. "I'm tired of this."

XVII

With Dog at their heels, snarling and snapping, the cattle abandoned all thoughts of defense and ran, bellowing in terror. Strung out and running, there were more of them than Gail had realized. Across their backs she saw old Willie waving and shouting, funneling them upward toward the wings of the cut, and she did the same. In moments the first of them darted into the narrow crevice, and a minute later the last of them followed.

Willie was grinning like a monkey. "That there Dog!" he shouted. "Ain't he somethin'? He's one reason I never had Injun problems up on th' plains." He clamped his hat back on his head. "You reckon that'll give us some travelin' time, missy? I'll call Dog back, so's we can—"

She raised her hand. Distinctly, over the racket of the retreating cattle, came the sounds of shooting. "Wait," she said. She turned and rode out away from the cut to where she could see up on the slope. There was no sign of Shanty. She rode out farther, circling. Then she saw him. He lay at the very edge of the south wall, not moving.

A cold fury blazed within her . . . all the pursuit, the fear, the repeated shocks of the past months welled up and became a searing anger. She wheeled her horse, drew her revolver and spurred toward the cut. Willie stared at her as she neared.

"What in hell are you—?" he started.

"I'm going to help Dog chase cows!" she snapped. "Are you coming or not?" And she was past, heading into the cut.

Willie shrugged. "Whatever you say," he muttered. "I got nothin' better to do today."

The cut was alive with sound now—lowing and clattering of maddened cattle ahead, the deep-chested fury of Dog, still deviling them—and the sounds grew as she spurred her horse to a run. As she rounded the second bend, she heard gunshots racketing back and forth between the closing walls and saw Dog at the heels of fleeing cattle. The beast heard her and turned, its ears coming up.

She pointed as Willie had done. "Go on, Dog!" she shouted. "Varmints! Get 'em!"

With this renewed encouragement, Dog almost tripped over his feet returning to his venture. Ahead of him, terrified cattle bunched and bawled as he redoubled his attack from the rear.

Another bend, and Gail could see the long, straight rise ahead. The entire cut was filled with running, stampeding cattle. Beyond them were mounted men. She couldn't tell how many, but she thought she saw four . . . then three . . . then they were out of sight.

A deep voice came from above, riding over the noise in the cut. "Holy Mother Mary," it said. "An' here I thought I'd seen it all!"

She hauled up short, skidding her horse full around, and looked up. Shanty sat at the top of the wall, his feet dangling as he cradled a bloody arm and stared on up the cut, where the chaos had gone.

"I thought they'd killed you!" she shouted.

"Well, I thought for a minute they had, too. Do you know who that was? That was Bull Mason."

"You're bleeding."

"That's because I have a hole in my arm. How am I going to get down from here?"

Willie was there then, reining in beside her. "Same way you got up, I reckon," he called. "They still runnin' yonder?"

"They were when I last saw them." Shanty tried to get to his feet, slid and almost fell from the ledge. He sprawled, then crawled back away from it. "Dog's coming back," his voice told them.

"Well, what do you want us to do now?" Willie called.

"Go on back where you were" the voice came back.

170

"I'll be there as soon as I can. Oof! Lord, a man could get hurt up here."

It was nearly an hour before he rejoined them at the west end of the gap, leading his horse and favoring his left arm. He looked them over, decided they were unhurt, and turned to Willie. "How did you do that, anyway?"

"Oh, the cows? Well, mostly Dog done that. But don't blame me for it. It was her idea." He pointed an accusing finger at Gail.

"Well, I thought you needed a diversion," she said, feeling guilty. "What were you up there for, anyway?"

"What was I . . . well, I was up there trying to drop a rock on those people, or at least maybe slow them down a little. Isn't that what you said to do? It was your idea."

"I also said to forget it," she snapped. "It was a rotten idea."

"Yeah, it really was. But I didn't hear you say not to. But that stampede, now—"

"Well, we had to do something! And I'm getting the impression that if John Thomas isn't around to do everybody's thinking for them, then no thinking gets done." She walked around him, looking at his injured arm. "Take your coat off and let me see that."

"Yes, ma'am." He began peeling off his coat. "It isn't bad, though. Bullet went on through. I've had worse. Uh, ma'am?"

"What?"

"A while back, what you said about Wolf and his . . . uh, violent ways. I thought you meant all that."

"I did mean it. John Thomas is decidedly uncivilized."

"Yes, ma'am. But I know I counted three dead men and two dead horses from up where I was. Not much left of them, either. You know, the floor of that gap in there right now looks like Wolf himself had been there."

Where the split peak gap emerged into eastward hills,

Bull Mason sat on a rock, muttering gloomy curses over and over as he wrapped shirttail strips around a bleeding leg and tied them off with twine. He had almost made it clear, running ahead of the bawling mass of beef that had thundered through the cut. Almost. Jake was gone, and Bull had seen Henry and one of the Aztecas go down in front of the stampede. The little Indian hadn't turned fast enough, then when his horse did turn it shied and bolted. For an instant Bull had seen the little black-coated figure on hands and knees, then the cattle had overrun him. Henry had simply become perpendicular to his horse in the confusion, and was still back there somewhere—what was left of him.

Bull had nearly made it. Shots in the heads of two cattle had given him time to turn and run, and he had stayed ahead of them through the cut and out into the slope where he veered away to the left and slowed, letting them go by.

All except one. A range bull, running with the herd, had somehow gotten to his left. He didn't even see it until it surged up under his horse with horns that threw and gutted the screaming animal, and a twist of its head that hooked Mason's leg.

Took a bull to slow down the Bull, he thought, oddly, through the red veil of rage that burned in him. The Indian must have been waiting over there, on the other side of the peak—the Indian they had told him about, the one they set the bounty on. The word was to be careful in going after him. He was mean, they said.

Wolf . . . that was his name. John Thomas Wolf. He must have been there, Bull thought. It had been a trap after all. The woman and the old man had gone through, then the Indian had choused a wild herd down on the pursuers.

One thing about it, though. Bull Mason was still alive and he had good reason to run them all down now. Plenty of reason, and no one left to expect shares in his bounty.

He finished his bandage and came down from his rock. He needed a horse . . . had seen a couple wandering around nearby. One was Jake's. It would do for his saddle.

Limping, he came down from his rock and looked around. The sun was well below the peaks now, and it would be dark soon. He debated about trying to get to the other side . . . they wouldn't have waited around over there; they would be on the move. Or maybe he should gather in a horse or two, let them rest and wait for morning.

A stink came to his nose and he whirled around. The one remaining Azteca stood there, a few yards away, gazing at him with expressionless agate eyes. His hands, arms and the front of his coat were splashed crimson with fresh blood, and he held his obsidian knife in one dripping hand. Bull hadn't even heard him approach, hadn't known he was anywhere around until he smelled him. Then, beyond him, he saw the source of the blood. The big range bull lay over by a standing rock, hamstrung and sliced open from breastbone to backstrap, parted ribs gaping.

The little man made no sign or sound. He just stood patiently, gazing at Bull Mason, and Bull felt his hackles rise. Deliberately he drew his revolver, cocked it and pointed it at the Azteca. The little man didn't seem to notice . . . or care.

Did he think he was bullet-proof? Bull glared at him, wanting to put a hole through him . . . or maybe five or six. Yet he hesitated. The range bull over there was no more than fifty yards from where he had sat bandaging his leg, yet he had not heard it die. How had he done that? A chill like the wind of evening crept along Bull's spine. He lowered his gun and backed away, still holding it. "Stay away from me," he rasped. "Do you understand? Just stay the hell away from me!"

He walked away then, and when he looked back, the

173

Azteca was leading his horse from the shelter of a cedar copse. Bull rounded up two wandering saddle horses, stripped his gear off his own dead mount, then gathered brush, built a small fire and rolled into his blankets. He didn't sleep well, but he managed to sleep off and on during the night.

With first dawn he saddled and packed, and headed again into the gap trail that cut the split peak. Glancing back he saw the Azteca mounted, following along after him. Like a dark little vulture, patient and implacable, just . . . just following along.

In Springfield, the man named Joy locked himself into his lantern-lit study to read again the long telegraph message from John Thomas, and to compare its information to what had come before: the messages from Leavenworth and Arkalon, also from John Thomas or relayed by him, the message from Jay Merrill in Kansas City about what had been found there, the one from Georgetown itemizing details about several recent sabotages of rail lines and telegraph lines in the western territories, incidents seemingly unrelated except that they all had the effect of shutting down communications out there and had all occurred since the army had pulled out after completing its track-down of Geronimo. Those and one other message that only Joy himself knew about, from Mexico. He would have liked to tell John Thomas about that one, but of course he could not . . . not now. The Director had been specific about that. Should any evidence come that Ernest Kichener might yet be alive, the Indian was not to know of it.

"It is clear that the only reason John Thomas Wolf has undertaken this trace," the Director had said, "is some sort of indebtedness he feels for Ernest Kichener. Kichener probably is dead. We have no reason to believe otherwise . . . but in case we *should* learn otherwise, we'll

174

keep that to ourselves."

The Director was gone now, back to Georgetown. But Joy had stayed on in Springfield to coordinate communications and wrap up loose ends. One of those loose ends, now resolved, was how the blood message had come to be painted on the wall of the study—this same study in this secure house. There had been a work crew at the house to repair shingles—all credential-checked men, except one who was a substitute. That one had disappeared from the job in progress, and the report had gone to Georgetown and lain unattended there for weeks.

John Thomas may be right about the modern administration of this organization, Joy thought. Such a thing wouldn't have happened in the old days. . . . Then he smiled, remembering. It wasn't the first time a secure house had been breached. The Georgetown house itself had been entered and searched by an outsider once, forty-six years ago. That outsider had been hardly more than a boy, then, but his demonstrated talents were part of the reason the general had recruited him afterward. That boy had been Ernest Kichener.

The General was gone now, and the Director was no General. But he *was* the Director. Joy put the secret message away. It required no response. It was enough to know that Ernest Kichener was alive, and that he was in Mexico and was doing whatever he felt needed to be done at that end. It remained, then, for John Thomas Wolf to do what was needed at his end, and for Joy to pursue matters here.

Maybe the Director was right, he thought. There was no way really to control John Thomas Wolf. Maybe it was best that he think Kichener was dead—if he in fact thought so—unless Kichener himself decided to tell him otherwise.

To work, then. The list of names in Wolf's latest message was ominous. Some of them Joy did not know, but some he did: a Congressman, a pair of high-level

175

Interior Department people, a career diplomat presently assigned to Mexico, two army officers and a senior supply sergeant. Quite a network, Joy noted. Mostly, these were people above reproach, but they were involved in something very nasty. Actively involved. He trusted Wolf's word, and his methods. If Wolf said these people were involved in a conspiracy, then they were. Something shadowy and ominous and very big indeed, and not a shred of real, legal evidence to use against them.

But, then, that's why this organization was established, he thought. The law is for dealing with those who are against the law. The organization devotes itself to those who are outside it.

Again he looked at the dark glyphs painted on the plaster wall. Nasty. Something really nasty. Something ancient and evil and alive, and with enough power behind it to have extended even here.

They had found the phony workman, of course—the one who painted those glyphs. But they hadn't learned anything from him except that he had copied them from drawings on a paper that he had carried hidden in his coat. The paper was on the way here now, by mail, and Joy looked forward to seeing it. Jay Merrill had mentioned in his wire that there was an odd thing about it; the last symbol had been altered, by someone using a different kind of ink than had drawn the rest of it.

The workman had been one of those they found in Kansas City—mutilated like the rest of them in that warehouse, each one with his heart cut out.

With the Kichener message locked away, Joy spread the rest of what he had in two stacks, intrigued at the way each began to unravel a story for him. One was the messages from John Thomas. The second stack was odds and ends, bits and pieces of information from other sources that each in its own way hinted at what John Thomas himself might have been doing or might do next—bits and pieces, Joy thought, that had the mark of

Wolf about them. The odd attack on a train in Missouri, the evidences there of a chase, and the finding of bodies in the hills, things that locally went unexplained. The report about a jailbreak—Joy had smiled privately at that one. John Thomas had need of Trooper, so he acquired Trooper. Very simple. Then there was the tragedy of all those unexplained drownings—it seemed a party of riders had broken through the ice, and there were no survivors. A few had been identified—drifters and toughs, border trash with money in their pockets. It had the mark of Wolf.

The woman who had hanged herself in a good room in a first-class hotel . . . a few odd sightings of gangs of men around the prairie settlements—nothing unusual in that, except that each gang had one or more small, dark-coated bald men among them—the theft of some fine horses at Trinidad. . . .

Joy copied the list of names Wolf had sent, then began the task of assigning known names to organization agents, and unknown names to the Georgetown research clerks for identification.

Where was John Thomas now? West . . . somewhere. West of Albuquerque. West and westward-bound, heading for the root of the problem. Doing things Wolf's way.

I wish you good hunting, John Thomas, Joy thought. With what I have here, maybe we can contain the problem, and I know now that Kichener is sighting in on the source of the problem. It remains for you to tackle the problem itself and eliminate it.

Does the Director understand? Does he understand you?

Probably not.

XVIII

Two days out of Albuquerque Wolf found the trail of Shanty and the others, angling southwest across the Rio Grande valley north of Socorro where the Rio Salado came down from the north plains.

"What's that crazy old coot takin' 'em this way for?" Trooper wondered. "I thought he was supposed to cut up around the Gallinas, but this is headin' us right into the Black Range."

Wolf ignored him, looking back across the valley. In the far distance, tiny specks in a clear sky, buzzards hung in slow spiral over the sawtooth crest of the Los Pinos. Somewhere in there was the split peak trail, and he wondered . . . but it was a long way back, and it could be anything.

"Let's go," he said. "Can you hang to these tracks?"

"I ain't blind, Wolf." Trooper looked at him accusingly.

"Then go find them. I'll be along."

Muttering sourly, Trooper headed out, splashing across the swift, cold Rio Grande, clattering up its high bank and pointing, as the tracks of Shanty's group pointed, at the fox-ears gap between the rambling Gallinas on the right and big Baldy Peak on the left, with the blue San Mateos far ahead and beyond them the Blacks.

Wolf watched him go, smiling slightly. Trooper could always be trusted to do exactly what he was told to do, as far as he understood it. A good man to have around in trying times—but a trying man to have around any time.

In a long and checkered career as a field cavalryman, Trooper had made sergeant seven times and sergeant major twice. He had also set a corps record for time on report and in stockade, and had finally been cashiered at entry rank. Trooper was surly, short-fused and pessimistic. He was a whiner, a complainer, a brawler and a troublemaker. He also was chain lightning with a pair of big, hard fists and the burly shoulders to back them up, and he was a better than fair shot with an issue carbine.

Wolf had found him at Fort Collins, years before, when what appeared a conspiracy to defraud the Indian agencies had turned out to be more than that—a conspiracy, in fact, to create a state of war between the Plains tribes and the United States government and thus nullify some treaties that were interfering with the goals of a consortium of San Francisco investors who had strong contacts in Washington.

They had sent for Wolf. More specifically, Ernest Kichener had sent for Wolf, and Wolf had come. They needed someone who could speak Cheyenne, think like a Sioux and act as ruthlessly as a white politician.

It had been a simple task, really. As Ralph Waldo Emerson had written, few conflicts of enterprise are so diametric and few grievances so devout that they cannot be reconciled if men are willing to reason together.

By various means—most of them devious and unscrupulous—Wolf had contrived to have the key men among the San Francisco combine and an escort of their friends from Washington make an appearance at Fort Collins. He had also chosen among the Cheyenne and Sioux a few real hotheads that their tribes might be better off without, and arranged a private meeting for all of these in a secluded canyon west of Flatiron Mountain. Every man who entered the "treaty" grounds, white and red, did so with the expectation of coming out extremely wealthy. As a matter of fact, none of them ever came out. No one had ever quite sorted out which ones among them killed which other ones, or over what disagreements, or how the two surviving warriors came to have drowned in Green Creek. And no one had ever found the four white men who were thought to have survived the fighting on the treaty grounds, though there was speculation that the avalanche in Twelve Mile Gulch might have caught them unaware.

A simple task. Wolf had arranged for them to reason together, and the problem no longer existed.

But he had needed help at one point, to create a diversion at Fort Collins to mask the departure of the uncredentialed negotiators. And that was where Trooper came in. Wolf had spotted him in a brawl at the sutler's sheds and knew he had found his man.

The diversion had kept most everyone at Fort Collins occupied for six days.

Afterward, it had taken a seven-A-one intervention to get Trooper out of Fort Collins, but Wolf had called on him often since then and the big man's thorough—if not enthusiastic—loyalty.

Wolf watched him now until he was out of sight, then the Indian turned and rode back across the benched valley of the Rio Grande, slowly working back and forth in wide swathes until he found what he was looking for. The buzzards above the split peak had left him with a hunch, and the hunch proved out. Shanty's party had company—two riders, staying far off their trail but following them nonetheless. From his saddle, Wolf studied the prints carefully. Three horses, two with riders. A big horse heavily laden, a second horse on lead behind it. And a second rider, hanging back at a fair distance, but not so far that the first wouldn't know he was there.

Twenty years earlier—after Appomattox and the end of war among the states—it had been said of young John Thomas Wolf, "That Injun can follow a trail faster'n most folks can make one." It had amused him even then, hearing that. They had just never understood, most of them. He had been, even then, a tracer. Tracking could be slow work, involving the eyes, the senses of touch and smell, and a knowledge of country. But tracing was something else. It was a game of the mind. Hide-and-seek.

Or run and pursue. The same thing.

And the mind often spoke best through hunches. Now his hunches told him several things: Something had happened over in the Los Pinos, that had not been fully resolved; the two who were following Shanty and his charges were dangerous and of no mind to wait; and Shanty and the others didn't know they were being followed. And a separate hunch said that the second rider was another of the Aztecas—the dark-coated little fanatics set loose from some remote hellhole and running loose now upon the land.

Further, there was something vaguely familiar about the lead rider . . . something in the set and pace of his mount's prints that spoke of how he sat his saddle and how he used his rein and spurs. Wolf felt this was someone he should know, someone he might recognize. But there wasn't enough to draw upon.

Whoever he was, though, there was a fair chance that Shanty and Willie didn't know about him, and an even better chance that Trooper might run right up on his heels in the mountains ahead.

John Thomas sighted on the gap between Baldy and Magdalena crests and began to trace.

Ce-Chinatl Ixtlic Tactli, priest of Huitzilopochtli, the god of the sun, found a clearing at dawn where he could stand to watch the birth of Tonaiu and sing his encouragement to the new day's sun. It was his purpose in life to witness the birth and death of each sun, to see that each was born healthy and died gloriously—a duty he shared with others of the *Taltzin*, priests like himself, if there were others present. But he was alone now, so it fell to him alone to be midwife, nurse and nourisher for Tonaiu each day.

The sun was not a god, as many of the ordinary people among his Quatemál clans seemed to think. The sun was

181

only a sun; but it was the gift of Huitzilopochtli, who was a god, and it was through the condition of each day's sun that the *Taltzin* could know the moods of Huitzilopochtli and when he hungered for *chalchinatl*, the precious fluid.

Tactli did not mourn for the priest Malinali, who had fallen under the hooves of beasts in the narrow canyon. Malinali's death had been sufficiently cruel that Tactli was certain he had gone directly to a glorious reward in the next world, without the necessity of ages of suffering before he could be admitted there. It was how glory was achieved, as Huitzilopochtli demonstrated through Tonaiu—to be born healthy, to live devoutly and to die harshly. Thus was the path of the *Taltzin,* and such was Tactli's fondest wish for himself as well.

Tonaiu edged above the toothed peaks in the east and Tactli studied it intently for signs, even as he sang his chant of encouragement. It was a healthy new sun, bright and vital, displaying none of the telltale messages that Huitzilopochtli was unhappy or hungry or ill. Therefore the new *tonaiu* did not require *chalcinatl* this morning. It was just as well. Tactli's only ready supplies of the human fluid now were the big pale-skin warrior—whom he needed to provide other sacrifices for the god—and himself. Offering one's own heart's blood was extremely difficult . . . and very final.

Sometimes the blood of beasts would serve, but it was dangerous to offer it. The god could be angered. Legends spoke of what might happen then.

Still, on the day when Huitzilopochtli had not been satisfied with the blood spilled in the canyon—when Tonaiu had hazed in the west and said that one who should have died had not—it had been Tactli's choice to spare the one remaining pale-skin and offer the blood of a bull instead. And Huitzilopochtli had been satisfied. Tonaiu had cleared. Deep inside, Tactli suspected that the god was exercising unusual patience because he knew of the work that was being done to raise him again to the level he deserved—chief god of all the world—work the ancients had prophesied. And deep inside, it was Tactli's desire to prolong his own dying—to remain in this world between Mictlan the dark place and Tonaiutlan the bright place—long enough to see with his own eyes the emergence of Huitzilopochtli on the shoulders of his old enemy Quetzalcoatl. For on that day Cem-Anahuac, the one world, would come out of hiding in the deep jungles to the south and begin to spread and grow as the ancient ones had promised . . . to grow outward over all the lands until Cem-Anahuac became Anahuactlan. Until the one world became the whole world. Until the day joined with the night, Tonaiu with Mictiu, Huitzilopochtli with Quetzalcoatl, and all of this world between Tonaiutlan and Mictlan were ruled by the Tenochca, his own people, bearers of the destiny willed to them in ancient times by the last of the devout Aztecatl.

For more generations than any could count, they had waited hidden, deep in their steamy jungles, for just this time to come.

Tactli himself had spoken with Kukulki when he came among them to tell them that the time was at hand—or at least with the small aspect of Kukulki that had shown itself, a large man with eyes as black as night in their centers and as red as morning all around . . . a man who seemed only a common Colchautl from the dry lands to the north, except that he spoke to them in the ancient Nahuatl language preserved by the priests and promised to lead them forth to Aztlan where the emergence of Quetzalcoatl as Huitzilopochtli was to occur.

The new sun was born and had begun its dying, and Tactli ended his chant. His task was done for now.

He was aware that the pale-skin had saddled his mount and ridden away, as he did each morning, not waiting for the new sun to be welcomed. It was a common sin among warriors of any kind, this casual indifference to the nurturing of the great god's gift. Even among his own

183

people, the Tenochca, those who went out to make war seldom appreciated the gods. But such was their nature. He expected nothing better. They served in their own way. A priest who had no warrior to command was a weak priest. At present, Tactli had only this one, and the creature was not even of his race. But he could still serve the cause—and when he failed he would serve once more, as *chalchinatl* for Huitzilopochtli.

Tactli went to find his own horse and put his saddle on it. The warrior was on its way to find those who fled from them, the ones the high priest Xochitli-Miqui had said must not be allowed to reach the place of Aztlan. Thirty priests and five times that many of the pale-skinned fighters had gone out to find them and stop them. The luck of the evil ones appalled him. So far they had not been stopped. But this one remaining warrior riding ahead of him now—this *Bulmesson* as he called himself in his strange tongue—might be the one who could accomplish the task.

Kukulki himself, Xochitli-Miqui had said, had decreed that the pale woman *Gelarken* and the man *Wulf* must not reach Aztlan. They had power to endanger the emergence of the gods.

On this morning Tactli had added to his chant a prayer—to Huitzilopochtli himself—that he give special strength to the man Bulmesson to stop the dangerous ones. He had also asked Tonaiu to bring more warmth to this high, cold country. The hairy ones—so much hair they had, on their heads and faces, some all over their bodies!—did not seem to suffer greatly from the cold. But Tactli had begun to think that even if he were to die today, even if he died without pain, just these past months of frostbite might have earned for him passage to Tonaiutlan.

The pale warrior was far away when Tactli set out on his path, just a tiny, distant figure, a speck of man on horse, climbing away toward cold blue mountains in the distance. But Tactli did not hurry. He would follow the man just as he had been following him. And he would be there with his obsidian knife when it was time.

Where the long slope crested before falling away to a maze of shallow canyons, Bull Mason stopped for a moment to look back. The Azteca was a mile away, but following along. A sigh that was like a deep growl rumbled in his chest. Stinking little buzzard. The farther away he stayed, the better Bull liked it. Spooky little carrion filth. With each day that passed, the presence of the freakish little men—even just this one—was more obnoxious. He wondered how Krell had ever gotten himself involved in a deal with such creatures . . . and he wondered more how he himself had come to be involved. But then, he knew the reason for that. Partly it was the money—a lot of money up front, a hell of a lot more if he could collect the bounty and the woman and the Indian.

But there was another side to it. Bull Mason had heard talk of John Thomas Wolf. Not many spoke of him, but some did, and as often as not there was hatred in their tones—hatred and a sort of dread. Nothing ever very specific, just that there were stories of this educated Indian who showed up sometimes, and where he went, havoc followed. And some said there was a connection of some kind between the Indian and Ernest Kichener.

Bull Mason had been face to face with Ernest Kichener once, a long time ago. Kichener was the only man who had ever really frightened him, and the memory of it had lived in his craw ever since, raw and bitter.

When men spoke of Kichener, sometimes they shook their heads trying to find words, then said, ". . . like a hawk. Just like a damned hawk stooping on a rabbit. . . ." When they spoke of John Thomas Wolf they were not at a loss for words. "Wolf," they muttered, as though that said it all.

And that was part of his reason for being here now, he knew. He would never again face Kichener—would

185

never know even how to start looking for him if he wanted to—but he would like to be the man who killed Wolf. It would clear the bitterness inside him if he could do that.

On the crest Mason swung aside a few hundred yards and got out his telescope. Over there on the next hillside he could see the thin traces of passage—recent passage. It was all the trace he needed. They were somewhere ahead, and not too far. The woman, the old man . . . and maybe the Indian. He hoped the Indian was there.

Returning to his own selected path he glanced back one more time. The Azteca was closer now but still some distance back. Stinking little buzzard, Bull thought again. He was really tempted to ride back there and kill the little filth. Despite the cold dread the blank-faced creature made him feel, he could think of no way he could stop him if he decided to just ride back there and shoot him down. So far as Bull knew, the only weapon the little bastard carried was that wide black knife with its jagged razor edges.

But if he killed him, how would he collect the bounty? He didn't even know where Krell was now, but he knew that the bounty depended on at least one Azteca witnessing the kills . . . or doing them.

He shrugged, turned and went on, down the short slope toward the shallow canyons, beyond which the land climbed again between Baldy, just ahead and on the left, and Magdalena, standing now due west of him, on his right.

Not far ahead were those he would find and kill.

XIX

"The reason we're headin' this way," Windwagon Willie explained, "is because that Injun wants to see that double valley I told him about, an' this is the straightest way I know of to get there. It ain't the way most folks might choose to get from here to Arizona, but it's the way to that place I seen."

He was talking mostly to Dog. The others might be listening or not; it didn't matter. He was used to talking to Dog. It was mid-morning, and they had ridden steadily since breakfast, topping out between Magdalena and Baldy an hour ago with the forested San Mateos on their left and the snowcapped hoods of Diamond, Black and Elk peaks standing like sentinels above their climbing ranges less than a day's ride ahead.

"Toughest part of it this side of Arizona is up yonder," he told Dog. "That way out yonder past the San Mateos is the Mimbres, an' we ain't about to try goin' up in there. But over there a little to the right, that whitetop there in the middle, that's Black Peak, an' you can see there's a sort of saddle between it an' the next one, which is Elk Mountain. Well, pay no mind to how cozy that saddle looks. Ain't but twenty-thirty mile from one side of it to the other, but by the time we cross it we'll cover a hundred mile or better. Wrinkly country ... real wrinkly."

"How do 'most folks' choose to go, Willie?" Gail asked.

Willie glanced around. He hadn't been particularly aware that they were listening to him, but she and the Irishman were both there, close by and interested. Gail was leading the spare animals, spelling Willie off while Shanty's arm got a start on mending itself.

Willie thought about it, then shrugged. "I guess most folks had they a mind to go to Arizona, they'd either slide on down to El Paso an' take th' train to Tucson or Yuma or someplace, or else head west out through Grants an' Cibola Pass, then follow the Puerco down into Arizona. That's the scenic route, seems to me. You know there's lava fields up yonder, where everyplace you look it's like there was these big black worms that petrified there, but if you bust through some of 'em they're hollow with tunnels inside. I wouldn't recommend travel there, though. Man could cut hisself to pieces tryin' to cross the lava fields. But on out past there, 'bout where th' Puerco starts amountin' to anything, why, there's big red cliffs that just go straight up from nothin' ... flat ground under 'em and flat on top, looks like th' Lord had started puttin' another layer on the world an' run out of plaster. Go out thataway, you could run off into the painted desert or come out on top of the Mogollon, but it's the long way around to get to where we're goin'. Crosses th' divide 'way up north of here."

"Divide?" Shanty asked.

"Continental Divide. Place where ever'thing on one side flows east an' ever'thing on th' other side flows west. Best I can figger, we'll cross it today our own selves. Happen you got a low opinion of folks in general, Shanty, you can step down there an' take a leak an' you'll be pissin' on everybody. Now that out yonder—" he pointed grandly off to their right—"all that is called the Plains of San Agustin. Never figgered out why, but I reckon they got to call everything something."

He was directing his monologue mostly at Dog again. Few people of Willie's experience had ever equalled Dog as a conversationalist. Dog tended to listen intently, to take pleasure from whatever information he might be receiving from Willie, and hardly ever argued. But now, for the past hour or two, Dog had seemed distracted. Sometimes he paced alongside Willie's horse, a willing recipient of the old man's views, but now and then he turned to circle back, his nose high, testing the air. And

188

each time, Willie would look back, squinting and shading his eyes, then seem slightly puzzled and continue on his way.

The repeated performance had left Shanty uneasy, looking often at their backtrail.

A ridge lay just ahead now, and Dog trotted off to see what was beyond. Gail watched him go, then asked, "Willie, what kind of dog is Dog?"

Willie wiped a sleeve across his whiskers. "Well, miss, in polite society he'd be what's called an embarrassment. His mama, she was a fine lady mastiff, brought all the way over from Europe by a Frenchman with th' aim of her makin' some good marriages. Maybe she did, afterward, but first she got loose an' taken to runnin' with a rough crowd. Best anybody knows, Dog's daddy was prob'ly a big old timber wolf. Makes a pretty good combination, far's I'm concerned."

"I never saw a dog so big."

"Not many ever did, for a fact. Ol' Dog, he eats about whatever he's a mind to if it don't eat him first, an' I believe he's managed to stay well nourished. I rigged a scale once an' weighed him. Two hundred an' thirty pounds he was. 'Course, he didn't really have his growth back then."

They rode on, and after a time Dog returned, tongue lolling out in a reassuring grin. He had found nothing ahead to concern him. But before falling in alongside Willie again, the huge animal paused once more, staring at the distances behind them, ears up and nose sniffing the air. They all looked back, and Willie said, "I don't believe that's Wolf back yonder. He'd have let us know it was him by now."

"But somebody's back there," Shanty rumbled.

"Dog thinks so, though for a fact I can't seem to get a look at him. Trouble with this high country. Man can't see a damn thing out here."

"Some more of those from the pass, then," Shanty

189

decided. "More than one, Willie?"

"I don't know. Seems to me like there's two or three folks back there, but they ain't any ways together."

"How do you know that if you can't see anybody?"

"I told you I don't know. Just sometimes I can see where I really can't."

Shanty sighed, checking his weapons. It went along with what Wolf had said about the old man. "Then, how far back would you say they are?"

Willie looked at the Irishman peevishly. "You got eyes. How far back there would you say you can make out from here?"

"I don't know. Maybe three or four miles."

"Do you see anybody?"

"No."

"Then they must be farther'n that. Shanty, sometimes you remind me of that varmint."

Gail danced her mount around, clearing the reined pack animals. "So what do we do now?"

They both looked at her blankly.

"Well?" She glared. "What do we do?"

"Beats me, Miss Gail," Shanty said. "I guess with Wolf not here you're the one with the ideas. What *do* we do?"

She hissed her exasperation. What would Wolf do now if Wolf were here? And where in God's name *was* Wolf, anyway? "Ambush," she said.

"Ma'am?"

"Ambush. That's what John Thomas would do if he were here, I suppose. Where can we find a place to lay an ambush?"

Shanty's grin split his whiskers in a toothy gleam of appreciation. "That sure enough sounds right to me." He nodded. "Willie?"

"Black Elk Saddle." Willie shrugged. "Like I said, that's almighty wrinkly country up there. But we better get a move on."

190

For the past two hours Bull Mason had been pushing his horse to its limits, far off the trail, circling high on the bulging slopes of Pelona Peak, riding to get ahead of those below, skirting the open plains. Only once had he seen them, but he had estimated their direction and speed, and with his telescope identified a place where he could wait for them—a gap between steep ridges where some old eruption or waterway had sheered off the trailing sweep of Pelona. The gap was in line with their direction. It would be a part of their trail. And above it, shouldering out from the first rises of Pelona, was a forested ridge where he could take aim with his rifle and certainly bring down at least two of them when they passed below. After that it would be easy. The Indian—Wolf—wasn't with them that he could see. Maybe he wasn't far away, but in the minutes it would take them to pass below the Pelona Ridge it wouldn't matter. He was surprised to see that the largest of the men was the big redbeard, the Irishman he had thought was dead back in the gap. Well, this time he would be. And the old man, too. With her protectors dead, it would be short work to run down the woman and give her to the Azteca. He could still go after the Indian when that was done.

In the hour since entering the forested slopes, Bull had seen no sign of the Azteca. He didn't think about him, either. He knew by now that the little creature would follow along, and would be there when it was time for him to be. The little buzzard. He pushed on until the slope became precipitous, a steep, wooded mountainside where aging drifts meandered among the boles of pine trees. When the horses started balking and pawing, fighting the uncertain slope, he left the extra animal and went on, pushing his mount by force of heel, thigh, rein and voice. The Pelona Ridge was near, and he knew its top was a near-level shelf. The slope bulged outward, and he inched around it, his horse skidding and struggling to keep its feet under it. Bull peered downward, back the way he had come, trying to see where his bounty was now, but he could not see the foot of the slope.

No matter, though. He knew where they had been, and when, and he knew they had been holding a steady cross-country pace. Predictable. If he couldn't see them, they couldn't see him either. All they had to do was just come on as they had been coming, and he would have them. They might never know what hit them.

The bulge veered inward again, and now he could see the outline of the ridge just ahead . . . but something else was there that he had not seen from a distance. From where he was to the extending ridge, the entire slope was a litter of deadfall. Avalanche-felled trees lay scattered upon one another, this way and that, a maze of uprooted trunks and sheered limbs. No horse could make it through that. With a rumbling curse he stepped down, drew his rifle and went on afoot.

The strew was less than a hundred yards across, but it was a head-high maze of fallen, thrown and twisted timber. He climbed, he crawled, he backtracked and burrowed, and he was sweating and panting when he reached the other side. But now the ridge was just beyond, and his prey would be in gun range soon. Where the mountain slope edged away toward the west, Pelona Ridge extended southward beyond it, its surface slanting outward to become a broad, sparsely wooded meadow. Catching his breath, Bull headed out toward its end at a trot.

From a distance he had seen a sheered slope directly above the pinched gully, where he could rest his rifle and direct his fire.

Come along, dummies, he thought. Just keep coming and I'll be right there waiting for you.

At the end of the table meadow he scrambled down a rock slope and crouched for a moment on the ledge below, getting his bearings. The ledge ran out a hundred feet beyond, where a rockfall had sheered it away, but he knew that its end was the prominence he had seen from a distance, and that the narrow trail was just below, fifty or sixty feet down. And beyond the shadowed deep was the face of another steep rise. They would have to come through there. He levered a load into the chamber of the rifle, putting the hammer on half-cock. Then he turned toward the end of the ledge . . . and suddenly the rolling clatter of hoofbeats echoed up from below—many horses, going fast. Rising above the clatter was the high, whining voice of an old man. "Come on! Come on! We ain't got all day, you know!"

Bull Mason froze for a moment in disbelief, then lunged and ran toward the sheer summit of the rockfall. He was almost there before he could see them, and all he saw then was horsetails and coattails, going away at a gallop, out beyond the narrow draw and climbing toward the Black Elk Saddle in the distance. Curses tumbling from his tongue, he raised the rifle and fired, levered it and fired again, then a third time . . . and knew that he had missed. They were too far away, moving too fast. Faces turned to look back, and he clawed out his telescope, raised it to his eye, stumbled as his boot turned a stone, and fell heavily just at the brink of the rockfall. The telescope spun away to clatter on rocks below, and he clung to keep from following it.

Trooper had just crested a winding ridge when he heard gunfire . . . somewhere. Three shots, he thought, though in these mounains he had no idea of its direction. It might be from ahead somewhere. Shanty was up there with the crazy old coot and that woman, maybe only a few miles now. Maybe it was them. He had been on their trail for some time, following it steadily, his eyes roving down and ahead for sign. But who were they shooting at?

Someone they had encountered ahead? The sound was of rifle shots, harsh and distinctive, shots fired in quick succession. Shanty carried a rifle, but Trooper had never known the Irishman to favor rapid firing. Maybe it was somebody else, then. But who? Trooper had seen no sign of any other passage . . . no other sign imposed upon the tracks that he was following, anyway. Many times he had seen Wolf scout out from a trail, looking for sign of tracers—other tracks off to one side or another—but Trooper had never figured out how Wolf seemed to know where to look to find such things.

Now he peered into the distance, shrugged and went on. He heard no further shooting. Whatever had occurred was done. Ahead a peak loomed on his right, mists forming on its shadowed slopes as the high, hazy sun quartered above it. He wished Wolf had stayed with him, or at least been a little more specific about when he would catch up. A few hours of light were left now, and he still hadn't seen those he was following. He couldn't follow trail without the light to see it, and the idea of another cold camp, alone out here in this wilderness, depressed him. He doubted whether there was a saloon within a hundred miles, unless he shucked it all and turned back toward that last little settlement he had seen from the western slopes—a little clutch of buildings off in the valley south of Albuquerque someplace. But there wasn't enough daylight left to get back there, either, he decided. There was another town—Socorro—off to the east someplace, but there were mountains in the way.

Grumbling under his breath at the injustice of it all, Trooper rolled heavy shoulders to ease the strain of burdening responsibility and headed on, following the trail that Wolf had set him to follow. Shadows crept out from the peak to the west, marking the daylight he had left, and the mists rolling up the slopes became a skitter of wind-chased cloud up near its summit, threatening to shorten the day even more.

He almost missed the sign, had to circle back and look at it again before he recognized it—someone had crossed the trail he was following. He got down and studied the sign. Two horses, one some distance ahead of the other. They had come from off to the left somewhere, and had crossed Shanty's group's path at an angle, veering more toward the rises pushing in from the right ahead while the group's tracks wound toward a break at the base of the looming mountain, heading for other mountains beyond.

Could these have been the ones who fired? Had they crossed trails and then returned, somewhere ahead, to fire at Shanty and the others . . . or be shot at by them? An urgency came to him, and he remounted and hurried on, glancing up often now toward the shrouded peak where errant winds scudded strings of shredded cloud like froth-patterns on a flowing stream. And now, he noticed, those same vapors had a scent to them as they touched erratically on the lower reaches—a scent that made him wrinkle his nose in disgust, and that made his flesh crawl. He had smelled it before, twice now, recently. The odor of the slaughterhouse. The odor those little bald brown men carried about them . . . the odor that had been as thick as rancid blood back there in Glorieta Pass, where that little creature had cut open Cecil Cobb even while Cobb was shooting him to pieces.

But the winds were fickle, and the odor, like the sound of gunfire before, had no direction to it. It was just there, a sourness on the winds.

Rounding a tall, ragged outcrop of dark stone, Trooper saw the tracks ahead climbing toward a narrowing cut in the shadow of a ridge—a steep, outthrust ridge which pointed out from the slopes above like a tail dragged behind the mountain.

Again hazes drifted overhead and darkened the land beneath, and Trooper's impatience grew as his feeling of urgency grew. Breezes drifted and the charnel odor teased him, suddenly sharp and near, then gone again, and he seemed to hear a voice somewhere, chanting.

Hauling on his reins, exasperated and worried, Trooper looked up at the haze-reddened sun just above the mountain's crest and pointed a demanding large finger at it. "Damn it!" he shouted. "I need more daylight! I got things to do!"

As though obeying his command, the high haze shredded again in the wind and drifted aside, and for a moment the sky was clear and the sun that shone there was a strong, trail-marking sun.

"Huh!" Trooper grunted. "Prob'ly the only thing in the world that ever pays any mind to what I want. The wind, for God's sake." He drummed heels, moving out, wanting to cover as much ground as he could before he lost the trial. A mile or two ahead, now, beyond the encroaching shadow of Pelona, good sunlight brightened gentle slopes where no shadows yet threatened.

If he could hold the track that far, he decided, then he might get in another couple of hours of good trail before he lost it. Maybe he would see them by then.

High above and now behind, on the dark-stone outcrop where Trooper had paused, Ce-Chinatl Ixtlic Tactli, priest of Huitzilopochtli, watched in wonder as the man rode away. Tonaiu had grown weak, then that man had come and ordered Tonaiu to recover . . . and Tonaiu had responded.

Tactli had seen many strange things occur in his life and was wise enough to know that most strange things were coincidental. Maybe this too was coincidence. Those were clouds up there, drifting with directions that only clouds could know, and maybe what had occurred was nothing more than a cloud drifting aside just when the rider decided to shout at Tonaiu. And yet, how did that account for the man shouting and pointing as he had

196

done. These people in this cold land knew nothing of Tonaiu. They knew nothing of Cem-Anahuac the one world or the ways of truth it cherished and taught to its chosen *Taltzin,* those who served the god Huitzilopochtli and attended the messages that came through Tonaiu the sun.

Tactli had lost his *Coatzitsi*—his warrior. He thought that Bulmesson still was ahead of him somewhere, but he wasn't quite sure where he was. This one who had passed, who had ordered Tonaiu to brighten, *looked* like Bulmesson, in many ways. Oversized, pale and hairy—of course, all of them were thus, all those the *peyotl*-eater Krell had rallied to serve Kukulki. When one had seen a few of them, it was as though one had seen them all. They were as alike as vultures in the sky or as so many sharks in a lagoon.

Yet . . . not before had he seen one of them speak to Tonaiu—point and speak in such a way that it could not be misunderstood what he was doing. Tactli had not understood the man's words, but their intent had been clear. The man had been concerned with the reddening and dimming of the orb, and had simply ordered the sun to brighten.

And it had!

Tactli did not know where to look for Bulmesson. But now he arrived at a decision. Bulmesson was, after all, only a hireling—one of those employed by Kukulki through the *peyotl*-eater Krell. This one who had just passed might well be another of the same, but he had done a thing Tactli had seen no other do—he had at least shown recognition of Tonaiu. Therefore, he might be of a higher order of barbarian than were the others. Surely the high priest Xochitli-Miqui would want this one to be observed. He would follow this one, at least for a time. Maybe somewhere ahead he could recover Bulmesson as well. Two *Coatzitsin* were better than one, and even if they should serve no other purpose, they could be a supply of *chalchinatl* for Huitzilopochtli.

Bull Mason did not see them pass. He was up on the blind slopes looking for his horses.

But on the finger ridges east of the trail was one who had seen them all, had watched everything that took place in the pass below Pelona. This one simply watched . . . and waited.

XX

From a distance Wolf saw him, a solitary figure sitting on a rock in the last rays of sunlight above Pelona's shadow. Casually he waited there, as though he had always been there, and as Wolf's eyes made him out, he knew that he too had been seen. He rode on, aware of the presence of the other but not intently so. There would be time to study him when he was closer. Now he rode at a mile-eating lope, but with his senses keen on the signs of passage before him and the story they told. Here Shanty had passed, with Gail Larkin and Willie Shay and their horses; there Dog had paused to mark a stone, proclaiming his rights to the territory; just there a single rider with a led horse had veered across the earlier tracks and angled upward on the mountainside—the ridge ahead suggested an attempt to ambush, and the pace of the rider confirmed it—then a bit farther on a lightly mounted horse had wandered through, as though its rider had lost his way.

And arrow-straight over it all, following close upon the path of the first ones, was Trooper's track, aiming at the cut below Pelona and the silhouette of Black Elk Saddle beyond.

As he neared, the person on the rock stood, raised a

hand, then climbed down and started walking toward the tracks to meet him. Wolf studied the man with hooded eyes. An Indian, stocky and solid, slightly bow-legged but with the steady grace of a walker. And the man seemed to know him. Wolf had the feeling he had been waiting for him there, and his fingers touched the butt of his holstered revolver. Yet the man made no suspicious moves. He simply walked down the slope from the finger ridges, leapt one little gully and clambered through another, then reached the overlaid tracks and stood waiting.

Wolf had never seen him before.

As he came closer he studied him. Apache, he decided. Not full-blood, but many were not. He reined in and raised a hand in salute. The Apache did the same, looking him up and down with eyes that missed little. Then in fair English he said, "You are John Thomas Wolf."

"I am."

"I am Dutchman. They thought you might come this way, so I came to watch."

"Who thought so?"

"Larkin . . . and the other man."

"What other man?"

"The one who put the wolf on the message of the Tenochca."

Kichener. It could be no one else. "Where is he?" Wolf asked.

"He went to Mexico. He said he would clip the serpent's wings. He told Larkin that you would be here soon. He said to hide and wait."

"Where is Larkin, then?"

The Apache spread his hands. "Hiding and waiting."

"Where there is a double valley?"

"No. That is where the Tenochca are. And Hall Kileen. But he is not far away. They have been looking for him, but Three People is with him. Three People knows how to hide."

"You have seen who passed here?"

"Lot of people," Dutchman said. "Larkin's daughter with a big red-whisker man and an old man I think I know, lot of horses on lead and a big dog. Then another one I think I know. The man the Mexicans call Toro."

Toro. Now Wolf knew why the track had seemed familiar. Once before he had seen Bull Mason. At a distance, but he had seen him. "Is he after them?"

"He was. Went up there, gonna snipe 'em from that ridge. But he missed. He's up there tryin' to find his horses. He won't find them."

"Why not?"

"I got 'em." Dutchman shrugged. "Then there was another fella, big man with a mustache and a carbine. He's got a Tenochca taggin' him now. He one of yours, or theirs?"

"He's Trooper. He's mine. You going to take us to Larkin?"

"Why I'm here," Dutchman said. "I'll get the horses."

The shadows had conquered all but the higher slopes now, combining with rising mists to blend distant land and distant sky so that the gleaming peaks of the Mimbres and the more distant San Mateos rode aloft like golden vessels afloat on seas of evening.

Working his way up the winding, climbing shelves and ridges, twisting this way and that with interlaced washes, coves and canyons, Trooper glanced gloomily at the sky where a hazed red sun was mashing itself against the tops of the far-off Tularosas. Every now and then the odor of carrion drifted to him and made his scalp crawl. These breaks could be full of those stinking little devils, for all he knew. And now for the second time he thought he heard a quiet voice somewhere, chanting.

"Losin' the light," he muttered to himself. "Can't follow tracks in the dark. I'll have to stop. Where in hell are those people, anyway?" By last light of a setting sun he urged his horse up to the top of a knob and stood in the stirrups, his unhappy eyes on the last rim of the failing sun. He cupped his hands and shouted, "Shanty! Where are you?"

And even as he shouted it the sinking orb flashed once among far-off peaks and sank from sight.

He listened, hearing only his own mournful echoes. Then he shook his head. "Guess that does it for today," he muttered. "Have to wait for morning now." He marked where he had last seen the tracks, then rode on ahead a bit toward a tumbled mass of rock that looked like it might offer some shelter for a camp. In lingering dusk he led his mount between standing stones the size of great houses and down an incline. The little stream he had expected was there—he had noticed spray on the winds and on the face of a spire that stood a quarter-mile away, at the head of the little draw hidden by the rocks. He drank from the cold pool there and let his horse drink; then a shift of wind brought the carrion smell to him again, and he wrinkled his nose. Were the little black-clad devils everywhere? He hadn't seen any of them; but he kept smelling them . . . and it was an odor he wasn't likely to forget. Visions danced in his head and in his throat: a nice, rowdy, smoky barroom someplace civilized where people killed each other with guns and bullets, not by cutting each other open and reaching in to fiddle with their internals; a place where a man could find himself a friendly brawl to shake off the dust of the trail and maybe a friendly bawd or two to drain off his accumulated annoyances; a place where a man could drink enough honest whiskey to finally drown the odor of death that clung inside his nose.

Distant, muted thunders echoed somewhere—a snow slope had let loose somewhere in the high-up peaks—and in its echoes he thought he heard the scuffing of a horse's hooves nearby. Leaving his horse still saddled, he climbed a rock and looked around. Pale after-rays still

201

lingered on the snowcaps in the distant east, though those to the west were now black silhouettes against a fading sky. For a time he scanned the countryside around, listening intently. He saw nothing, heard nothing more. But then, again, errant-winds shifted, and the rancid-sweet odor of old clotted blood was there—a warm, near-at-hand odor not exactly like carrion but similar. It was like—he tried to put a memory to it, and found one. It was like the odor of a German cellar in the fall, the fetid, cloying smell of collected blood setting up in buckets for the making of winter puddings.

"I don't know how long I can stand this," he muttered sourly. "Damn Wolf anyway, always sendin' me off where I don't want to go. . . ." He sighed. "Well, a waterhole's no place to be."

Trooper scuttled down from the rock and picked up the reins of his horse. Carbine in one hand, reins in the other, he retraced his path up from the stream, between the standing rocks, and paused. In the shadows he had seen something move. "Who's there?" he called. "Wolf? That you?"

Again he thought there was movement, quick and furtive, and he raised the carbine . . . but there was nothing to shoot at. Only shadows among the tumbled rocks. But now the odor of death was close and strong. Vividly he recalled the scene above Glorieta, the little black-coat clinging to Cecil Cobb like some monstrous spider, slashing away at him, cutting him wide open even while Cobb's bullets tore through him. That stinking little devil had made no sound . . . no sound at all. But the smell had been there, as close as it was now. Trooper turned full around in the failing dusk, his carbine cocked and close-hauled at his side. Maybe the shadows had moved, just over there . . . he squeezed the trigger and the big, stubby gun flared in the darkness, its roar caroming back and back from stone surfaces. He heard his bullet strike rock, heard its shrill whine as it ricocheted off into the dark sky. "Shit," he muttered, then he shouted it. "You can have the damned waterhole! Take it! I'm gone! Just get the hell away from me!"

With a final pivot he swung aboard his prancing horse and hit heels to its ribs, trusting his memory of the terrain southward. There should be a few hundred yards of running room out there before the next canyon dropped away. He ran, letting the hooves thunder beneath him, trying to estimate distance. When he reined in and stepped down his foot slipped, and he clung to his saddle horn while rocks and loose gravel clattered away in darkness below. Another step, and—"Christ!" he muttered, finding solid, level ground again. But at least now, at least for the moment, the crisp winds that wandered about him were only mountain breezes, clean and fresh with the scent of high country.

Leading his nervous horse, moving slowly, guided only by unreliable starlight through the tendrils of cloud that drifted low above him, he walked for an hour, zigzagging this way and that, always pushing southward, away from the haunted waterhole with its stinks and moving shadows. "Wolf," he muttered over and over, "I don't know if I could get it done, but right now I believe I'd try to kill you was you to show up. Where in hell are you, anyway?"

He came down from a rock flat onto a narrow, snaking ridge that angled upward again, winding this way and that until it widened and entered timber. He was a hundred yards into the rising forest when he realized he could barely see at all. In the shadows of the conifers, even the occasional starlight was no help. He worked his way between dark boles, as much by feel as by sight, beginning to wonder where he was and whether he would ever be able to find the tracks he had left at dusk—tracks he was supposed to follow to catch up with the others. He was just making up his mind to stop and try to hole up when a shadow moved, a big shadow among shadows, almost in arm's reach. He gasped, started to raise

203

the carbine—

"You beat anything I ever saw," Shanty's chiding voice told him. "First you stand around hollering, then you ride in the dark, then you take to walking in circles. What in God's name do you think you're doing, Trooper?"

"Well, I'm tryin' to—"

"Never mind. I figured I'd better come get you before you walked off a cliff. Where's Wolf?"

"If I knew that," Trooper snorted, "I'd be emptyin' this carbine in that general direction right now."

The place Willie had found for them, up in the forested crags that were the beginning of Elk Mountain, was not the ideal ambuscade that Gail Larkin had wanted. "It's decidedly difficult to ambush people," she had grumbled, "if they can't find you." It was, though, a snug and comfortable campsite with two caves under a beetling jut of caprock, a small flowing spring and sheltered graze below for the animals, the entire site about three acres of isolation with a surrounding rim where Dog could patrol. And when Trooper told them about smelling Aztecas down in the tumblestones, Willie sent Dog to do that.

They had much to tell, and questions to be answered, but there was no hurry. It would all have to be told again when Wolf found them. In the meantime, it was Gail's suggestion that they give the stock—and themselves—a day to rest. And none disagreed. Dog had brought down a mule deer on the way up to Black Elk Saddle, and Willie broke out his beloved salt pork and onions.

"We be in Arizona directly," he told Gail. "Not but a hop, step an' jump from here. These mountains"—he waved a gnarled hand generally westward—"they're rightly more part of Arizona than they are of New Mexico. They're the Mogollons, run off yonder to the Mogollon Plateau, which is about the only place in Arizona that a man can really see anything—'ceptin' the desert down south, an' that's just all red an' gray most of the time. Everyplace else is all cut up with mountains an'

204

canyons an' cliffs an' big rocks . . . everywhere you look there's somethin' in the way so's you can't see the scenery. Shame about Arizona. Real shame."

Nearby, Trooper snorted and rolled over, pulling his blankets around his ears. "Crazy old coot," he rumbled. "He'll be dead an' gone fifty years an' his mouth will still be runnin'."

Willie glanced around. "Varmint. Anyways"—he turned back to Gail—"if that double valley Wolf wants to see used to be Aztlan, then we'll be there directly. It ain't far past White Mountain, an' you'd be able to see that from here if it wasn't for all this mess that's in the way."

"My father believes that all this was Aztlan," she said. "Not just some valley, this whole part of the country. Aztec glyphs have been found as far north as Colorado and Utah. The thing nobody has ever been sure of is where was their cultural center. That's what he went to Arizona to find. It always puzzled him, all the time we were down in Mexico . . . if a band of Aztecs did escape from Cortes and take a sacred relic back to Aztlan to hide, they wouldn't just hide it anywhere. They would have had a significant place in mind. And to Aztec thinking, that place would be the spot where their heritage began . . . the place they first organized to worship their sun god and make war on their neighbors. He said he had an idea where that place might have been. The template stone was a key to it."

"Wonder who else had a look at that thing," Willie said.

"Nobody. Father was careful about that. The others may have known about it, but he never let them see it. He had already found out that Kileen was dangerous. That's why we left Mexico when we did. Father didn't want Kileen to get hold of the things that might lead to Aztlan. And he just didn't want to have anything more to do with Kileen, either."

*   *   *

Some wandering prospector or lost traveler once had named this place Haunted Butte, maybe because the wind off the desert seemed to grieve as it twisted and writhed through the canyons to the south, and its voice across the misnamed ridge above the hidden valley was a mournful whisper as of lost souls wandering here and there in some world nobody could quite see. The name stuck because there were people there from time to time, and what others had called the place they called it, too. Bits of history, wind-worn marks of trial and failure, could be seen here and there about the place: fallen remains of a stone cabin where once some recluse had slept while plodding the wild lands about, looking for gold or gems or some other kind of dream; the skeletal remains of an overturned wagon deep in a dry gorge; a stone mound on a hillside with the stump of a wooden cross atop it . . . monument to something nobody would ever remember. And in the valley, on a sandy flat where sometimes grass grew, stood a cluster of buildings that once had been a ranch. The buildings remained, but not those who had put them there, the only trace of them the weathered "K-" carved into the roofbeam of the main building. "K-Bar," the place had been. But not anymore.

And beneath the visible marks of people and histories around Haunted Butte were other traces, far older: here and there crude drawings on slabs of rock, steps and handholds cut into a cliff, remains of wicker-and-clay basketry in a cave. The Apache and the Zuni had known Haunted Butte, each in their own time, and before them people who may have been Navajo and others whose name for themselves was known to no others now. Yet even they had felt the ghosts of others past here, and had found evidences of man-made structure in hidden places sundered now by old earthquakes or mostly buried beneath volcanic cinder.

And it was these ancient ones—or certain ones among them at a particular time—who most interested those who now occupied the spread that had once been K-Bar.

The buildings still stood, and those who came made use of them because they were close to the north crest of Haunted Butte, from which could be seen the two valleys that once had been one.

The land around—endless miles of sundered mountain and desert—had not always been as empty as it was now. Even a decade or two before, there had been little ranches tucked here and there among the hills, even a tiny settlement or two within fifty or sixty miles. Few remained now, though. Years of exploding warfare between the army and the Apache—years in which it was the white settler who was erased from the scene—had ended just a season past with the most concerted campaign ever mounted in the southwest, the hunt for Geronimo. It would be a few years before the land began to fill again.

Which was what Hall Kileen had in mind. Not many settlers outside the towns had deep roots in Arizona yet. He had counted on them doing just what they did, when the Apaches broke loose again. Many of them had just hauled up and gone on, with no stomach for Apache warfare anymore. It was as well. He had assured Kukulki that it would happen, and he wouldn't want to disappoint Kukulki. The man had too many strings in too many places.

But it had gone just as he said. Now there were a hundred armed hardcases on the old K-Bar . . . not counting Xochitli-Miqui and his little band of fanatics in their own camp across the way. Standing at the lip of Haunted Butte, his coat pulled tightly around him against the morning chill, Kileen glanced eastward. A half-dozen stained tents and a pile of stone . . . to Xochitli-Miqui it was a city. The stinking little primitive had no concept of the good things this world had to offer, the comforts and luxuries that would flow in abundance to Kileen and Kukulki and those they chose to share with. The Quatemál had no idea that he was being used toward such a purpose, and Kileen wondered if it would have mattered to him anyway. In a pen near the stone pile, bound and haltered, were a half-dozen or so desert Indians and a couple of Mexican peones, and Kileen knew that there was one fewer than had been there the evening before. He knew because the top of the stone pile was scarlet and shiny.

Would it matter to Xochitli-Miqui that he was being used . . . that he and all his "priests" were simply pawns in a game financed by Kukulki and orchestrated by Kileen? Maybe not. As long as the Tenochca had *chalchinatl* to offer to their sun god, nothing else ever seemed to matter to them.

It still mystified him that Kukulki had ever managed to find the little tribe of jungle recluses, but he had. And he had seen the value of them when Kileen spoke to him about the Aztec legends.

There had never been more than forty or fifty of the little black-clad priests among the primitive Tenochca of the jungles. Kukulki had shipped nearly thirty of them north—by jungle trail, by forced march through the mountains to avoid scrutiny of the Mexican authorities, then by cattle car through Chihuahua and night crossing into Arizona Territory. Of the twenty-eight Kukulki had sent, twenty-three survived the trip. Now fifteen remained below Haunted Butte. The rest had gone out with Krell and the Grimes woman, and with Kukulki's associates from Kansas City, to find Gail Larkin and to make sure no more Kicheners came west to mess things up.

But there was a problem there. He had received word that another agent was on the way—an Indian named Wolf. He had word of his progress as far west as central Kansas . . . then he had heard nothing more. Had they stopped him? Kileen was sure they had. He had people on all the rail lines and main trails, even patrolling the Puerco Valley and the mountain trails north of White Mountain.

But if they had stopped him, then why had he not

heard of it? And where was Gail Larkin? He needed her—either in his hands or safely dead, it didn't matter—to smoke out that bastard Larkin with his waystone. It would save them a lot of time and energy if they could pinpoint the hiding place of Montezuma's mask. Otherwise, they could only dig and dig again, and hope.

And Kukulki's patience would wear thin before very long.

In the distance northward the double valley spread away, a three-mile-wide depression bastioned by harsh ridges and cliffs along its margins, yet between these mile after rolling mile of gentle fields, meadows and streams that fed from springs above the headwaters of the Black River—that might once have fed a deep, clear-water lake nestled in the valley. Kileen could see it that way—the way it surely once was—although now it was changed. The cone that clove the valley midway was not an ancient feature, just an old one. And it had risen abruptly, violently, possibly just in a matter of hours or days those few centuries ago. It had thrust itself up from some hell below and poured molten stone up and down the valley in a rift that rose as high as the protecting walls around it, with the cone itself standing even higher. Atop the cooling lava it had rained ash and detritus, covering what was left of the gentle valley floor—a thick carpet of red and gray cinder that only a few hundred years of erosion had swept away along the sides, to expose traces of what might have been there before.

And somewhere out there—somewhere within sight of where he stood now—Kileen knew that the survivors of that holocaust had taken shelter, waiting out the worst of it. And from there they had gone forth, finally, seeking a new homeland.

A hidden rift? Caves or tunnels? Somewhere, right out there, was the spot they would have looked back on, and committed to lore and legend. And it would be there, at that spot, where their successors returned to hide the one artifact that embodied all of their legends . . . the mask of

Huitzilopochtli, the mask of the last emperor Motec'zoma Xocoyotzin. The eagle-head sun mask of Montezuma, largest single gold artifact known to have escaped the treasure ships of the Conquistador Cortes and the key to the legend of the return of Aztec might.

For months, Kileen had orchestrated a search for the missing Frederick Larkin, but he seemed to have vanished . . . though Kileen felt he was somewhere not too far away, hiding and waiting.

XXI

Kichener would clip the serpent's wings, he had said.

"How is he going to do that?" Wolf asked the Dutchman. "What does he plan?"

"Didn't say," the Apache said. "He just told Larkin you'd be coming along by and by, said you'd figure a way to take care of things up at this end."

Damn Kichener, Wolf thought. It was always the man's way . . . always expect another to do what you knew he would, whether he knew what that was or not. And then the humor of it tugged at his cheeks. Kichener knew him well. And even if Kichener had left a specific plan, with details, he would have known Wolf would do things his own way. So he just left it simple—no details at all.

"There's about a hundred of them over at Haunted Butte," Dutchman said. "That fellow Hall Kileen, he's in charge there. Most of the ones he has with him are hardcases. He's brought them in from all over. His recruiter is an easterner named Krell, was down in Mexico for a while and got tangled up with some Tarahumaras. Story is they thought about killing him, but then they got the idea it would be funny to feed him

210

peyote and see what he'd do. They'd never seen a white man walk the wonderways. First two buttons they gave him, he decided he could fly, and they had to carry him down from a clifftop and never did figure out how he got up there. So they didn't kill him; they just kept him for a while and fed him cactus buttons. Then when they got tired of him they sold him to a big Mexican *don*. Got a price for him, because Krell knows how to find guns for hire. That's what he used to do."

"Not anymore," Wolf said. "Krell won't bother anybody now."

Dutchman glanced at him, then shrugged and turned his attention back to the climbing trail.

"What are they doing at Haunted Butte?" Wolf asked.

"Digging. Not right there, but within a mile or so north. Kileen thinks he can find Montezuma's mask."

"Can he?"

"Larkin says he's close. He knows the general area, but not exactly where to look. That's what Larkin knows, and that's why Kileen wants Larkin."

"How does Larkin know where it is?"

"Little flat rock he has, it tells him."

"The template stone? How does it tell him?"

"He knows where to stand to look through it. When he can do that, the sun-sign on it will be sighted on where the sun mask is. You ought to know that."

"How should I know?"

Dutchman glanced at him again. "You're Indian. So were the people who made the template. That was a dumb question, too, because you already knew the answer."

Wolf nodded. He had been curious how the half-breed Apache might answer that, but of course he knew. It had always amused him, how difficult it was for most white men to follow Indian logic . . . or *any* straightforward logic, for that matter. The old scholar Saquo-yadi, whom the whites had called Sequoyah, had said it simply: "Tell a *yoneg* a thing is here, and point to it, and he will search everywhere looking for it. Ask him why he searches everywhere when it is here, and he will say it must be someplace else because it is too easy to find here. So you find it for him and show it to him, and then he'll never trust you because he will think you tricked him."

It was so true that even the whites made jokes about it. He had heard the story of the man going up and down the street looking for his hat . . . someone asked him where he lost it . . . he said, "Down there in that alley." They said, "Then why are you looking out here in the street?"

"Because the light is better here," he explained.

The white man has always been amusing to the red man, Wolf thought. But so often it had been a bitter humor. He knew that there had been Cheyenne at Sand Creek who had considered Chivington a real joke . . . for a while.

"They're up there, a mile or so." Dutchman pointed. Wolf nodded. He had already seen where the camp must be.

"How many of the Aztecas does Kileen have with him?"

"'Bout a dozen and a half," Dutchman said. "Aztecas . . . that's good. They think they're Aztecs, all right. Call themselves Tenochca."

"Where did he get them?"

"Same place he got Krell, I guess. That bigwig *don* down in Mexico. Makes everybody call him Kukulki. Owns about half of Mexico."

"Strong man."

"Real strong. Ranches, railroads, banks, you name it, he's got it. Apache don't know much about him, except he controls about everything in his part of the country, and he's a *Kligwi* . . . means he's crazy. Thinks he's god or something. But a lot of the Indios down there, the ones that talk Nahuatl, they think maybe he is, too. If he can show them a sign, they'll follow him to hell and back. And he's just crazy enough to take them there, too."

"How many Indios would follow him . . . if he could show them a sign?"

Dutchman thought about it for a minute or more, then he shrugged. "Maybe a million, maybe more. Tribes all mixed up in Mexico, but not as much as folks think. There's Chichimecs and Tarahumaras and Tehuanes . . . Pimas and Mapines, even some Ulumiles and Toteacas, all scattered around where folks don't bother them much . . . then there's a lot of just Indios that could be most anything and a little Spanish. But what's gone is the old languages. Not many of them left, but one is. Nahuatl. Aztec language. Spanish isn't the first language of Mexico. Not yet it isn't. Nahuatl is."

"Do you speak it, Dutchman?"

"Little bit, not much."

A tawny gray shape moved, above and ahead of them, and Dutchman shaded his eyes.

"That's just Dog," Wolf said. "He's with us."

"Yeah, I saw him before, but I didn't believe him then, either."

Wolf cupped a hand at his mouth and trilled a coyote song. A moment later Shanty's shaggy head appeared above the stone ledge where Dog paced. Wolf raised a hand, and Shanty waved back.

Dutchman raised his head, nostrils flaring. "Smell that?" he asked.

"Yes, I smell it. Azteca."

"Tenochca. Not far away. That's the one that followed your man. Stinks to high heaven, doesn't he?"

"That's probably what he has in mind. He's a priest. He wants his god to smell how holy he is."

"You've seen what they do to people?"

"I've seen it."

In high morning they came up to the sheltered camp, to a chorus of greetings.

"John Thomas, where have you been?" Gail Larkin demanded.

"Where in hell have you been, Wolf?" Trooper glared. "You damn near got me killed!"

"Man with a rifle back there someplace, Wolf,"

213

Shanty said. "We got past him, but he's still out there, I guess. And Trooper has been smelling Aztecas. . . ."

Windwagon Willie cocked a thick silver eyebrow at him, then looked at Dutchman skeptically. "Wolf, you know that's a 'Pache there with you?"

Gail noticed the newcomer for the first time, and her mouth opened in surprise. "Dutchman? What are you doing—"

"He's Dutchman," Wolf told them. "He's on our side. He knows where your father is, Miss Larkin."

"He's alive, then? Dutchman, will you take me to him?"

Willie raised a warning hand at Dog. "Don't chew on that 'Pache, Dog. He's on our side."

"Just like always," Trooper grumped. "I ask a civil question and never get any answer. Same old damn thing, all the time."

Wolf stepped down and handed his reins to Trooper, glancing at Shanty again. "What happened to your arm?"

"We had a run-in with some folks back a ways," the Irishman said. "I got nicked, but we put a stop to that business. We ran a herd of cows over them . . . well, *they* did, anyway." He lined a thumb at Willie and Gail.

Wolf pursed his lips. "So that's what happened. Whose idea was that?"

"Hers," Shanty said. He grinned. "The lady didn't want to do anything violent or murderous or anything, so she just stomped a stampede over them. Gently, though. She did it real gently."

Wolf regarded the girl thoughtfully, black-agate eyes revealing nothing. "Very thoughtful," he said. Then to all of them, he added, "All right. Somebody get Dutchman some coffee, and I'll take reports. You first, Shanty."

An hour later he knew all that had occurred, and all the impressions of each of them, and Willie and the Dutchman were comparing notes on trails and routes

214

while Gail changed the bandage on Shanty's arm.

For a time Wolf walked the perimeter of the sheltered place, studying terrain and thinking. Dog paced at his side, waist-high and massive, as though realizing that this was the human in charge at the moment, and that where he went interesting sports and pastimes were likely to occur.

After a while Wolf returned to the camp and got Shanty and Trooper aside.

Of the sullen man he asked, "Trooper, what were you shouting about out there, last evening?"

"What?"

"Shanty said he heard you shouting, off in the distance, about sundown. Then he heard your carbine being fired a little later. What were you doing?"

"Aw, well . . ." Trooper scuffed his toe, embarrassed. "Well, if you must know, I was aggravated. I mean, you set me off to follow a trail I couldn't hardly see anyways, an' then it started to get dark—"

"Who were you shouting at?"

"The sun! Dammit, Wolf, I was feelin' cranky, all right?"

"You shouted at the sun?"

"Well . . . yeah, I guess so. But dammit, I needed the light. Anyhow, when I hollered th' clouds broke up an' I got in some more trailin' time."

"The clouds broke because you shouted?"

"Oh, hell, no. I know better than that. It just happened, is all. What difference does it make?"

"When did you start thinking there were Aztecas around?"

"Well, I guess it was right after that. Then when I got down to the water it smelled like there was a whole tribe of them little stinkbugs. That's why I shot. I thought I saw one. That's all."

Wolf rubbed his chin with a thumb, thoughtfully. Then he looked at the sky. High sunlight above Black Mountain reflected dazzlingly from the snowcapped peak of Elk Muontain towering above them on the west. Southwest winds were at work up there, peeling shreds of mist away from Elk's cap, filaments of gauze against the deep blue of high-mountain sky. Without looking around he asked, "Shanty, can you sing?"

"Not very well," the big man admitted.

"What songs do you know?"

"Well . . . *Mother McCree*, I guess, and maybe a little of *Down to Dublin Town.* Why?"

"*Down to Dublin Town* will do. Practice it. But quietly. Don't let your voice carry."

"You want me to sing, Wolf?"

"Just practice. You can sing later. Trooper, is your carbine loaded?"

"And when was it ever not?" Trooper countered, insulted.

"Then get a saddle on one of those horses. I have a job for you."

Muttering and shaking his head, Trooper went off to get a horse. While he waited, Wolf walked across to where Gail Larkin sat by a small fire, and squatted beside her, gazing out at the rises that climbed away like stairsteps toward the high slopes of Elk Peak. "They'll be waiting for us, you know," he said. "Just the other side of that mountain . . . or another day or two beyond. You'd be safer here than out there."

"I'm not going to be left behind," she said flatly. "Besides, you—"

"I don't need you. Dutchman knows where your father is. He can take me there. Besides, you never did know, did you?"

"Well, not exactly. But I know the general area."

"Dutchman knows exactly. Why don't you just wait here. I'll see that it's safe, and I'll leave someone with you."

"Who? Shanty? Haven't you saddled that poor man with me long enough, John Thomas?"

"Not Shanty. I'll need him. Willie, maybe. Now that I

216

have the Dutchman to guide—"

"It's out of the question, anyway," she cut him off. "I told you I'm going to find my father. If you leave me here, I'll just go alone. So let's not argue about it."

"Stubborn woman," he said. "Do you know what those people will do if they get hold of you?"

"What? Kill me?"

"They'll use you to smoke out your father. They need that template stone he's carrying. And I'm going to be busy enough, without worrying about you."

"You? Worry?" Her laugh was a prod. "I don't think it would matter to you if they *did* kill me, John Thomas. It wouldn't matter if they killed me and my father both . . . would it? To you, I mean?"

"Yes," he said quietly. "It would matter to me."

She gazed at him, letting her eyes follow the harsh, chiseled profile of him, the sun-dark skin, the unreadable agate eyes. "It would? It would really matter to you?"

"Then they'd have the template stone," he said.

Her eyes flashed. "That's what I thought!"

"You are a burden I don't need," he explained simply. "Those people over there, they know we're on the way, and they know we have made it past their outer defenses. So they'll be looking for us. And I have things to do over there. I don't need extra problems."

"You sound as though you know what you're going to do."

"I do."

"What?"

"I'm going to stop them. That's what I came out here for."

She raised her head to stare at him, trying to look down her nose but still amazed at the arrogance of it. She opened her mouth, then closed it again. "I'm going," she said. "If you think I can't pull my own weight—"

He shrugged and stood, not looking at her, and she noticed that his gaze was now fixed on some point out in the rises toward Elk Peak . . . but not high up. Some

217

point not far away. She tried to follow his gaze, but saw nothing.

Without looking around he raised a hand in a quick signal, and a moment later the Apache was beside him. Wolf pointed. "There. Is that him?"

Dutchman squinted, shading his eyes. Then he nodded. "That's him. Closer than I thought."

Gail peered into the distance. "Who? Who do you see?"

Wolf ignored her. To the Apache he said, "You remember which of those horses the gunman was riding?"

"Yeah. The big black."

"Put a saddle on it, and saddle your own. Edge on out of here, downslope north, and get out of sight. In a little while you'll hear a shot. When you do, head for that ridge where you found the horses. Go halfway, and leave Mason's horse where he can find it."

"Why do you want him to have it back?"

"Because I need him mounted, not walking. Go."

Dutchman went. Still staring toward the west, trying to see what the Indians had seen out there, Gail asked, "What are you doing now? That Mason, is that one of those men after us? Why are you giving him that horse?"

"It's his horse," Wolf said. "I don't intend to give him one of ours."

Trooper came then, saddled and mounted, his carbine across his saddle and a sour look across his face. "All right, Wolf," he sighed. "What do you want me to do?"

Wolf pointed westward. "Do you see that jut of rock out there, Trooper? Half a mile, not much more . . . where the slope falls away to the right. See it?"

"I see it."

"All right. That Azteca that followed you . . . that's where he is. He's right under that jut, just waiting there. He'll be in plain sight when you top out on that first rise, and his horse is off to the left, not a hundred yards from him."

218

"Good. I'll go kill the stinkin' little—"

"No. You stay away from him. Don't get near him and don't let him get near you. Remember Cecil Cobb."

Trooper shuddered, remembering. "Then what in God's name do you want me to do, if I'm not supposed to kill him?"

"Kill his horse. One clean shot, kill it and head back here. Don't waste time."

Gail's face went pale and her mouth opened, but Trooper was already on his way. Standing beside Wolf, she watched him ride off down the first slope, disappear for a minute in the maze of gullies at the foot of it, then reappear, going up the far slope. She could see the jut of rock Wolf had pointed out, but if there was an Azteca there she could not see him. Minutes passed and Trooper diminished in the distance, a rider going away, approaching the top of the far slope. She watched, chewing her lip. Finally he topped the slope and stopped there. Slowly, then, they saw his carbine come up, saw his head go down to its sights, and saw the tiny jerk of his body as he fired. Then he reined around and spurred his mount to a long-strided run, downslope and coming back. He was well along before the hollow crack of the carbine came to them, backed up by echoes from the peaks around.

Gail let out a long-held breath. "He did," she whispered. "He went out there and shot that poor horse. No questions, you just told him to and he did." She whirled to Wolf. "Why, John Thomas? Why did you have him do that?"

Inscrutable eyes lowered to meet hers. "We're leaving here in a little while," he said. "Back there to the north, there is a very bad man without a horse. Over there, the way we're going, is a very bad Azteca with a horse. Now it's going to be the other way around."

"But why?"

"Because I don't want to have to fool with them," Wolf said. "I'll let them fool with each other. I have other things to do."

"You think . . . you think they'll kill each other?"

"Maybe. At least maybe we'll only have one of them behind us when we go, and not two."

XXII

Had there been neighboring haciendas for comparison, the *casa grande* at Rancho Cuautemoc would have been the showplace of showplaces. Even among the great houses of Mexico City, the sprawling mansion would have been noteworthy, and certainly nowhere north of San Luis Potosi or west of Coahuila and Zacatecas was there anything even remotely approaching it. Stone carried down from Sierra de la Madera formed its walls and the walls of its four courtyards, set in place with shell mortar from Bahja Kino and dressed with the white limestone of Tlaxcala. Red clay tiles from Nuevo Leon and blue clay tiles from Jalisco dressed its roofs, and the interior floors were of the finest Torreon slate.

How many Sonoran peones and Aconchi Indios had died in the construction and preparation of the hacienda was not known, nor was such of any real concern. For Hacienda Cuautemoc was the favored residence of Don Juan Ascencion Acuna, *patron* and *hidalgo,* whose holdings ranged from Chiapas to Michoacan, from Tamaulipas to Sonora and whose influence was felt from Guadalajara to Veracruz and even—very strongly—in Mexico City.

A scholarly man, some said of Don Juan Ascencion. A linguist, a student of pre-Conquistadorean Mexico and a patron of the sciences, he was considered by some to be a luminary among those who dabbled in archaeology and anthropology because of the excavations he had endowed, the expeditions he had sponsored into the remote regions.

A treasure hunter, others muttered under their breaths, recalling the controversy a few years before when the name of one of Don Juan Ascencion's imported scientists—Hall Kileen—had been linked with the abortive uprising of peones in the middle provinces . . . recalling also the bitter disputes that had raged over Don Juan Ascencion's proposal to raze a large portion of Mexico City so that he and his hirelings might dig there, seeking the lost Aztec treasure of Cortes. Some muttered still about such things, but not loudly. Don Juan Ascencion Acuna was a powerful and influential man.

Kukulki, he named himself. An affectation, of course, a source of amused winks among the fine folk of Mexico—an old Indian word that struck the great man's fancy. Kukulki. Few knew or cared what it meant, though among the Indios and the field peones throughout Mexico, most knew its meaning and none laughed about it. Kukulki meant Quetzalcoatl, and such a name was not to be taken lightly. Though centuries had passed since Cortes and Alvarado and the flood of bishops and priests that had followed them, Catholicism had never replaced the older, darker beliefs among the Indios, the Mestizos and others of the servant classes. It had only cloaked and hidden them. Quetzalcoatl would return, the legends said. Quetzalcoatl would return with his old enemy Huitzilopochtli on his shoulders, and Cem-Anahuac the one world would rise again, strong in the spirit of two gods become one. Cem-Anahuac would arise, and the one world would dominate the whole world forever.

The legends were powerful. Just as the night sky Mictaiu supported the birth each day of the sun Tonaiu, so would the god of darkness Quetzalcoatl support the rebirth of the sun god Huitzilopochtli. And the sign of the coming of these things would be seen in ancient Aztlan, where it all began.

To those who still celebrated the feast of the skulls along with All Saints' Day, and who still closed their

221

prayers at mass with the unsaid words, *Ayyo Tonaiu,* such thing were as certain as anything else in their world. They believed, and they waited, and the Spanish language still came grudgingly to their tongues.

Don Juan Ascencion Acuna named himself Kukulki, and among those who knew its meaning most were willing to believe . . . if the signs appeared. Yet some who had met him face to face had another private name for him as well. It may have come from his startling and intense red eyes with their black irises, or from the little forests of wooden crosses that grew above unimportant graves where his great works proceeded. The name was Diablo, and to the eyes of those who saw as much logic in welcoming the sun at morning as in fingering the beads on a rosary, Diablo and Kukulki were names that could be carried by the same person.

To those who had not been taught to distinguish between mysteries, all mysteries were equal.

Few outside of his own associates, though, had seen the man called Kukulki in recent times. For more than two years, Don Juan Ascencion had remained in the relative seclusion of Rancho Cuautemoc, coordinating the movements and the comings and goings of others in far places but seldom venturing out himself. It was accepted of a man of his station that he should employ others to represent him in those far-flung places where his interests lay, and he worked that acceptance to good measure. If those in Mexico City and Washington and the territorial capitals who dealt with his emissaries suspected that Don Juan Ascencion Acuna was a rich, eccentric Mexican and nothing more, it served his ends very well. If those outlaws and gunmen, those *pistoleros* of two nations who drew pay from his henchmen, never knew that Don Juan Ascencion Acuna existed, that was as it should be. And if a million or more peones and Indios scattered among the remote deserts and mountains were willing to believe that the old ways still could return, nothing suited him better. Kukulki did not trust

222

Hall Kileen, but he did trust the man's expertise. Kileen would find the Mask of Montezuma. And when he found it Kukulki would use it to gain that which he desired—control of a land area of more than eighty thousand square miles, an area that would be a private empire at his command.

Then it would be his turn. For so long he had gone to those in power and paid homage, to build his fortune and his base. When this was done, then they could come to him, and he would decide who would receive what, and what would be the price.

From the window of his great hall he looked out on a bleak and arid land which soon would blossom with spring rains. The window faced northward, and in the distance a tiny engine pulled tiny cars along the new rails that in appearance connected Nacosa to Nogales and the trade center at Tucson—that in fact connected holdings of Kukulki to the heart of the Arizona commercial routes. The railroad, the trains that ran on it and the ground it crossed belonged to him. One day soon it would be that railroad that would carry an army of neo-Aztecs northward to establish a new empire in old Aztlan.

In the nearer distance *vaqueros* were beginning the spring roundup on the upland shelves that were foothills of the Sierra Madres, and peones worked the fields down by the river, putting late corn into fields that had already produced a first crop of winter vegetables. The plodding workers and their animals were dwarfed by the shining new trestle that crossed the river and its floodway, a rail spur just now being completed, its glinting tracks leading directly to the long warehouses going up adjacent to the west courtyard wall of the hacienda. Kukulki's red eyes glistened as he gazed at those warehouses. Within a month there would be barracks covering the hundred acres beyond them, barracks all the way to the river. And by early summer those barracks would be full of men . . . men ready to ride north, to reclaim Aztlan in the name of Quetzalcoatl and Huitzilopochtli, to do what they and their ancestors had waited for centuries to do, and that only he, Kukulki, could lead them to do. On the bleak slopes of old Aztlan would arise the splendor of Mepitlan, the new empire. And he, Kukulki, would be its emperor.

Smiling, Kukulki strode across the great hall to the west windows, the better to see his preparations. At a glance, he could see a hundred men or more there, all working for him. Some were putting the roof on the main warehouse; ordinance and arms already purchased waited now in a dozen secret places in Mexico for shipment here as soon as that was done. Others, a dozen or more, were out beyond, setting final spikes and testing the switching gear on the new rail spur. It had been completed only two days ago. The Yanqui expeditor Don Ernesto was with them out there, his white hair glistening in the sun when he removed his hat, pacing up and down the last section of track, pointing at this, inspecting that . . . the man was a perfectionist, it seemed. Again, Kukulki smiled to himself. He could use more perfectionists.

It had been a stroke of fortune when Don Ernesto was referred to him. He gathered that the man had a shaded past, somewhere in the Estados Unidos del Norte. He didn't even know his full name. But the man knew how to get a task completed. Under his direct supervision, work on the spur had increased by half, and its completion time had been cut by a third. It was on that basis that Kukulki had set the man to one more task—the construction of ramparts on the northwest courtyard wall from which Kukulki's *pistoleros* could supervise the arrival and organization of his troops when the time was right. Nothing must be left to chance.

And already Don Ernesto had begun the work. Timbers and milled lumber were stacked beyond the wall, and planking, structures and nailed frames were stacked everywhere. At the moment only a dozen men were actually within the courtyard; he noted with satisfaction that his guards were in place and were watching them carefully. They were setting rails on ties, just as he had watched them do on the rail spur beyond the wall. It was Don Ernesto's suggestion that the wall ramparts should be mounted on rails so that they could be rolled into place above the wall when needed, then rolled back into the courtyard and into tall covered sheds when not in use.

"This is such a gracious *palacio*," the old man had said in his quiet manner, "it would be a shame for its elegance to be diminished by such mundane structure when it is not needed."

Thus sheds were being built against the wall of the great house itself, tall structures that would be trimmed and decorated to resemble appendages of the house. The rails between the sheds and the wall would be masked by plantings of flowering shrubs and would become simply part of the landscape.

A stroke of fortune, to have acquired Don Ernesto. Kukulki congratulated himself. The man was an engineer, an expeditor and a thoughtful planner. In the three months or less since his arrival at Rancho Cuautemoc, much had been achieved. And to top it off, he was interesting company for an occasional evening of wine and conversation. It was rare in these desolate lands of northern Mexico to find a guest who could converse intelligently—who could discuss the philosophies of Plato or Correon with equal skill, who could provide insightful comment upon the methods of Machiavelli, assess the significance of the emerging German state and recite Coleridge, all in one evening.

He expected to be paid handsomely, of course, for his work here. But then, considering what he had accomplished, his demands were not unreasonable. Not that he would receive them. Kukulki smiled. Unfortunately Don Ernesto now knew far too much about Kukulki's base of operations ever to be allowed to leave alive. But still, while he lived, he was a pleasure to have around.

Far in the distance, he watched the tiny train pass the flagged spur and creep on southward toward his marshaling yards on the main line at Hermosillo. He squinted. For a moment he had had an impression of a second train on the line, miles to the north. But hills intervened and he saw nothing. A trick of the light, he felt. There was no other train due today.

Beyond the courtyard wall, Don Ernesto had completed his inspection of the final tracks and was walking toward the house. He had guest quarters in the back apartments, on the ground floor off the small dining room.

Kukulki walked to a table and lifted a silver bell, rang it briefly and set it down. An instant later a side door set into the walnut paneling opened silently, and a servant was there.

"Send my respects to Don Ernesto," Kukulki said. "When he has refreshed himself I shall be in the small dining room. He will join me for a glass of wine."

"*Sí, Patrón.*" The servant closed the door and was gone. Kukulki went back to the window, standing close to look down at the clutter in the northwest courtyard. A shame that the small dining room has no windows, he thought. We would be able to look directly out at the work being done on the rampart sheds.

Possibly Don Ernesto would have a suggestion for the opening of that wall, when his construction was done.

Kukulki waited a full hour before retiring downstairs. He was met by a servant in the central hall, who bowed and scurried across to open the door to the small dining room for him. He entered and the door was closed behind him. Wine and glasses had been set out on a serving bar, with his preferred chair in its usual place, its back to the solid outside wall so that he could face the door and the northside windows. A second easy chair had been set in place a modest distance away; his servants had been carefully trained, and lived in fear of him, which was how he wanted it to be.

He frowned heavily when he looked around the room. He was alone. It had been his intention to keep Don

226

Ernesto waiting for a time, as was his custom. It was presumptuous of his guest to allow it to be otherwise.

But then there was a quiet tap at the side door, and Don Ernesto entered. "Good afternoon, *Patron*," he said. "Thank you for inviting me. I believe this will be a most entertaining hour."

Kukulki tipped his head, peering at the man. He did not look quite as he had before. His clothing . . . his manner . . . something was different. Instead of the threadbare tweed and rumpled pants he usually wore, Don Ernesto now wore a tailored suit of fine dove-gray material, spotless linen shirt and elegant black boots. He even carried a hat—a fine beaver felt in black with a flat crown and elegantly swept brim.

But it was more than the clothing. Something in his stance, his walk, the way he held his features—it was as though the shabby old expatriate had fallen away and in his place stood a lithe, virile man whose advancing years were only a badge and not a burden.

Don Ernesto raised a brow, almost a mocking thing, but not quite . . . nothing Kukulki could put a finger on. "Have I surprised you, *Patron?* I do hope you are not upset."

"Not at all." Kukulki shook his head and crossed to the serving bar. "But those clothes . . . I had not seen them before. I had no idea you had lived so well."

"Traveling clothes," Don Ernesto said. "I thought it a good idea to give them some use."

"Yes, of course." As was his custom, Kukulki poured their drinks. It was an old habit, from times when he had been less sure of those around him. He handed a glass to Don Ernesto, who had placed his black hat on the dining table beside.

Why does he carry his hat? Kukulki wondered. Is it to complete the costume? Does he try to impress me?

Kukulki crossed to his favored chair and sat, then waved a casual hand to Don Ernesto to be seated. "The work goes well, Don Ernesto," he said. "You have ex-

227

ceeded my expectations."

"I shall exceed them again, *Patrón*, I assure you." The man sat and sipped at his wine, then touched a tongue to his lips. "Ah, *Patron*, no one can question your good taste. Vintage Chevignon."

"I am glad you approve," Kukulki said, a bit sourly. What was the man doing? He seemed quite forward, as though he had forgotten his station in this house. He shrugged it off. "Well, Don Ernesto, what shall it be this evening? Philosophy? Military strategy? Poetry? What would you prefer?"

Don Ernesto regarded him for a long moment with eyes that Kukulki had not noticed before—eyes as level and gray as pond ice, so cold that they seemed to burn him with their intensity. Their surveillance made him want to look away . . . to squirm. "I think I would prefer to discuss history this evening."

"History?" Kukulki blinked. "What kind of history?"

"An interesting kind. The history of oblivion."

"What do you mean by that?"

"It is rather a favorite of mine," Don Ernesto said. His voice was a purr. "A specialized field of history. The history of those grand schemes that never came to pass and those great events that never happened. Have you never considered the subject, *Señor Acuna?* That is surprising, considering that you have just become part of the subject."

"I . . . *what?*" Kukulki surged to his feet. "Have you gone mad, Don Ernesto? I will not stand for such talk." He stepped to the table, picked up his bell and rang it strenuously.

Don Ernesto sipped at his wine, his gray eyes level and aglow with a cold fire. A moment passed and he clicked his tongue, as though in sympathy. And now Kukulki saw something he had not seen before. Where Don Ernesto's coat was parted at the waist was a hint of dark wood and metal. He was carrying a pistol. Kukulki rang the bell desperately.

The silence that followed went on and on. Then Don Ernesto said, "Sit down, Kukulki. No one is coming."

Kukulki glared at him, then strode across to the door. He tried its latch, could not open it, and pounded on it with his fist. Don Ernesto sat quietly, watching him. Kukulki crossed again, to the rock wall behind his chair, and tugged at a satin strap. It came loose at his pull and fell to the floor.

"I told you no one is coming ... *Kukulki*," Don Ernesto said. He pulled a watch from his vest pocket and glanced at it, then closed it and put it away. "Your interest in rails is most appropriate, you know. The railroads have changed history in many ways. I think the changes will continue, don't you?"

"I don't know what you're talking about!" Kukulki whirled on him. "If you think you can—"

"Why, I am talking about history," Don Ernesto said quietly. Then his voice became suddenly commanding. "I said sit down, Kukulki! Now!"

Kukulki sat.

"Not so many years ago," Don Ernesto said, again quietly conversational, "there was a man who set out to split a nation apart for his own purposes. You've never heard of him, but his name was Manchester. He lived in Boston. That man amassed a great deal of wealth and power, Kukulki. Then he decided he wanted more. He had a different idea of how the country should be apportioned, and his idea was that he could split it down the middle, separate the east and the west, and wind up a sort of king when the dust settled. Does any of that sound familiar to you, Kukulki?"

"You are a madman. I don't know what you're talking about."

"Of course, you've never heard of Anthony Manchester, because everything he tried—everything he did, the whole magnificent, glorious scheme—just didn't happen. Do you understand, Kukulki? That's what I mean by oblivion. Anthony Manchester manipulated a government, an economic system, the industry of a nation and millions of people. But everything he did came to nothing. As far as history is concerned, Anthony Manchester never existed at all. Appropriate, don't you think?"

Kukulki writhed and fidgeted, his red eyes glaring at the other man with pure, malevolent fury. And in the quiet of the walled room, somewhere in the distance, he thought he heard a rail engine, its pistons throbbing, its iron wheels clicking steadily on polished rails.

"Then there was a man named Adolphus Meers," Don Ernesto said. "You might have heard his name. He had quite a reputation before he decided to become an empire shifter. A really nasty man, Kukulki. You would have liked him, I think. I'm sure it seemed to him and his partners that their plan—they had a nice, inoffensive name for it, the 'Mississippi Combine'—was just on the verge of succeeding. If it had, of course, the United Staes Civil War would have been much earlier, much bloodier, and would have ended without any particular victor . . . except themselves. But you don't know about any of that, because it never happened, Kukulki. It came to nothing whatever. So much nothing, that not a handful of people in the world have ever known what they tried to do. And that's just as well. History is tidier if it isn't cluttered with the grand notions of overblown conquerors who failed."

Kukulki's eyes wandered to the drawer of the lampstand at his side, and his fingers twitched.

"It isn't there, Kukulki," Don Ernesto assured him. "There is no gun in that drawer." Again he looked at his watch and put it away. The faint sound of iron wheels had grown in volume, but still was muffled by the walls.

"There have been so many such incidents," Don Ernesto said, "that one wonders why an intelligent man like yourself has never questioned what happened to the ones who failed. Your little primitives, for example . . . your Tenochca, from the jungles. In a generation, none of them will remember what you tried to use them for. Hadn't you ever considered that? You were never their Quetzalcoatl, Kukulki. It has been unkind of you to ever let them think you were."

"Who are you?" Kukulki sputtered. "I don't know what you want of me!"

"I think you might have heard of me, Kukulki." The quiet voice now was as cold as the burning gray eyes. Casually, Don Ernesto arose, strode across to the dining table and picked up his hat. "When you sent your clever message to be painted on a wall in Springfield, it was my blood you thought would paint it. That was unfortunate for the Tenochca you assigned to collect the . . . what is the word? Ah . . . *chalchinatl*. Yes. You see, it was that priest's own blood that went to make the painting, and the message you worked so carefully on . . . well, I added a stroke or two of my own. It probably is achieving its purpose about now. What do I want of you, Kukulki? Nothing at all. You never existed. As to who I am, well, some poetic souls have called me Nemesis. But my name is Kichener. Ernest Kichener."

The sound of a thundering engine was a roar now, a thunder that shook the walls of the solid room. Kichener put on his hat. "Good-bye, Kukulki," he said. "A few of us will remember you. But not many, and none for very long."

The engine that raced down the spur track was unoccupied by the time it reached the border of Rancho Cuautemoc's *casa* grounds, but its boilers were pressured, its coal box was full, and its throttle was open all the way. The northwest courtyard wall exploded as it thundered through, clacking from spur track to garden track without a shudder, to slam into the windowless wall of the small dining room of the grand house.

When *vaqueros* came in from the high pastures to see what had happened, they found the house virtually destroyed. The rogue engine had gone all the way through, finally blowing its boilers on the far side of the house. On the grounds outside they found six dead guards, but no one else. The field hands were gone. The servants were gone. Everyone was gone, except one. Digging through the rubble, they found what was left of the man who called himself Kukulki. It took a long time to determine who he was, but then someone found his head in the east garden, half-hidden by the wreckage of the engine. The face was still recognizable, and the red-black eyes were wide open and staring.

They searched through another day, but there was no one else there.

XXIII

On a day when warm southwest breezes thawed the winter deserts and brought high banks of clouds to stand above the shrinking snowcaps to the west, Diego Torreon—trim in frock coat, belled britches and riding boots—stood on the boardwalk outside the *oficina de telegrafo* at Paso Portales, thumbed back his hat from above heavy brows and smoked a cheroot while he waited for his guest to complete his business inside. People strolling the walks and streets in the warm sun glanced at him as he stood there, and some of the glances lingered. Yet none of them were likely to know him. They noticed only a well-tailored, oddly striking *caballero* whose years were betrayed only by the streaks of gray at his temples . . . and possibly by the cold steadiness of dark eyes that seemed to see everything and say nothing.

It had been pleasant, this small time of working together with his American counterpart—the description brought a slight tug to his lips, a faint pleasure at comparing himself to the little-known yet almost legendary *Halcón* from across the border. Only three times in all the years that each had served his own interests by serving those of their separate countries had they actually met, and Torreon thought with ironic amusement how nearly—each of those times—they had come to being on opposite sides. And what a shame that would have been, for only one would have survived any such encounter . . . and he was not at all sure it would have been him. Though the *Norteamericano* was older by many years—sixty-five years old, Torreon's private records said—the years meant nothing. Rarely was there such a one . . . and what a blessing that there were never more than a few such. A few were more than enough. Ernest Kichener . . . Diego Torreon . . . possibly the man Jean-Claude Duval whose name had filtered down from Canada. . . . Anything more than a very few such would be far too many.

Still, from hints that Kichener had made in these months they had worked together to—as Kichener put it—clip the serpent's wings, Torreon gathered that there was at least one more, and that that one also was at work, somewhere to the north. Something related to the business here in Mexico. Wolf, Kichener had said. But was that a name or a symbol? Their work lent itself to symbols and dramatic appellations. Torreon himself had been called Tarantela in those small circles where he was discussed at all, and he knew that Kichener often was referred to as Hawk. Was this Wolf, then, another *nom de guerre?* Quite possibly. But Torreon had promised himself that he would investigate when this business was done. It was well to know who else was out there, just in case they should someday meet.

The door opened behind him and Kichener stepped out, snugging his hat down over ice-gray eyes.

"It is done?" Torreon asked.

"It will be. Detail work back east. But I know some people who are very good at detail work. And on their behalf and my own, Diego, I thank you for your assistance."

"It was a pleasure. As I told you, I had a score of my own with Señor Acuna. You offered me a means to settle it. Ah . . ." He grinned. "Such marvelous inventions, railroads. Not often suited to purposes such as ours, though. Too expensive."

"I rather enjoy allowing the . . . ah . . . client to finance his own retribution. In this case it was expedient. And satisfying. The sort of thing Wolf might have conceived."

Torreon raised a dark brow. He would not press, but he was curious. "This Wolf, he is another, like us?"

"Of course. We can't live forever, my friend."

"Ah. I see. The hawk has a protégé. One day I will have to consider such, as well. God help us if we die and leave it to the *politicos* to replace us by appointment, *sí?*"

"*Sí.*"

"Will you go south with me now, to Mexico City? There is still much to do before Kukulki is once and for all erased."

"There is much to do in both our countries. No, I have other places to go, on business similar to yours, Diego."

"Then we part again here," Torreon said, nodding his acceptance. "One question, though, Ernesto—how does a hawk keep a wolf on the string?"

Kichener glanced at him, faint amusement in his eyes. "What would a *tarantela* want to keep on a string, Diego?"

"Only a little bird, Ernesto. Though maybe not so frail a bird as it might seem."

"Then you already have a candidate in mind."

"*Quien sabe?*" Torreon spread his hands. "A bird is thrown from its nest, one waits to see if it can fly."

"But you need a string. Yes, I have a string on my wolf. He thinks I gave him his life."

"And did you?"

The gray eyes shone with humor. "If he thinks so, what else matters?" He held out a hand. "*Adios*, Diego

Torreon, until another time."

On a snow-clad trail in the high reaches of the San Francisco Mountains, where high timberline was near at hand on the peaks and spires, they came up from Black Elk Saddle to where a sprawl of tumbled lands lay before them. Escudilla Peak stood white-topped to the north, towering above its cousins, and nearer at hand, ahead, lay the treacherous reaches of Mapletop. Beyond, the vast distances rolled away across a world of steeps and gashes, a crazy terrain that had built itself, all blindly, without any help from the Almighty.

Willie dismounted and stood, a gnarled hand atop his hatbrim to give him more shade for his old eyes, then he pointed. "You come lookin' for Arizona, Wolf. Well, there she is. Ain't she somethin'?" He walked forward a few steps, and when Dog paced alongside him, he waved the huge animal back. "We got to do this right, Dog. Now you just wait a minute."

"Crazy old coot," Trooper rumbled absently, then turned to look back over his shoulder. He had been doing that since the day Wolf had had him kill the little Azteca's horse. Sometimes he seemed like a man haunted.

"Varmint," Willie muttered, not looking around. Then he removed his hat and held it at his breast. "This here bein' the fifteenth day of March, eighteen hundred an' . . . what year is this, again?"

"Eighty-seven," Gail said, fascinated.

"Eight-six, isn't it?" Shanty squinted his eyes in thought, then nodded. "That was last year. It's eighty-seven."

Willie glanced around at them, perturbed, then returned to his ceremony. "This here bein' the thirteenth day of—"

"Fifteenth," Shanty suggested.

"What?"

235

"A minute ago you said it was the fifteenth."

"Well, if that's what I said, then that's what it is. This here bein' th' fifteenth day of March, eighteen hundred an' eighty-seven, I do hereby cross from New Mexico Territory—God save its soul—to Arizona Territory which ain't got one to worry about. God never had nothin' to do with Arizona." He took a long step, across an invisible line, and put his hat back on his head. Getting a boot into his stirrup, he swung monkeylike into his saddle, then looked back, past the lagging Trooper. "I think that varmint's right, Wolf," he said. "There *is* somebody back yonder."

"How many?" Gail shaded her eyes, looking back.

"One, I reckon, but I keep thinkin' he's there, so he must be."

"That's what I've been thinkin' too," Trooper snorted.

"What varmints think don't count," Willie proclaimed coolly.

Neither Wolf nor the Dutchman looked back. They knew what was behind them.

"Three People and your father are there," Dutchman told the girl, pointing southwestward. "Eagle Springs. Maybe sixty miles."

"Be sixty miles if this was God-fearin' level country," Willie said. "Prob'ly more like a hundred, busted up like it is."

"Sixty miles," Dutchman repeated, and led the way.

Throughout the long days, across long miles of rugged high country, Wolf had quizzed various among them at each resting, and Gail Larkin had made it her business to listen to as much as he would let her hear . . . and to do some quizzing on her own to fill in the blanks. She had seen parts of Arizona before, with her father on a long-ago expedition to study Anasazi ruins up in the plateau country between the Puerco and Little Colorado rivers. Now from Windwagon Willie she renewed old memories of locales, terrains and distances, and from the Dutch-

236

man she dragged details of the area where her father had thought he would find the ruins of old Aztlan. She had no doubt that the double valley Willie had seen, its silhouette matching the template stone her father had found, was the location. And she suspected that Wolf knew—or had deduced—something further about exactly where to find the sun god mask, though he would say no more about it. But she was sure it had to do with the template stone, and she searched her memory to see the little flat artifact again . . . a rectangle with rounded corners, the inscribed winding cut nearly from end to end, which could in fact be a landscape in silhouette, and the little sun-sign that she had always thought should be in the sky over mountains—if it were in fact a silhouette template—but which Wolf saw as symbolic of a place past and therefore below the horizon . . . thus below double valleys as the stone would show it.

And in the center of the sun-sign, a tiny hole like a pinhole entirely through the stone. Hardly noticeable, except that it was centered in the symbol. She had thought about mentioning that to Wolf when she finally recalled it. But he had been behaving in a particularly close-lipped and arrogant manner just then, and she had kept it to herself. Let him notice such details on his own, she decided. He's so damned much the expert here, let him see it for himself.

Like the whorls and patterns on the face of the stone— flat agate, she thought it had been, or a patterned flint— the pinhole might mean something or it might be just a characteristic of the little slab of rock on which the old message had been cut.

But she listened, and she questioned, and details came clear in her mind. The place where her father was waiting was a high valley between cliffs, in the rugged, rolling lands just below the Mogollon rim, in that area where the plateau swelled upward toward the White Mountain Range. Well within what the government had designated as the San Carlos Reservation. Three People—she

237

recalled the bizarre Englishman with the Indian name fondly—had friends there among the Apache and their occasional Zuni trader guests. It was as safe a hiding place as any he might have found in the vicinity of Hall Kileen's operations.

Kileen, she learned, was working from an abandoned ranch at Haunted Butte, a short day's ride from where Larkin waited. And Haunted Butte, by Willie's description, was the prominence from which the silhouette of the double valley matched the incised wiggly line on the template stone.

Between the Apache valley and the base at Haunted Butte, both Willie and the Dutchman described terrain that was wild and precipitous, a thirty-mile-wide expanse of peaks and breaks, gorges and canyons, cliffs and pinnacles cut through by a sand-bottom gorge where a little stream flowed down from high springs to join a tumbling, narrow river that flowed eventually into the Gila, down where the deserts began.

Ahead of them now, within the range of this day's ride, was the cloven far slope of Mapletop, and there the trails forked—west toward the Apache valley in the White Mountains; southwest toward Haunted Butte. By morning they would be on one or the other. More and more through the long days, John Thomas had kept his thoughts to himself, and each evening she had noticed his concentration. Sometimes he paced; sometimes he drew elaborate designs in sand, then studied them, wiped them out and drew them again. But he said little to the rest of them, except occasional questions put to Willie or Dutchman, and she noticed how Shanty and Trooper— who knew him better, or at least longer, than the rest— stayed apart from him and left him to his thoughts. For a time she did, too. Then her patience wore thin.

Now she caught up to him on the trail and paced her horse alongside his. "I want some answers," she stated.

He glanced aside at her, his eyes distant and cold.

"I mean now," she said. "I want to know where we're

going and what you have in mind when we get there."

"We're going where you wanted to go," he said. "I'm taking you to your father."

"Fine. Then what?"

"He's safe where he is, Dutchman says. You'll be safe there, too, if you can behave yourself."

"We're going to stay there?"

"You are. I have other things to do."

"What other things?"

"What I came for. You don't need to know any more about it."

"Damn you, John Thomas," she spat. "You owe me more than that."

"I owe you? Why?"

"Because I came to you for help. Because if it weren't for me you wouldn't even know where to look out there or who to look for . . . to do what you came to do. Do you think I don't know why you're out here? And about those people you work for, and—"

"I don't work for anybody. I do things on my own."

"Of course. But what you do on your own you do for them. Do you think I can't deduce from what I see and hear? Do you really think I believe that place in Springfield is just a residence? I found it, remember? I followed you there, *Mister Hide-and-Seek,* and you never even knew you were being followed. What gives you the arrogance to assume you're the only one who can sort things out?"

A wry grin tipped the corners of his mouth. "You *did* pay for lessons, didn't you? All right. Your old friend Hall Kileen has got himself mixed up with some very nasty people, and he's out there trying to find Montezuma's mask. You said he almost started a revolution one time. Well, if he gets his hands on that mask, this time there won't be any 'almost' about it. The reason I'm out here is to stop him."

"I know all that. What else?"

"What else?"

239

"You have something more in mind than to stop Kileen. What is it?"

"To make sure that what he's trying to do can't ever be done again."

She thought about it, and paled. "The mask? You intend to destroy the mask, don't you! You can't do that, John Thomas. That artifact is priceless. My father has spent years just to get on the track of it. Why, just *finding* it will resolve most of the questions about Aztlan . . . and the mask itself, imagine what can be learned from that! About the Aztecs, where they came from, why they were like they were . . . maybe we can even learn something about the Toltecs from it. Don't you see—?"

"Don't *you* see?" His voice was harsh, almost a growl. "You've seen the Aztecas, Gail. Think about them. They're nothing but a handful of primitive fanatics. Tragic little anachronisms who believe the sun god will come back and give them glory. But imagine millions of true believers like them, armed and set loose by some madman somewhere. *That's* what the Montezuma mask is all about, Gail. 'Those people,' as you call them, are convinced that it would be best if the mask is never found. *Never*. And I happen to agree. That's why I'm out here."

She stared at him. "You are going to decide history single-handed? You're going to be the ultimate judge of what all the rest of us can and can't do with a precious artifact? But that . . . that makes you worse than *them*, John Thomas!"

"Did I ever say I wasn't?"

She raised a stubborn chin. "Well, you won't get it, then. Kileen might or might not find it, eventually. But you don't have a bloody army to dig around for you. You'll never find it without my help."

He smiled again. "I take it there's something about the template stone that you forgot to tell me when you described it."

She clenched her jaws, not looking at him.

240

"I assume there is a second opening in the stone, besides the horizon line."

How did he know? Still she said nothing.

"There has to be, of course," he continued. "Those people didn't go to all that trouble just to memorize a horizon. That stone is meant to pinpoint a particular place that they didn't want to forget . . . not a valley, but a precise point in that valley. Maybe a cave opening, or a volcanic shaft. As I see it, the stone is a sight to show where that exact point is. And I suspect the second hole in it is a pinhole, probably right in the middle of that inscribed sun-sign."

She sighed. "All right. You have deductive reasoning. But you still won't find it without the stone itself."

"Your father has the stone."

"But you don't. And you won't get it."

"Yes, I will. Otherwise your father won't get you. You keep forgetting your own revelations, Gail. I am *not* civilized."

She sighed and turned away, truly hating the Indian beside her. And yet, over and over, a tiny thing rang in her mind, a thing significant all by itself. It was the first time John Thomas Wolf had called her by her given name.

When the sun stood low ahead of them, pressing its shield into the glowing tumble of tall clouds that stood far off beyond the mountains, Wolf guided them off the winding trail and up a bare slope to where a wind-carved rock spire jutted upward, a great stone sentinel standing alone, its top visible for miles.

"We make camp here," he said.

The others gazed around them in confusion. It was a poor place to stop, exposed to view, unsheltered except for the single rock spire, not even good graze for the animals, although there was vegetation above and what might be a spring-fed tank.

"We could make a few more miles," Dutchman said. "It's still early."

241

Wolf looked at the sun, sitting atop the distant clouds. "We stop here," he said. Then he turned. "Shanty, have you been practicing your songs?"

"I remember a couple of them, Wolf, but I sure never was any kind of a singer."

"It doesn't matter, as long as you're loud. How's your arm?"

"All healed over. No problem."

"All right. I want you to climb up there and stand on top of that spire. Right up on top. And when you're there, you face the sun and spread your arms out and sing."

Shanty gawked at him.

"Just do it," Wolf said. "Get up there and sing and don't stop until you can't see the sun anymore."

XXIV

That Injun . . . that Wolf . . . John Thomas Wolf . . . I'll kill that son of a bitch when I find him . . . the thoughts were curses, whisper-curses that went around and around in a dull fury as Bull Mason pulled himself up the sheer face of a cold mountain. Handhold . . . pull. Toehold . . . push. Spread and cling. Handhold . . . pull. He concentrated and climbed. Kill that Injun son of a bitch. Find him and kill him.

He didn't think about the Azteca. Stupid, stinking little savage, all he had done was exactly what that Wolf had set him up to do. It was Wolf's fault. Bull climbed and his fury pushed him onward.

Just lucky to be alive, he knew. Just lucky the wind had shifted like it did in that little canyon . . . lucky he had seen how the Aztecas worked before . . . lucky he had thrown himself clear just as the Azteca came from the shadows with that damnable black knife, striking like a snake strikes ... lucky to have had that rolled blanket over his shoulder to take the cut. He had bled a little, from the nick on his chest right at his breastbone and the glancing cut on his shoulder, and was bruised from falling and rolling down that rocky incline. Lucky, though, that he *had* rolled. Had he stopped, the Azteca would have struck again. Hadn't even got his gun out. There had been no time ... no time at all. Stinking little spider had been all over him, just like that ... all over him, striking with that black blade, then taken his horse and was gone.

That was what it was all about. The horse. Wolf had set it up that way. When he got on his feet and backtracked, he had seen it all. Killed the Azteca's horse, left one for Mason, so the Azteca had come for *him*.

Now he was afoot in these mountains, and the Azteca had gone with his horse ... gone on, following ... following as he always did. Stinking little blood-bather. All that Injun's fault. Find that Injun and kill him. Handhold and toehold. Pull, push ... climb. One thing a man afoot had going for him in these mountains. He didn't have to follow the trails. If he could climb and knew the land, he could cut straight across. And Bull knew the land. He had holed up in these mountains before. The trails wound and curved and cut back and around, with the rise and fall of the steeps. But he knew where they went. Handhold and toehold. Pull, push. Climb. Know where the son of a bitch Injun is going. Volcano valley below Mogollon. Seen it. Krell said enough to know where. Climb.

Ayyo, Tonaiu, gift of the god. *Ayya, Huitzilopochtli,* was it your wish that the Bulmesson once more postpone his dying? Your servant offered his *chalchinatl* as the signs decreed ... yet your *tonaiu* sprang too quickly into the sky. Its brilliance reflected on bright stone dazzled these eyes, made this hand to miss its mark. You gave

Bulmesson another day of living, and gave to me your *Taltzi* this animal so that I can follow those ahead. It must therefore be your wish that it be so. *Ayya, Huit-zilopochtli. Ayyo, Tonaiu. Nocipa.*

Through the long, hard days and the long, cold nights Tactli clung to the trail of the people moving westward. Frostbite was a constant torture in his feet and the fingers of his left hand, and he suffered constantly from hunger, although he had sometimes found food. But these things did not matter. He alone, of all those who had begun the journey, remained now to follow those the high priest Xochitli-Miqui had described. Possibly he, Tactli, *had* been selected by Huitzilopochtli to prolong his dying long enough to witness with these eyes in this world the ascension of the waiting gods.

The legend was coming to the fullness of its time. Mictlan and Tonaiutlan together for the first time . . . Quetzalcoatl with the face of Huitzilopochtli . . . Aztlan revived! Aztlan and Cem-Anahuac the one world that would become the whole world. Just as Huitzilopochtli had promised his chosen people the Mexíca . . . just as the Mexíca had passed along that promise to the Tenochca with the teaching of their ways. Generations beyond counting ago, yet never had their *Taltzin* doubted, and now it was to be true.

Even in this desolate, frozen place, this country where nothing of value could grow and the air was hard to breathe and a cold like nothing Tactli or any of his people had known made toes and fingers begin to die . . . even in this alien land, his fervor warmed him and gave him strength. *Ayyo, Tonaiu!* With Tonaiu in his eyes he rode on, holding to the signs of passage of those not far ahead.

High clouds beyond far mountains said that this day's *tonaiu* would die alone, beyond the view of those who might sustain its strength, but in this season—even far to the south where Tactli's accustomed places were—such was not uncommon. It was only that a *tonaui* sinking behind clouds before its dying should have encouragement to fortify it for its lonely journey down to death. Otherwise there was always the fear that the new *tonaiu* born after *mictlix* and the dark hours might be feeble. Tactli felt concern as the sun edged down toward the distant clouds. He was alone now and had only his one voice to chant to the vanishing *tonaiu*. Malinali was gone. So were Tequatl and Sontec . . . the winds had told him that. And Yaoli, Chimecat and Huexotl, all dead now at the bidding of Huitzilopochtli. Only Tactli of all those who went out had not been so honored. Only his voice remained in these angry lands, to guide the cloud-threatened *tonaiu* to a strong and flowery death. He remembered when it had seemed that the large pale man had spoken to Tonaiu, but he was sure now that had been only an appearance. The pale ones knew nothing of the gods or their ways. Tactli saw a crest ahead where he would be able to see Tonaiu clearly, and Tonaiu also to see him. He would sing to the sun with his single voice. It was the best he could do. And if tomorrow's sun was weak, then he would overtake the ones ahead and collect as many hearts as he could for rich blood to offer to Huitzilopochtli.

He topped out on the crest and started to dismount, then stopped, staring ahead in amazement. For there, just beyond the swell of a rising slope, rose a high natural pedestal of stone. And atop the pedestal a thickset man with flowing red whiskers alive in the wind, his arms outspread, bellowed a chanting lyric toward the dying sun. Even here, Tactli could hear the voice. Not the words, but the voice, and this time there was no question. It was a chant. It was a sacred song. The big outlander was singing encouragement to Tonaiu, and Tactli knew that Tonaiu responded. It was no weak and supine sun that sank into its bed of cloud off beyond the mountains, but a sun full of vigor, ready to fight to the last upon entry into Mictlan. A glorious sun to die a glorious death and send forth the seed for a strong and vigorous sun tomorrow.

In his stunned awe, Tactli did not even think of adding

his own poor chant to that ringing bellow from the man atop the pinnacle. He simply watched, listened and felt a thrill of promise.

Quetzalcoatl, encouraging Tonaiu. A tall, red-bearded man, as much an omen of the gathering of night as though he had been a winged serpent, he was allying himself with the sun.

It had been foretold. Now Tactli watched in wonder as the first part of the legend began to unfold.

"Did you see him?" Wolf asked the Dutchman as shadows closed over the top of the spire and Shanty stopped his hollering and started down.

"Plain as day," the Apache said. "Right back there on that ridge. Tenochca on a horse. Looked like somebody had stole his teeth, too. Or like he'd swallowed them."

"He thinks he's seen Quetzalcoatl," Gail said, glaring at Wolf. "You're not even going to tell Shanty what that means, are you?"

"I'll tell him the Azteca will be following him now."

"And will you tell him what that little fanatic will do when he finds out Shanty *isn't* his god of night?"

"Trooper has seen what the Aztecas can do. He'll know what to watch for." Wolf scanned the ridge east of them. The sun was gone now, behind standing clouds, its last rays climbing away up the slopes of Mapletop to flare and glisten on the snows up there. The Tenochca had been on the ridge, watching, and the horse he had been on was the same one they had left for Bull Mason. Wolf nodded grimly. So far, so good. No one was in sight now on the ridge, but he hadn't expected to see him again when the sun was gone.

"Trooper," he called, "you and the Dutchman can take the horses up to that water. Then bring them back and close-herd for the night. We're camping right here. No fires after dark. Dutchman and I will share the watch. The rest of you get plenty of sleep. Tomorrow comes early."

Shanty had come down from the spire, brushing himself off and grinning through his whiskers. "I told you I couldn't sing," he told Wolf. "My dear grandmother in County Cork is turning over in her grave right now at what I've just done to *Down to Dublin Town*."

"Well, she'd better get used to it. You've got it to do four more times."

"I have?"

Gail had wandered close to listen, and Wolf sent her away with a look. Then he said, "First thing in the morning, you go up there again. Be there at dawn. Face east, and as soon as you see the sun you start singing. Loud as you can. Keep at it until the whole sun is above that ridge."

"You sound like you won't be here."

"I won't. But there's an Azteca back there, and I want him to think you're a god or something. You convince him and keep him convinced. I want him to follow you."

"Where am I going?"

"You'll come to a fork. Take the left trail. Tomorrow night and the next morning, find another high place and give your grandmother conniptions. Then go on, and do it again next sundown. I think that should do it."

"Okay, then what?"

"Then you break trail." He squatted on the sandy slope, and Shanty squatted beside him. With a knife point Wolf drew a map. "Trooper goes with you, and Willie. There's a double valley . . . about here. Two high mountain peaks this side of it, you'll go between. Let Willie make trail. He knows the way. Have Trooper circle back when you can. He can make sure that Azteca is following you. Second evening out you should be almost in sight of the valley. Sing for your trailer one more time if you can do it safely. Then break trail. You figure out how; but I want you to lose that Azteca right there, so he'll go on down to that valley. Aim toward the south end of it, place called Haunted Butte. That's where I want him to go. But not you. You and the others hole up. Keep an eye on that place if you can, see what you can see, but don't be seen. You wait there. I'll be along eventually."

"All right, Wolf." Shanty nodded. "Where are you going?"

Faint sounds came from the tank above, where Dutchman had taken a pair of horses. Trooper was coming downslope with a watered pair. Wolf glanced up the slope, then back at his drawn map. Casually he wiped it out with a hard hand.

"That girl," Shanty said. "You better keep an eye on her. She's slick as a gambler's fingers when she wants to be. And she isn't happy about any of this. I can tell. I've been watching her."

"I know," Wolf said. "In the morning, you and Willie pull out. Let Trooper hold back out of the way with the extra horses. Once that Azteca has passed, he can turn them loose. We won't need them again. Drop the saddles and gear in a gully someplace. Trooper can circle around and catch up with you before you get to the fork. Got it?"

"I've got it, Wolf. But listen, what I said about that girl, I'm serious. She's quick, and she's smart—"

"And she's gone," Wolf finished for him.

"What?" Shanty stood and looked around. The Indian was right. There was no sign of Gail Larkin. She had disappeared. "Where'd she go? She was right here just a—"

Wolf picked up a saddle and started toward where Trooper was corraling the stock. Shanty paced alongside him, perplexed.

"I have to find her father," Wolf said. "He has something I need."

"Yeah, but Dutchman knows where—" Shanty broke off again, looking up toward the tank.

"Yes, he's gone too, Shanty. Dutchman's Larkin's man, not mine. He and Gail weren't going to take me to her father. Not unless I'd do things their way. But this

248

way they'll take me there." He picked out a horse, slipped a headstall on it, then tossed his saddle aboard. "Trooper, bring my gear," he said.

Trooper brought his saddlebags, bedroll and tie-ons. Wolf stowed everything in its place, glanced at the evening banners above the western clouds, and swung aboard. "You know what to do, Shanty," he said. "I'll be along."

As he rode out, Willie looked up from where he had their supper boiling in a pot. "Where's he off to now?" he asked.

"He's off to where he intends to go," Shanty mused. "That's Wolf. He wants to do things one way, and folks set out to do them another way, they all wind up doing it Wolf's way anyway."

Someone had sabotaged telegraph lines north from Cuautemoc, and certain vandalisms had disrupted communication from Nogales to Tucson in the wake of the army's withdrawal from the Geronimo campaigns. Thus some time had passed before news of the death of Don Juan Ascencion Acuna made its way into the mountains and finally to Hall Kileen. The message was vague as to what had happened to Kukulki, but this much of it was clear: Kileen no longer had a partner in Mexico. It would have been shattering news had Kileen not from time to time harbored thoughts of how to cause such an event himself. But he had, and so had ready ideas on how to adjust the operation at his end.

Kileen had never shared Kukulki's grandiose notions about carving out empires and the like. Such schemes, he felt, were bulky and clumsy and slow to pay profits. Better simply to establish nuisance value, and then to collect on it. Such had been his original idea anyway, before Acuna had come along with his money, his influence and connections—all too good to pass up, of course—and his somewhat different ideas about what

249

could be accomplished by starting an uprising among primitive and fiercely devout people.

It was a minor readjustment, really. A man who had the power to unleash revolts could name his price not to. And a man who had the Mask of Motec'zoma and knew how to use the old legends would have that power. The mask . . . and someone to wear it. That would have been Kukulki's role once the mask was recovered—and in the past two days there had been a discovery in the digs that suggested he was very close. Kukulki had been fluent in Nahuatl. It was how he had managed to recruit the little Tenochca priests. He knew the "sacred" language, and he knew the legends.

But he didn't need Kukulki, and he didn't need his madman schemes of empire. Power had one purpose where Hall Kileen was concerned. Power was a tool for the amassment of wealth. With a million or so simple Indios and Mestizos ready to do his bidding, there were people in Mexico City who would pay handsomely for his alliance. And with half of Arizona Territory wide open to invasion by such a force, he was sure there would be ways to negotiate with Washington to his advantage.

Kukulki had, of course, had the power to amass an army. Money would buy such things. But without a goal of empire, armies weren't needed. The hundred guns he had around him at Haunted Butte, along with the little terrorist force that his Tenochca could become once he showed them their sun god . . . these and Vittorio's Mescaleros to spread the word south into Mexico . . . they were enough for what Kileen had in mind.

Had the digs not become promising, he might have had some doubts. But two days ago . . .

He reined in at the dig site on the slope of the old volcano and handed his reins to one of his gunnies. Sweating men stood aside as he walked up the slope to where timbers supported a shelf of black stone above a slanting hole. Picks had broken through a thin flow of lava stone here, and there had been emptiness beyond.

And in the emptiness was a framed rectangular opening —arch stones set in place centuries before and then covered by molten rock when the cone created itself. And beyond the opening were steps cut into older native stone, steps that led downward. Each day now he came here, inspecting each new find, knowing that this was a place of the ancient Mexíca and that it was from here that their journey had begun so long ago.

With a digger preceding him with a torch, and two of his guards at his heels, Hall Kileen stooped to enter the portal and went down the ancient stairs. Twenty-five feet below he paused, looked around. It had been a building, and the broken portal had been a roof opening. The room he stood in here was approximately fifteen feet to a side, and ten feet high, the timbers of its ceiling still sound. That had been puzzling, until a peripheral dig had proven that a second story had sat atop it. The devastation of the lava flow had literally melted that second level and had made of it a dome that shielded the lower floor from both the heat and the pressure of flowing rock above.

And there were other rooms beyond this. Already they had broken through in two directions. The artifacts were poor. Little had been left behind by those who had left this place. Bits of clay pottery, a broken *maquáhuitl*— stone-edged sword of the warlike Mexíca—shards of obsidian and flint, and bits of corn husk and woven reed . . . and, in a tiny chamber sealed off from the adjoining room as though a wardrobe closet had been stuccoed over, the mummified remains of a man, a woman and two children.

Kileen felt inclined to gloat over just these things. Those of his one-time peers who had scoffed at the idea of Aztlan having been north of the Sonoran deserts, what would they give now for an opportunity just to study these poor artifacts? Maybe, he thought, some of them might have their chance before long. Maybe once he had what he wanted, he would then invite a few among them to come here and see what he had found. But it would

251

cost them. It would cost them dearly.

Today's digging had produced nothing. A wall had been broken away, but beyond was solid black lava stone. Nothing there to find.

But he was right. He knew . . . intuition that was as keen as morning sunshine told him. Here, somewhere nearby, was the golden mask of the god Huitzilopochtli. Motec'zoma's lost treasure. The key to his own grand fortunes.

One entire wall of the latest room was a beehive of niches, ancient frames set in a mortar made of reddish mud and fibers. A sleeping room. Remains of a woven rug dissolved under his boots as he paced the small area, studying the walls. Finally he pointed at the sleeping wall. "Try there tomorrow," he said. "Pull all that structure away and break out the wall. There should be another room beyond."

And somewhere, he suspected, another entrance. If those Aztec refugees from the steel of Cortes had brought the mask back here—and if this building were its hiding place—they would have had a way in.

XXV

The Dutchman was good. Both of them, Wolf realized as he knelt on a moonlit slope to study a print which was no more than a scuff, were good. For two riders to leave so little trace, they both had to be good at covering their trail. He wasn't surprised about the Dutchman. That Apache had lived his life in this kind of country and knew its ways. But he was surprised once again at how capable Gail Larkin could prove to be. She hid it well, but now and again . . . she was good at this business.

Even in daylight, they would have been difficult to track.

He studied the scuff, then looked out across the land ahead, seeing its wild contours. A madness of moonscape ... Coleridge would have known words to do it justice ... or Emerson, for that matter, and probably better. The earlier word-workers would simply have described country like this. Emerson with his philosophies would have looked at its chaotic extremes and sought unities and commonalities. The old preacher had always seen patterns where others saw none. Patterns like the way that broken ridge out there sloped more steeply to the right than to the left, and how the walls of the canyon beyond were serrated by erosion. Dutchman knew this land, but Wolf knew trailing. To the right would be rockfall, to the left a passable way ... and beyond that, out where that slope reared up like the first of a series of giant steps climbing toward the top of that crusted peak, was where the canyon would come out. And over there, beneath that high outcrop, would be a stone path where a man might go if he was trying not to be tracked. Dutchman would know about that.

White teeth glinted in a dark, shadowed face, a grin of savage pleasure. It *was* a pleasure to track people who knew the ways of evasion. Of course the Dutchman knew. And surprisingly, so did Gail Larkin. A natural talent.

Ralph Waldo Emerson would have sought the unity of ideas and found direction in them. John Thomas Wolf sought unity of the elements and the terrain, and knew his direction. Afoot, he led his mount up a steep shoulder, then mounted. The moon was higher in the sky when he dismounted again, this time on a wide ledge above an outcrop, and squatted at its lip to watch small figures pass by in the canyon below. They were riding almost abreast, Dutchman guiding, the Apache at home in Apache mountains.

He watched where they turned, saw them out of sight, and studied the terrain again. Then he mounted and set out cross-slope to be where they would eventually come.

253

This leapfrogging of trail would give him direction, and at some point the direction and the lay of the land would tell him the destination.

It was not yet morning when he knew where to find Frederick Larkin.

Frederick Larkin, Ph.D., awoke when the first rays of morning sun touched high peaks beyond the valley, throwing back rose tints to light the hidden cove where they had set his hut. For a moment he thought Three People had returned, then he wondered why he had thought so. Three People might be gone another week, south someplace where there were telegraph wires, trying to get a message out to Kichener's people. They had waited for weeks now, and nothing had happened. And then those people down by the butte had begun to dig. Something had to be done, so Three People had gone. Why had he thought he was back? Something . . . some hint of presence . . . he came fully awake and sat up. Out in the cove, near the little waterhole the dripping springs fed, was a saddled horse. He could see it through the interwoven sticks that were the screen and camouflage of this hut the Dutchman had built . . . a shelter almost invisible in a place that would be hard to find. Yet *someone* was here.

He leaned to pick up his crutch, then stood, supporting himself on it, mentally cursing for the thousandth time the hole he had stepped in and the slowness of mending of a broken leg. And as he stood a shadow moved, and he looked around. The man was only a few feet away, in shadows, squatting on his heels beside the heap of packs and supplies against the stone rear wall. He squinted, and Indian features in a shadowed face gazed back at him, expressionless.

"Doctor Larkin?" the man said. "My name is Wolf. You sent for me."

"How did you get here? How did you get in without—"

"I had no reason to wake you." He stood, glancing down. "Dutchman didn't tell us you had a bad leg."

"He didn't know. It just happened two weeks ago. Where is my daughter? Where's Gail?"

"She'll be along," Wolf said. "Dutchman's bringing her. I came on ahead to look things over. That valley out there . . . it's the one, isn't it?"

"Yes. I'm sure it is, although I haven't had a chance to verify it. Those men down there. Do you know about Hall Kileen?"

"I know. Do you know what he's doing now?"

"He's digging. Down at the south end of the valley, just in from Haunted Butte. He has diggers . . . I think they're Mescaleros. They're excavating a site, and from what I can see it's only a matter of time before they find the mask. They must be close to it. I don't know how Kileen could be so exact, but there he is."

"You can see the digs from here?"

"No. That volcanic ridge hides the actual site. But I see them coming and going, and I can see the butte out there beyond. I can estimate. They are close, Mr. . . . ah, Wolf."

"Your daughter calls me John Thomas," the dark man said easily. "You've talked with Kichener. What did he tell you about me?"

"Not much, except that he would be in Mexico and I should try to send for you. That you could help. I didn't do anything right away. It was only when I didn't hear anything from him. I became concerned, so I sent a wire to Gail and then started up here. I really thought I could just come up and find the mask and get out with it before those people showed up. But I was too late. And I don't know what you can do, either . . . unless maybe you brought the cavalry with you?"

"No cavalry." Wolf shook his head. "Just a couple of friends, but they should be enough."

Larkin pushed aside the screen and stepped out onto the cove, Wolf following him. "I don't see how," he said.

"I've thought about it. It might be just possible for a man to slip in there—if he knew exactly where to look—and find the mask. But getting away with it is something else. Kileen has an army over there."

"Getting away with it may not be the problem," Wolf said. He walked out to the cleft of the cove, where juts of stone flanked a steepening gravel slope that became a cliff, falling away toward the wide valley far below. It was as Willie had told him, a wide, once-gentle valley whose floor once must have been verdant meadows. But only the edges of those meadows remained. Almost from the foot of the cliffs, harsh slopes arose, climbing toward the broken cone of a comparatively recent volcano, a mile or two away. The rest of the ancient valley, he knew, was beyond that ridgelike cone. The volcano and its debris lay like a great, scaly snake occupying the valley. Its flow had gone both directions along the lower reaches, spreading lava in wide, ropy layers for miles each way. It had been a rift eruption, probably many smaller cones opening and growing along a fissure, but the central cone, facing upon the valley's southern end, was the highest. Probably it was the one that had erupted secondarily after the lava flows had stilled, throwing cubic miles of detritus into the stratosphere on clouds of steam, to fall back to earth as a rain of red-gray gravel, blanketing everything around.

A few miles south, beyond the volcanic slopes, was the mesalike feature called Haunted Butte and beside it a lesser valley where tiny buildings stood—the abandoned ranch where Hall Kileen made his field headquarters. There was movement out there, people and activity.

Larkin came up behind him, leaning on his crutch—a medium tall, fair-featured man of middle years, robust good health impeded now by the splinted and mending leg and the awkward crutch.

"I stepped in a damn hole," he said, at Wolf's glance. "Been all over the world and never a scratch, then I come up here and step in a damn hole."

256

"Here?"

Larkin's grin was rueful. "Out there. I got nervous waiting around. Thought I could slip in and maybe find the hiding place before Kileen got too close to it. I went at night. I couldn't get to the butte to sight in; but I knew generally where to look, so I tried. And stepped in a damn hole. Clean break, but I had a devil of a time getting back here so Three People could set it."

"You haven't used the template, then."

"You know about that? No, the sight-point is the top of Haunted Butte. Kileen's people were all over the place. I couldn't get there."

"Maybe I can," Wolf said.

"I don't see how anybody can now." Larkin shook his head. "Maybe at night, but there'd have to be at least a little light to get a fix, and he has diggers and gunmen everywhere down there. And then the Tenochca . . . you know about them?"

"Yes. I've met some."

"They're absolute fanatics," Larkin said. "All the old Aztec blood-rituals and none of the civilization that went with them. It's all they live for . . . to kill, to sacrifice to their god."

"Do you know where he got them?"

"An associate of his, in Mexico. Power-mad bastard. He and Kileen make a good team. This isn't the first time Hall Kileen has tried to build a revolution, you know."

"Your daughter told me. But not details."

"Details? I don't know for sure. We were associated then, in a way. Separate expeditions, but we were working the same area. Pre-Columbian ruins, probably Mayan, though I thought—still do, in fact—that they might have been built on the remains of a Toltec structure. Thought Kileen was working the same thing, just a different part of it. Then the idiot dynamited his own digs—no telling what he destroyed—and somehow convinced a lot of the people in the area that their government was trying to wipe out their villages. Oh, I

257

know. It's preposterous, but he did. He was trying to extort money from one of the state offices or something. It will be years before anyone gets a chance to work any of those sites there again. The man is a lunatic."

"Is he in the habit of doing archaeological excavation with blasting compounds?"

"Hall Kileen might do anything. I'd be surprised if he doesn't have plenty of explosives right there at Haunted Butte, just in case."

"He could destroy his site."

"He wouldn't care. All he wants is that gold mask."

"What do you think is under that lava flow, Dr. Larkin?"

"A city," the man said. "A city of the ancient Mexíca. An absolute *wealth* of information about those people."

"Uh-huh," Wolf muttered. "And the mask?"

"The mask is the key to everything," Larkin said. "It's the artifact that will validate all the other finds."

"Meaning?"

"The Motec'zoma mask is a validated artifact, Mr.— ah . . . John Thomas. Cortes and his scribes actually saw it. They had it in their hands. It is accepted without question as a major artifact of the Aztec empire in Mexico. Of course, then it disappeared. But don't you see, if there are ruins under that lava, and if the mask is there, then that means that those people who stole it away from the conquistadores—those Aztecs, four hundred and fifty years ago—they brought it here and hid it. The mask will be the proof that this was Aztlan!"

"And if you didn't have the mask?"

"Without it? Why, we wouldn't have found anything, really. Maybe some old Indian ruins, but who's to say they are Aztec? There are Indian ruins everywhere. These would just . . . just be some more. That's all. But the mask is there, John Thomas. I know it is. And if we . . . if you can get to it before Kileen ruins everything . . . it's Aztlan, John Thomas! Aztlan! One of the great mysteries of the ages, the actual location of the first homeland of the Aztecs."

Larkin's eyes glistened, focused far away. Wolf sighed. He would have no ally here. Faint sounds drifted from the shoulder beyond the cove, and a moment later Dutchman rode into view, Gail Larkin following close behind. Her eyes went wide when she saw Wolf, and she spurred her horse past the Dutchman, down into the shielded cove, then jumped down and ran to her father. Her gaze on Wolf was a hard glare. "How did you get here?"

"The same way you would have if the roles had been reversed, I suspect. I knew where you were going, so I let you show me the way."

She turned, frowning at Dutchman. "You said we weren't followed!"

"We weren't." The Apache shrugged. His dark eyes went to Wolf, alive with curiosity. "He didn't follow us. He traced us. I wouldn't have believed it."

"Father, we can't let him get to the mask," she said. "He will destroy it. He has told me so."

"Destroy . . . the mask? But you can't!" Larkin looked stricken. "It's priceless. I told you—"

With a shrug, Wolf turned away and started for his horse. He was done here, and wasting time. Behind him he heard the hammer being cocked on a pistol. Without turning he said, "Put it away, Gail. You don't have a chance."

"Put it away," Dutchman echoed him. "He can kill you."

"He wouldn't—"

"Yes," the Apache's voice was soft, "he would, I think."

Wolf walked to his horse, swung into his saddle and glanced back at them. "Too bad," he said. "I thought we might all be on the same side." He turned the animal then, drummed heels and went up the slope to where the hidden trail began at the shoulder. He didn't look back again; and a moment later he was out of sight.

"I thought he could help us," Gail said. "I really thought he would, too. I should have remembered. He told me he wasn't coming out here for my reasons. He said he was coming for his own."

Larkin stared at the faceless slope where the Indian had gone. "But to destroy the mask? Why? I don't understand."

"I do," she said. "In a way, I see his reason. Even if we stop Hall Kileen, there might be other Hall Kileens one day."

"But the mask . . . it would go to a museum. It would be protected. There are ways. . . ."

"Those ways aren't his ways, Father. I've seen him work. He doesn't leave loose ends."

"Well, he won't get it," Larkin said. "Without the template stone, he won't find it. We'll just have to do this ourselves. Dutchman, will you help?"

"Sure." The Apache stepped down from his saddle. "I guess so, if you have an idea how. Might even find some friends if you want them."

"Who?"

"Cousins." He grinned. "White Mountain Apache. Still a lot of young bucks in these hills that might like to have some fun."

"We can use some help," Gail decided, noticing her father's leg for the first time. "What happened to you?" Then, "Oh, I'm so glad to see you. I was afraid—"

"Stepped in a hole," he said, then braced himself on his crutch to return her hug. "And I'm glad to see you, too. I'm just . . . well, I thought from what Mr. Kichener said about John Thomas Wolf, that . . . well, I guess I was expecting a miracle or something. So much for that, though. Maybe with Dutchman's 'cousins' we can make our own miracle. I guess we have to try. At least I didn't give him the template."

She stepped back, her eyes widening again as an intuition that was almost dread crept over her. "The template! Where is it, Father?"

260

"It's packed away in there." He pointed. "In the shack."

"Show me," she said.

A half hour later they walked again to the clifftop and looked out across the valley. Where was John Thomas? What did he intend to do?

They had searched through all the packs and the sacks. The template stone was nowhere to be found, and there was no remaining doubt who had it.

"He was here when I woke up," Larkin said. "Right in there with me. All the time we talked, and I told him about Kileen's digs and showed him where they were working . . . he had it all the time."

Gail's mind whirled, thoughts fitting together to form tentative ideas, ideas that might become plans—and through it all a cold anger at John Thomas Wolf. He could have *asked!* He could have given her father a chance; he could have debated it with him, compared reasons and goals, done him the honor of letting him decide. He could have . . . but no. He couldn't. It wasn't his way. And for her part, could she have shot him when she had the gun pointed at his back? Somehow she knew that he was right, and so was Dutchman. Somehow, even then, he left nothing to chance. He could have killed her. But could she have killed him? She didn't know. But just for a moment there. . . . "We *will* need some help, Dutchman," she said. "How many people do you think you can find?"

XXVI

Ce-Chinatl Ixtlic Tactli had lost Quetzalcoatl. Somehow, just in those last few rises and falls of the land, the red-bearded man and those with him had disappeared, and now there was not even a trail to follow. Worse, he had lost his horse somewhere—the beast had wandered away during the dark hours of night—and he was now afoot. Still, he felt elated as he stumped along down punishing slopes on feet that oozed dark blood from raw cuts that he could no longer feel. He *had seen* Quetzalcoatl, had even heard the human aspect of his voice as he sang encouragement to Tonaiu morning and evening. There could be no doubt of it anymore, no coincidence. Quetzalcoatl had come, was even now in the world and would soon resurrect his old enemy Huitzilopochtli so that Cem-Anahuac could arise and conquer the world. The legends were coming to pass.

And though he had lost Quetzalcoatl, he had found his way back to his brothers. Just ahead now was the encampment of Xochitli-Miqui and the other priests, and the high priest himself stood watching him approach. He raised his hands in salute to them; then the world spun about, and he found that he had fallen. He sat dazed for a moment, feeling Tonaiu's warmth on the scant stubble that had grown on his head recently—there had been little opportunity to shave it off, even though he knew it made him less presentable to the high god to have his head darkened by hair like ordinary men. But Tonaiu beamed upon him and his warmth was a pleasance. He could hardly remember the last time he had been warm. There were hands on him then, and others around him, and they lifted him and carried him to where Xochitli-Miqui waited.

The high priest stared at him without recognition until Tactli spread his right hand in the blood sign upon his chest and said, "Revered one, I am Ce-Chinatl Ixtlic Tactli, your son. I have come to tell you that Quetzalcoatl lives on this world. I have seen him myself." Then Xochitli-Miqui returned his salute, and they carried him to the mound upon which was their stone altar and set him where he could rest. Some looked at his dying feet, but they turned away. There was nothing they could do.

Already the darkness of his *chalchinatl* had drawn long streaks up his legs. His feet were dying, and they sent their death upward to claim more of him.

But they gave him water and some boiled grain, and one of them used his own obsidian blade to shave the stubble from his head. And when he had rested he told them of Quetzalcoatl. They had many questions for him, determining whether he might have dreamed the visions or otherwise imagined them. But finally they were satisfied, and Xochitli-Miqui himself proclaimed it. The god of night, the god of Mictlan, the feathered serpent who could appear to men's eyes as a red-bearded man, had come and certainly would be coming here. And when he came, he would raise the great and wrathful Huitzilopochtli and set him on his shoulders, and they would be as one god.

"And this our brother, who has seen the god before anyone else and thus brought the word, this worthy and devout Ce-Chinatl Ixtlic Tactli has earned the highest of rewards," he said. Then he raised his face and his arms. "*Ayyo, Tonaiu. Ayya, Huitzilopochtli.* Accept this most worthy one."

They lifted Tactli, removed his black coat and laid him on his back atop the altar pile. Then with his own obsidian knife, Xochitli-Miqui himself extracted his beating heart and offered his *chalchinatl* to Huitzilopochtli and to Quetzalcoatl. Quetzalcoatl had shown himself to Tactli. Thus it was fitting that Tactli should be the first to nourish both of the gods who were to become as one. It was a great honor.

Afterward one of the priests asked, "Revered one, shall we tell the man Kileen of the news Tactli has brought?"

Xochitli-Miqui thought it over, then said no. Though the man Kukulki had delivered them to the man Kileen, still Kileen was not Kukulki. And Kukulki had not proven himself to be Quetzalcoatl. Not yet. They would know soon enough if what the outland promisers said was

263

true. They would wait. Certainly if the man Kukulki was in fact the god Quetzalcoatl—in which case it must be him that Tactli had seen—and if the man Kileen was favored of him, then Quetzalcoatl surely would inform Kileen himself that he had arrived. The Tenochca would wait and see.

There was much activity now on Haunted Butte and out on the volcanic field north of it where the digs were in progress. Even some of Kileen's gunmen had been pressed into muttering service carrying stone, wheeling barrows and setting timbers. Stripped to the waist in the warm sunlight they worked side by side with Mescalero and Mestizo diggers and hated Hall Kileen for what they were doing, though the promise of vast rewards kept them at it.

And among all the activity, one Indian more or less might go unnoticed.

Wolf had combed out his hair and sheared it in the Apache manner, and tied a band around his head. The stained leggings and dark loincloth he wore were Apache, the sweat-stained pouch and slim knife at his waist were Apache, and the heavy boots he wore were suitable Apache wear. They could have come off a dead cavalryman.

For a time he hauled debris from the cave opening, working with others to stack it aside and go back for more, saying nothing. Then when long racks of ancient wood began to come out of the hole—some internal structure being dismantled to clear another surface for breaking through—he took a load of these in his turn and walked purposefully away, toward the butte. Several others, uncertain where the old structures were to go, followed him. And when one of them asked an armed guard where the materials were supposed to be, the man simply sneered, jerked a thumb over his shoulder and said, "Wherever they headed you, just keep goin'.

Nobody tells me anything."

At the very foot of the bluff Wolf set down his load. Then as others came to deposit theirs he busied himself stacking and arranging the pieces in a manner that suggested he knew what was supposed to be done. Within minutes he was alone there. With one quick glance around he headed up the slope toward the top of the butte. It was a long climb, but he moved steadily and with purpose, not looking around or back.

At the top of the slope, where red caprock jutted upward in a serrated face, he noted the foot trail veering to the left, and he ducked right, out of sight behind a wind-carved rib of stone. There he paused, looking and listening. No one had noticed him. There were no alarms. He braced himself against the sheer rock face and began to climb. From below he had seen a distinct outthrust in the caprock, now just above and to his left. It had the appearance of a wing stage, very much as he had seen in opera houses in the cities—smaller, abutting stages at each flank of a central stage, platforms for supporting choruses in works done in the Sicilian or Andalusian manner or for performances of the Greek classics. He had noted it, the outthrust of reddish rock, and had made an assumption. If he noted it now, heading south from the lost central city of Aztlan, then others too might have noted it . . . maybe even those shadowy others of that many centuries before. It was a thing common among people—when doing a significant thing, try to do it in a significant place. And a significant thing of the time had been the carving of the contours of the template stone.

The outthrust was a bulge, almost a shelf of stone. He reached the jutting underside and eased around it, finding finger-and-toeholds in clefts and crevices, climbing like a spider on a wall.

Just below the top he found verification. He would not have seen it, except for his fingers finding a slight declivity that was not quite like the other declivities they had found. It was an incised pattern, almost scoured away by the winds of centuries—a wavy line with a sun-sign just below. The wavy line—he could barely see it, it was so old—was a duplicate of the incision in the template stone.

Then he was at the top, and he rose to look, then ducked back. There were men there, and a structure, a small shedlike building well back from the lip of the mesa, something not visible from below. And one of the men was Hall Kileen. Gail's description of the man had been accurate—tall, ascetic, with limp straw-light hair and watery blue eyes.

He heard their voices. They were almost directly above him. And in the distance, indistinct, someone was shouting and the voice was approaching. He waited, heard those above him go quiet, then he could hear the words. "You better come see this! Those stinkin' little bastards just sacrificed one of their own kind! My God, broad daylight, they stripped him down and cut him wide open, just like they been doin' with them Meskins we give 'em!"

Other voices, scuffing of feet . . . Wolf peered over the top again. The men were hurrying away, toward the east lip of the mesa, all except one who seemed to be standing guard at the shed. And he also was looking in the direction his companions had taken. Wolf went over the top and sprinted toward him.

The man on guard was distracted, watching those who had gone to watch the Tenochca camp. He never knew what hit him. The shed's single door had a cast-iron padlock, but on the back wall was a high window for light and this was not as secure. Wolf prowled the little building, noting and itemizing its contents. Larkin had been right. Kileen was prepared to blow the digs to shards if that was what it took to find the sun god mask.

Outside again, he glanced eastward. The others had arrived at the east rim, and as he watched, first one and then another sank from view, going down a trail over there. Wolf gathered up the inert guard and his rifle and strode the fifty yards to the north rim, coming up on the "platform" of the wing-stage outthrust. He dumped the guard and the rifle over the edge . . . bad place for a fall, he noted, a man could break his neck. Then from his pouch he took the template stone.

Centuries before—how many centuries? Six? Maybe eight? Or more than that?—a person whose descendants would fortify a marshy lake and build upon it the city of Tenochtitlan, a warrior race who would dominate Mexico driven by sadistic priests of an insatiable god, back then that person had stood on this very shelf incising patterns in a small, flat stone. Patterns with which to recall and relocate a place devastated and left behind. Smaller than hand-size, the stone was smoothed, striated fossil rock, less than a half-inch thick. It had been broken—breaks occurring at the points at each end where the incised line approached the edge—then carefully mended. Even its colors seemed Aztec: the red of flowing blood, gray of antiquity and little bands of white that gleamed like divine purpose. Gleason had said that to the Aztec, everything meant something, even the colors of a glyph.

Wolf held the stone out before him, half arm's length and then slowly outward, letting its incised slit mold itself to the near horizon of valley rims and fissure cone. From here, from its end, the great snake of the lava bed had the silhouette of a rounded cone rising from the floor of a wide, gentle depression. At almost arm's length the horizon and the incision coincided . . . perfectly. And abruptly, at just that point, the pinhole in the middle of the sun-sign gleamed with brilliance. He lowered the stone.

A little above where the diggers were at work, above and back, up the slope of the volcanic field, a surface caught the sun's light and reflected it brilliantly—only one of many such points of light, but that one was the one the stone signified. He squinted, shading his eyes. A small jut of lighter stone standing above the tumbled surface, emphasized by the dark of shadows at its base.

Wolf put the stone away and lowered himself over the edge.

Hall Kileen was jumpy. It wasn't any one thing that did it, but a combination of factors that fed his intuition and said that not everything was right. Something about Kukulki's death . . . not that he minded, it was a blessing in fact, but why just now? Such a coincidence, that the man would die just as everything was coming together for them. And where was Krell? He should have been back before this. All the best of the hired gunmen, and some of the Tenochca, had gone with him to make sure there were no more interruptions from those people back east. But there should have been word by now. Krell should have been back. *Somebody* should have been back. Or there should have been messages. And the failure to locate Frederick Larkin or his daughter. He knew Larkin well enough to suspect that he was somewhere nearby. He *would* be nearby with a project like this under way. The man was incapable of *not* being in the vicinity when the secrets of the Aztecs were being uncovered. But they had found no trace of him. And his daughter—they had known where to look for her, so why had they not sent word that she was found?

Kileen had been uneasy about Larkin's daughter ever since the sweet deal in Mexico had gone sour. He had never quite learned why that failed . . . only that it had, and without the alliance of Don Juan Ascencion Acuna he would have been in serious trouble there. But he had always had a nagging suspicion. Somehow, Gail Larkin had been involved in his failure. Not the father, but the daughter. Her, and that cold-eyed, meddling Hidalgo, Diego Torreon. Kukulki had mentioned something once, about Torreon. Dangerous, he had said. And another he had mentioned, Ernest Kichener. Somehow associated with the one Kileen had been warned about, that Wolf.

He was so close! So close to finding the mask of

Motec'zoma and the key to his ambitions. A matter of days . . . even hours. It was there somewhere, in those digs. And yet he was jumpy.

Odd little things bothered him now. Why had the Tenochca sacrificed one of their own? He had never known them to do that, unless they simply had no one else. But he kept them supplied with victims. And then this strange thing . . . the shed guard who had fallen of off the edge of the mesa. Why? What was the imbecile doing out there, that he should fall? Had he seen something at the digs? Walked out for a closer look? If so, what?

It puzzled and bothered Kileen, and he paced the mesa's lip, scanning the work in progress out there, wondering what might be wrong. Small in the distance, the diggers and the carriers worked, their movements a regular pattern with few variations. He looked, looked away and back, then peered, squinting in the bright sunlight. One figure had separated from a group of figures out there, one man climbing rapidly above and away from others. A moment later the figure disappeared, then reappeared again, still higher and farther back on the incline. Kileen watched, puzzled, then turned to one of his guards.

"Who is that out there?" He pointed, turning to look again as he did so.

"Who?" The guard peered.

"That one above, where—" he broke off. The figure was no longer in sight. "Give me that glass," he said. With the telescope extended he studied the area out there, where the man had been. Nothing. Just the tumble and clutter of the slope—jutting stones here and there that had ridden the crest of the ancient eruption, and the tumble of detritus that had covered its cooling flow.

"I'm going down," Kileen said. "Two of you come with me. I want to look at that slope above the digs."

* * *

The glinting stone was a free slab. Though it appeared to jut intact from the volcanic stone at its base, that was an illusion. In an ancient time someone had made it so, and fit it so perfectly to its base that only a person knowing precisely which stone to study would see that it only rested in place. With quick movements that gave the appearance of casual rest, he knelt and strained against it, corded muscles standing in his shoulders and arms. Reluctantly at first, then with startling ease, it pivoted on one corner and lay aside.

The opening beneath was a shaft, less than three feet across, smooth-walled and dark, a hole leading almost straight down into the solid lava stone below the tumbled detritus. A cool breeze, bearing the faint odors of dust and antiquity, seemed to rise from it. Without hesitation Wolf let himself down into the shaft, bracing his back against one side, feet against the other, and reached overhead to replace the capstone above him. The rock pivoted smoothly into place, and he was in complete dark.

He freed a shard of pumice from the neck of the shaft, held it for a second, then let it drop. Its muted impact when it struck a surface below was almost immediate. Twenty feet, possibly. Not much more. He could ease downward that far, tensing and relaxing his legs in turn, sliding his back against the smooth, cool stone. But once down, there would be no coming back unless. . . . Bracing himself where he was he fumbled for his waist pouch, found a candle and a match, and lit the wick. Barely able to move in his strained position, he explored the bit of shaft wall that he could see, and that this fingers could reach. He found no toeholds—nothing. Only the smooth dark wall of a shaft going down into the earth. If the ancients had used this as an access to somewhere, they must have had ladders or ropes. And yet, when he lifted the capstone, there had been moving air. It could mean another opening somewhere.

Best to slip away, come back with rope and a lantern,

he decided. And maybe with some help, or at least someone to give him a diversion if he needed it. Carefully, painfully, he dug his fingers into the rough neck of the shaft above the smooth lava walls, and raised himself until his head touched the capstone. Then he wedged there, got his hands under it and lifted . . . and stopped.

Through an exposed crack he saw the slope and the mesa beyond, and in the distance there were men mounting horses, men who seemed to be looking directly at him. He eased the stone down. They had seen him, then . . . or had seen something suspicious. They were coming to investigate.

In darkness, Wolf began relaxing one leg and then the other, his back sliding on the smooth wall of the shaft, a few inches at a time, letting himself down.

XXVII

Ten feet down, the shaft ended. Wolf clenched his teeth, turned loose, dropped and landed crouched on a surface that crunched beneath his boots. Echoes, hollow with their own reverberations, ran around him and died. For a moment he waited, immobile, his senses testing, then he stood and reached above him and to each side. His fingers found nothing. He got out his candle and relit it, then looked around. The little flame reflected dully from a dark surface several paces to one side, a surface that rose and curved like the inside of a bell. Dimly, above, he saw the bottom of the shaft from which he had fallen. Beneath his feet was gray volcanic ash, an undulating floor that crunched and crinkled in tiny protest as he moved his feet. He squatted again, looking more closely. Just at his feet were indentations in the silt, little conical holes where something had rested. He found two of these, and something far more interesting—two sets of human footprints, clearly delineated, leading off into the darkness opposite the visible wall. The prints were smaller than his own feet, footwear flat-soled without a raised heel. They went away side by side, and at each few steps an imprinted line appeared between them as though something carried had occasionally dragged.

Lighting a second candle he set it in the sand-ash where he was, then arose and began to explore out from it. The place he was in was an underground cavern, but unlike limestone caverns he had seen. Its walls and roof were a uniform dark gray stone, swelled and rippled here and there but not rough to the touch—smooth as lava flow is smooth. He walked completely around the interior surface, looking for openings or other shafts, finding none. It was as though he were inside a bubble—a huge, dark stone bubble maybe thirty paces across, its lower half buried in the coarse pumice-sand of its floor. Like being inside a great bell set mouth-down on a dark beach. A bell with three protrusions into it. The second time around he concentrated on these. The first was a featureless blob of stone, extruded inward from what might once have been a fissure. It hung above the sand floor, the size of a boulder, an ugly growth on the smooth bell surface. The second was a steep pile of broken stone, rising from the floor to high on the curving wall. Rubble which had poured in through a break? It appeared so. He made no judgments about it.

At the third he saw the footprints again. Backtracking them, he walked to where he had left the extra candle, snuffed it, put it away, then followed the tracks again. They went directly to the third protrusion, and this one he studied with care. It was obviously a man-made structure—a corner formed by two sloping walls made of cut and fitted blocks of a light stone that could have been coarse marble. The blocks were massive appearing, each one at least three feet across at its lower edge, each one slightly tapered and sloping inward—or outward—toward the lava bubble wall.

He ran his fingers along some of the joints, finding traces of what might have been limestone mortar. He dug at the base of the stones, a foot deep and then two. They went on down at the same slope . . . how far? He pictured the old volcanic field as it appeared from outside, imagined that this was a building that had stood on the original surface and been buried there. He decided that where he stood must be at least thirty feet up from the original base of the structure. And sloped walls. A pyramid? The material he had read at Gleason's house had suggested that the early Aztecs were not builders, that they had learned the skills of building from Toltecs or others. The structure he saw here suggested otherwise.

He held the candle high, studying the top of the wall, where it disappeared again into the dark bubble, fifteen feet or more above his head. The stonework continued without change.

And yet the two sets of footprints came directly to the wall of this buried structure and ended there. Whoever had come before had gone through. He knelt, studying the wall with eyes and fingers, and found a variation. One stone, just above the sand on which he stood, had been tapered inward at its top edge, for two-thirds of its length. And in the underside of the stone above were deep grooves. Again he ran his fingers around this one, and found no mortar. He got his fingers under the stone, under the grooves, and pulled. It moved slightly, grating as it slid an inch from its socket. He paused. A trap? People had gone from this place, not expecting to return. Might they have left some nasty surprises behind them? Such things were not unknown. Standing, he studied the wall above the loose stone. The next one up was solid, its corners resting on two other stones, not on the loose one. He turned and walked away, toward the center of the great bell, then turned back for a longer view. As he turned, the sand floor caved below his foot and he jumped back. Something had given way beneath the coating of volcanic ash, and bits of it sifted through, leaving a shallow depression. The shifting also had revealed another feature—a long railing or wall-top of the light-colored stone, barely hidden by the pumice. He brushed sand away, studying it. Its top had been barely a foot beneath the surface, and as he revealed a double arm's length he found the remains of clay troughs fixed to it with mortar. Stubs only, but identifiable.

This, then, explained the bubble of lava. Steam. The structure in its center had been a well of some kind, or a cistern. A large container of water. The lava flow had overrun it and trapped its exploding steam in a bubble within the lava itself, then had solidified. And that explained the shaft as well. It was where the steam had escaped.

He made his decision, returned to the marble wall, crouched and pulled at the loose block. Once, twice . . . his muscles bulged, tendons crackled . . . then it was free. A narrow block, no more than ten inches thick, it was set high in a sloping wall and intended for opening. The surrounding wall was a good two feet thick.

He leaned into the dark hole where the stone had been and saw nothing. Just dark space beyond.

Again he lit his second candle, knowing that he might lose it now. Leaning through the hole he reached down as far as he could and dropped the feeble light. It fell only a few feet, rolled and stopped, and the surface beneath it was a sandstone floor, long and narrow, like a shelf built inward from the pyramid wall. He swung through the hole, let himself down to the shelf and retrieved his candle. To his right the shelf extended beyond sight. But after he had gone ten paces there were stone stairs, a narrow, unrailed staircase pitching steeply downward into darkness.

He counted twelve steps to the bottom, scant treads half the depth of his foot but nearly fifteen inches high, and no more than two feet wide, with precipitous darkness on each side. A vertiginous staircase, even if one could see. Finally he stood on the floor of the ancient structure and circled its interior, his eyes seeking out every detail the feeble light could show him. There was no pumice-sand here, no volcanic ash, just an inch or two of sifted fine dust over every horizontal surface. A large, square chamber with stone benches against straight high walls on two sides, facing across a wide, paved floor. One of the other walls was bare of ornament except for a narrow, higher bench at its very center. A throne . . . shelf for a shrine . . . he could not tell what it might have been. Simply a cut stone shoulder high and flattened on top, the size of a small chair seat. Its sides were unmarked pale stone. He circled past the foot of the soaring staircase, which grounded in the exact center of the room, and again found the two sets of footprints, angling away ahead of him. He stepped over them carefully, then went on, counting his paces. The room was no more than thirty feet across, and Wolf estimated quickly, a low whistle forming at his lips. The pyramid must be a hundred feet across at its base outside, maybe a third again that. No wonder it had breasted the volcano's surge and survived. Lava had buried it, but could not collapse those mighty walls and had cooled too quickly to burn through their stone.

Reaching the far wall he found the largest artifact—a flat, grooved stone resting on other stones, its surface waist high, and at its feet a stone container like a vat or short trough.

Aztec. Here it had begun. Here was the sacrificial altar, and this pyramid had been their great temple. Deduction told him that the opening he had come through would have a mate in the opposite wall—one facing east, one facing west. Portals for the rays of the morning sun and the evening sun. Access for the sun god.

Wolf raised his candle high and peered upward, into the cavernous dark height of the place, an idea forming in his mind. The light was not enough to show him anything, so he set the thought aside for the moment and returned to the double set of prints. He knelt to study them. Two people had come down those pitching stairs and at their base had stopped and walked around, a jumble of prints there. And here again he found the two clear depressions, this time in old dust only partly obscured by the newer dust of further centuries. Two marks, a little more than a foot apart; just as under the shaft in the lava bubble. And from there the footprints angled away again, in tandem as before, toward a corner of the room to the left of the altar stone. He followed them and knelt at the wall by another moveable stone, but this one was smaller and lighter. It was almost no effort to pull it aside. Its weight could not have been more than a hundred pounds.

And beyond it he found Aztecs . . . two mummified bodies, side by side, each with a gaping slit in its breast. The body on the left still held a stone knife in its outflung hand, and its other hand was inside its own ribs. The cubicle in which they lay was a tiny, low-ceiling room with no other apertures except the single, moveable stone.

"Murder and suicide," Wolf whispered, shaking his head. He looked down again at the mummy on the left. "You certainly had your beliefs," he said.

Backing out, he closed the stone door.

He found what he was seeking almost immediately. The Aztecs had left them laid neatly along the row of benches nearest to the cubicle—two long poles of ancient wood, dried rock-hard now by the ages, with shorter rods spanning between them at intervals and the dry remains of fiber binding. It had been a ladder. Wolf lifted one of the long poles, braced a foot against it and pulled. Rather than bending, it shattered.

"Won't be a ladder again," he muttered. "But it might make a probe."

Carefully he lifted the second pole, raised it upright and carried it back to the center of the temple, at the foot of the steep stairs. He set his candle on a tread, raised the pole and prodded upward with it, into darkness. After a moment he felt it touch something, and above a metallic "chunk" echoed dimly from the walls. He felt with the pole, trying to see with it what was above. He raised it higher and felt something below it, partially taking its weight. He edged it aside and felt an obstruction that gave with his push.

Bracing his feet then, he raised the pole so that its butt was shoulder high, estimated locations, and swung it as hard as he could. Something gave before it, a dry hiss like fabric tearing. He followed the swing and ducked aside as something solid and heavy fell where he had been, ringing echoes violating the ancient silence of the temple. Air gusted in its path, and his candle winked out.

He laid the old pole aside carefully, got out his other candle, lit its wick and knelt.

Cortes's scribes had not done justice to the mask of Huitzilopochtli. Those old Spaniards had been seeing it as gold to be melted down, gems to pry loose. Their sketch and description had been an insult to a work of high art. The mask lay face up beneath a cloud of settling dust, its gold surface as brilliant now as it might have been centuries before, red and green stones twinkling and glinting around its periphery. Beaten and shaped from solid gold, the mask was nearly twenty inches in diameter, its serrated rim—delicate flame-spurs carefully shaped—forming most of a circle. From its center a proud beak thrust out, the hooked beak of a great eagle, and on either side of that stared the frowning, slanted eye sockets of a bird of prey. The eyes were apertures, the eyes of the mask from which its wearer's own eyes would look out. Sweeping gold plumage curved down from the sides of the beak, framing a gap in the circle that would leave the wearer's mouth and chin exposed.

And around the eagle face, carefully molded, were squared glyphs of the Nahuatl sign writing, each set with stones so that the very colors of the gems became a part of the meaning of each symbol. And around it all, the sunburst rim of golden fire. He rubbed away its coating of dust, fingering each meticulous feature, and the thing glowed warmly in the candle's light, its eagle face staring up at him, inhuman and implacable.

Huitzilopochtli. God of the sun, ruler of day, promiser of a world to his chosen people. Huitzilopochtli, ravenous flaring champion of a warlike people. Huitzilopochtli, whose only sustenance was human blood.

This was no artifact made by people in the wilderness of Aztlan, not even the people who had constructed a temple that defied volcanic flow. But this *was* the construct of their children, and in time it had been brought back to the source . . . to wait.

If ever a thing were made to kill for, Wolf thought. It was the mask's only purpose.

He picked it up, studying it. Heavy . . . at least thirty pounds. The gold of varying thicknesses to form an eagle face in front and depressions for human features behind. Three solid metal loops on the back side, one near the top, one on each side—loops for thong or strap to hold the mask on the head of its wearer. Through the centuries, how many people had seen this mask? Probably thousands . . . but except for the priests and maybe the emperors—and of course a few Spanish invaders—probably none had seen it and lived.

"*Ayyo, Huitzilopochtli,*" Wolf muttered, "I have a different use for you now . . . but it might not be all that different in its outcome."

Hours had passed since he first came down the shaft into this forgotten place—maybe a day or more. Hunger and thirst gnawed at him, but he ignored the torments. There were more important things to think about . . . like getting out of this tomb. The shaft he had come down was out of the question, even if he had a way to reach it and climb to its top. People outside had seen him. They might not find where he had gone, but they would be there if he came out.

But, there had been moving air at the shaft. For air to move, it must start somewhere. And for cool air to rise on a warm day, there must be force. The wind would be from the southwest. Would have been then, at least.

He pictured again the valley and its terrain, as he had scouted it, as he had seen it from atop Haunted Butte. Between this end of the old flow and the mesa was open ground, simply rises leading to the mesa's slope. But west of the mesa were scour lands, a wilderness of breaks, boulders and gullies on climbing ground . . . a place of sentinel stones, where tall, grotesquely beautiful towers and spires of red and pale sandstone stood like monuments to antiquity, shaped and scoured by wind-borne sands over the centuries.

Older than the volcanic field? Maybe older than this rift flow, at least. The kind of land that would have tossed and fought the runnels of lava, where winds from beyond might have cooled their outer shells even as they flowed—like the "tunnels" in some of the older volcanic fields farther east.

Wolf tucked the heavy mask under his arm, picked up the old wood pole and walked to the wall opposite the altar stone. No temple with its sacrificial trappings inside would be served only by high windows. There would have been a door, somewhere.

XXVIII

Partly by logic and partly by surmise, Gail Larkin led Dutchman and his "cousins" cross-country to within a mile of the hidden croft where Shanty, Trooper and Willie waited for Wolf. With a dozen White Mountain Apache at her back and Dutchman by her side, she set a precarious course across the wild lands between Natanes

279

Rim and the Mescals at a pace that worried even stolid Vicente, most seasoned of the young bucks who had taken Dutchman up on his suggestion of "one more big out."

"This woman, she got sand in her craw," Vicente observed as they went down a precarious shelf at a high lope on the horses she had shown them how to find—horses Shanty had left behind.

"Blood in her eye," Dutchman corrected him. "That sonabitch Wolf, he made her mad."

To desert fighters still stunned by the scope of the recent southwest campaigns, Dutchman had given them all the reason they needed to ally with the Larkins in an adventure. Sure, the army and the agent told them they had to stay on the reservation now, he had said. But nobody said if there's a bunch of unauthorized rock-busters digging up reservation property, that they shouldn't go run them out and maybe keep whatever they left behind. Besides, Larkin could be trusted to pay fairly for services rendered. And who could say for sure that those hooters *weren't* on reservation property? If not, they were close.

Only the Dutchman's carefully cultivated Indian inscrutability concealed his amazement when, on their second day out, Gail led them through a maze of trackless canyons, up a long gully, across a rock ridge and down a cactus-strewn slope, then reined in her horse, got down and studied the bare ground there, her eyes rising slowly to a prominence less than a mile away. She stood. "They're over there, the other side of that rise. But Wolf isn't with them. Where did he go?"

"I don't know where he went," Dutchman said. "I'm not even sure where *we* are. How'd you learn to read ground that way?"

"By paying attention." She got back into her saddle. "Well, come on."

Beyond the rise were rocks and a glimpse of the hues that said water beyond. As Gail led past a standing stone, a huge shape appeared beside it, holding a rifle that pointed beyond her at the trailing Apaches. Without lowering his gun, Shanty removed his hat. "There you are, Miss Gail. Hello, Dutchman. Who are they?"

"They're with us," Gail said. "Where's Wolf?"

"Don't know." Shanty lowered his rifle and put his hat on his head. "We thought he was with you. He just told us to hole up and wait, so here we are."

She rode on down to the hidden tank, a file of Apaches following behind her, each of them studying Shanty with curious eyes as they passed him. When the last had gone by he shouted, "It's all right, Trooper! They're ours!"

Trooper came out of hiding, followed by Windwagon Willie, and two of the Apache warriors found themselves clinging to pitching, spinning mounts when Dog appeared on the path beside them, grinning up at them in happy anticipation.

Willie shouted, "Dog! Leave them Injuns alone! You already et!"

Trooper took an instant dislike to Vicente. He hated to see an Apache wearing an old blue shirt with sergeant's stripes. But he kept the grudge to himself. Wolf had long since made it clear to him that there were a lot more white men running loose wearing buckskins than there were Indians wearing military garb, and that they probably came by their apparel less honestly. When the horses were tended and what introductions could be tolerated had been made, Gail climbed with Shanty up to a ledge that provided a view of distant Haunted Butte and the activities there.

"They got a regular dig going on over there," he said. "All told, there's maybe a couple of hundred people, but most of them are diggers. Dutchman told us they had a hundred gunslingers over there, but I haven't counted more than about thirty."

"There may be a hundred," Gail said. "What are your plans?"

"Ma'am?"

"Your plans. What do you intend to do?"

"I don't know, miss. Wolf just said for us to wait, and he hasn't come back yet. I was hoping he was with you. Did you find your father?"

"I found him all right. So did John Thomas." She was about to elaborate on that, then changed her mind. "We left Father where he is. He has a broken leg. He stepped in a hole. But he's all right. What do you mean, you don't know what you intend to do?"

"Why, just that, miss. Wolf hasn't come back, and—"

"Oh, I know. Until John Thomas says what to do, nobody does anything!"

"Well . . . uh, what *should* we do, miss?"

"What we all came for," she decided. "Those men down there are looking for an old mask that they aren't supposed to have. My father is supposed to have it. So I believe we should go down there and get it."

Shanty edged back from the rim of the ledge, then turned to look down into the little camp at the tank. He made a show of counting, then turned back to her. "There's fifteen of us here, miss. Mostly Apaches, at that. Make that sixteen if we count yourself, miss. Throw in old Willie and Dog and it still comes out only eighteen. Now, that's pretty long odds, even if Wolf was here to—"

"To what?"

"Well, whatever he'd do. I don't know."

"I know what he'd do. He'd go down there and get that mask."

"That sounds right. How?"

"By behaving in a sneaky, scheming, murderous manner. How else does he do *anything*?"

"Sort of like stampeding cows over folks caught in a narrow canyon, miss?"

"Well, it's the sort of thing he'd consider, isn't it?"

"Seems just like him. It really does."

"Then that's settled. We can't accomplish anything up here, so we have to go down there."

"Yes, ma'am."

"At dark. What's over on the other side of that mesa?"

"That mesa's a butte, ma'am." His whiskers mostly hid his grin.

"Admire it some other time, please. What's beyond it?"

He shrugged. "Wild country. Pretty broken up. What Willie calls scour lands, with big rock formations, canyons, breaks. Nobody over there that we know of. They work pretty much from this side."

"Then we'll work from there," she decided. "I want you to go down and tell the Dutchman everything you've seen out there, especially how they deploy themselves at night. Tell him when it gets dark we're going across the slope out there, into the scour lands, and I don't want anybody to see us on the way. You and the rest figure it out. Just get us there."

He stared at her, round-eyed. For just an instant he'd had the illusion that John Thomas Wolf was talking to him. "Yes, ma'am," he said finally. When he was gone Gail stayed on the ledge for a time, trying to see details of what those people were doing out there, trying to see the terrain as it might look from the top of Haunted Butte, trying to imagine where the pinhole she had seen in the template might have fallen on the mass of volcanic land beyond.

For hours they had searched the area where Kileen had seen the man disappear. By fives and tens they walked the bulging slope, crossing first one way then another, searching for caves or hidden portals, anyplace that a man might hide. They poked among rocks, pulled away brush, and found no holes larger than a snake might use. And Kileen watched the search with angry watery eyes and crawling intuition. He had seen the man disappear. Something was very wrong, and he wanted to know what it was. Still, they found nothing. Finally he posted two gun-guards there to watch the area. "If anybody comes here, I want to talk to him," he said. "If anybody shows up here, anybody at all, you are to bring him to me."

They had found nothing in the dig below and had run out of walls to break through. One of the teams, though, had found another fault nearby with what might be another bulding below it. They would work that one and see. But after that, if they had not found the mask, Kileen decided he would let his instincts have their way. Up here, where he had seen a man disappear on the bare slope. There was something here. He felt it. Something here to find.

He called in his foremen before heading back to K-bar. When they were gathered, he showed them the area where the guards were posted. "I'll want picks and drills up there, and all the men as soon as they've checked out that latest fault. And get some carriers up on the butte to empty that shed and bring everything over here. Maybe picks and drills will open this slope up for us, but if it doesn't we'll blast it out. I'm through with this brush and teaspoon business. Now get them moving."

Why had he heard nothing from Krell? Where were all the men he had sent out—to find the Larkin girl, to make sure those people back east didn't send any more meddlers to interfere? And who *were* those meddlers? Kukulki seemed to have known. Agencies, he had said once, darkly. Agencies that are secret because the countries they work for are not. Agencies set aside from the structure of government for the sheer purpose of frustrating anyone who might have the genius and the power to operate outside those impeding structures to achieve his own ends.

Kukulki had not told him much about that, only that there were such agencies and that they must be dealt with. When Kileen had mentioned the name of Diego Torreon, he had seen a hot hatred grow in Kukulki's red-black eyes. And there had been the name Kichener as well. Kileen did not regret the death of Kukulki. His only regret was that Kukulki had died without telling him everything he knew about such problems. The Mexican had kept it mostly to himself to deal with those matters, except for having Kileen send his best gunmen—men the lunatic Krell had assembled—eastward to stop any shadowy others who might try to come. It was to Krell he had given the name of John Thomas Wolf . . . to Krell and those Tenochca he had sent with him.

Where were they all now? Where was Krell? In evening light Kileen climbed again to the area they had searched, his sense of impending . . . something . . . still troubling him. The guards there identified him and made a show of being on guard. Once more he walked the area where the man had disappeared. Nothing. Nervous and irritated, he turned to watch the beginning of transfer of the blasting materials. Already, parties of carriers were forming up there, on the butte, and lines of men were starting down on the east slope carrying parcels.

Chipping away at these old rocks could take years, he thought. I don't have the time to spare. Around him the face of the volcanic slope seemed to stare back at him, inert and impervious, uncaring.

Damn you! He kicked at a jutting light stone. Don't keep your secrets from me. I need them. I've waited long enough for what I want. You owe me!

He stopped then, scarcely breathing, and nudged the stone again. It had moved! Kneeling beside it, he grasped and lifted; it moved again, and he saw the cunning set of it into a natural socket of the lava. Not a random stone jutting above the flow. A trick! He cursed the ancients who had done this even as he began to smile grimly. The stone was a lid. A lid to hide something beneath. He stood, beckoning to the guards.

"Move this rock aside," he told them. "I want to see what's under it."

Miles to the north, in the hidden cove at the basin's lip, a man named Three People stepped down from a tired horse and wiped sweat from the balding head above his beaded Zuni headband, enjoying the cool breeze on his long, bare arms. He had packed away the stiff and binding clothing of his heritage as soon as he was safely away from the little perimeter of relative civilization that was Tucson, and had changed back to the garb of those people he considered his adopted kin . . . all except the gold-rimmed spectacles that hung from a thong at his neck. He raised those spectacles now and peered through them as Frederick Larkin emerged from his hut, leaning on his crutch.

"You're looking well, Frederick," Three People allowed. "Quite getting the hang of the extra leg, I see. Jolly good. Sorry to say, though, I bring no news. I wired off about the Wolf chap, as you requested, and waited around the bloody place two days before they answered, but all they had to say was that Wolf was out."

"He's out, all right," Larkin said. "Out here. He was here and I spoke with him. But the man is some kind of maniac, according to Gail—by the way, she was here too; she's in excellent health and gives you her regards—but by the time I knew he wasn't to be trusted, he already had the template stone and was gone with it. I thought you'd never show up."

"Oh, I say," Three People said. "That is a bother, isn't it? But where is Miss Gail? And Dutchman? Are they about?"

"No, they took off after Wolf . . . or something. Blast it, everyone has run off and left me here. Do you have an extra horse?"

"Just back at the springs." Three People nodded. "Where do you intend to go?"

"Down there." Larkin pointed. "Montezuma's mask is there, I'm certain of it. But I'll be damned if I'll let Hall Kileen get hold of it to make trouble, or John Thomas Wolf to destroy it."

"Destroy it?" Three People was flabbergasted. "Oh, I say. He wouldn't do that, would he? I mean, that's hardly the civilized thing, is it?"

"He isn't civilized." Larkin was already heading for the hut to get his things. "He isn't civilized at all."

In the murk of a buried temple, Wolf lifted a stub of candle before a shoulder-high stone shelf and decided that one thing it might be was a lever. It was the logical place for a door, the only logical place in this vault of ancient death and worship. It lay directly across from the stone altar, in line with the base of the soaring stairway to the sunwindows above. The ancestors of the Aztecs might have had a logic all their own in many ways; but they were people, and people tended to be consistent within their logics. *Their* logic, as he analyzed it, would have dictated an entrance here. He studied the stone shelf, applied his weight to it, pushed it this way and that, and then thought Aztec.

Those who had entered here, except for the priests, had never been intended to leave, and the building of the place would reflect that. Getting in would have been easy, getting out difficult—unless you were a priest and knew the secret. And yet, right here, at this point, would be the way. What would a person trying to escape from sacrificers in here do, if he got free? Beat on the wall, probably. Try to push through it. Maybe notice the shelf and try to climb up on it, seeking a doorway above. What would he not likely do?

He would not likely try to lift it.

Setting his candle aside, Wolf bent his knees, put the flats of his hands against the underside of the shelf and pushed upward. The sudden result almost knocked him down. The shelf swung upward easily, and the stone at his back swung inward, pushing him aside, and continued to swing until it lay flat on the floor at his feet, a door become a porch. Beyond was a rectangular passage barely large enough for a man to traverse. Four feet high, two feet wide, he estimated. And it led off into darkness.

Picking up mask, pole and candle, he entered and had gone three steps—bent almost double under the roof of the passage—when a paving stone gave slightly beneath his foot and he heard and felt the door closing behind him. He pulled the pole's length through just before it snapped shut, then squatted on his heels to look back. Plain, flat stone barred the way he had come. He reached the pole back to tap it, then push against it. It didn't move, and in the candle's light he saw a broken slab of stone lying just at the edge of the passage, the stump of another lever-stone above it. *Not* easy in, then, he corrected himself. A secret both ways. The priests didn't take any chances. And no way in now. With the lever gone, no way to return. He turned and went on, noticing that the air here did not move. It was dead, enclosed air.

Fifty feet along he found the end of the passageway, a shattered slab of stone with gray-dark rock beyond. He sighed, wondering what the chances were that there had been another water sytem on this side of the temple. There was only one way to find out.

Carefully he laid the heavy gold mask aside, leaning on the passage wall, and the stub of candle beside it. Then he backed away a half-dozen yards and hefted the ancient pole in both hands, its butt under his right arm. Thrusting it before him like a lance, hampered by the tight space and low ceiling, he braced himself and charged the lava stone barrier.

The tip of the pole collided and shattered in ringing shards, its stump thudding again and again at the stone as Wolf rammed it forward. Then there was another sound, a crackling of a different tone, and suddenly the air was alive again as the dark stone shattered and fell in a rain of ragged slabs, piling up to almost fill the sudden opening there.

Wolf put down what was left of the pole, retrieved his candle and held it close to himself. He was bleeding from a half-dozen cuts—both hands, his right arm and his side. Splinters of the ancient, rock-hard wood had gouged and cut him. But nothing had gone deep.

He knelt at the pile of dark fragments and took several deep breaths. The air was clean and cool, and it came from somewhere. With a sigh, he began to dig.

XXIX

Willie and the Dutchman planned the route, and did it well. By the time the sun had set they knew the general route that they would take to slip across enemy country, to get into the scour lands beyond Haunted Butte. And by the time it was full dark they had every step of it pinned down. Vicente and several of the Apaches sat around them, listening, occasionally one or another going up to the ledge to observe the route and judge its secrecy, and finally Vicente nodded his agreement.

"No problem from here to the creek," he told Dutchman. "Then from where that gully starts north of the buildings, no problem from there on . . . not for an Apache anyway. Gullies and washes all the rest of the way. Mescaleros might see us go by, but what do they care? They're just here to dig and make some money. Only problem's from the creek to the gully. Those little stinkbugs down there, they got eyes."

Dutchman repeated the comments to Willie, who asked Shanty about it. Shanty shrugged. "Miss Larkin says we do it, and Wolf isn't here so I guess we do it her way. She said for us to figure it out."

"Never knowed an Irishman yet that wouldn't let a woman tell him what to do," Willie observed. "But I reckon we'll get there. Ain't anything an Apache can do that me and Dog can't do better."

"You and Dog aren't going," Shanty said. "You can wait here."

"I be danged!" Willie snorted. "You think I come this far into this godforsaken country that me and God both forsook twenty year ago, just to hang up here by this waterhole an' miss all the fun? Not any way in hell am I not goin' on this jaunt, Irishman. Just make up your mind about that."

"Well, I'll talk to Miss Larkin about it if you—"

"Nothin' of the kind," Willie said. "I never was no Irishman. You go ahead on and go over there because that woman says to. That's all right with me. But me, I'm goin' over there with you because I feel like it. Now hush up about that." He turned back to the conference.

Trooper had come up from the tank in time to hear part of it. Now he curled a sullen lip. "Crazy old coot," he said. "Just might get himself killed, that's what he might do. Crazy as a loon."

From a few feet away, Willie turned to frown at him. "Varmint," he said, then ignored him and told Dutchman that whatever suited him for a route would just make everybody else right tickled.

With dark, Gail came down from her perch and told them, "Mount up and let's get started. I hope you've decided on a path."

They had, and they did, and in the dim starlight a young woman, an old man, an Irishman, the Dutchman, a dozen White Mountain Apaches, Dog and Trooper came down from the hills to snake a silent and covert course through the very heart of Hall Kileen's enterprise. From the slopes they crossed the little stream that fed from the springs above into the creek beside K-bar, then circled wide around the dark and reeking little camp of the Tenochca, waded the creek and crept the half-mile to where a little dry wash curled in from the north. Once into the gully they were out of sight and remained that way for more than six miles before emerging into a bizarre land of standing rocks, scoured cliffs, abrupt small canyons and knife-lipped breaks, due west of the lava bed that was the beginning of the volcanic field.

Maybe a few Mescaleros saw them, but they had no reason to mention it. And except for them, only one other person was aware that they had passed. Cha-Quitl Xacali Imli, priest of Huitzilopochtli and emissary of the Tenochca, had been standing watch for the anticipated appearance of the new moon which must feast on stars for thirteen passages of Mictlan in order to grow gorged and content before it sacrificed itself to Tonaiu. He had seen shadows moving and had crept closer to them—so close that a creature among the night things had growled in the darkness. And he had inherited then the task that the god had bestowed upon the recent and revered Ce-Chinatl Ixtlic Tactli—the honor of observing Quetzalcoatl in the hour of his return.

Tactli's description of the appearance of Quetzalcoatl in his guise as a mortal man had been precise. Even in the dim starlight Imli recognized the huge man with the beard. He went immediately to Xochitli-Miqui and woke the high priest to report what he had seen.

And Xochitli-Miqui understood the thing that they must do. Quietly, he assembled them and instructed them. Silently they descended upon the fenced enclosure where were kept the sacrifices Kileen had provided. Systematically and in total silence they dispatched them one by one, obsidian knives glinting in the starlight, hands and arms glinting as darkly with fresh blood, and as the last one's heart was laid upon the pile of stones to await Tonaiu's pleasure at morning there was fresh light in the sky. A tiny bright point shot across the heavens, and at that instant the new moon arose above the eastern peaks to begin gorging itself on stars.

The knowledge of Xochitli-Miqui was confirmed. It was nearing time to witness the rebirth of Huitzilopochtli on the shoulders of Quetzalcoatl. Single file, the priests of the Tenochca departed their enclosure and set out the way that Quetzalcoatl had gone.

*   *   *

Once in the breaks, and with the Dutchman guiding now, they circled north and then east until they were at the very edge of the lava field, with the monument rocks climbing away behind them. In the pale glow of a new moon the land at their backs was a freakish landscape of canyons and crests, cactus and cedar shrubs, and here and there the natural monoliths of sandstone where ancient winds had shaped the land by cutting most of it away. And before them was the dark swell of the rising lava, great areas of it obscured by ash and new soil, interspersed with stretches of solid or broken volcanic stone. The ragged verge between lava bed and monument breaks ran off to the north in great swoops where two natural forces had collided in ancient times, then solidified and become changeless.

"We'll have to wait 'til dawn," Gail decided. "We can't move any farther without light. We'd kill the horses out there on that ruck."

"So come dawn," Shanty pushed, worried, "just what is it we intend to do?"

"I need to get up there on the butte," she said. "If that damned John Thomas hadn't . . . never mind. I just hope once I see that valley from up there, that I can remember that template well enough to get an idea where to look."

"For the mask, or for Wolf?"

"Probably both. Don't worry, Shanty, if we find John Thomas, you can have him. And good riddance. It's the mask I'm after."

"Vicente says there's an old trail on this side of the butte," Dutchman said. "Says an Apache could get a horse up there if there was a little light."

She peered at the dim outline of the butte, then back at the lava field. "Good. That's where I'm going. You go with me, Dutchman. Two of us will be enough. We won't be staying long."

"How about the rest of us?" Trooper wondered. "You gonna leave us here in this hellhole?"

"Not everybody," she decided. "By the time we get up

topside, there'll be enough light to see where those people have been digging. I want that stopped, right now. Shanty, you and Vicente and these others, as soon as you can see, you get out there on that rise. Find some cover and see if you can't run off anybody who tries to get to the digs. Just for a little while. It will give us cover. As soon as we come down, you can pull back into these breaks. We'll join you here, and then I'll know what to do next."

"You don't know what we're going to do after that? Miss Gail, generally when we set out on a job with Wolf, he knows beforehand what we're going to do. At least, it seems like he does."

"Well, I'm not Wolf," she snapped. "So we do this my way."

"At least *that* sounds like Wolf," Willie Shay offered.

Gail looked around at him. "I'd as soon you wait back here, Willie. That could get rough out there."

"I be damned," the old man bristled. "I never claimed tc be no fighter, but me and Dog don't back down from a bunch of—"

"We all need someone here to cover our return," she added. "Trooper will stay with you. Two guns should do it."

"Me stay with this crazy old coot?" Trooper's whine rose in pitch with each word. "Ma'am, you gonna need this carbine—"

"Right here," she said. "I need it right here when we come back."

Willie glanced across at Trooper. "Varmint," he muttered.

"So it's settled," Gail said. "Let's pull back into those rocks there and get some rest. It's going to be a busy morning."

Beyond the crest of the lava bed, out of sight of the west slope, men worked by lantern light. Having found

293

the shaft into the rock, Kileen had changed his plans and his schedule. The contents of the emptied shed were stacked now, near the hole, and he had men working there, making rope ladders and torches, assembling digging and drilling tools, preparing an assault on whatever might be in the hole below. A man with a torch had been lowered down there, then raised again to the surface, and Kileen's watery eyes glowed as he heard the report. A big cave of some kind, with what looked like a piece of a building sticking out of one of the walls and a high rockfall across from it. And footprints. There had been people down there.

Kileen pieced it together and could almost feel the solid weight of the sun god mask in his hands.

As tools and equipment were assembled, they began lowering them down the dark shaft.

There must have been a lake in that valley—centuries back when it was a valley. An obstructed stream that had become a lake, and when the rift opened. . . . He was in darkness now, relying on his hearing and his innate sense of direction, using his dwindling matches and the stubs of the two candles only when he could no longer find a way. How far had he traveled, here in this dark maze? Miles.

At first there had been only a tunnel, smaller by far than the little entryway of the old temple. A gap where plastic rock had flowed and arched over a knee-high wall of stone that deflected it and left a tiny space. For most of that he had had to drag the mask behind him on a thong made from strips torn from his britches . . . inching along on toes and elbows, not knowing at each moment whether there would be space enough to go on, knowing only that there was no way to go back.

Then the floor beneath him had dropped away in darkness, and he had clung by his knees, searching with fingertips for a surface. A series of rough shelves, down and down, deeper into the rock mass. But then there had been water . . . a tiny stream that was no more than a trickle. All that was left of what might once have been a river. He had rested there, drinking a few ounces at a time, until his belly ceased to knot and his head was clear again. How long? He did not know. Maybe he had slept.

But beyond had been rising slopes, shelves and shoulders of sandstone, with lava stone overhead. He had clicked his tongue, clapped his hands, and finally howled like a coyote, and the patterns of the echoes told him of a labyrinthian enclosure where sometimes the ceiling was a hundred feet high. Vaults and tunnels, paths that led somewhere and others that didn't, and still he pushed on. Twice he had found little shafts where ancient steam had risen to the surface. Once he had even had light—a tiny beam, high overhead where sunlit sky shot down through an inaccessible little fissure in the distance. But to his eyes it was light, and for once he could see what was around him. It had to have been a lake once, tunnels and vaults created by flash-vaporized steam that defied the burning mass of the lava and held it away until it could escape.

Again there had been cool air and the suggestion of an opening above, but though he had circled and peered for long minutes he had seen nothing. Not even starlight.

He made sounds and heard echoes and went on, and then there was nowhere to go. For a long time—an hour?—the surface beneath his feet had been rising—rising and changing. Where there had been the dry crunch of pumice-sand at each step, there now was intermittent fine sand strewn with bits of gravel and chunks of sandstone. It continued to rise, and the echoes nc longer were distant.

"Don't close on me, *chito*," he murmured.

Yet the ceiling above was now just over his head. He could reach up and feel its whorls and striations, and the walls of this tunnel were closer than before. He walked or., and a piece of ceiling hit his head, a heavy droplet of lava stone cooled in the act of falling, suspended now for eternity. He eased around it, exploring it with fingers that ached and bled, and started on again, but now bent low. Abruptly the slope of the floor increased, and his feet slipped in sliding sand. He fell, rolled over and dug out a candle stub and a match. Just ahead, a few feet above, the tunnel ended. Red-sand floor rose sharply to meet the dark ceiling, and there was no opening. Red sand met gray stone, and that was the end of the path.

"Arizona's red and gray," Willie's voice explained in his mind. Everywhere you look, red and gray, he'd said. Well, it's red and gray inside, too, Willie.

Climbing to the top of the sand slope, he dug with sore fingers, the sand flowing back around him. He worked on, pulling sand away, burrowing into the mass of it with his back against the cold rock of the ceiling, hands digging fast to keep air space around him. Each time he stopped, even for a moment, the sand sifted through and threatened to bury him. Then his fingers found an edge to the stone above, and he wriggled deeper into the sand to get a purchase on it. Both hands turned upward, fingers curled around the perceived edge, he gripped and pulled . . . and a piece of the stone split off in his hands, not much more than an inch thick.

Panting and sweating, trying to keep his lungs filled in a closing shroud of sifting sand, he turned himself over, face up, his nose only inches from the stone above. He paddled his elbows in the sand, getting his forearms upright, and braced both hands against the rock. With a heave that crackled tendons and strained bulging thews within his sweating skin, he pushed. He sensed—and maybe heard—a faint, shrill crackling sound that seemed to go on and on, radiating away from him. He increased the pressure, ignoring the deepening sand that now muffled his ears. Again the crackling. . . .

Rock split and sharded, exploded away above him, and the sand atop it came through to bury him where he lay. Lungs burning, ears ringing, he held his breath and clawed upward.

Dawn was only a suggestion above the White
Mountains when Dog came to his feet, growled deep in
his chest, and padded away into the darkness, his ears
high. Shanty had just rolled over in his blanket, coming
awake, and he raised himself on an elbow, trying to see
where the beast had gone. He picked up his gunbelt,
strapped it on, and stood. Around him in the gloom he
sensed others awake, and raised a hand to assure them.
He would investigate it himself. Gail Larkin and the
Dutchman had been gone for an hour, and he had set out
no more guards when the last two Apaches came in.

In the gloom he heard Trooper's mutter, "Damn dog
probably smells a rabbit," and Willie's response nearby,
"Varmint."

On silent feet, with skill belying his size, Shanty crept
away from the dark camp in the direction Dog had gone.
Ten minutes out he found the animal, crouched on a
shelf of stone, ears up and tongue lolling, watching
something in the shadows below. He crept to the edge and
looked down, squinting.

Among the shadows a shadow moved, and John
Thomas Wolf said, "Don't just sit there, Shanty. Give me
a hand with this thing. It's getting heavy."

XXX

In the first paling of a new dawn Hall Kileen climbed
past the digs and strode to the crowd gathered around the
shaft, awaiting him. His watery eyes narrowed as he
counted them . . . then counted them again. Thirty,
thirty-two, he stopped and glared at those who waited
there. "Where are the rest? I said everyone!"

"We're all that's left," a heavy-jawed man told him sourly. "There's been some difference of opinion about going down in that hole."

"*What* difference of opinion?" Kileen squinted, making out faces in the uncertain light. "Where are the Indians?"

"Th' Mescaleros? They're gone. Left in the night. They said before that they wouldn't go down there. I guess they meant it. Most of the Mescans went, too."

"They just . . . left? Damn them!"

"We're about it, Kileen," the same man said. "An' we been thinkin', workin' down in a hole like that ought to be worth maybe twice per man what you offered. You didn't tell anybody we had to go down in a damn hole."

"You all agreed to stay on until we found the mask!"

"Times change," another man said, grinning.

"But you're all willing to dig? For more money?"

"No other way," one said. "You call the shots, Mr. Kileen. But we're changin' the rate. If you don't like it, you can do the rest of this by yourself."

Kileen fumed, glaring at them, but could see no way out. He was *so close!* So very close to the sun mask. "All right," he whispered, almost choking. Then again, "All right! I'll pay. But I expect every man here to dig and carry for that money."

They muttered among themselves, then one said, "Agreed. But if we find other holes past this hole, we'll talk about it some more."

"Then get those ladders down. Is everything I ordered down there?"

"It's there."

"All right. Four of you stay up here. The rest take torches and get down there. We're wasting time."

"You comin' down, Mr. Kileen?"

"As soon as I've had a look around on the butte. In the meantime, you know about the stone structure that's down there. Use picks and drills. I want to see what's on the other side of that wall by noon."

298

He turned and strode away, heading for his saddled horse, muttering curses as he went. Behind him the men watched him go and some shook their heads. "Sonabitch is crazy," one said. "I toted crates down that shaft yesterday. We ain't gonna find anything there. Just some more Indian ruins, that's all."

"You suppose he'll pay when he comes up empty?" another muttered. Then he looked around at the rest. A tough enough crew, brawlers and drifters, even a couple of fair gunhands among them. He chuckled. "Yeah, I guess he'll pay, all right."

The four who were considered best with the guns at their belts remained on the surface. It was their decision, and they enforced it.

Footing was tricky in the predawn light, but Kileen led his horse out to the edge of the plate and mounted, glancing aside as he did. Then he squinted. There was someone coming, a man on foot, coming up from the creek. He paused. One of the workmen changing his mind? He peered at him. A big man, limping and sore-footed . . . heavy shoulders above a belted waist . . . the man was close now, and he could see shadowy features. Someone he had seen, but didn't really recognize.

"Who is that?" he called.

The man came on. "You're Kileen, right?"

"I am. Who are you?"

"I was with Krell. I'm after that Injun, Wolf. Has he turned up here?"

With Krell? "Who are you?" he demanded.

"Mason. Bull Mason. Did Krell get here? What's happened?"

"Krell hasn't come back. What are you talking about?" The man was close now, and Kileen felt an almost physical shock at the intensity of him. "Answer me," he said.

"Then you don't know about Wolf? Well, he was ahead of me, mister, and if your people didn't nail him, then you got trouble because he's had plenty of time to show up."

Wolf. The one Kukulki sent Krell and all the best men to stop. Here? Now? Suddenly he felt cold. He squinted, looking back at the top of the shaft, then turned toward the butte. Someone was up there, silhouetted against the sky. He pointed. "Up there. Take one of those horses there!"

The man looked, then shook his head. "I don't know who's up there, but it's not Wolf. I know Wolf."

"Then wait here and watch. I want to see who's up there."

"I'll wait. Where are the rest of the Tenochca?"

"Rest of the...." Kileen peered toward the camp across the creek.

"Oh, they're not there," Mason said. "Place stinks of them and there's bodies all over, but there's no Tenochca there."

This time Kileen swore aloud. What had happened in the night? Damn the darkness, why wouldn't dawn come? He needed to see. Again there was movement atop the butte. Without looking back he headed that way, his fingers touching the butt of the revolver at his belt.

There was enough light in the sky to show horizons, but nothing more. Yet it was enough. Gail Larkin stood at the lip of the rock outcrop on the butte and imagined the template stone as she remembered it, and her breath caught in her throat. The horizon was as it should be. It was the place. But where her memory placed the little sun-sign with its pinhole center, the murk below horizon held the glow of torches and lanterns. She was too late. Kileen had found the hiding place. They were out there now.

Without turning, she said, "They've found it."

"The mask?" Dutchman asked.

"The place, at least. Did you look in that shed there?"

"Empty," he said. "But I can tell what *was* there, and

300

not long ago. I've smelled dynamite and blasting caps before. Looked off the east rim, too. No smoke or lights at the house or the Tenochca camp. Looks like everybody around here is out there on the lava."

"All right, then." She thought rapidly. "If they've found the mask, then we have to take it from them. Go on back to the others, Dutchman. Your Apaches will be heading out there in a little bit. You have a look and see what the situation is, then pin those people down if you can. I'll wait for light, see what I can see from here. You watch me and I'll watch you. You remember the semaphores, Dutchman?"

"Arm signals? Sure." His teeth glinted in the predawn gloom. "Just like we did in Mexico."

"Leave Wolf's people out of it if you can. I don't trust any of them anymore."

"I might make the sourpuss and the codger stay put," he allowed. "But I expect that big Irishman does about what he wants to . . . unless you tell him, or Wolf."

"Just do your best, Dutchman. Go now."

She heard the scuff of his horse's hooves going away as she perched at the lip of the outcrop, waiting for light. Somewhere, elsewhere, another horse was moving. But in the valley shadows it was hard to know just where.

The sky had a pink cast between the thrusting peaks to the east, and the snowcap atop distant Bald Peak seemed to float in the far sky on corona wings when Wolf sluiced himself with water from a cold canteen and put on clothes to replace the tattered rags he had discarded. Shanty handed him his spare gunbelt, and he buckled it on, then hoisted the big Colt to check its loads, all the time listening to the words of the Mescalero that Dutchman's "cousins" had brought in.

They had found the shaft, and Kileen intended to dig in the dome beneath. Picks and drills. Thirty or so left over there, all the tools and the crates from the shed now

301

down in the cavern. Rope ladders, torches and lanterns. "Crazy men go down in holes to dig holes," the Mescalero said. "We decided none of us is crazy. Lot of others left, too." He paused, then added, "No little stinkbugs over past the creek this morning, either."

"The Tenochca?" He turned his head to gaze at the Apache. "They left, too?"

"Not very far. They're over here now." He turned to Shanty. "We saw you go by last night. Helped make up our minds about pulling stakes with this crazy outfit. Stinkbugs saw you, too. They followed you. You want to know where they are?"

"How much?" Wolf asked.

"Fifty dollars. Save you havin' to find 'em yourselves."

"Pay him, Shanty."

Shanty squinted, counting out money, and handed it over.

"They're right over there." The Mescalero pointed. "Not half a mile. They been watchin' you all night."

"Then let's give them something to see," Wolf said. He hoisted the gold mask, then took it out of its wrapping blanket, and the Mescalero's eyes went as big as dollars. A few feet away Willie Shay said, "My, oh, my!" Trooper's "Jesus God!" echoed him, and everyone around crowded in for a better look. None except Wolf and Shanty had seen it unwrapped. In the rose glow of predawn it seemed to shine with a light all its own.

"Lord have mercy," Willie breathed. "Now ain't that there somethin'!"

"Montezuma's mask," Wolf said. "More blood has stained that trinket than anything before or since, and not a smudge on it." He hefted it and handed it casually to Shanty. "Get some straps on these loops there, Shanty. I'd like to see how it looks on you."

Shanty gazed at the brilliant thing as one would gaze at a snake, revulsion clear in every feature. Even his beard seemed offended. He looked at Wolf, a gaze that was a plea. "Aw, Wolf, I don't want to do that. This thing. . . ."

Holding it easily in one hand, he crossed himself with the other.

"Do it, Shanty," Wolf's voice was gentler than before. "This time that mask will be on the side of the saints."

With uncertain feelings, Shanty set about doing as he was told. And while he laced straps and tested their measure, Wolf told him the rest of what he was going to do.

On a sloping sandstone ledge twenty feet above a cedar slope, Xochitli-Miqui sat cross-legged watching the eastern sky. He was bone-weary, hungry and homesick; but a rich anticipation glowed in his simple heart, and he waited for the coming of a morning that would be as no other morning had ever been.

At his side sat Imli, and the others huddled about them, shivering with the cold of dawn and with their own nervous anticipation. Quetzalcoatl was down there, visible even from here . . . Quetzalcoatl in the guise of a mortal man, though his sheer size distinguished him from the ordinary men around him. Yet, how could such a one—lord of Mictlan, owner of the night, feathered serpent of the shadow world, a god second only to Huitzilopochtli in his power—how could he *not* be larger than ordinary men, even when appearing as one? And they had all seen now that he was indeed bewhiskered. Tonaiu would show them whether his whiskers were the color of blood, as Tactli had thought.

Mountain horizons in the far distance became more distinct by the moment, and the clarity of sky said that Tonaiu shared their anticipation. The very sun, it seemed, waited like a nervous bride to celebrate the return of the heralded one—god before and god forever. . . . "*Ayya, Huitzilopochtli,*" Xochitli-Miqui murmured, and a chorus of murmurs around him echoed the devotion.

"Look," Imli said, and pointed a quivering finger. In

the shadowed, jumbled land below, shadows were coming toward them. Horsemen in the pale dawn, winding upward through the stolid sentinels of rock, Apache riders . . . and Quetzalcoatl, carrying something in his hand. The breath caught in the throat of Xochitli-Miqui. Paling dawn had brought color, and the beard of Quetzalcoatl reddened with each moment. And the thing he carried seemed to glow.

Upward they came, toward the shelf where the Tenochca waited, spreading as they came. Then one by one they halted until only Quetzalcoatl and one other still moved up the slope, among colors coming alive as dawn brightened the sky. As one, the Tenochca turned, staring at Quetzalcoatl as he passed, looking straight ahead, red beard flowing in playful breeze, the thing he carried glinting, seeming alive—a thing with the profile of a great eagle, beak outthrust.

Just beyond them Quetzalcoatl stepped from his horse to a stone atop which were other stones, then to a higher one and to one higher than that. Above and behind him clifftops came alive with the first touches of a new *tonaiu* waiting to be born. Again Quetzalcoatl arose, and again, and stood atop a formation of striated red rock, his back to them. Xochitli-Miqui and the rest watched with huge eyes, no longer even aware of the line of mounted Apache just below them . . . or of the dark man who sat his saddle just beyond them, watching them intently.

Tonaiu's rays walked down the cliffs, and then Quetzalcoatl's shadow was on them. He turned, facing the sun, and on his shoulders was a glory of brilliance that was like the sun itself. He spread his arms, seemed to swell in size, and in a voice that rumbled and echoed, he chanted, "O oi wint dahn ti dooblin tahn wass of a moornin foin whin spring wass green an fayre coleen sh' promiss ta be moin . . ."

Shaken and humble, dazzled beyond wit, the Tenochca came to their feet as one, their murmurs almost lost beneath the rolling thunder of that mighty voice. "*Ayya,*

Huitzilopochtli . . . Huitzilopochtli ya nechca . . . Huit-zilopochtli nocipa . . . ayya . . ."

Quetzalcoatl/Huitzilopochtli completed his song of rebirth, and there was a ringing silence in the hills. Then, blood-red beard streaming beneath the awful visage of the master of the sun, he turned his face to his Tenochca, pointed at them with a huge hand, then swung it eastward to point to the lava beds in the distance.

In stunned obedience Xochitl-Miqui clambered down from the rock shelf, the rest jostling one another as they hurried to follow. In single file they trotted past the silent, watching Apaches on their skittish horses and headed down the slope.

Of them all, only one, Cha-Quitl Xacali Imli, hung back, looking over his shoulder. To him had fallen the honor of observing Quetzalcoatl in passage, and he felt as though his heart would burst at the glory of it. With sudden resolution, when they filed around a stand of rock, he stepped aside and hid himself among cedars. As observer of Quetzalcoatl, it seemed to him, he should observe who followed the reborn Huitzilopochtli and who, if any, did not. For if any did not, then they could provide *chalchinatl* for his first breakfast.

The Tenochca went away down the slope, and after a moment the Apache filed past . . . then behind them Quetzalcoatl/Huitzilopochtli, both faces now plainly visible as he carried the eagle visage at his shoulder, and another rider, the dark man who was his escort. There were none left above. Imli followed them silently.

In breaks below they paused for a time, where others may have been; then they went on, and Imli climbed a spur of stone to look down into the canyon where they had been. They had gone on, but one remained there that he could see—an old man with snow beneath his hat and a beard like mountain snow below his chin. Imli waited for a time to see if he, too, would follow. Then when it seemed he would not, Imli climbed down from his stone and took out his blade of obsidian.

XXXI

From the east rise of the butte, even in the uncertain light of dawn, Kileen knew who it was that he saw crouching on the north rim. He knew, because it could be no one else. He paused for a long minute, letting his eyes sweep the mesa top. She was alone. Just one horse—her horse—over by the storage shed. And just her, alone, motionless at the rim, her attention fixed on the torches and lanterns out on the lava slope. They still shone out there, though muted now by the lightening sky above. Men would be descending into the natural shaft out there by now, and he knew she was watching that.

Leaving his horse at the top of the trail he strode toward her, walking as quietly as possible but with firm purpose, and the revolver in his hand didn't waver.

Maybe she didn't hear him, he thought. But it wouldn't matter. He crept to within a few feet and started to speak, but she spoke first, not looking around.

"Hello, Hall," she said quietly. "You've found it, haven't you?"

So she had heard him. Even identified him. But, again, it didn't matter. "I have its hiding place," he said. "The template stone would have helped, but I found it anyway. Ah . . . I trust your father is well, Gail?"

"Much better than he'd be if your killers had found him, Hall." Still she didn't look around at him, just continued to gaze off to the north. Why was she so cool . . . so indifferent? Certainly she knew he had a gun in his hand? He cocked the hammer, letting her hear it. Still she didn't turn, but now there was a mocking edge to her voice. "Doing your own dirty work these days, Hall? How the mighty have fallen."

"You and your father had your chance in Mexico," he hissed. "You could have joined me. We could have been very rich. Why did you betray me?"

306

"Betray you, Hall? We were never in it with you. All I did was help expose you. And I did that gladly. I won't expose you again, though. I won't settle for that this time. I want the sun mask, Hall. My father wants it. If you have it, then I'll take it from you."

His chuckle was dry and brutal. "You are a nervy bitch, aren't you, Gail. But you won't do anything. Do you know why? Because I have a gun pointed at the back of your head, and I intend to use it."

He thought she would respond; but at that moment sunlight struck the top of the butte, and among the tumbled lands beyond something flashed with the brilliance of another, smaller sun. Both of them turned to stare at it, dazzled by the brilliance there. Something mirror-bright with the hue of gold.

Gail recovered first. "So you *don't* have it," she said. "It's Wolf, then. Somehow he—"

Kileen stared across the distance, her words bringing realization to him. "Wolf? Then, that's who I saw . . . but how . . . ?" He jerked his head around as she moved, and the little muzzle of the gun she held was a blackness like that shaft out there on the lava bed.

"Good-bye, Hall," she murmured.

Three high-velocity slugs from a 32-20 revolver burned through him before he fell, but the last two were wasted. The first had entered at his chin and fragmented the top of his skull. He tottered and pitched forward, and Gail sprang out of the way as he hung for a second at the lip of the rock, then disappeared below it.

"You had a gun," Gail breathed. "What made you think I didn't?"

Dutchman was just entering the breaks when he heard the gunshots, and he swung his horse around, spurred to a high place and looked back. Though the new sun was in his eyes, he could see Gail Larkin up on the rim and knew she had seen him. Her arms went up, then out, and he read the signals as he had those years before in Mexico.

He watched for a moment, then rode higher on the ridge and around a rock spur. From there he could see what she saw. Vicente's Apaches, afoot now, were coming out of the breaks and climbing the lava shield, strong legs carrying them at a fast trot. And just behind them was Shanty, carrying something wide . . . and John Thomas Wolf.

And there was someone else out there as well, approaching the shield's crest. Little, dark figures. The Tenochca! He rode into the clear and wagged his arms where she could see. Yes. He saw them. He would go. But her response was negative, followed by signaling so fast he could barely read it. She saw something else, something he could not see from where he was . . . he could not make it out. Something beyond . . . there was desperation in the wild swinging of her signaling arms.

There were more gunshots then, from somewhere farther up in the sentinel breaks—crash of a heavy carbine fired again and again, rapidly; a roll of drumbeat thunder that crashed and echoed and then went mute.

Xochitli-Miqui and his brothers came over the shield of the volcano's flow to where they could see the men around the hole, and stopped there. Xochitli-Miqui squatted on his heels, and the rest clustered around him, a tight little knot of black-clad figures, childlike faces under bald domes, expressionless, simply watching and waiting.

Thirty yards away, where bits of paraphernalia littered the stoney ground around the dark shaft, the four gunman-guards stared back at them, open-mouthed. They were still staring when a commanding voice almost on top of them said, "You men! Raise your hands!"

As one they spun. The man there, just above them on the slope, was an Indian, and there were other Indians beyond him—Apaches. But he was no Apache.

"I said raise your hands," he said, his fingers at the butt of a Colt at his hip.

Two of them hesitated. Two went for their guns and an instant later crumpled as thunder rolled across the valley. Wolf swung to face the other two. "How about you?" he purred.

They raised their hands, and an Apache disarmed them.

"Down in the hole," the shooter ordered. "Go on, *chitos*, there's plenty of room down there. I've been there."

Reluctantly they moved to the shaft, and one and then the other disappeared down the rope ladder.

Vicente offered the extra guns to Wolf, who waved them away while he reloaded his own.

"Didn't know a man could draw and shoot that fast," the Apache said.

Wolf put away his Colt. "Neither did they."

"Any other way out of that hole?" Vicente wondered.

"Not anymore."

The Apache grinned. "You want me to cut those ropes?" He paused, reconsidering, then pointed at the cluster of Tenochcas. "Let's put the stinkbugs down there with 'em . . . *then* cut the ropes."

Shanty came over the crest, still carrying the sun mask, and all the Tenochca rose to their feet, gazing at him in wonder.

"Wolf, please," Shanty begged. "Let's get rid of this thing. I don't like it a bit."

"In a little while, Shanty," he said. "Right now, you just play god for these people while I find Hall Kileen."

Without a backward glance he walked away, down the strewn shield, thoughtful eyes on the K-bar buildings some distance away. Those shots he had heard . . . from the butte and then the unmistakable bark of Trooper's carbine from the west . . . not knowing the whole situation made for loose ends. Wolf didn't like loose

309

ends. And where was Hall Kileen? Could he be with the workers down in the hole? No, not likely. Not this early.

Back near the shaft, most of the Apaches fingered their guns and kept nervous eyes on the clustered Tenochca. They had all seen what the innocent, bizarre little foreigners could do. The Tenochca ignored them. They ignored everyone except Shanty, and the eyes they fixed on him were bright with adoration. Shanty watched Wolf disappear among standing rubble down the shield, and swore fervently under his breath, hating everything about this situation.

Vicente strapped on the gun Wolf had rejected, crouched and tried to draw it as he had seen Wolf do. His efforts seemed to him painfully slow. He dropped the gun into its holster and went to look down the hole in the rock. It was like a big tube, straight down to its end, and below were men moving around. Shadows and torchlight and a big stack of crates and kegs lay directly under the shaft. As he watched, a shot boomed hollowly down there, and a bullet chipped rock twice coming up the hole, then ricocheted into the sky. Someone had seen him looking down and tried to shoot him. *"Hijo de puta,"* he muttered.

Two rope ladders were suspended down the sides of the shaft. Wolf hadn't said not to cut them. For that matter, he wasn't here for Wolf's benefit, anyway. He had come with Dutchman. He drew his knife and cut the ropes. When the first ladder slithered down to sprawl across the stacked crates, there were shouts from below. He scooted around the hole and cut the other one loose. "Gettin' out of there is the least of your worries, *perros,*" he muttered. "Those are dynamite crates and that keg on top is blasting powder and you damn fools are runnin' around down there with torches."

Unused torches lay nearby, where a fire had been built to light them, and he was tempted to drop one in to see what would happen. He stepped over to them and thrust

310

one of them into the fire, then raised his head. Someone was coming, on foot but walking strangely, coming over the lava shield from the east. He couldn't see the person yet. Rock intervened. But beyond where he would be, in the distance at the edge of the flow shield, a man stood, holding two horses, and Vicente knew him. It was the crazy Englishman who thought he was a Zuni, the one named Three People.

Down the slope to the south, abrupt and furious, guns spoke. Shanty lurched to his feet, still holding the detested sun mask on his shoulder, muttered, "Wolf?" and set off toward the sounds at a lumbering run. The mask lay where he dropped it, gleaming in the morning sun.

Wolf had gone a hundred paces down the lava field, following the twisted path among dark stones, when he heard behind him the soft whisper of metal clearing leather, the double click of a hammer being cocked even as the gun came out and a deep, rasping voice that said, "I knew you'd be here, you son of a bitch."

Pure reflex began a dodge to the side, his hand going to his gun automatically, but it was too late. He felt the cold fire of a bullet piercing his side, and gunfire hammered and echoed around him. The impact of the shot twisted him and started him down; but his gun was out now, and he let the force carry him full around, firing even as he saw the grinning face of Bull Mason just yards away. Mason fired again, then stiffened and jerked as Wolf's gun bucked and thundered, putting burning ball after ball through him.

Wolf sprawled on his back on cold stone and didn't see Mason fall. But there were no more shots. He lay for a moment, blinded by pain and shock, trying to find a conscious thought to cling to. Only one came, and he fixed on it with his entire attention. Words on old paper: "The way to have a friend is to be one." What did that mean? Who . . . then he knew, and a sob racked him, a

311

sob that became laughter, bubbling up inside him and making his lungs breathe, his heart beat, his head begin to clear. Emerson! Ralph Waldo Emerson. I didn't understand the man's reasoning then, his mind told him nonchalantly, and I still don't. Why would anybody say a thing like that?

But it had got him to living again, at least for now. He tried to sit up and raised his head far enough to see the crumpled body of Bull Mason a few feet away; then dizziness washed over him. He fought it back. He had things to do and no time to lie here bleeding. The job wasn't done yet. The sun mask, the Tenochca, Hall Kileen . . . he fought dizziness and sat up. He couldn't see what the bullet had done to him behind, but where it came out in front said it had done some damage. How much? He couldn't tell. Then there were people around him, and he reached up a hand. "Help me up, Shanty. I have things to do."

No time to find Kileen now. That would have to wait. But he could do that which remained to be done at the lava shaft.

With Shanty helping him, he stood, feeling unaccountably weak. "That was Bull Mason," he said. His voice sounded too far away. "He shot me from behind."

Shanty rolled the body over with a big boot. The three bullet holes in Mason's chest were only inches apart. "Last mistake he ever made, I guess," he said.

Wolf felt his knees buckling, but Shanty turned and caught him before he could fall. The big man turned him around easily, supporting him and looking at his wounds, peeling off his shirt as he did to make binding. He was just tying it into place when Wolf's eyes focused and he scowled. "Shanty, where is the mask?"

"Right up there. I dropped it. Don't worry, it—"

"Go get it. Quick. Pick it up and hold it."

"Wolf, you've got—"

"Now, Shanty! I'll be right behind you."

With a shake of his head, Shanty hurried off, Apaches clearing a path for him. Wolf thumbed cartridges into his revolver and started after him, concentrating on staying on his feet. There was no telling what the Tenochca would do if. . . . Ahead he heard voices, one louder than the rest, shouting in a language that was like the singsong chants he had heard—all ululating tones, clicks and chirps. Rounding a stone he almost bumped into Shanty, then went on past him, his hand on his gun butt.

On the clear rise, vivid in morning sunlight, the Tenochca were spread an arm's length apart, each with his obsidian blade glinting in his hand. But they were going upward, away. And beyond them, facing them, shouting at them in Nahuatl, was Frederick Larkin. He held Montezuma's mask in his right hand, leaned on his crutch with his left, and was backing away as he shouted.

The little dark figures advanced on him, crowding him back, and he scuttled aside awkwardly to pick up a lighted torch from the fire. He thrust the sun mask under his left arm with the butt of his crutch, lifted the torch and waved it at them, still shouting. His crutch slipped on a stone, and he lurched, then righted himself again and scuttled back. His foot found emptiness, and he teetered for an instant, clawing at air, still hugging the gold mask and waving the flaring torch. Then he was gone. Wolf caught Shanty's arm, staggering. Behind him Vicente said, "There goes the powder," and Wolf understood.

"Run, Shanty!" he shouted. And fell.

Dizzily he felt Shanty's arm around him, scooping him up like a rag doll, and pounding pain inside him as Shanty ran, Apaches sprinting past him down the slope. Shanty tossed him into the shelter of a lava-stone shelf and dropped in beside him, and both lifted their heads to look upslope as the ground vibrated as if from an earthquake.

Upslope, dust and larger matter erupted from the opening of the shaft, and the lava shield bulged upward visibly with the ringing sound of shattering rock,

313

throwing dark-clad little figures about as a cloud of smoke and dust spread above them, hiding the sun with its shadow.

Reluctantly, slowly for a moment and then with a roar, the bubble dome collapsed upon itself, and a wide crater appeared where the clear shield had been. Rubble rained into it from above, little avalanches poured into it around its rim, and the cloud of gray smoke and volcanic dust hung over it in silence as though impervious to the light winds of morning.

XXXII

He lay beside a desert stream, weak and light-headed from loss of blood, not trying to sort out the impressions that came to him, just letting them tumble around in his mind and form their own patterns. He could put them into logical order later.

Hall Kileen was dead. That was clear, though how he came to be dead was something of a mystery. Gail Larkin had something to do with it.

The Tenochca were gone. They had all fallen into the crater when the cavern blew up. Three of them had lived to climb out of that hole, and two of those didn't make it. Vicente and a couple of his friends had seen them and decided they should stay in the hole. They'd had a glimpse of the third, but missed him. But he was gone.

These things he had learned from Shanty while the Irishman worked over his wounds. Then he had slept for a while, and fought fever dreams that were like being buried alive in places where the ceiling was dark stone and the floor red-gray pumice, and all the walls closed down on him so that he could never move again. Then there had been sunlight and blue sky again, but nothing would hold still and be restful. Much about that would remain unclear, because the impressions were old and distant: Gail Larkin standing above him with what might have been tears in her eyes and saying, "I should have killed you, John Thomas. I could have. I know that now. I should have, too." The Dutchman beyond her, holding the reins of saddled horses, and someone else there—a tall, balding man with a Zuni headband and glasses—a man who leaned over him curiously and said, "Bit of a waste, that. Larkin, I mean. Hardheaded chap most ways, but the lass will miss him."

And then Shanty again, shaking his shoulder gently. "Wolf, listen. Pay attention. Trooper . . . Trooper's dead, Wolf. One of them, he went after Willie . . . Wolf, listen! Wake up! It's Trooper, Wolf. He shot one of them off Willie, then the little bastard got him instead. Wolf! . . ."

He slept. He dozed and awakened to firelight and starry sky and the droning of Windwagon Willie's voice. ". . . just don't see why he did that, Shanty. All those years I wandered around, always expected somebody'd kill me sooner or later. But nobody ever even tried. Then finally somebody tries to kill me, and that . . . that damn varmint . . . he steps in an' takes it hisself. Why did that varmint do that, Shanty? Shoot, he never even hardly tolerated me, far as I could see."

Wolf lay on soft blankets and watched the old man's words soar away into the starry desert sky, then when they came back, he collected them and stored them away to think about when he could. And Shanty was saying, ". . . didn't find him, Willie. Those Apaches don't miss much, but they couldn't find that Azteca. Are you sure. . . ?"

"Sure I'm sure," Willie said. "Trooper killed him dead. Still shootin' when th' little stinker cut into him. But they won't ever find him. Old Dog . . . no, you stay put, Dog. I'm talkin' about you, not to you. Ol' Dog, he buried the stinker. Buried him six or eight different places, best I could tell. He just kept doin' that. He'd drag him off someplace an' bury him, then he'd sniff the sand and decide he's ripe so he'd dig him up again, then have it all to do over. I finally made him quit."

Dog. Wolf felt a chuckle rise in his throat, but it hurt and he fought it away. And slept.

And didn't like any of the dreams that presented themselves to him. At least, those that he knew to be dreams, he rejected. He had no use for dreams. Dreams could take charge if you let them. But man is in charge. Man has a life, and he is in charge of it and in charge of everything in it. Each man is in charge of his universe, and what he does within it he must do in his own way. Who had said that? Himself? Partly, maybe. But someone else before said part of it.

Ralph Waldo Emerson.

High spring lay on the Kansas hills, greening the walnut buds outside the window of the Leavenworth boardinghouse where John Thomas Wolf, dressed in traveling clothes, folded shirts into a slim leather valise and laid a few books and an extra gunbelt atop them. He closed the valise and paused to look out the window again. There was still that extra shadow beneath the tree. The shadow of the tree's trunk, merging with the shadows of interlaced boughs . . . and an extra width to the shadow as though someone were standing beside the tree, just out of sight and just standing there, waiting. Not Shanty. The Irishman had gone ahead to the depot, to buy their tickets. And yet it was not some casual passerby just pausing there. The shadow said patience and purpose.

He buckled the straps on the valise, lifted it and left the room without looking back, leaving the door open so the proprietor would know he had gone. He collected his door-string counter and dropped it into a pocket, then went down the stairs and out. In front of the house he turned left, walked to the walnut tree and said, "Enjoying the breeze, Mr. Joy?"

The dour man stepped around the trunk and gazed at him. "You're looking fit," he said. "Any remaining problems?"

"If you mean the wound"—John Thomas shook his head—"no. Most things heal."

"I'm glad of that," Joy told him. "The Director would like to see you."

So soon again? John Thomas squared his shoulders. "I have other plans, Mr. Joy."

"Oh, I don't mean in Springfield or Georgetown, John Thomas. He's here. We just arrived and he does want to see you. Your train will wait. Your Irishman will see to that."

"All right." John Thomas shrugged. "Where?"

"At the post office."

They walked together along sun-dappled streets, and Joy let them in the locked back door of the sturdy building which served both as Leavenworth's post office and as postal center for the military enclave nearby. The postmaster let them into his office and waved them through to a second door. Joy opened it and Wolf stepped through. The man who stood to welcome him was Ernest Kichener.

"Director, huh?" John Thomas frowned at him.

"An interim measure only." Kichener shrugged. "Just while a few adjustments are made in the Civil Service System and the political appointment process. My immediate predecessor made the recommendations himself . . . along with his request for a different line of work. Sit down, John Thomas. Tea?"

Joy left the room and closed the door quietly. Kichener poured tea.

"It is unfortunate but necessary," the man called Nemesis said, "that an organization that officially does not exist, by the nature of our country's system cannot be funded from the public treasury. My own preference has been to allow the unruly to stand the cost of the problems they cause. This"—he handed a thick wallet across to the Indian—"was the household fund of a man named Kukulki. He doesn't need it anymore. It is yours. If the sun mask could have been recovered, then it would have reimbursed you for your efforts. But my predecessor was right; Montezuma's mask needs to remain buried . . . at least for a time."

"Someone will find it again, you know," John Thomas said.

"Yes, and when that happens there may be problems again. There are always fanatics, and always people to find them and use them. But then—" he smiled, a cold, gray smile that matched his piercing eyes—"I think there are always those who rather enjoy putting a stop to such things, don't you?"

"There seems to be a few."

"That's all it takes. A few. There is a man in Mexico, his name is Diego Torreon. I've known him for a long time. He helped me when I was there. He enjoys such sport from time to time. And I expect his protégé will, as well."

"Protégé?"

"A little bird," he said. "Nicely put. Her name is Gail Larkin. I wouldn't be surprised if you should meet her again."

Somehow, he wasn't surprised. She had learned rapidly.

"There's one other thing, John Thomas," Kichener said. "I have done you an injustice and I wish to correct it now. I believe you feel . . . well, beholden to me."

"I owe you my life." John Thomas shrugged. "I suppose that *is* 'beholden.'"

"And unfair." Kichener nodded. "You believe that because I have allowed you to believe it. It was a string I had on you. Well, you can have your string back, John Thomas. You owe me nothing whatever. Nor do you owe anything to the organization."

John Thomas regarded him, Indian eyes as cold and expressionless as the gray ones looking back. "You're cutting me loose?"

"As loose as you want to be. Now"—he picked up a heavy envelope from the desk—"I understand you are on your way to California."

"A lecture assignment." Wolf nodded.

"Yes. As it happens, there is a situation out there that has gotten entirely out of hand, and neither the legal nor military systems can seem to get at the roots of it. Would you like to take this information along with you, to study at your leisure?"

"Why should I? You just gave me back my string."

"No reason you should, unless you want to. You have done very well with a string on you, John Thomas, but I think you'll do better without it. It is entirely up to you, you see. But is an interesting situation."

"Why me?"

"Why not? It's up to you."

John Thomas sighed. "If I take on this . . . this task, I'll handle it my way."

"Of course," Nemesis told him. "There is no other way."

Epilogue

He had come a long way, but he knew now he could go no farther. He had thought he might go home, but he really had no idea of where home might be, except that it was somewhere south. He had come as far as he could . . . but it didn't matter. Nothing mattered anymore. The legend had come to reality, and reality had exploded into oblivion, and there was nothing left for him in Cem-Anahuac the one world. There was nothing left for the world itself. Tonaiu still came and went, but it was only Tonaiu. Huitzilopochtli was gone. *Ayya, Tonaiu,* all that is to be is now past.

Alone and starving, forever lost and no longer able to wander, Xochitli-Miqui sat on a hill and waited for the world to end.